Finding
Eden

Other Books by Jeffrey S. Crawford

<u>Non-Fiction</u>
Image of God
On a Ship to Tarshish

Finding Eden

Jeffrey S. Crawford

HILLSIDE HOUSE
PUBLISHING

Finding Eden
Jeffrey S. Crawford
Hillside House Publishing

Published by Hillside House Publishing, Springdale, AR
Copyright © 2019 Jeffrey S. Crawford
All rights reserved.

Cover Design by Tori Lasater
Binocular Graphic: @Depositphotos/Taigi

Library of Congress Cataloging-in-Publication Data

Library of Congress Control Number: 2018911940
Jeffrey S. Crawford

Finding Eden
ISBN: 978-1-7327596-0-2

Printed in the United States of America.

For Garrett
My son, my friend

PROLOGUE

Field Journal – Day 30, September 15

I think we are lost.

But that wouldn't be the first time! Not with this group of yahoos. This has to be – what - at least number ten? What an amazing trip it's been though. We just hit the one-month mark away from home, so I did some reflecting as we hiked today. Picked up this journal from a street vendor last week and thought it might be a good idea to record some thoughts, so here goes. Let's see...thirty days, three continents, and at least 120 miles of hiking.

It's just gotten better as we've moved from place to place. Europe was great. People were nice. Yeah, everybody does the "backpack through Europe" thing. But still, good way to break in the gear and get our legs under us. The Middle East was next. One word: AMAZING! And boy, talk about edgy. Lots of Muslims. Trying to just blend in and not stick out. Not too easy for four white guys from the south. Well, I guess Alberto is Hispanic but it feels all the same when everyone is speaking in Arabic, and you're not sure what you're eating pretty much everywhere you go.

My parents think the whole thing's crazy and they are probably right. Ah well. You only live once. In and out and back in, via Turkey and then a plane to Egypt.

And now here - wherever here is. Haha. Anyway, just a couple more weeks and then back home, just in time to enroll for the spring semester. That will definitely make my folks happy. Been a nice break though.

None of it would have been possible without Jake. Or I guess I should say, Jake's money. Or I guess I should say, Jake's parent's money! Anyway, he's cool and they're cool and what a gift. The whole thing has been on the cheap, but it does take some bling to fly and rent vehicles. But now we're just walking - six days and at least 50 miles on this leg. Pickup is in three days. Jake says he's got it figured out, so for now, I'm not going to worry about it - just gonna crawl in my sleeping bag and get some shuteye.

Field Journal – Day 31, September 16

A great day today - the weather was perfect. No more than 80 degrees and not a cloud in the sky. Lots of wildlife. If I were alone I'd probably be scared, but not in a group - especially our group. I love these guys. We've truly seen the world together. And not the usual places - we've gone and are going places no one goes. At least people like us.

We are really remote now. Haven't seen anyone really since the first day of drop-off. But all is well. I know it. Jake says we are right on track and ready for pickup in just two more days. I can't believe it - two more days and we start the journey home. SO much fun today.

Ryan was cracking us all up with his singing. He just makes up these crazy songs. Makes the hiking not so bad, that's for sure. If I'm honest, my feet are sore and I'm tired of the miles. It will feel good to drive again.

We sat around tonight over dinner eating our freeze-dried packets – tonight was something like meatloaf – talking about all the food we are looking forward to eating when we get home. For me....I can't wait to throw down an entire meat lovers pie from Pizza Hut. Okay, I'm torturing myself now.

Alberto's already asleep in the tent we share. Ryan and Jake are down by the little creek next to camp looking for exotic fish. I'm just enjoying the fire and staring at the stars.

The sky is different here than at home. The stars are all in different positions, and I can see constellations and stars here that you don't see at all in Texas. I have never felt so far away from home as I do right now. And I've never felt so small before. If there is a God up there, and if he really did create all this, then he surely is a big God.

Field Journal – Day 32, September 17

Such a frustrating day. Jake insisted we were right on track, but now I'm convinced he's full of it. There is no doubt that we are still lost, and this time I think we are really lost. Jake was so sure when we started off today. But I know we have walked in circles. We've passed the same boulders, the same trees, the same water - at least three times. I know it. Jake says no way. He's sticking to his guns but I can see it on his face.

For some reason the GPS thing we brought isn't working either. That was news to me. I was trusting Jake. We all were trusting Jake. I don't even know how long it's been out. Jake says since today but I don't think I believe him. We are supposed to be at the pickup point tomorrow by the end of the day. So I'm a little freaked out about that.

Jake says that once the sun comes up, we need to be up and ready to haul out of here. He says that if we just mark the exact spot that the sun breaks the horizon, we will know for sure which way is east, then we can hike exactly opposite of that, to the west, right toward pickup, and until we hit something that matches our topo map. That sounds right. I think that's right. But man...I'm nervous. There was a lot of yelling over dinner - mostly all of us at Jake. He's gotten quiet on us. Nobody's really talking to each other right now. But I think we are all thinking the same thing. It's time to go home.

I'm sure we will be fine. Yes. We will be fine. I'm gonna keep telling myself that. The power of positive thinking, right? We will make the pickup and ride out of here. Bus it back to Cairo. Then on a plane back to the good ol' United States. This time next month we will be back, things will be calm, and we will all be laughing about this over some Mexican food and a round of beers at El Rey's. God, I hope I'm right. Please, Lord, let me be right. I can't believe I'm praying! I must really be desperate. Haha. That's right. Keep laughing. Keep praying. Keep positive. Time to close my eyes. Tomorrow's going to be a long day I think.

Field Journal – Day 33, September 18

I'm so tired…my watch says 12:30 a.m. It's dark - so, so dark tonight. We missed pickup. Of course we missed pickup. We have no idea where we are. We were up early, ready to head west once the sun came up, but it was cloudy. Go figure! The only cloudy day the whole time we've been out here. So we decided to follow the muddy river we've passed the last two days.

Jake's not talking much but Ryan says that the rivers on our map all seem to run pretty much east and west. Sounded like the best idea considering.

All morning we just walked, a little chitchat but not much else. Around noon we got so excited because we ran into a small village. It was the first sign of anybody since the small town where we were dropped off. It was so strange. They looked like Massai, but there are not supposed to be any Massai anywhere close to where we are. But they were also very different than the Massai I've seen. Very little clothing and only men in the village. What's that all about?

I'm not sure you can even call it a village, just some mud huts with thatch and a burn of thickets surrounding it all. And where are the women and children? Every place we've gone since Cairo has had children everywhere. I think we surprised them as much as they surprised us. They were nice at first, but a little standoffish. We offered them some of our leftover packets of food. We don't have much left to trade. One man brought out a bowl of some kind of raw meat, soaked in blood with flies swarming it. Absolutely nasty! They used hand motions and their strange language to insist we eat. No one could understand anyone. It felt tense so we all tried it -

hardest thing I've ever done. Only one bite and I gagged the whole time. We all did. We weren't hungry much anyway, just desperate to get out of there.

Ryan showed them the map, trying to get them to help us, and they got very agitated. He kept pointing to the spot where our pickup point was. I don't think they understood at all. I think they thought we were trying to find something else and that made them even more angry.

Then two of the men ran to one of the huts in the back of the yard. We could hear angry shouts but we had no idea what was being said. All of a sudden the two men came running out with an old man between them. Old is an understatement. This guy was ancient. Skin so black from the sun and so wrinkled with time, wearing only a loincloth. He had no teeth and was clearly blind. When they got about twenty feet from us, he shook off the other two and walked straight toward our group. I swear he could see us, but how?!

The old man - must have been the chief - began to chant and stomp and then from the back of his loin cloth he pulled a knife made of some sort of bone material! The two others snatched the map from Ryan and began to push us out of the yard. Everything went to crazy after that. Alberto was pushing through three of them trying to get the map. Ryan went after Alberto and the old man slashed him across the side with the knife. Jake yelled and threw his pack at the old guy - I grabbed Jake and we ran. Alberto and Ryan tore away and followed. The whole group chased us for at least a hundred yards, and then just stopped and formed a line. They began to chant and jump, in a strange rhythm. Were they cursing us? It was clear we were to leave. Immediately. So we ran.

Skirting their camp, we just took off and stopped after ten minutes or so.

We found shelter under a tree to look at Ryan's wound and to regroup. It's pretty nasty looking – a wicked gash just below the left side under his rib cage. Maybe six inches long or so. Ryan put on a strong face saying it didn't hurt much, but I know it has to. After a short rest to dress Ryan's wound, we took off again. We are all pretty shook up. We just need to get out of here. We decided to hike even after sunset. But there's no map and Jake's pack had our spare food, what little we had left. We finally stopped, just because we can't go any further tonight. It smells really odd where we are. I'm writing all this down because it feels important. We need help.

Field Journal – Day 34, September 19

Morning - *Bad just got worse. We slept in more than we wanted to. Just so tired still.*

Ryan is sick. His side is killing him and none of us feel quite right. Lots of stomach cramps. I think we should never have eaten that bowl of whatever we were given yesterday. I have no appetite at all, which is okay because all we have left are some power bars and trail mix.

We've decided that our pickup team we hired will come back today since we didn't show up yesterday. They would have to, right? Then if we still don't show up, they will come looking for us. That may be our best chance. It's just before noon and we are about to get going for the day - try to find the river again and keep following it.

Evening – *We could only go a few hours today. Ryan is just too sick. He keeps apologizing to us. His cramping is worse than ours and his side looks really bad. We still have a few bandages left, so that's good.*

We found the river again but stopped late afternoon. We decided we needed to stay rested. Alberto has started cracking potty humor jokes to cheer us up - sort of goes along with all our intestinal issues. Haha! Thanks Alberto. Love you man.

It's very strange here. The longer we walked and followed the river today, the more the vegetation and scenery changed. This whole time everything has looked the same: arid climate, short brown grasses, acacia trees here and there, etc. What you'd expect. But now everything is…I don't know, greener. More lush and just…more. The area feels different too. And that smell - what is the deal with the smell? So bad and pungent and getting stronger. I've decided I'm done panicking. It is what it is. We have each other and something will happen to get us out of here.

Field Journal – Day 35, September 20

Morning – *Something is out there. We could hear it all night long. Like we are being stalked. Alberto joked that it was a lion. Do they even have lions in this part of the country? No way it's a lion, right?*

Ryan is bad. Real bad. It was hard to wake him up this morning. His wound is infected I think.

Alberto is still cracking jokes, but it's not funny anymore. Why's he doing that?

Jake won't talk to anyone. He just sat around the fire last night and stared at the flames. I think he's blaming himself. I told the guys last night that we have *to stick together. We have to. All we have is each other. This is the part in the movies where everything goes from bad to worse. But this is not a movie. We are going to be okay.*

Please God, let us be okay. There I go praying again. I don't care. We need all the help we can get. I don't know if we can travel at all today with Ryan the way he is. Everyone is just laying around anyway. I'm going to walk a ways down the river and explore. See if I can see anything.

Evening – *Jake is gone. What the heck! I was gone about two hours and when I got back he was just…gone.*

I don't like where we are camped at all. When I went down the river, I noticed that there is no wildlife at all here. No birds, no insects, no ground or tree animals of any kind. And it's so quiet. How long has it been this way? I got to a point on my morning hike where I couldn't go any further because the terrain just rose up so high on the bank, and I would have had to cross over to the other side to keep going.

Before I turned to come back, I looked across the river and my eye caught the only thing I've seen alive out here. Sitting with just its upper torso and head showing above a large boulder was what looked like an eagle. But it was not like any kind of eagle I've ever seen before. Incredibly huge! And terrible looking with white, red, and gold plumage. And his eyes – he kept staring at me. Like he was warning me to stay away, to go back. I couldn't take my eyes off of him. And I didn't! I just eased away walking backwards until I was around the bend and he was out of sight. So creepy.

Ryan is sleeping and Alberto keeps telling knock-knock jokes.

"Knock, knock."

"Who's there?"

"Jake."

"Jake, who?"

"Jake the SNNAAAKKKEEE! SNAKE! SNAKE! SNAKE!"

He just keeps saying this over and over again, pointing at the river and laughing out of control every time he says "snake." I think he's lost his mind. I hope Jake just went to explore like me. Come back, Jake. Wherever you are, come back!

Field Journal – Day 36, September 21

Morning – *Jake never came back last night. Jake, where are you? Ryan won't wake up either. He's burning up with a fever. Alberto. Oh man. Alberto is bad. I can hear him in his tent just mumbling and laughing. Every once in a while I hear the word "snake." God, I don't know what to do! I'm not sick anymore and now I'm getting hungry.*

I'm gonna go soak some dirty clothes in the river and try to cool Ryan off. I feel completely alone. Except for that thing that keeps walking around our camp at night. What is that?

There is seriously nothing alive around here. Not even mosquitos, I've realized. It's crazy. But then there's this thing. And the eagle from yesterday. Is it the same thing? Can an eagle stalk? At one point I stepped out of my tent to go pee, and about 20 yards away I saw a pair of red eyes just staring at me! Red eyes? What kind of animal has red eyes? Yes, I feel totally alone right now and totally freaked out.

Evening – *I don't want to go to sleep. It's late, past midnight. Watch says 1:00 a.m. About an hour ago I was drifting off and I heard this awful scream. It sounded like someone was dying. Seriously. It was so horrible. And it went on for over a minute. I ran from my tent - it was coming from the river. Then all of a sudden it stopped. I yelled for Jake over and over again. Please Jake - I hope you heard me brother! And then this light. Right across from us on the other side of the river. Maybe 200 yards away, like a rod or shaft of fire, not very big, but distinct and bright. Then the smell. The same sickening smell that won't go away. It became overwhelming. I bent over, wanting to throw up.*

When I looked up from doubling over it was just…gone. Am I hallucinating? Losing it, like Alberto?

Ryan is bad. I think he might die. Oh God, please no! Alberto never came out of his tent today. He's just whispering "snake, snake, snake, sssnnnaakkkeee…" over and over again. When I try to talk to him, to get him to eat something, he just says it louder until I leave. He's not dangerous, I hope. Is he? Oh man. Nope, I'm definitely not sleeping tonight.

Field Journal – Day 37, September 22

Morning – *Ryan died last night.*

Despite my best attempts to stay awake, I fell asleep. I woke up and he was standing over me, wide-eyed. He was just staring at me...and then he pointed. Off into the distance. He looked right at me and said as clear as can be, "Go." I was shocked, horrified! I jumped up and grabbed him by the shoulders as he collapsed in my arms. But his fever was gone. I thought he had turned the corner. I couldn't believe it! I laid him back in his tent and then went back to my post by the fire. I tried so hard to stay awake, but fell asleep again.

When I got up this morning to check on him, he was just gone. No pulse No breath.

I'm so sorry Ryan. So, so sorry. Please forgive me! I tried not to leave you alone.

I went and told Alberto and he just laughed...

"Knock, knock."

"Who's there?"

"Ryan."

"Ryan who?"

"Ryan the...LION!...LION! LION! LION!!!!"

More laughing and totally freaking me out. What am I going to do?! I guess I should bury Ryan. Or should I not and just wait to be rescued? I can't leave him here. What would I tell his parents? Surely there's a search party looking for us by now. It's been four days. I'm so tired. So hungry. I'm going to go check out the river where I heard the screaming last night....

Evening – *So. Much. Blood! Oh my gosh, I went down to the* river's edge and what a mess of blood and gore. Nothing recognizable at all. I don't know if it's human or animal. I've never seen anything like it.

Oh Jake! Jake. Jake. Jake. He's not coming back, is he? That has to be him. Or what's left of him. I'll never be able to get the stench out of my mind. The smell of death. And that other odor just won't go away! What is it? What is any of this? What did that to him? Did that red-eyed whatever it is take him? I am so scared. So, so scared. I've got to hold it together. I don't want to sleep and I don't want to be awake either. This place is hell. I want out. Please, God, send someone to find me.

Field Journal – Day 38, September 23

Morning – *I have to leave. I have to leave. I have to leave. NOW. I can't believe what I just saw! Oh man, Alberto! And Ryan, what happened to Ryan?!! Dear God…I am running….*

Evening – *Okay, I'm going to try to write all this down. I'm not sure I can trust everything happening to me. I'm so exhausted and so hungry. My food is totally gone. I left everything behind. I ran with only my pack and personal items. Oh man, Alberto.*

I woke up this morning and I couldn't hear Alberto in his tent, so I went to check on him. Empty. First time in days he'd come out. I looked all around for him, calling his name.

I didn't want to go back to the river. Oh, the awful river! But that's all I could think of. And there he was…on the other side! He'd swum across to the other side and he was just standing there with no clothes on…totally naked. His back to me - like he was looking at something.

"Alberto!" I called to him. He turned around and had the biggest smile on his face. His famous Alberto smile. And then he threw back his head and yelled, "SNAKE!!" Before he finished – it happened so fast. I didn't even see where it came from. Yes…IT! Oh, it was a like a flash of white and red and gold and I thought I saw fur and also that horrible beak. The eagle! But no! It wasn't! I don't know what it was, but it took him. It just took Alberto. It picked him up and crushed him and then he was gone. I don't even know where. Up. Away. Back. I can't say. It's like I didn't see what I saw. But I saw it. And I don't even know what I saw. Tears in my eyes, I just

*yelled and cried and called and then...I ran. I ran to camp -
and Ryan. Oh, poor Ryan. His body, gone.*

Just gone!

Like Alberto.

Like Jake. They're all gone, except for me.

Field Journal – Day 39, September 24

I had to come back to the river. Oh, I didn't want to, but I can't just roam around out here going in circles. The river is my only path, my only way to freedom...hopefully. I didn't go back to camp though. I'm sitting right now, downriver as far as I can go on this side. Same place I was a few days ago...where I saw that...thing. That thing that got Alberto. Oh, Alberto....

I'm going to keep my fire going all night and rest. I'm so hungry. So utterly exhausted. I've got to find some food. Tomorrow, I'm going to swim across. I have to. It's the only way. I'm going to swim and then I am going to run. Downstream. And keep running. Away from here and away from that thing.

I don't know what's going to happen to me. If anyone finds this journal please get it to my mom and dad. Mom, I love you so much. I can't get your pretty face out of my mind. Please forgive me for not being a better son. Dad, you were right. I never should have done this stupid trip. I pushed it too far. I love you Dad.

Field Journal – Day 40, September 25

I did it. I made it across. And I ran until I collapsed. No sign at all of the eagle-creature-thing. Thank you, God. I have no idea how far I've gone.

It's even greener and more lush here. Like I've entered a jungle almost. Still no sign of animals of any kind. But the smell is gone. The air is so much sweeter! I went as far as I could go before the sun went down. I laid down thinking this was it. I can't go any further.

Then I looked back across the river and began to cry! There is a grove of trees, maybe just 75 yards on the other side. There's what looks like fruit hanging from them! My heart leapt. I had forgotten what hope felt like.

I'm going to sleep now and tomorrow muster my strength to swim back across. I think this is a good sign. I might make it out of here after all. See you soon, Mom and Dad. Too tired to write any more. Going to sleep now....

Field Journal – Day 41, September 26

OH GOD!
PLEASE!
NO!!!

CHAPTER ONE

Phineas T. Crook bolted up in bed.

Alarm blaring.

6:00 a.m.

Another "dream," if that is what you can call it. More like a premonition covered in dread. One of those dreams that you can just barely get your mind around as you wake up. The images and details slipping away like sand running through your fingers.

It had been, what, a month or even longer since the last one? It was so easy to lose track as the days turned into weeks.

Until another one hit.

The images, the horror, the feeling of wrongness and hopelessness.

Then…wide-awake, shirt soaked with sweat. And always, always the details just falling away, no matter how hard he tried to concentrate and hold on. Just to find some meaning in it all.

Sometimes the dreams or visions or whatever they were would come in waves. Happening every night for three, four, or five days - like torture. Then they would just…be gone. Sometimes they invaded once a week and other times once or twice a month. But always the same - dread without meaning.

No matter. It was time to get up because the students would be waiting at 8:00 a.m. sharp for another Monday morning lecture on biblical hermeneutics.

Phineas T. Crook, that would be *Dr.* Phineas T. Crook, was the esteemed associate professor of preaching and pastoral ministry at Oklahoma Baptist University. Esteemed may be too proud of a word, especially in light of his ongoing reputation. But he did hold the Sam and Martha Goodman Chair for said position.

Dr. Crook resided alone in the little home he had purchased three years ago on Broadway Avenue in Shawnee, Oklahoma, just minutes from the campus known as Bison Hill. He liked the little mid-century house very much, but he hated the loneliness of it all. Hopefully, prayerfully, it wouldn't always be this way.

Ring…Ring…Ring…!!

Jolted from his thoughts, Crook rushed to his charging station, grabbing his cell and quickly unplugging it.

"Hello?" he answered, still shaking off the aftermath of his dream.

"Phin! You awake?" That's how everyone who knew Phineas Crook well referred to him – *Phin.*

"Oh…good morning, Max. Yes, I'm awake. What's up? A little early to be calling, isn't it?" Phin asked, eyes rolling as he sighed to himself.

Dr. Max Allred was the assistant dean of the Hobbs College at

OBU, and Phin's best friend. He'd been the one to recommend Phin for appointment to the faculty at OBU, the one to insist to Phin that this was something he simply must do after his decision to resign as the senior pastor of Covenant Baptist Church in Oklahoma City. Those were dark days for his good friend, and Max felt it his duty to help his old college roommate reinvent himself. He also knew the tremendous potential that Phin held intellectually and spiritually. Phineas Crook would be a gift to the university they both loved and attended together as students so many years ago.

"Look Phin, sorry to call so early, but the dean has asked to meet with you and me together this morning before your classes begin. He wants to do it at seven-thirty," Max explained.

"What's this about, Max? Please don't tell me the school's bent out of shape again because of my *personal* interests."

"Look, I don't know. I can't really talk about it with you over the phone right now. I've just been asked to call and make sure you show up. Don't worry, I'll be in the meeting too." A pause. Then Max continued, "Look, Phin. Everybody likes you. The students *love* you. That goes a long way and you know it. Just relax and I'll see you in forty-five minutes," Max hung up.

Forty-five minutes? It was already 6:45! Phin had completely lost track of time. Lost in thought. Paralyzed is more like it.

Dang! he thought, *I hope this isn't the beginning of something bad.* As he said this to himself, he was thinking about the "dreams" and not the meeting.

Dr. Phineas T. Crook, took a quick shower, threw down a bowl of Cheerios and an orange, and grabbed his Harris Tweed jacket along with his leather satchel as he ran out the door.

Oklahoma Baptist University is a small liberal arts university of roughly two thousand students. Located just forty minutes east of Oklahoma City on Interstate 40, the school was founded in 1910 by the Baptist churches of Oklahoma, and has maintained a strong reputation for producing ministers and missionaries. But it's also known for its excellence in business education, nursing, science, and a host of other disciplines. A hallmark of an OBU education is the close link between faculty and students. At a school like OBU, the faculty also live under certain *expectations* - that they will not wander too far from the doctrinal tenants of the Baptist faith, and that their public reputations will not serve to tarnish the good image of the university. Not just anyone can be an OBU professor.

The student experience at OBU is tied hand and glove to strong and real relationships with those same faculty. Everyone knows that college is a time to learn and grow and explore new ideas. Sometimes those ideas are not necessarily a part of one's upbringing, especially in a state like Oklahoma and the surrounding states of the Midwest and Southwest where OBU draws from primarily for its student body. Individual faculty quickly form individual reputations among the OBU community. Students are continually drawn to those professors that have a penchant for the eccentric, the unusual, or the perceived "out of bounds." It's all a part of the coming-of-age cliché: to know and understand oneself.

On this cold February Monday morning, Phin whipped into his faculty parking spot located just behind Montgomery Hall, home of the Hobbs College of Theology and Ministry. It was 7:28 a.m. as he stepped out of his car, the bitter wind that comes "sweeping down the plains" slapping him in the face. *Why does it always seem to blow harder on campus?* Phin thought as he sprinted through the back door and up the stairs, bypassing the elevator. He didn't like to be late, ever.

The dean's office was located on the second floor. The best office in the building overlooked the majestic Oval of the campus, dotted with other class buildings, dormitories, and administrative offices. The central point of the Oval was the beautiful Oval Fountain itself, either frozen over or simply turned off this time of year.

Like most professors' offices, the dean's office sported an impressive library with one notable difference - it was enormous in size. Floor to ceiling, wall-to-wall bookshelves filled with a lifetime of collected works, special and rare editions, classics, and an assortment of various artifacts of academia. To step into the dean's office for the first time would truly set one aback. Phin had been in the office so many times now that its aura no longer affected him. It was still early as he arrived so not many were around yet - not even Carol, the dean's assistant.

Taking a deep breath and calming himself, Phin moved on through the open doorway. *Why was he so nervous anyway?*

"Ah, Phin, come on in! We just got here ourselves and were chatting," greeted Dean Reynolds, rising from his leather desk chair. Max Allred rose from where he was seated as well. *Of course...Max is already here*, Phin bristled.

With a round of customary, good morning handshakes, Phin and Max settled into guest chairs spaced evenly apart on the opposite side of the dean's desk.

"Okay," Phin thought. "Here we go."

CHAPTER TWO

Dr. Clayton Reynolds had served as the dean of the Hobbs College for seventeen years. He was forty-seven years old, having come into the position at a remarkably young age. Handpicked, he'd been plucked from one of the Southern Baptist seminaries by the search committee. "A prodigy in theology and philosophy" was the label he carried into the position. Reynolds was also good with people. All put together, it made for a rare combination. Because of his tenure, Reynolds was now firmly entrenched as a major gear in the university machine.

It is always a challenge to keep a school like OBU firmly planted in its historical and theological roots, while also staying relevant in an ever-changing world. Prior to Dr. Reynolds' assumption as the dean of the Hobbs College, the school had, some would say, *drifted*. Reynolds had fought the hard fight to right the course and set a new direction; one that made the administration and the trustees immensely relieved and happy. Dean Reynolds knew what he wanted, not tolerating anything or anyone that gummed up the works.

On top of all that, Clayton Reynolds was a sharp-looking and impressive man. Standing just at six foot three inches, he was well-built and muscular, the exact opposite of the two other men in the room. He looked older than his years, with his hair being on the saltier side of a salt and pepper mix. The man commanded respect.

"Phin, thanks for coming in early," the dean was all business this morning. "I'll get right to the point because I know you've got a class to teach. I've asked Dr. Allred to join us because I know you two are close, and because I think we need to make sure we are all on the same page when we leave here."

Dr. Allred. *Okay, we definitely aren't here to shoot the breeze*, Phin thought. This was a formal job evaluation. No doubt about it.

He was actually glad Max was in the room. Yes, they were good friends and had been since attending OBU together. Phin and Max saw eye-to-eye on many things, although they both took very different paths after graduating. Max taking the more formal route in academia, Phin going off in search of himself and God as a missionary on the African continent.

Phin would always be grateful for Max's presence in his life. They were both now in their mid-thirties, and as the two friends joined Reynolds in his office on this very cold Monday morning, it struck Phin: this trio of men shared a deep love for OBU. Yes, they had that one thing in common, but they were each vastly different from one another in so many other ways.

After losing touch through the twists and turns of the post-college years, Max and Phin had reconnected while Phin was still overseas. He would later return to the United States with his doctorate under one arm and a wife under the other. Those were the best of years. After what most would label an adventurous life abroad, Phin was ready for something a little quieter by way of pace of life. He and Autumn were madly in love and ready to start a family. No more adventure. No more crazy. Those days were over. Just a quiet life as a pastor, taking care of people. Preaching the Word of God. Raising kids in the suburbs of Oklahoma City, taking them to Thunder basketball games. He could see it all in his mind's eye. Then it all had come to an end....

Max and Phin sat quietly, Max stoically even, as Dean Reynolds continued, "Phin, your tenure with us the last three years has been a good one. There's no doubt you are one of the most popular professors on campus."

There was a "but" coming. Phin could feel it. Why hadn't Max said anything yet? That was just like him to sit there, overshadowed - overpowered really - by the persona of the dean. *Come on Max, help me out here, buddy*, Phin pleaded within.

Max Allred was very average when compared to... well, just about anyone. He was average height. Average build. Brown hair. Not dark or light, just...average. Even his personality was average. Not too high and excited, and not too low and dull. Just right in the middle. It made him the perfect person to serve under a man like Reynolds as the assistant dean. The dean would never feel threatened, and Max would never challenge. Hiring Max was brilliant on Reynolds' part because, as a graduate of OBU, Max understood many of the finer points of how the university lived and operated, which made him invaluable to a man like Reynolds, who would always be an outsider.

"But, Phin..." and there it was - the *but*. "I want you to seriously consider whether or not you still truly fit at a university like OBU."

"Why would I do that, *Clayton*?" Phin quickly shot back. Almost too quickly. If the dean was going to call him by his first name, he could do the same, couldn't he? Just a slight move on his part to bow up. Phin was definitely not like Max when it came to jockeying with the dean.

"Why in the world would you even ask me that? I love it here. I love what I do. I love working with the students. You just said yourself that I am one of the most popular professors on campus. Help me understand."

So this is how it's going to be, Reynolds surmised. Okay then, here we go. "Phin, I think you know what I'm talking about."

"Of course I know what you're talking about, *Clayton*. Why are we beating around the bush with all this popularity crap?" Phin shot back. He had no patience for playing political games. He did love his job, and he knew the administration would be hard-pressed to release him. Phin wanted to seize on this to his advantage.

Reynolds bristled as Phin continued, "Please, let's just cut to it - I want you to say it straight out. Say what the problem is...what we all know it to be. Say it with Max sitting here just staring at us. Go ahead, I'm all ears."

The room fell silent. Max sat wide-eyed, the dean composing himself to continue. Even Phin was surprised at how strong he had come on. "Very well. Look Phin, you *are* a good teacher...great even. But it's about your interactions with students and those outside the university when you are *not* in the classroom. Your personal interest...obsession actually, is staining your reputation."

"What you really mean is that it's staining the reputation of the university," Phin inserted.

"Phin, it's the same thing. The faculty, the students, the administration, it's all the university. You can't separate one from the other," Reynolds countered. "When students attend one of your dorm floor lectures, or when you draw any kind of crowd on your personal lecture circuit, people don't just see you, they see Oklahoma Baptist

University. It's all one and the same and you know it."

Phin did know it but he didn't like it. In a very real way, being a sitting chair at OBU gave him the clout to travel and lecture and propose his ideas and interpretations no matter how unorthodox they might be. That was really what this was all about. That's why Dr. Phineas Crook was sitting in Dean Clayton Reynolds' office on a Monday morning, just before a class, seemingly being asked to resign. Orthodoxy.

Phin sat silent for a moment, contemplating how to continue. "Okay, you are right. I understand, Dean. So let me ask because I want to be clear," Phin had cooled a bit. "Are you asking me to resign my position on the faculty at OBU?" Phin tensed again waiting for a reply.

"No...I don't think we are there yet, Phin. But I want you to understand. There's pressure. Real pressure coming from outside this office. Certain trustees don't like what they are hearing. It's all second, third hand - whatever. But they don't like it."

Reynolds went on, "When the trustees aren't happy, they put pressure on the president. When the president feels pressure, he pushes on the provost. When the provost feels pressure, he pushes on me. And when I feel pressure, I push - "

"On me," Phin cut him off.

"Yes, you've got it," Reynolds agreed. "Phin, you know that I advocate for my faculty."

"Yes! He sure does, Phin. He's in your corner." Welcome to the party, Max. *Nice time to speak up*, Phin was thinking, perturbed at his friend. *Why are you even here?*

It was true. Dean Reynolds did have a reputation for hiring faculty he liked and respected, then standing by those men and women through thick and thin. If they were even having this conversation it was because, Phin knew, he was feeling the heat from above.

"Yes, I do and I appreciate it, Dean," Phin replied, ignoring Max. "I do know that and I appreciate it. My intention is to never put the university or you or anyone," eyeing Max with a smirk, "into a bad position on my account. You say that I'm obsessed. I don't know, maybe I am. I like to think that I'm passionate. Am I driven by that passion? Yes, absolutely. You both know," Phin's voice rising, his excitement beginning to permeate the room, "that what I am doing, *on my own time*, that what is compelling me and pushing me forward in all of this is not academic. No sir...for me, this is *real*. For me this is *everything*!"

Phin finished much stronger, much louder than he had intended. He couldn't help himself. The room was once again silent. This time the tension between the men had drained. Clayton Reynolds sat staring. Max just looked down. The silenced dragged out.

Until finally...Dean Reynolds' slowly and thoughtfully broke the silence, "Phin...do you really, honestly, in your heart of hearts, with the full engagement of logic and reason believe that the Garden of Eden still exists and can be found?"

It was Phin's turn to be stunned.

This was the first time that Dr. Clayton Reynolds had ever asked this question in a way that Phin actually believed that he wanted to know an answer.

No mocking.

No derision.

No placating.

No humoring.

Something had shifted in the room. Something had changed. Phin could feel it. Max could feel it. The books on the shelves could even feel it.

"Yes sir, I do," came the answer from Dr. Phineas T. Crook.

CHAPTER THREE

Staff sergeant Billy Warren readied his military issued M27 IAR, affixed with an ACOG Squad Day Optic. A weapon designed for only one purpose - to kill.

This was a solo mission. No backup, no support. He would go in and not come back out.

Looking to his left and to his right, and again to his left, he popped up from the depression he'd been lying in and sprinted toward the first out building at the edge of the small town. His heart was racing, blood pumping, palms moist.

This was real. As real as it gets.

Sergeant Warren was career military. He joined the Marines right out of high school, making his parents proud. He had served in multiple theaters of conflict across both Iraq and Afghanistan, mostly covert and in conjunction with "friendly" nationals in both countries. Since the official end of the war, the media and Washington played up the role of the United States military as "special advisors" on the ground.

Sergeant Warren laughed every time he heard the term.

"Special advisors, my foot!" he'd say to his men. "This is my special advisor!" hollering as he held up his automatic assault rifle. "And it has two bits of advice for anyone on the other end of it: run or die!" his men whooping it up as he lowered the weapon, big giant grin on his clean-shaven face. Billy Warren was a serious fighting machine, trained by the Marines with two objectives: protect and kill.

The scourge of the Middle East and Northern Africa known as ISIS had been the dominating focus of his time on the ground. Yes, Sergeant Warren had multiple confirmed "kills" to his name, and he'd been wounded more than once in return, his body bearing the scars of his sacrifice for his nation.

Now he was ready to sacrifice again.

Warren had three targets that were his primary objectives. His secondary objective included killing any other bad guys that got in his way.

This mission, like so many before it, was off the books, and no one would ever know it happened. The only sign being, hopefully, a byline from Syria on page four of the *New York Times* or the *Washington Post* announcing the death of "high ranking leaders" within ISIS.

Pulling up his HUD (Heads Up Display), Warren took one more quick look at the digital images of the three "targets."

Muhammad al Shanees, Alexander Jabar, and a woman, Miriam Akbar. All three were bad actors, responsible for kidnappings, beheadings, and at least six suicide bombings in Europe.

The recent bombing attempt on the subway system in New York

City was traced back to this trio as well. Only by the grace of God did U.S. intelligence services intercept the would-be bomber. The documents taped to the explosives in his backpack were the break the government needed, and the reason that Sergeant Billy Warren was sent to this little desert hamlet in southeastern Syria known as Ghouta.

Parachuting in about a mile outside of town, Warren had made his way under the cover of darkness to the edge of town and waited. He was now fully engaged, and having memorized the layout of the village, was ready to execute the mission.

Ready, *GO!*

Rounding off the corner, Warren sprinted down the quiet street between a canyon of open-windowed buildings. Some two stories tall, others three and even four stories. Classic Middle Eastern architecture, the buildings shown with the battle scars of the years of civil war within Syria.

The territory that Ghouta lay in was now firmly under ISIS control, this little unassuming village becoming one of the many headquarters of operations for the multi-headed monster.

Tonight, I'm going to cut this head off! thought Warren as he moved in stealth mode to his first checkpoint, ducking behind a pile of tires about two hundred yards inside the interior from where he started. He was doing good. Not out of breath yet, heart rate calming. All business, just like he had been trained.

Waiting only ninety seconds to assess the new vantage point, Warren made a quick check of the rooftops and the side street he had just moved through.

No sign of detection. Excellent.

Steeling himself, he eased slowly from behind his tire barrier and verified that his next pathway was open. This one was behind a series of buildings just off a main street.

Not an ideal path.

Satellite imaging showed this to be the most direct route, certainly better than the main street that ran parallel. But back alleys are unpredictable and this one was extremely narrow, maybe four feet wide at most, so if there were any surprises, there wouldn't be much room to maneuver.

Ah well, this is urban warfare, Warren knew - hazardous at every turn…and deadly.

Warren shot his body to the corner of the alley and immediately entered, moving low and quiet. He relied on his night vision to step over and avoid trip hazards: trash, broken toys, and anything else that lay in his way. About halfway through he heard a sound and saw movement just up ahead and to his left. Pinning himself against the stone wall, Warren's reflexes kicked into action. He launched himself toward the movement.

Better to be on the offense and own the element of surprise, the sergeant knew.

He found himself pinning a helpless and homeless old man to ground, his hand over his mouth to keep him from crying out. The city was likely dotted throughout with many more just like this one, run out of their homes either because they had been destroyed in the fighting or because ISIS had commandeered the property for nefarious uses.

There was that moment of realization: *This is not a hostile. He's a victim.*

Without another thought, Sergeant Warren sunk his knife deep into the chest of the old man, squeezing him tight, holding him firm as the life faded from his eyes.

There was no other way, the mission could not be compromised. Collateral damage. That is what they call it in military terminology. Warren could not risk a cry of warning or fright from the old man. The mission was too critical. He knew this was a possibility, even a likelihood, and had come to terms with it before even saying yes to the mission.

Sorry old man, Warren thought, as he eased off of the now lifeless body and resumed his movement through the ally.

Arriving at the exit, Warren found himself at a "T" that dumped into a larger street. Checking both directions, he once again made his move, this time turning left and moving quickly, hugging the side of the building. It was deathly quiet now, and dark. The only sound, that of a barking dog in the distance.

For the next twenty minutes, Sergeant Warren weaved his way with precision through the maze of pockmarked buildings and burnt-out cars.

At last he arrived at his destination - a small compound of buildings behind a chain-link fence topped with razor wire.

Laughing to himself at the pathetic excuse for security, Warren made quick work of clipping his way through the fence. He chose as his breach point an area where, on the other side of the fence, was some garbage and concrete blocks stacked as much as three feet high, a perfect place to reassess and prepare for the assault.

Now, it was show time, thought Warren, smiling to himself. *It's about to get fun!*

CHAPTER FOUR

W arren checked his weapon one last time taking in the situation.

About thirty yards ahead standing at the corner of the main building were two guards, both with what looked like Russian-made SKS rifles slung over their shoulders.

Figures the Russians would be involved, Warren mused, *either directly or indirectly*. Their intelligence had been correct again. If the intel was *still* correct, then on the second floor of that same building all tucked nice and neat into bed would be al Shanees, Jabar, and Akbar.

Both guards were lazily smoking, basically looking bored and uninterested, not paying attention to anything.

No doubt they drew the short stick for the midnight shift, Warren thought, smiling once again to himself. He liked to find the humor in dangerous situations, keep the atmosphere light. *Can't give into fear*, he knew. He also knew that these two would not be the only ones lurking about. There was likely one to three more stationed at the other buildings or just walking the perimeter.

Sergeant Warren's plan was simple: a head-on, fast assault. He'd belly crawl as far as he could, get as close as he could. When he knew he could go no further without detection, he'd lay on the ground and put two rounds through the forehead of each guard.

Then he'd storm the building and run the stairs to the second floor. Infrared imaging showed only three rooms on that level. He should be able to check all in less than thirty seconds, identify the targets, and eliminate them.

By that time it would be obvious to everyone else sleeping in the other buildings what was happening. They would converge on his position. But at that point it wouldn't matter anymore.

Crawling ever so slowly, Warren slithered his way toward the corner of the building from his hiding place. He could feel his heart rate climbing. Taking slow deliberate breaths, he worked to calm himself, all the while continuing to move - to creep - closer and closer to the unsuspecting soldiers.

He was maybe thirty feet away now. Easing his rifle into position ever so quietly, he sighted the first guard, all the while preparing to train his sights on the second as soon as he pulled the trigger.

If either one were to glance to their left and down they would surely see him laying there. It didn't matter though, he was close enough now that he could improvise.

A nice clean head shot, Billy, he said to himself. *A nice clean*...holding his breath, Warren wrapped his index finger around the trigger...*shot*.

A massive thud slammed into Sergeant Warren's back, intense pressure but no pain. Simultaneously, he heard the crack of a shot being fired... but not from him!

What the…?! Warren's mind raced. *The roof!*

He had missed the guard on the roof. Probably out of sight on the other side of the building.

The guard had likely made his way to the edge and glanced down. Even covered in camo, he had seen the shape of a man laying in the grass and dirt, training his weapon on his two unsuspecting friends.

Warren had been a sitting duck!

Then crazy happened. Warren jumped up as the other two guards looked his way and scrambled to pull their rifles off of their backs.

Billy was slammed again by another round, this one in the right shoulder.

He was already throwing his own M27 up to the same shoulder, firing a quick blast of three shots. He saw the guard on the roof disappear behind the ledge in a red mist.

One down.

Turning his weapon on the other two guards - one sprinting toward him yelling something about Allah in Arabic - Warren fired and took him out cleanly with a single shot to the face.

The man fell hard, and Warren ran over the top of him as he fired into the chest of the other guard.

Two down.

Three down.

Under normal circumstances, the shot to the back and the shoulder would have been the end of the mission and the end of Billy Warren.

But these were not ordinary circumstances. Warren was laughing to himself again as he burst through the front door, immediately bounding up the small flight of stairs just to his right.

Gotta find the humor, keep it light, stomp down the fear, Warren was saying to himself, also aware that maybe he was having too much fun with this one.

At the top of the stairs was a small hallway - two doors on each side and one directly in front.

There's no way anybody's asleep anymore, he knew. But it didn't matter now.

Which door? A one in three chance.

Warren charged straight ahead, busting the door down and off its hinges.

He recognized them immediately.

Muhammad al Shanees was standing on his bed in the corner, still in his nightclothes. Arms and hands out in front of him, he was obviously pleading for his life.

Alexander Jabar was kneeling over the side of his bed, frantically trying to wrap his hand around something underneath, looking up wide-eyed with fear.

Pop, Pop!

And then another *Pop, Pop!*

No thinking, no hesitation. There had already been enough of both.

Only execution. Literally.

But wait! What about Miriam Akbar? Of course! There's no way she would be sleeping in the same room as the men. Not in a Muslim culture.

Rookie mistake.

Fatal mistake.

Sergeant Billy Warren knew it before he heard the shuffle behind him. There was no time to turn around as the metal bar came down on his arm...hard.

CRACK! He heard the snap as his weapon went flying.

Then another blow, this one across the back of the head, sending him to the ground.

He began to twitch, his body not working properly. He was lying on his side, helpless. As he stared across the room into the eyes of the two dead primary targets, a pair of boots slowly came into his view.

Primary target number three.

Miram Akbar kicked him over onto his back, sitting down heavily on his chest, a look of evil in her eyes. She had a devilish grin on her face as she...observed him. Like she was studying a dissection in biology class.

Sergeant Warren just smiled back.

Then he began to chuckle - out loud.

Gotta find the humor, keep it light, stomp down the fear.

Akbar began to chuckle too, a fiendish laugh originating from the pit of hell itself.

And then...lifting a long, brutal knife from behind her back, Miram Akbar slowly and deliberately drove the knife through the forehead of Billy Warren, all the way to the back of his skull.

*Gotta find the humor...no fear...*these were Warren's last thoughts as, painlessly, everything went red and then black.

CHAPTER FIVE

"Yes!"

"We have a confirmed termination. Targets eliminated and active connection severed," the excitement in Tony Chen's voice was contagious. He and Osmond Jenks were all smiles, high fiving each other, whooping it up. Like two teenage nerds who just hacked the Pentagon.

They actually were nerds, just not teenagers. Chen and Jenks were co-heads of the Body Residence Grouping Project. They affectionately referred to it as the BORG Project because they were both Star Trek fans. They were also arguably among the brightest minds in artificial intelligence application research in the world; landing both of them had been a coup for LaPhage Industries.

"Beginning body residence restoration," it was Jenks' turn to steer. "Doc, how are we looking?"

"Vitals are stable and his brain synapses show normal activity," replied Dr. Mark Sayer. "He should be coming around any moment."

"Sergeant...can you hear me? Sergeant Warren? Billy...come on brother. Open your eyes, you're back," said Chen. He was standing over Sergeant Warren in his standard uniform of faded jeans, Chaco's, and a tank top of some solid color - today it was green. He gently tapped Warren's cheek as he continued to lay back in what they called *The Chair*. He was still, unmoving, as he had been for the last two hours and thirteen minutes exactly.

"He's okay, right?" It was General Myers' turn. A consummate Marine, he was genuinely concerned about one of his "boys." "This is all still normal, isn't it?"

"Well, normal is a relative term, Sir. Since this our first time in a real theater of conflict with the Robatar, nothing is truly normal yet," said the black spike-haired Chinese tech genius. "But if we are comparing to our controlled test runs, then yes, we are all within our acceptable parameters...oh, look, here he comes...."

There was a twitching movement in Billy Warren's fingers and feet as the reconnection was setting in, his breathing becoming more excited as he crossed from one reality to the next.

His eyes popped open, body suddenly tensing.

"Whoa," he squeezed out, "now that was one heck of an out-of-body experience."

"Welcome back, son," said the general.

"How'd I do, sir?"

"Mission accomplished. You did well. Now take it easy." Looking to the doctor, "Can we set him up?"

"Sure," Dr. Sayer moved over to The Chair, pressing the button that righted it to a sitting position. "Here, take a sip of this and just

44

relax," urged the doctor, handing Warren a cup with a straw.

"Okay, all very impressive, but can we go over one more time what it is exactly that we have just seen?" This time it was Admiral Watkins who emerged from the background with a question.

He had been sitting quietly during most of the operation, whispering comments or asking questions to his colleague, General Myers. Both men represented the Department of Defense and had been assigned to the BORG Project as military liaisons. Both had been given the authority to classify the project and its beta operations. They were here today to see what it was they had given their thumbs-up to, and assess its viability for military application.

In an ironically funny sort of way, Chen and Jenks weren't in the business of hacking the Pentagon - they were now actually working for it.

"What you have just seen, Admiral, is the future," it was the voice of Ruth LaPhage. She had entered the lab sometime during the operation, having observed the whole event as the other five in the room stood transfixed in front of the video wall. The group had watched the events of the operation in Ghouta unfold in real time. The vantage point was unique because they had seen it all happen the same way Warren had seen it, as if his eyes were their eyes. As it turned out, Sergeant Billy Warren had been the perfect choice for this first, real-world test of the Robatar.

Ruth LaPhage strode over to the two military men, arms crossed, a formidable presence of confidence. She stood her own next to them.

"Project BORG is everything we had hoped for and promised. We've just seen the ultimate test with smashing success," she was smiling from ear to ear.

"Yes, we have, indeed," said Chen. "And Sergeant Warren is back with us none the worse for wear. Sergeant, how are you feeling now?"

"Pretty good, actually. So we did it? It worked? That all *really* happened?"

"Oh yes, it did!" exclaimed Jenks.

"Tony, now that we've seen it all in high definition and in real time, go ahead and unpack for us one more time exactly what it was again that we saw," urged Ruth.

"Sure thing, Ms. LaPhage. Okay, as you know, our artificial intelligence, or AI, research has made significant strides in the last four years. Especially in its application to the biomedical field. We've been able to integrate AI into a whole new generation of prosthetics for victims of amputations."

"The prosthetics of the last one hundred years look like wood stumps compared to what we've been able to do," inserted Jenks.

It was true.

Fed mostly by the extreme wealth of its founder, Charles LaPhage, LaPhage Industries had been a small player in the AI field but it had quietly, behind the scenes, been making huge strides in research and development.

Charles LaPhage had a passion for doing extraordinary things to improve the quality of life for all people. It was also personal to LaPhage. His beloved wife, Mary, suffered from diabetes and had undergone the amputation of one leg. The old generation of prosthetics was just unacceptable to Charles. There had to be a better way.

Pouring massive amounts of cash into outside-the-box thinking and testing, LaPhage Industries burst onto the scene publicly when they posted a video of Mary - walking, running, *playing tennis* - with a prosthetic that functioned to the level of a *real* limb. The impossible had been achieved.

The LaPhage Limb, as it came to be known, really did make the prosthetics of old look like Captain Hook's peg leg.

"That's right, " Chen continued. "Artificial intelligence is basically a computer's ability to think and act on its own. But even the best AI has to be steered and directed. No AI is truly autonomous. So the breakthrough for us came when we bridged the gap between the brain and our proprietary AI chip in a fully functioning robotic prosthetic."

"The LaPhage Limb," said General Myers.

"Yes, the LaPhage Limb," came Ruth LaPhage. "Consider an arm or a leg that is artificial, but can function and be controlled fully by the brain. Go ahead Tony, keep going."

"Right. What we have been able to do is insert a tiny neuro-implant into the base of the frontal lobe of the brain. This transmitter wirelessly sends signals to the AI chip in a new robotic arm or leg. Then the chip takes over and just *knows* what to do. But here's the exciting key that makes it all possible: the neuro-implant is two-way, so the AI chip is continually sending back to the brain signals of its own. This creates the sensation of *feeling*. Even pain receptors are restored. So you have this back-and-forth exchange of information between the brain and the chip and *Voila*...The LaPhage Limb!"

"Amazing..." said Myers. "Simply amazing."

"Yes, it is, General," said Ruth. "The LaPhage Limb has transformed the life of every single person that has received one. Universally we are told, and even my mother testified, that the LaPhage Limb is nearly one hundred percent like having a real arm or leg. There is absolutely nothing a person cannot do with one of our next gen prosthetics."

"So all of this has opened the door to what we just saw in what way, Ms. LaPhage?" asked Admiral Watkins. A man of few words, he was obviously curious and fascinated by what they had just witnessed.

"That's where Project BORG comes in," replied Chen. "Oz and I...I'm talking about Osmond here...so Oz and I began to play *what if*. So what if - instead of just an arm or a leg - what if we connected the neuro-implant in the brain to a fully functional robotic instrument? But it would have to be something that fully mimicked human form, or else it would confuse the brain."

"Yeah, like you couldn't connect it to a robotic spider because the brain has no reference point on how to use eight legs," said Jenks.

"If you go full body, you have to be working with something that has two arms, two legs, all ten fingers and toes, eyes, ears, you get it? The whole works. So full body means full *humanoid* body," continued Chen.

"This would have been impossible even ten years ago," said Jenks. "We just didn't have the right tech in place for optics, audio, plus the necessity for high-powered computing in a super small digital format."

"But that's all changed," back to Chen. "We have it all now, the full package in a complete human-form robotic apparatus. Once again, the full connectivity to a real human brain is key because an AI chip on its own just won't cut it. You can't send a computer to do what we just did and expect any measure of success. It just can't act and *react* like a fully trained soldier."

"And that's what we just now saw?" Myers inserted. "Sergeant Warren's brain was connected to...what do you call it again?"

"The Robatar," said Jenks.

"Yes, the Robatar. And this *Robatar* went in and took out the enemy just as if Sergeant Warren were there physically and in person. Do I have it right?" asked Myers.

"Why do you call it a Robatar?" interrupted Admiral Watkins.

"Yes, you have it exactly right, General," answered Chen. Turning to the Admiral, "And the word Robatar is a cross between the words *robot* and *avatar*."

"I came up with the word!" Jenks gloated, apparently pleased with himself.

Chen just rolled his eyes, "Obviously we all get what a robot is, but an avatar is basically a digital character that represents who a person is in a video game or some online platform. Like I have created an avatar of myself for when I play *Fallout* or some other first-person shooter video game. What we have done with Project BORG is marry together a real human-form robot with the human brain. The best way to describe it is that when we connect a subject's brain, he leaves his own body, in a manner of speaking, and he *becomes* the robot. Controlling every aspect of the machine. Thus it becomes his Robot-Avatar…his Robatar! Make sense?"

"Yes it does. Fully," said General Myers. "You said that this all works because the robot or the chip or whatever sends back messages to the brain so that it can feel sensation. The LaPhage Limb feels pain, right? What about this Robatar? Good Lord, what did we just subject Sergeant Warren to?" The General was obviously concerned with the physical implications of what they had just done to a real man.

"Don't worry," answered Chen. "We have the ability to set tolerances for the LaPhage Limb and for the Robatar. Remember, we are dealing with artificial intelligence. There's a balance between what the brain tells it to do and what we allow it to do via programming. Obviously, we turned off all pain receptors on the Robatar. That's why the good sergeant was able to get up and just keep going, even though he was shot twice. Either one of which could have been fatal if he had really been there in person."

Admiral Watkins again, "I don't understand how this link works. We're sitting here in Fort Worth, Texas, and the Robatar is in Syria. I get how an arm or leg is connected, but how are we making this happen half a world away?"

"Because my father has three satellites orbiting the earth that beam a near-perfect signal between this room here, and whatever country we position one of the others over," said Ruth. This news raised the eyebrows of the general and admiral. Apparently LaPhage

Industries was more *industrious* than most people realized.

In fact, everything about today's military test in Syria was fully and completely off the books. Even the president was unaware. Myers and Watkins were there to see the final product of what LaPhage Industries was offering to the military. The operation was classified, and had a problem occurred, all involved would have denied any knowledge.

"General...Admiral...what we have seen here is the dawn of a new day," Ruth began to build her case. "With zero casualties or fatalities, our military, *with the help of LaPhage Industries*, was just able to execute a successful operation, covertly, in another country, and take out three of the top terrorist leaders of ISIS."

Sergeant Warren couldn't hold back any longer and jumped in, "Wait just one second!"

He was obviously agitated.

"What do you mean by 'successful' and taking out 'three'? That witch, Akbar, kicked my butt and drove a stinkin' knife into my robotic skull! How's that a success? They now have the Robatar and all the tech that goes with it. And by the way, I hear what you're sayin' about the pain thing being turned off, but it still ain't no walk in the park getting killed!"

Everyone just stared.

"I'm sorry, Billy," Ruth moved over to Sergeant Warren, placing her hand gently on his right arm. "I thought you understood. The moment she stabbed you in the head and severed the connection, it triggered the self-destruct mode on the Robatar. There was an explosion - a big one - precisely measured to take out the whole compound and everyone in it. No one survived. And if they even bother to wade through the rubble, all they'll find of the Robatar will be some charged chunks of unidentifiable metal. The world will just assume we hit the target with a drone strike. So, you see, it was a success, Billy. *You* were a success."

It was Sergeant Warren's turn to just stare. "Well, I'll be..." he trailed off.

Ruth patted his shoulder, moving away. Dr. Sayer moved in to do another check of his vitals.

There was something magnetic and beautiful about Ruth LaPhage, that's for sure. She had a grace about her as she walked and moved, yet at the same time she exuded confidence. She was never seen around LaPhage Industries without wearing her stereotypical white lab coat. Most likely her attempt to mute any ill feelings others may have about her being Charles LaPhage's only daughter - that somehow she had come to the head of the company without earning it - and to also look the part of a serious scientist.

In truth, Ruth LaPhage was as brilliant as she was beautiful, with her piercing green eyes and striking red hair, always pulled back in a ponytail. She had graduated with honors from MIT and had worked for some of the leading bio-tech companies in Europe, like Mak Labs, The Schluberhause Research Forum, and others.

That was, until the accident.

While building her own name and reputation in Europe, Charles and Mary LaPhage had been in a serious accident while vacationing in Utah.

It was a strange occurrence that sent her parents' Land Rover careening off the edge of the road and into a gully as they were driving up Big Cotton Wood Canyon outside of Salt Lake City. Charles LaPhage was known to never touch alcohol and the toxicology report confirmed that he was clean.

That was three years ago.

Questions about the accident's cause plagued Ruth's mind to this day. But the end result was that her mother was dead, and her father incapacitated to the point that Ruth was forced to come home and take the reins of LaPhage Industries. There was no other family to fill the role. The only other children the LaPhages ever had was a son, Ruth's older brother Jacob, who had died in another tragic accident years before. That left Ruth as the only one to do it.

She was the catalyst behind Project BORG, and while no one in the world knew it yet - save the six individuals in that room - at the age of just thirty-five, she was on the verge of leading a paradigm shift in how humans interacted with technology.

"Gentlemen - excuse me - *Admiral*," Ruth's steely eyes drilling into Watkins, "and *General*," a softer look at Myers, "I hope you can appreciate what we've just seen today. The LaPhage Robatar changes everything. What we are talking about is far more sweeping in scope than just one operation to take out three terrorists - three terrorists that most people have never heard of. Imagine the application just for the military. We can send our best trained men and women into any context regardless of the danger. They can move with a boldness that has never before been seen, without fear of injury or death. They can even take on damage, as we have seen today, and keep going!

"Certainly the Robatar is not unstoppable," she continued, "but it is the next best thing. If a mission is not fully successful, if the Robatar is compromised, it simply detonates. Leaving behind no trace that it - that *we* - were ever there. No dead bodies, except for those that deserve death. Ideally, the Robatar can accomplish its objectives without detection, and remain for whatever time is necessary after the hostiles have been eliminated - collect intel, search for records, maps, whatever could be useful for future missions, and then upload images of what it finds in real time. We've never had anything like this available to us before. In the ideal scenario, the Robatar egresses in stealth, just the way it enters, and we extricate it and repurpose it for another mission.

"But that's just the military application. Consider first responders. Robatars that can go into burning buildings and bring out survivors.

Or move into avalanche areas, or scale down dangerous mountain slopes to stranded hikers. *Any* situation too risky for human life is now the playground of a LaPhage Robatar," Ruth's enthusiasm was winning the moment.

General Myers and Admiral Watkins were sold. These were tough-minded and tough-bodied military men. They had both lived and breathed the hell on earth known as war. Both understood clearly the implications of what they were seeing and hearing, because they had both seen and heard the agony of too many young men and women mangled by the ravages of armed conflict.

The LaPhage Robatar would not put an end to war. No. Nothing could ever do that. But it would certainly save lives. United States American lives. And it would help make sure that the United States was the winner.

"Thank you, Ms. LaPhage," it was Admiral Watkins who spoke for the two of them. "I'll admit I was skeptical. Even as we watched Sergeant Warren in action today, it was very difficult to believe that what we were watching was real. It looked more like watching a video game that my grandson plays. One of the *Call of Duty* games, I think it is. But when you wrap your mind around the fact that what we were watching was no game at all, but as real as any war can be...well, I am indeed impressed."

Tony Chen and Oz Jenks were both smiling.

Tony winked at Ruth and mouthed, *I told you so*, about to explode with delight.

Dr. Sayer sitting next to Sergeant Warren looked satisfied.

Ruth LaPhage beamed, "Thank you, Admiral. I am glad to be of service to my country. My father would be thrilled. He was - *is* I should say - a proud American and feels it his duty to leverage his resources for good and against evil. I am just glad I can see this dream come to fruition. So...I trust we are clear to continue testing?" she asked, "We have a series of other real-world scenarios we would like to run the Robatar through. And obviously, Sergeant Warren is ideally suited to continue as our primary driver of the Robatar."

"I'm good if you are, Admiral," it was clear that General Myers was on board. He was the easy one to sell going in. They all knew it.

"Thank you, General. Yes, Ms. LaPhage, you are clear to continue. I don't think I need to say it, but just continue with the protocol we have set, and keep sending us your results via the encrypted channel we've been using," concluded Admiral Watkins.

"Can somebody get me out of this dang chair?!" Warren was done. Ready to be moving again. That elicited a few chuckles in the room.

"Sure, Billy, thank you so much again. I assume you are on board and ready to continue with the program? I'm sorry if I was being presumptuous earlier. I didn't intend to speak for you," Ruth said warmly.

"Absolutely, I'm on board! Are you kidding me? Just as long as somebody can get me a pizza and a beer. I'm starving," another round of laughter in the room.

It had been a good afternoon.

"Dr. Sayer, are we good here you think?" Ruth asked.

"Yes, ma'am," replied Sayer. The good doctor had been with LaPhage Industries as an original hire of Charles LaPhage, his discretion and professionalism unquestioned.

"Let's just get you reconnected, Sergeant, before you go trying to storm out after that pizza of yours," Sayer said.

Sergeant Warren worked his way to the edge of The Chair and swung his body to the side.

"Okay, left arm first," directed the doctor.

Warren lifted his left stump and Dr. Sayer attached his prosthetic, his LaPhage Limb. Checking the neural connection, Sayer confirmed a green status.

"Are we good, Sergeant? Everything feel normal?"

Warren flexed his fingers and worked his arm. "Yep, feels A-Okay, doc."

"Very good, now the leg."

Next Warren lifted the stump of his left leg, severed just above the knee.

Sergeant Billy Warren had been a victim - one of the many victims of the bombing of the U.S. Embassy in London five years ago. Forty-seven dead and twenty-three more wounded.

It was a suicide bomb like so many perpetrated by ISIS around the world.

Sergeant Warren had spent two months in a coma at Walter Reed Medical Center in Washington D.C., followed by eight months of rehab, having lost both his left arm and left leg.

It was a difficult adjustment to life without two limbs. It meant the end of his military career and the beginning of a life he knew nothing about.

Then he heard about the LaPhage Limb.

That was two years ago and that's when Sergeant Billy Warren had been reborn.

It was a sweet moment the day Ruth LaPhage, aware of his Marine training and combat background, came knocking on the door of his one-bedroom apartment.

LaPhage Industries was about to begin trials on a new project. The Body Residence Grouping program it was called. Or Project BORG.

They needed a volunteer, but not just any volunteer. They needed Sergeant Billy Warren. If he was willing.

And oh, he was willing.

For you see, after waking up from his coma and finding himself mangled and broken, Sergeant Warren had wanted to know what happened. That's when he was told about the bombing. A bombing planned and orchestrated by Muhammad al Shanees, Alexander Jabar, and Miriam Akbar.

"Now then, how's that, Sergeant?" asked Dr. Sayer.

Jumping out of The Chair, Warren hopped up and down a couple of times, shaking the leg in between.

"Good as new, Doc! You the man." Looking over at Tony Chen and Oz Jenks, "You two nerds take it easy." Then a high five for Chen, who was all smiles.

He turned to his superiors and snapped to attention, offering a crisp salute. Admiral Watkins and General Myers returned the salute.

"At ease, Marine. You take care of yourself now," Watkins offered with a proud look in his eye.

As Sergeant Warren shot his way to the door, he made one quick glance back at Ruth LaPhage, and offered a wink, "Ruthie! I'll catcha later!"

Then he was out the door.

Walking down the hall, Warren stopped at the elevator and swiped his security card. The doors opened and he stepped inside, beginning the ride to ground level and the cafeteria.

In his mind's eye he could still see Miram Akbar, sitting heavy on his chest, cold eyes staring and laughing out loud.

Sergeant Billy Warren couldn't help but to chuckle under his breath, "Looks like I'm the one that got the last laugh."

CHAPTER SIX

"Dr. Crook!...Dr. Crook, can you hold up please?"

"Oh sure, Jason, how's it going today?"

Dr. Phineas Crook was nearing the bottom of the steps, exiting Shawnee Hall after his hermeneutics class, which came after his tension-filled meeting with Dean Reynolds earlier that morning. Phin had spent the last fifty minutes lecturing on the importance of context when seeking to apply meaning to the biblical text for today. "You have to constantly ask yourself, 'what did this mean to those reading it back then, in the day,' in order to migrate that understanding to today's culture," Crook preached. "It's all about context, context, context!" he'd boomed. Then they spent the last twenty minutes of the class applying this principle to Exodus 32 and the famous golden calf incident in the Old Testament, the infamous scene when God's people had forsaken God by pooling their gold jewelry and ornaments together to fashion an idol. The whole camp slipped into a drunken orgy, and all the while, Moses was on top of Mount Sinai receiving the Ten Commandments of God, designed to chart a path for how the people were to live. Besides the story being filled with deep irony, it was also rich in *context* when it came to seeking the meaning *then* in order to find meaning for *now*.

Phin had done this lecture numerous times throughout his tenure at OBU, so while his voice was running on one track, his mind had been running on another, the aftermath of his meeting with the dean and Max still raw.

Jason Morris hurried down the stone steps to join Phin. "Thanks, Dr. Crook, I'm doing fine. I've got a break before my next class and was wondering if you had a few minutes to talk about tonight's lecture?"

"Sure, let's go over to the GC. I need some coffee," Phin replied reluctantly, careful not to let it show. He technically had the time, but what he really wanted to do was retreat to his office and just be alone. It had been a long, restless night followed by the events of the early morning. But Jason and Phin were close and he relied on Jason for a lot of things these days. As his student assistant, Jason graded many papers and assignments for most of Phin's classes, sitting in on some classes he had already taken, just to take roll and observe.

Jason Morris absolutely worshipped Phineas Crook. As a senior major in religion, Jason would be graduating in a few months, and he wanted to spend as much time as possible with his mentor, to soak up as much knowledge as he could before he moved on to graduate school. In his time at OBU, he had taken every course that Dr. Crook taught, and he had spent eight weeks one summer with Phin working an archaeological dig in the Negev region of Israel. The two had taken an extra week to jump over to Iraq and do some "off the books" exploring of the Tigris and Euphrates Rivers region. It had been fairly safe, but there had also been a few harrowing moments, especially for two academic men with not a lot of formal contingency training for the unexpected. In the end all had gone well, that summer cementing Jason and Phin's relationship.

Phin had grown to love the young man as a dear brother, leaning heavily on him, maybe *too* heavily at times. Jason also traveled with Phin when he conducted his lectures, mostly at other colleges or universities in Oklahoma, Kansas, Texas, or Arkansas. Anywhere that was within a half-day drive, they could do with no trouble.

The two chatted easily as they made their way to the Geiger Center, known as the GC to students and faculty. The GC was the center for student life on campus, containing the cafeteria on the second level, and a grill, bookstore, and lounge area on the main level. The grill *proudly* serves Starbuck's coffee, so Phin ordered and received a tall Pike's Place black coffee for himself, and a hot chocolate for Jason. They found their way to a quiet corner, commandeering a couple of seats.

"So I've got your updated slides ready on the Mac. I've spoken to the media director at ORU and I think they are all good on their end. I'm going to drive up early, maybe leave around four o'clock this afternoon, and make sure everything is good to go."

"Perfect. I really appreciate you taking care of the details as always, Jason. Don't know what I'd do without you, man."

"Hey, no problem. I really think we will have a good crowd tonight. The dean of their religion school says they've been talking it up since the semester began, and there's a lot of buzz on campus among students and faculty both."

Oral Roberts University in Tulsa was one of the larger schools Phin had been invited to since he began the lecture circuit. The title of his presentation, *Finding Eden*, had been provocative enough that it easily generated interest in some of the smaller regional colleges. But Phin's reputation had been growing, and larger schools were now becoming interested in what he had to say. But not all the attention was positive. There were numerous skeptics, mostly his peers in the academy that thought he was a kook. Some even accused him of being an opportunist who surely did not believe the things he purported, that he was in it only for the money.

That made Phin laugh. *The money!* How crazy was that? For one, Phin charged nothing when he conducted his lectures. Some accused him further of attempting to build an audience for some future book deal he was working on. Well, there was, in fact, a book deal. And yes, he was working to build an audience for it, but money was not the motive. Not at all. Phin was driven by one motive and one motive alone. Knowledge. People needed to *know*. They needed to know that the Bible was real - that there was a literal reality to the places and events that were in it. And, for the ultimate skeptic, they needed to know that there was indeed a God. If he was right, if everything he theorized and believed about the Garden of Eden was true, it would be the ultimate vindication – for the doubters, the skeptics, the trustees, everyone.

"That's outstanding. Listen, Jason, this is a significant event tonight. ORU is a highly respected school and we can get some real mileage off of this. I want to record everything this time. At least three angles on the video, got it? I want to begin exploring a social media presence with my work on this. Take it to the next level. I just feel that now is the right time."

"You got it, Dr. Crook. I've got two buddies working on media degrees that will be with me. We will take care of everything."

There was an awkward pause and Jason continued, "Dr. Crook, I hope you don't mind me asking, but is everything okay? You seemed a little bit off today in class. Like you just weren't quite yourself."

Phin shifted uneasily in his chair, taking another sip of his coffee. "I'm fine, thanks Jason. I've just been going through another wave of dreams the last few weeks. I had one this morning even. Very hard to describe, like I've shared with you."

He didn't like to talk about the dreams. For two reasons mainly: one, there wasn't much to say. Besides waking up in a sweat with an overwhelming sense of wrongness and dread, there just wasn't anything to talk about. And two, it was embarrassing. Phin didn't like to be vulnerable, as was the case with most men, but especially with a student. The only reason Jason knew was because they'd spent so much time together, traveling and sharing hotel rooms. The first time Jason experienced one of Phin's dreams was when they were sharing a tent in Israel, and Phin had cried out as he woke from one of the nightmares. Phin explained it away easily enough, that was until it happened the next night, and every night after that while they were in-country. He had to finally level with Jason just so he wouldn't worry.

"Do you think the dreams are tied to what happened to your wife, Dr. Crook?"

Phin winced at the mention of Autumn. Jason knew he had hit a nerve. "I'm really sorry, I've just been thinking about how long you've been having these dreams. Years now. And just how bad you say they are. It seems like it could all be tied, at least timing-wise, to losing your wife."

Phin didn't want to go there. No other topic was more sensitive, more painful to Phineas than the loss of his wife, Autumn. She had been his everything. There was not a day that went by that he did not find himself mesmerized by her memory. She was, without a doubt, the most beautiful woman, inside and out, that he had ever known.

"Look, Jason," Phin stood abruptly, "if we're all good here, I need to get going. I've got another class to teach today and I have to go over my notes and some new angles on research before tonight. I'll see you in Tulsa, okay?"

"*Oh geez*, I'm sorry, Dr. Crook. I didn't mean to upset you," Jason replied also standing, hot chocolate in hand.

"It's fine, Jason. Really. Don't worry about it. I really do have to get moving today. I feel like I've been behind since waking up. We're all good for tonight and I know you're on top of the details. Thank you. I mean it."

Jason made a move to his bag. "Oh, I almost forgot. I've got a campus map for you," he said, pulling out a file folder and handing it to Phin. "Inside is a parking pass as well. You'll find some other details that might be helpful. Just text if you need anything."

Phin gave Jason a thumbs up and another *thank you* as he headed out the door of the GC toward his office in Montgomery Hall. As he walked across campus, he found his mind drifting away to thoughts of his beloved Autumn.

The first time Phineas Crook laid eyes on Autumn had been during the last summer of his Ph.D. studies at Oxford. After serving as a missionary in East Africa for several years after college, Phineas had applied and been accepted to the prestigious English institution, the second oldest in the world of its kind.

It was a lazy Saturday afternoon and he was taking a stroll through Christchurch Meadow when he happened upon a group of three girls laid out on blankets having a picnic. Their banter caught his attention and he knew immediately from their accents that they were Americans. Phin always enjoyed running into Americans when he was abroad. It had been many years since he'd been home. He was always curious about news from across the pond, and to see what states and cities his fellow expatriates were from. It never ceased to amaze him at how small the world was and the connections that could be made.

Thinking that Phin was an Englishman, he immediately caught the eyes of two of the girls. His good looks didn't hurt either. Phin was not what one would call buff or muscular, but he *was* wiry and fit. He walked with an ease, his mussed brown hair and boyish looks adding a certain charm to his jovial personality. As soon as he had opened his mouth, though, he read their disappointment. *Just another American.* It was written all over their faces. The third girl was unengaged from the other two. She was reading a book, obviously too engrossed to look up. But *she* was the one that made Phin's breath catch in his chest.

"And what is your name?" were the first words he spoke to this unnamed beauty, trying to engage her.

He would never forget her response. The first words she spoke to him....

"*Not interested*," came her curt reply, head still buried in her book.

"Well that is an *interesting* name," came Phin's witty reply. He was game to play if that's what she wanted to do.

She just sighed and lowered her book, finally lifting her eyes to meet his. That is when Phin found himself truly taken away. She had a perfect complexion; her skin...oh so smooth and pure with just a hint of tan, or was it just her natural tone? Whatever it was, it was perfect. *She* was perfect. She had brown hair that looked like a drape of fine silk hanging to just her shoulders. Her eyes were a majestic hazel that he would later discover seemed to change to match whatever color of clothing she wore. Obviously, she was fit with toned arms and legs. She cared about taking care of herself. Phin couldn't look away.

After a moment of silence, she just laughed. "Is that really the best you've got? *Well, that is an interesting name.*" She said the last part, lowering the tone of her voice to match his. She was mocking him! Phin loved even that about her.

He smiled, "I'm Phineas Crook. I'm from Oklahoma." That's all he could think to spit out. All three girls laughed this time.

"Be nice to him, Autumn."

"Yes, be nice to *Phineas*. He just a friendly boy from *Oklahoma*."

Why was that funny? Phin thought. His name or that he was from Oklahoma? Which was it? But it didn't matter. He now knew her name: Autumn.

"It's nice to meet you, Autumn," Phin said, hand extended in a very formal manner.

Autumn looked at him and then his hand. Her *perfect* lips reminded him of a rose bud. That was the word that kept coming to his mind as he stared at her. Perfect. Perfect. Perfect. She really was perfect in every way that he could see.

She reached out, taking his hand in an equally formal handshake. "My name is Autumn Eden Rose. Nice to meet you Phineas Crook from Oklahoma." Autumn *Eden Rose*. Yes, of course, that would be her name. Like the Garden of Eden and with lips like that. Just perfect.

Withdrawing her hand from his, she broke the tension, "Well, I guess we're all done here!" she exclaimed to the group. She reached down and began to gather her belongings.

"Wait," Phin nearly shouted, panicked. "You have to let me take you to dinner tonight." Did he just say that?

"Autumn never let's anyone take her to dinner, Mr. Crook." It was one of the other girls. What was her name? *Who cares*, Phin thought.

"That's right. Autumn is waiting on Mr. Perfect to come along and sweep her off of her feet. She's a picky one, she is," came the other girl. No idea what her name was either.

"There's a little place over by the school. It's called the *Eagle's Nest*. I'll walk by and pick you up…six-thirty? *Wait*…I don't know where you are staying…it doesn't matter…please just say yes," Phin was fumbling all over himself and all over his words. He sounded nearly desperate.

Autumn's two girlfriends just giggled again. They were having a great time, at his expense.

And then Autumn said, "Yes."

The laughter stopped. The girls just stared.

Phineas stared. "Yes?" is all he could get out.

"Yes," came her reply a second time, a matter-of-fact tone.

"Autumn, you're not serious...you can't!" exclaimed her friend. "We don't even know him."

"Yes, we do. He's Phineas Crook from Oklahoma," her beautiful hazel eyes bearing into Phin. A slight smile was beginning to crack her face. And then....

Autumn Rose finished picking up her things, and as she made the turn to walk away she gave her friends a bit of a smirk. "I'll see you at the *Eagle's Nest*, Phineas. Six-thirty p.m. sharp. Don't worry about coming to get me. I'll meet you there."

She smiled full on at him. A glorious, beautiful, carry-me-away-to-heaven smile.

Her friends just stared, paralyzed.

"Perfect," Phin found himself saying. "Just perfect."

CHAPTER

SEVEN

It was dark by the time Phineas pulled his Toyota Corolla into the parking lot on the map Jason had given him. The ORU campus has a certain presence about it as you come through the main entrance, passing the famous giant "Praying Hands" statue indicating that you have arrived. Just after six o'clock, he was about an hour early for his presentation. The weather reports predicted a winter storm coming later that night, maybe as much four to six inches of snow. *Great*, Phin thought genuinely, *as long as I can make it back to Shawnee, maybe it will be enough to cancel classes tomorrow.*

Phin easily located the Hammer Center and found Jason waiting for him outside the Fenimore Room, which would host the night's event. There was already a small crowd of students and others gathering in clumps and talking amongst themselves. Phin's adrenaline started to flow the moment he walked into the lecture hall. He loved the thrill that came over him in the moments before he spoke in front of a crowd. As he and Jason made their way into the room, he caught the attention of several eyes, people who recognized him from posters and social media posts the university had been networking around. The Fenimore Room was equipped with a state-of-the-art audio/visual setup. Its large screens and audio setup would make for a dynamic impact as Phin cycled through ancient texts, both biblical and extra-biblical. He and Jason had also worked to produce a series of short videos that graphically told the story of God's paradise on earth. *A little theatrics never hurt*, Phin believed.

At exactly seven o'clock, the room was maybe seventy-percent full, at least two hundred in attendance. The lights went dark. A musical score began to rise and fill the room, sounding like something written by John Williams for a Steven Spielberg movie. The screens popped to life as a deep-throated voice began to recite the most ancient of texts:

In the beginning, God...
In the beginning, God...created...
And God saw that it was...good...
And the LORD God planted a garden in Eden...
And there he put the man whom he had formed...

A spotlight broke the darkness of the room as Dr. Phineas T. Crook stood center stage in its glare. For the next ninety minutes, Phin spoke, fueled by an internal energy that propelled him in a way that made him feel as if it wasn't even him doing the presentation. Almost like an out-of-body experience. There was also a wit, charm, and charisma about Phin that captivated the audience.

The *Finding Eden* presentation was a mixture of apologetics, archaeology, and speculation. Phin built a strong case for the existence of God. But not just the existence of any God. No, he built a case for the God *of the Bible*. This was vitally important to the whole of his argument, his belief system. At a school like ORU he was, for the most part, preaching to the choir. But Phin was clearly speaking to another audience, one that went beyond who was actually in the room this evening.

Next he turned his attention to the Bible itself. The Bible is many things to many people. To some it is merely a book of myths - nice stories that teach morals and principles of truth. To others it is the real story of a group of nomads called the Hebrew people. People who thought they were God's special people. To this group, the Bible holds shades of truth, but it is still a mythology, although a mythology about a real group of people. As one moves along the spectrum of views on the Bible, various groups emerge, embracing increasing levels of truth and myth. There are nuanced discussions about metaphor and allegory. Finally, the spectrum ends at the position advocated by Phineas Crook – that the Bible is true and is itself Truth in a very literal sense, especially regarding those books of the Bible that tell a historical story.

Methodically, Phin made his case for this level of literal truth in the biblical text. This in turn set matters up perfectly for the case for Eden and its garden. A real garden in a real place called Eden. Since the Bible speaks to all kinds of geographical landmarks - rivers, mountains, cities, many of which are still identifiable today - then it stands to reason that Eden itself still exists, surmised Phin. *Somewhere...on planet Earth. Just because we don't know where it is, doesn't mean it's not there. Waiting to be found.* With great fervor, Phin dove into the latest archaeological research before moving onto the final stage of the lecture.

"What if we could find Eden? What if? Imagine how such a discovery would change everything. If a real Eden - *when* the real Eden

- is found, the Eden of Genesis 2, then it will be impossible to deny that the Bible, *all* of the Bible, Genesis through Revelation, is true. Not metaphor. Not allegory. Not myth. But true. And the God that stands behind such truth is himself real and true." On cue, the lights once again eased down as Phineas finished the presentation, booming out six final words, synced, as in the beginning, on the screen one at a time.

Undeniable.

Truth.

This...Would...Change...Everything.

A round of applause followed a dramatic pause. Even some whistles were heard, and a scattering of people stood in appreciation.

The lights came back up to full to reveal Jason Morris behind the lectern. "Thank you everyone. We will now take a round of questions from the audience."

Phin spent the next half hour fielding a variety of questions about his research and about specifically *where* he believed Eden to be located. As good and well executed as the *Finding Eden* presentation was, there was always a flat element to it in the end. People wanted to know the location of Eden. They expected that this would be the big reveal of the night. But this was one trophy that Phin had determined to keep inside the closet. Was it because he didn't know the location of Eden? That he lacked confidence in his research and theory? Or that he was saving the location, keeping it only to himself for his own personal reasons? It was impossible to tell, and no coaxing could get Phin to show his hand.

"So Dr. Crook," came the voice of a young man, probably one of the college students, "it feels like you are just toying with us. Teasing us. What's the point of the last two hours if you aren't going to tell us where Eden is? I feel like you've wasted everyone's time." There was a hint of hostility in his voice.

Phin was used to this. "The point is this: before you can go looking for Eden, you must believe. At least believe to a point. Let me ask everyone here a question that will illustrate my point. How many of you in this audience believe that the Bible is true?"

It was a loaded question on a Christian campus like Oral Roberts University. Nearly all hands went up.

"Now let me ask you another question: how many of you have ever thought about actually going and searching for Eden? Much less finding it?" Predictably, no hands.

"You see, *that* is *the* point. You say you believe but you really don't. There is more skepticism in this room than most of us want to admit. Because belief equals action. People believe that Noah's ark is real. And that belief has led to countless attempts to find it. Even though no definitive proof of the ark has been found, people still search for it. Why? Because they *believe*, that's why!" Phin's passion was evident. "But no one has ever sought the Garden of Eden. In spite of saying they believe Eden was a real place, besides perusing a few maps of rivers and such, no one has truly gone looking. That's because they don't really believe. Belief...is...action."

"What kind of action have you put to *your* beliefs, Dr. Crook?" A new voice chimed in. This one a mature male voice coming from the very back and to the right. The lighting on stage made it difficult to make out any features so far back in the room.

"Excuse me?" Phin came back.

"What kind of action have you put to your beliefs?" came the voice a second time. Phin strained to put a face to the form. "You say belief equals action. Exactly what kind of action have you taken to find the Garden of Eden? The garden that you so passionately say you believe in?"

Phin was slightly annoyed. There was something behind the tone and presence of the voice that bothered him. "Well," Phin began to

70

answer, "I'd say first and most obviously, I am here. Tonight, I am here with you, a winter storm on the way, even. Because *I believe,* I have come here to plead my case."

"Oh, come now, Dr. Crook. Tonight is nothing more than an intellectual exercise, a mere show if you will. There is no real action here, only words. If you say you believe and you say belief is action, then show us something real. Show us the itinerary you have created to actually go and find this Eden you are so passionate about. Give us dates and locations. Show us the team who believes enough to go with you, to put feet to their faith. Is there even such a plan in the works?"

The crowd began to grow restless. Phin could tell that he was on the edge of losing them. Two and a half hours and the crowd was slipping away in a matter of moments because of...who was this guy anyway? Was he part of the university? No way he was a student.

"Look, I don't know who you are or who you represent -"

"I only represent myself, Dr. Crook," came the voice, cutting Phin off. "And what difference does it make to the issue of belief and action? Can you answer my question, sir? *Where* is the plan of action? Or do *you* not truly believe, as you have accused us all of here tonight?"

"The kind of action you are talking about requires *funding,*" shot back Phin. "And no small amount. Just because I have not initiated a search does not mean I won't. Yes, I have a plan, and yes, I have a location. But no, I am not going to say where. Not yet, and not here. There are issues to be considered. Many, many issues. Issues of timing and as I also have said, issues of finances."

Phin surprised even himself with his admission. It was the first time he had been goaded into revealing that he indeed knew where Eden was located. Or at least that he believed he knew.

"More words, Dr. Crook. Let's see if you truly are a man of action. What would you say if I told you that I was ready to fund your expedition in search of Eden to the tune of one million dollars? No strings attached. Just an open door for you to put your belief into action. What say you, Dr. Crook?"

The crowd was stunned into silence. This was an unexpected turn. Totally unforeseen. Yet Phin didn't believe a word of the so-called proposal he was being presented. Convinced it was a set up of some sort, Phin just stood there. He could feel his face growing flush as he broke into a sweat under his shirt and on his forehead. Could the audience see how uncomfortable he was? This voice was seeking to expose him. To paint him into a corner and ruin him. Phin decided to call his bluff.

"I'd say this," he began with as much boldness as he could muster. "I'd say that you have come here tonight, clearly with a motive that goes beyond discovery and inquiry. I'd say that you are sitting on the back row of the room, in the most unengaged position in the room. That you are hiding who you are and don't even want your face to be clearly seen. I'd say that unless you can come forward right now and present a check for one million dollars to back your challenge to me, then I'd say sir, that *you* are the one that is all words."

It was a gamble. But Phin felt confident that common sense was on his side. Who in their right mind would do such a thing, just walk up and hand him a million dollars? Yet, the tension was thick as all heads turned to stare at the figure with the voice. Instead of a reply, what they got was a dark silhouette silently slipping out the back door.

Only a few students remained in the Fenimore Room, still surrounding Phin, the mood light and jovial. The evening had ended well on a high note. Phin had been vindicated with the exit of the nameless stranger. He had recaptured his audience, many of whom hung around for a time before heading out, the winter storm bearing down at any time.

"Jason, you and the guys need to hit the road," Phin called over to his student assistant who had finished packing away their gear.

"Sure thing, Dr. Crook," came Jason's quick reply. "What a great evening!"

"Oh yeah, one for the books for sure. Let's you and I break it all down back on campus tomorrow."

"You got it. I'm gonna have Mark and Toby start working first thing on some video clips from tonight. Even some of the Q and A stuff was good. I think we can pull together several great moments to push out on our social media campaign."

"Sounds great, but let's stay away from Mr. Millionaire if you know what I mean," came Phin with a small laugh and thumbs up. While he tried to generate some humor on the outside, something about the mysterious visitor continued to stick to Phin, nagging at the back of his mind.

Jason laughed in return, "Yes sir! I read you loud and clear."

Meanwhile, outside the campus entrance and two blocks away, a black SUV sat parked but running, next to a curb and under a street lamp that was burned out. A Tesla silently slipped in behind the SUV and shifted into park, headlights still on. After a few minutes that seemed just a bit too long, the door to the Tesla opened, and a slender figure made its way to the driver's door of the SUV. The window came down as a female voice began. "You did well tonight. Exactly as instructed. I watched the whole thing from the other side of the room."

"You were there?" a surprise in his voice. He had never seen who it was that hired him, so it would have been impossible to recognize anyone in particular. He assumed that he would be the only player in the room tonight.

"Here's the other half as promised, *Mr. White.*" Not his real name. A gloved hand passed a brown sack containing the balance of his payment. They didn't know who he was and he didn't know who they were. That's how the game was played. And this had been an easy game. Just a part to play. Follow the script. In and out. A max of two and a half hours of his time. As a bonus, this job didn't have any messy cleanup involved. He was amazed at the amount *they* were willing to pay for such a simple job. *Ah well, what do I care,* he thought. *As long as it's green and unmarked, it's good.* He stuffed the sack quickly into his canvas carryall on the passenger seat.

"Nice doing business with you. If you ever need anything else, you know how to reach me." He was done here for tonight. But he was definitely interested in future business transactions with this one.

No other words were spoken, and he never saw her face. Nothing more than that slender figure and red ponytail as she turned and walked back to her car.

CHAPTER EIGHT

Stepping out of the elevator, Osmond Jenks took another pull on his Mountain Dew. He was deep in thought as he made his way down the underground hallway in the deep basement region of LaPhage Industries. Only those with the highest clearance were allowed on this level that contained the most sensitive projects at various stages of development. Oz didn't really know what all went on down here. His lab was the only one that his retinal scan granted him access to.

Oz's Converse All Stars were the only things that broke the silence as he squeaked his way down the tiled hallway. There were three security checkpoints that he made his way through, each with massive steel doors that effortlessly slid open and closed as he moved toward his destination. There were no security guards, although Oz had no doubt his every move was being monitored and recorded. LaPhage Industries left nothing to chance, especially down here.

In his first year as an employee, Oz had worked on the main levels. The public levels. He had been involved in simple projects, all involving artificial intelligence application. It had become clear to his supervisors that he knew what he was doing and had potential to be trusted with more. As a graduate of Georgia Tech, working for a company like LaPhage Industries had been a dream come true for this Alabama native. His big break with the company came when he was pulled onto the LaPhage Limb project. That's when he met Tony Chen. The two immediately hit it off. What truly impressed the powers-that-be was that the product of both Oz and Tony working together quickly became greater than the sum of their parts. They shot to stardom as the dynamic duo of LaPhage Industries, and that's when they caught the eye of Charles LaPhage.

After the accident that left the founder incapacitated, and the ascendency of Charles' daughter, Ruth LaPhage, Oz and Tony found no problem gaining the trust of their new leader. Ruth viewed the duo as brilliant but also naïve. Therefore, no security risk at all, warranting her full trust.

Ruth LaPhage had an *idea*. A grand idea and these two were the ones to help her see it become a reality. Besides, if they were to pose a risk or become a threat with the knowledge they now carried, they were the type that could be easily intimidated and scared into compliance.

But there would never be an issue Oz Jenks and Tony Chen. They absolutely loved what they did, both believing they were ushering in the future. Rounding the corner to the right, Oz walked the final thirty feet of hallway to a door on the left embedded in the wall. The sign simply read LP-6, denoting it as LaPhage Lab number six. But to

Oz and Tony it was their inner sanctum, the home of Project BORG, a place they dubbed *The Lair*.

It made Oz smile and gush with warm feelings every time he thought about a guy like him in a place like this. He had near limitless resources at his disposal, and *carte blanche* to experiment and innovate. Oh, how he craved to brag to all his family and friends who thought that he was a hopeless geek who would never be able to make a living at what he loved so much – full immersion in the world of virtual innovation and AI exploration. But he couldn't tell anyone. Not a soul. He understood the stack of papers he'd signed, and LaPhage Industries was good, *very* good, at making it crystal clear that any breach of confidentiality would be met with immediate expulsion from the company and enough lawsuits to make sure he'd never have so much as a stick of gum to his name ever again. Oz also sensed that LaPhage Industries was willing to go to other extremes to ensure that their intellectual property – that would be code for *secrets* – was never exposed. Oz was sure that those *extremes* would involve certain things being done to his body that he didn't want to think about. So Oz didn't think about it, at least not very often.

It didn't matter because he wouldn't tell a soul, and besides all that, he had Tony. They were not only professional colleagues, but had become close friends as well. It was scary how much they were alike. Both loved sci-fi, movies, computer games, and soda with lots of caffeine. Oz had even begun to view Tony as a soul brother of sorts. They shared thoughts about everything, not just their work at LaPhage Industries.

Oz stood in front of the door marked LP-6 and waited as a pinhole located right at nose level shot an invisible beam across his face for one final retinal scan. Then Oz placed his thumb on a scanner just to the right of the door jamb. Two seconds and then a beep. As a final security check, he pulled a swab from a small dispenser next to the thumb scanner. He mechanically swabbed the inside of his cheek and then deposited the swab into a tiny receptacle where the sound of a *swoosh* sucked it away. Waiting another seven seconds exactly - Oz had it timed down perfectly - another beep, and then the door slid open, allowing him access to the Lair.

LaPhage Industries was serious about making sure that no one unauthorized got into LP-6, or any of the other secured LP labs for that matter. It made Oz cringe to think that if someone dug his eyes out for the retinal scan, they would still have to cut off his right thumb. Still yet, they would need a *fresh* sample of his DNA. Unauthorized access was therefore virtually impossible. To Oz it had just become routine, something he did each and every time he came or went.

The Lair was kept on the dark side, lights dimmed with several incandescent lamps scattered around. This was their personal preference, they just liked it that way. Overhead fluorescent lights were anathema. Pizza boxes, Whataburger sacks and cups, and numerous gaming magazines littered the spacious lab. There were a multitude of computer stations, a new beta version of The Chair, and two additional Robatars also occupying the space.

Oz made a pit stop in their personal bathroom to take care of business. He took a quick glance at himself in the mirror as he was washing his hands. Today was Marvel day and he wore an Iron Man t-shirt under his white lab coat. He made a fast check of his moppy, sand-colored hair. Oz wore stereotypical brown plastic round-rimmed glasses over his brown eyes - his complexion showing with just a hint of scarring from the acne of his teenage years. Making his way back into the lab proper, he eyed Tony in the corner at his primary terminal working hard, totally zoned out to Oz's arrival. He was wearing his typical headset and probably listening to his Mumford and Sons playlist.

Oz snaked his way over, planting himself at his own terminal just

78

opposite Tony's. It was easy for them to talk across the table from one another this way, pushing data from one person's screen to the other as part of the discussion if needed. Jiggling his mouse, Oz's screen popped back to life. He keyed in his password with one hand while reaching over with the other and digging into a burger sack. *Is this one from today or yesterday?* He couldn't tell. He fingered a wad of cold fries and shoved them into his mouth. *Definitely yesterday*, he discovered.

Glancing back to his screen he noticed that his diagnostic had finished. He began to scroll through the pages of coding, line after line. To most this was a foreign language, but to Oz these were the notes of a majestic symphony. Just as he was swallowing his day-old French fries, he paused. Leaning in, he scrolled back a page, then two. Ever so slowly he marched forward, soaking in each letter of coding. Then he stopped. Staring hard, he leaned in closer still. Did he just see what he thought he saw? And what exactly was he seeing anyway?

"Tony, you need to check this out," his eyes still on the screen. "Tony! Hey bro, you need to see this...." Oz chunked a fry at Tony Chen's head. Still nothing. Tony was totally zoned out.

Standing and raising his voice louder, Oz lobbed the whole sack and its contents at Tony's head. Pushing back and throwing off his headset he shot back, "Bro! What's the deal?!"

"I said, *you've got to see this.*"

"See what? Your high score on Galaxian?"

"No stupid! I ran the diagnostic on last week's field test again."

"And what? Did the coding glitch show up again?"

"Yes, the glitch, for sure. But I went ahead and ran a level two pushback analysis and diagnostic. I wanted to look at the exact data sets we were getting back from the AI chip in the Robatar, to see if there was a link."

It was standard operating procedure for Tony and Oz to run a full set of diagnostics on the data from each of the Robatar field tests and scenarios. In the early days, this was how they identified faulty coding being sent from the human brain via the embedded neuro-implant to the Robatar's AI chip, which was then used to steer the Robatar into full auto mode. The early testing was disastrous as the Robatar acted confused, stumbling around like someone who was drunk. It was quick work to analyze the data and to recode for correction. Ironing out the finer movements of the Robatar had taken more time, but in the end, they had conducted numerous simulations that ran flawlessly. The real world tests provided for more minor glitches in how the Robatar behaved, but even those were eventually corrected. All of that led up to last week's stunning success in Syria. The after-test diagnostics had become virtually routine, even boring. Until the glitch they found in this new batch of coding.

"And?" Tony was curious now. What could possibly be the issue? They had not run pushback analyses since the early days when they were having so much trouble with the Robatar.

"You just need to come look at this. Here, let me send it over to you." Oz feverishly punched the keys, pushing a shared screen to Tony. "Take a look at this page, go down about halfway and start there. This is the sync point for the glitch we saw on our normal diagnostic."

"Yeah, got it. Looks like there was something weird happening on the Robatar end too."

A normal analysis always checked the coding on the receiving end - the Robatar end. Tony and Oz checked to make sure the signals from the human brain were received properly and then translated into the correct actions by the AI chip. All of this added up to the Robatar actually functioning the way it was designed. In the case with the Syria scenario, it was Sergeant Billy Warren's brain that was pushing data or code to the AI chip of the Robatar. The initial analysis of the operation had shown the coding to be perfect, as expected and hoped for, with one small exception, or glitch. Not sure what the glitch even meant, Oz had decided to run the pushback analysis. A level two test that analyzed not only the data going from Billy's brain to the Robatar, but also the data being *pushed back* to Billy's brain. It was not protocol to run the level two push back, because as long as normal diagnostic analysis showed no anomalies, and as long as the subject - Billy in this case - was doing fine, there just was no need.

"I know, definitely weird," replied Oz. "Now watch this. I'm gonna scroll on down a couple of pages and look what begins to happen in the coding." Oz's heart rate rose once again as the suspect data came into view. He waited for Tony to see it too. And there it was.

Tony's face fell, his mouth falling open. "Holy..." he trailed off. "You gotta be kidding me."

"I know. That's exactly what I thought too, but it's right there, in all its digitized glory."

"How's this even possible?"

"I don't know, but if this is saying what I think it's saying, then we have a *big* problem."

"Big problem doesn't even touch this, Oz. But bro, do you realize what this means? We've crossed over into the impossible, man. Into the freaking Twilight Zone. This is not even supposed to be theoretically possible for another generation!"

"And yet this."

"Yeah...and yet this...."

CHAPTER NINE

Phin could go no faster than 45 mph. The snow had begun to fall before he made it back to his car after the lecture on the ORU campus. By the time he hit the Turner Turnpike headed southwest toward Shawnee, the snow had picked up even more. He was only fifteen minutes on the highway when the ground was completely covered with a blanket of white. The road itself was starting to slick up. What would normally take just over an hour and a half to cover the one hundred miles between the two cities was going to take him at least twice that long. As he crawled along, his windshield wipers worked feverishly to keep up with the snow that would turn to ice once it hit the glass. Visibility wasn't *too* bad if he just took his time.

Phin hated driving in the snow. He didn't have the confidence that he could react quickly enough if things went bad and he began to slide. Or if he could react in the right way. Something about sliding on ice dictated that you turn the steering wheel in the *same direction* of the slide, contrary to what your brain would automatically tell you to do. Oh well, he'd just make sure he went slow enough so that wouldn't be a problem. The other thing Phin hated about driving in the snow was the other drivers. Just because he decided to play it safe didn't mean anyone else would. *It seems like everyone is driving faster on this stuff than me.* A semi truck blew by just as he was thinking that exact thought. The force of the side draft rocked his little Toyota, the truck spraying up onto his windshield a layer of snow and muck. Phin had to work the wiper fluid, jetting a fresh coat of clean liquid to clear his view. This, of course, added to the ice buildup on his blades. With each car or truck that passed him, a fresh coat of dirty road slush threw itself back onto his windshield and the process started all over. But the semis were the worst.

The heater in Phin's car was blowing hard, keeping it nice and toasty in the cabin. On the way out of town, he took the time to stop and pick up a hot chocolate from a local coffee house called Holy Grounds. It was just off the ORU campus, which made sense, Phin thought. A Christian coffee house – at least Christian in name – next to a Christian university. No coffee for him - not this late. He wanted to crash as soon as he got home without waiting for a caffeine rush to wear off.

As Phin took a cautious sip of his *very* hot chocolate, another semi ran past him. More crud on the windshield. More wiper fluid.

Phin was thinking back to what had turned out to be a night that exceeded his expectations. The crowd had been greater in number than he would have thought, especially with the snowstorm coming. He'd have to remember to write a letter of thanks to Dr. Hammond in the school's religion department. He had been the one to issue the invitation to Phin, and the one who pulled the strings to get him access to Fenimore Hall. He had also likely been the lead voice in the promo on campus, which generated the healthy turnout. The crowd had been surprisingly energetic, the atmosphere charged the moment the presentation had begun. And the facilities had been top-notch. Fenimore Hall was more than he could have hoped for as a venue. Jason and his media buddies had really beefed up the sound and video component of the lecture. The overall effect had been just awesome. Phin really couldn't be more pleased. But then there was *that guy.* So strange had been the whole exchange. Phin had never experienced anything quite like it. Oh sure, he'd had his share of unusual encounters with unusual people. That was just the nature of public speaking, whether it was behind a pulpit in a church or a lectern in a public hall. When you throw in the topic that Phin spoke on, you are bound to have a few crazies come out of the woodwork. But this...this stranger had been different. It left Phin feeling chilled, and not because of the below freezing temperatures outside.

Whhooooossshhhh!!!!....Whhoooosshhh!!!! Two semi trucks this time. One after the other. It was nearly impossible for Phin to see the road as he plowed through the fog and mist and snow of the blowback. *Man, this is bad,* Phin thought. *Reminds me of....*

Wyoming. Phin and Autumn had found themselves caught in a spring blizzard outside of Cheyenne, Wyoming. They'd been on a mini vacation of sorts. A road trip through the Rockies. Three days skiing at Vail, and then a quick stop to see some friends in Boulder. Autumn had wanted to take a one-day side trip to the Cheyenne Mountain Zoo. They were just too close to pass up the opportunity. Phin and Autumn loved zoos. It reminded them of some of their more exotic outings in the wild in the time they spent overseas. They had a checklist, of sorts, of the various zoos in the United States, and the

Cheyenne Mountain Zoo had an empty box by it. So on a whim, they took off late one afternoon. Cheyenne was an easy drive up I-25. Or so they had thought. They had neglected checking the weather.

The blizzard had been bad. A complete white out. Near zero visibility as the sun had gone down shortly after making their way through Fort Collins. Wisdom would have dictated that they stop, but they pushed on regardless. Just over the Wyoming State line, the weather became more than Phin wanted to fight. At the first exit that looked like anything, he made his move to the exit ramp. That's when he lost control. It happened so fast. It always does. The next thing he knew they were off the road and through a barb wire fence. They were all right, of course. They hadn't been going that fast. But it was a complicated task getting the help they needed to get their car unstuck and to a hotel for the night. The paint job on the rental car was a total mess, and so were Phin's nerves. As they lay in bed that night, in a smoking room of the very cheap Happy Trails Motel, Autumn just giggled about the whole thing, snuggling in close to Phin. She was not one to be easily shaken, always rolling with the punches and finding a silver lining in any of life's clouds. Phin found strength in the way she approached life. A life that was now over.

As he continued his trek down the turnpike toward home, the snow coming down and cars and semis continuing to speed past him, Phin's thoughts were now squarely fixed on Autumn. Oh, his sweet, precious Autumn. How he missed her. Her smile, her smell, everything about her was intoxicating to Phin. There was not a day that went by that he did not think about her. Not a single one. If he were not careful, he would find himself carried away into another world, another life. One filled with the joys of his dear Autumn, whose presence would change the temperature of any room she entered. Most days he did not allow himself to go fully there. He couldn't afford to. Not just because he had responsibilities, but because it was too painful. Too painful to live in a world that had been lost. On this snowy night, however, driving toward his little house on Broadway Avenue, he had nothing but time. So he allowed himself the space to drift back in time.

Autumn Eden Rose had been perfectly made by God for Phineas T. Crook. No other woman *got* Phineas like Autumn got him. No other woman could. Phin had a long and complicated heritage with lots of baggage. She made him feel *normal*. Phin was never more himself, more energized and full of life, than when he was with Autumn. She truly made him complete. He was the same to her. Autumn was special, and while it was true that she was picky when it came to her taste in men, that was only because she had been waiting for the right one to come into her life. She had been waiting for Phin. She loved his sense of adventure, how Phin was never satisfied with the *status quo* - always pushing the limits - striving and dreaming and visioning for more.

Theirs had been a whirlwind romance. From the time of their first date at the Eagle's Nest that night, oh so long ago now, it had only taken six months for them to marry. Autumn had simply said goodbye to her two girlfriends when it came time for the trio to return to the States from their holiday abroad. They were aghast at the whole thing, convinced that Autumn had fallen under some sort of spell. And she had, really. She'd fallen under the spell of love. Phineas Crook from Oklahoma was whom she was going to marry. She'd known it instantly, which is why she'd said yes to his awkward and bumbling invitation for a date. She'd been waiting her whole life for Phin. Just as he had been waiting his whole life for her. They didn't want to waste any more time before beginning their new life together.

Phin was nearing the completion of his doctoral work at Oxford and had been invited to stay on as a research fellow. This would allow Phin the space he needed and desired to write and explore some of his own peculiar topics of interest while taking care of what the university needed from him. Autumn and Phin had extraordinary freedom to travel and explore as they enjoyed those early years of marriage. Autumn brought a nice family trust into the union, which gave them the financial means to be adventurous. And adventurous they were. They spent time on every continent of the planet save Antarctica. The young couple was rapturously in love with each other. They were in like mind, soul, and spirit. For Phin it was as if life did not begin until there was Autumn. He often thought of his biography in two parts: before Autumn, and with Autumn. What had he done to deserve such fortune from God?

Their life together during those years abroad made the world feel small, like their own personal playground. Cities like London, France, Barcelona, Cairo, Beijing, Sao Paulo, Buenos Aires, Istanbul, and Jerusalem - just to name a few - became second homes as friends as close as family were established and cultivated. A memoir could be written about their exploits as the young couple globetrotted their way from one location to another. As the years began to tick by, another desire began to creep into their hearts. A desire that could not be met via another adventurous encounter. The desire for children. It was time for another chapter, a whole other volume to be written in the lives of Phineas and Autumn. After much discussion and even prayer, they made the decision to come home. Back to the United States. It was not an easy decision. Phin was resistant to return to the States, but he knew it was the right thing. The children they hoped to have should be able to know their grandparents, Autumn's parents. Phin had run from his past long enough, and it was time to face certain demons. With Autumn by his side he could do it.

But where to move to? It had been so long since Phin had lived in the United States. All of his connections and networks were international. Except one – Max Allred. His ol' college buddy. They had stayed connected through the years, and Max had come to know and love Autumn as well. Max was teaching at OBU and knew the Oklahoma landscape of churches well. He had just the place for Phin and Autumn. *Oklahoma? Are you serious, Max?* That had been Phin's first reaction. Out of all the places he could go, surely not Oklahoma, nearest to the root of it all for him. But Max was insistent, and when the search committee of the Covenant Baptist Church saw Phin's resume and met him and Autumn, they were convinced God wanted him to serve as their pastor. It was a radical shift for sure, but he and Autumn quickly saw themselves fitting and growing toward new kinds of dreams and new kinds of adventures – with children.

Then it all came to an end. A horrible, awful end. Phin and Autumn had gone to Oklahoma City to celebrate their sixth wedding anniversary. They had chosen the Redrock Canyon Grill for an outstanding dinner that included short smoked north coast salmon finished off by the house-made key lime pie. *So good.* For the highlight of the evening they attended the off-Broadway production of *Les Misérables* sponsored by the Oklahoma City Theater at the Thelma Gaylord Performing Arts Theatre. It was one of their favorites, having seen the original production in the West End in London. They sat through whole show, arms linked, Autumn's head on Phin's shoulder. After the show they were making their way back to their car in the cold January night.

"I just can't believe it's been six years," Autumn's voice trailed off as they walked.

"I never knew six years could be gone so quickly," replied Phin. "I can't imagine my life without you, E." He sometimes called her that, his special *E*. As in Eden, the Garden of Eden. "These past six years really have been like living in God's Garden of Eden. I love you so much."

"Oh, you're so sweet, Phineas."

"No seriously. I *cannot* imagine life without you. I'm the luckiest man on earth, Autumn. I don't know why you ever decided to marry a guy like me. You could've had so much better -"

"Shhhh....don't say that, Phin," she cut him off. "I couldn't have had any better than you. Plus, you're the man that I want to be the father of our children."

That was becoming a raw topic. For two years Phin and Autumn had tried to have children, but to no avail. They had recently begun to see a fertility specialist, so hope had been renewed.

"I hope that's true, honey. I really do. Sometimes I get so discouraged."

"It will happen, Phin. I've prayed and I believe that God will make this happen for us." She stopped walking and turned to face him. She was stunning, her face glowing in the moonlight. Phin was convinced that she grew more beautiful with each passing year.

Choking up, Phin whispered, "What have I done to deserve you, my precious E?" He gently eased a few strands of her perfect hair behind her ear. "Sometimes I think you have more faith in God than me, and I feel guilty." Autumn reached up and placed a delicate finger over his lips as if to shush him. Her hazel eyes bore into his, and then she leaned into him with a soft kiss.

"Ahhh...look at the cute couple!" It was a gruff voice that cut through the night air, breaking the moment. Startled, Phin and Autumn pulled from each other only to discover that they had been approached by three rough-looking men.

"Excuse us," Phin said, grabbing Autumn's hand and beginning a move past the one who had spoken. He was wearing baggy jeans and a red Kansas City Chiefs coat. All three had the obvious smell of alcohol on their breath. Phin cursed himself for being caught off-guard. He was usually better than this, having traveled so much in unfamiliar places.

"Whoa, hold on just a minute there," retorted the guy in the Chiefs coat. Phin's quick assessment was that he was the leader. The other two - one in a camo jacket and the other in a gray hoodie - took a step closer. It was a cold night, the alcohol was surely what was keeping them warm. "We're looking for a little help here. You see, we ain't from around here as you probably guessed. But we've got an invitation to the Petroleum Club for dinner." The sarcasm was thick in his tone. "We just need a little help with directions, you see. Now, you nice folks can surely help us out, am I right?" The Petroleum Club was an exclusive club located on the upper floors of the Chase Building in downtown Oklahoma City. There was no doubt these three didn't belong.

"Over there," came Phin's reply, pointing to the skyscraper with the word Chase lit across the top. Impossible to miss.

"Well....." laughed the leader of the group. The others continued to move in. Autumn was squeezing Phin's arm tighter. "How 'bout *that*! You see that boys? It's been right there, staring down on us the whole time! We must be a bunch of idiots." The three of them laughed at this. The leader stopped laughing, looking at Phin square on, "You think I'm an idiot don't you?" He and Phin locked eyes.

"No sir, I don't. Now, if you'll please just excuse us..." Phin made another move and this time was stopped with a hand to the chest.

"Now just hold your horses there, okay?" Things were taking a turn that made Phin very nervous. "I know you *must* think we're idiots. Because it's cold out here tonight. And we, being from out of town and all, aren't dressed for this kind of cold. Are we boys?"

The other two responded with a short laugh and a hungry look in their eyes. "No, we ain't boss. It's a cold one for sure."

"Yeah, so you see, you must think we are idiots if you think we're gonna walk all the way over to that building." Now he was pointing to the Chase building, maybe five blocks away. "So let me tell ya what I think is gonna happen right now. I think we are all gonna go get in your car, where it's nice and warm you see," he said this looking at Autumn, licking his dry chapped lips. "And you're gonna give us a ride right over to the Petroleum Club. That can be your way of apologizin' to us for calling us *idiots*. Now how's that sound to you?"

"Look we don't want any trouble, okay?"

"Oh, it's no trouble at all," he said with a grin, reaching up and taking Phin by the arm.

At the same time the thug in the camo jacket reached up and ran his hand through Autumn's brown hair. "You're pretty," he said, leering at her.

"Hey!" Autumn slapped his hand away. Phin reacted to his own arm being taken hold of by pulling back.

"We're done here." There was force in Phin's voice. He was finished playing the polite card. "Come on honey, we're out of here." He had Autumn firmly around the waist as he made a push past the three men now pressed in close. Then things got out of control. Phin felt a sharp pain to the back of his legs as he was kicked, sending him to his knees.

"Come here, sweet thing!" It was the camo jacket talking again. "How 'bout you warm me up." He had grabbed Autumn and pulled her close, wrapping his arms around her from behind. She gave a grunt and cried out Phin's name as she struggled to free herself. Phin's adrenaline kicked in when he heard and saw Autumn. He jumped to his feet and rushed toward his wife. Then he was clotheslined, hard, falling on his back. It was the guy in the gray hoodie - he was standing over Phin with a wild, crazed look in his eyes, and he began kicking Phin in the gut.

One.

Two.

Three times.

Hot pain shot through Phin's insides. He thought his gut was going to explode.

The guy with the Chiefs coat had moved in on Autumn, Mr. Camo jacket still holding her strong. "That's right, baby. Why don't you warm us both up? You look hot enough to me!" Then Autumn went crazy. She let out a primal scream, kicking the leader in the groin with ferocious speed and force. He was caught completely by surprise. What these three thugs didn't know was that Autumn was trained in martial arts self defense. And she was good. Real good. She threw her head back, catching the guy in the camo jacket off his guard. *Snap.* His nose, broken, began to gush blood. He released Autumn as he cursed, grabbing his face and doubling over. She made a move for Phin, who had grabbed his attacker by the leg as he tried to kick him a fourth time. Yanking hard, he pulled, gray hoodie and all landing down on top of him in a heap. The two began to scuffle as Autumn screamed again.

BOOM!

It was like the sound of a canon going off. Phin froze and the guy in the hoodie jumped up. A loud silence fell on the group. Autumn was staring at Phin with tears in her eyes. Phin wasn't exactly sure what had happened. His gaze broke away from hers as he looked down at Autumn's stomach. A blossom of red was growing and spreading. Everything began to move in slow motion.

"NOOOOO!" Phin was screaming. He tried to get to his feet, but something wasn't working. A broken leg maybe.

The leader in the Kansas City Chiefs coat was standing just feet from Autumn with a smoking revolver in his hand. He had a look of wild fury in his eyes as he thundered one step at a time right up to Autumn who was beginning to stagger. *"Son of a....!"* he yelled as he drew back the butt of the gun, throwing a vicious punch into the side of her head. Something cracked and she fell like a sack of dead weight.

He just stood over her, glaring, as if trying to decide what to do next. Then, as if overcome by evil itself, he reared back and gave her one more cruel kick to the side of the head.

"NOOOO...nooo...no!" It was Phin again, desperately crawling toward his bride. The ringleader turned his gaze on him and raised the gun one more time.

Whoop-whoop! It was the sound of a police car racing toward the group. All three thugs turned as the officer inside began to bark orders to stop. In unison, the three ducked into an alley and ran.

Phin painfully made his way to Autumn. "Don't leave me. Don't leave me." There was desperation in his voice. He was putting pressure on her abdomen, trying to stop the flow of blood from her gunshot wound. "Autumn, can you hear me? You have to hear me. Don't leave. I love you. Don't go. Please. Oh, God, please! Don't take her from me. Autumn can you hear me?" Tears were cascading down his face onto her cheeks, his face rubbing against hers. With his other hand he was gently stroking the wound on her head as if he could take it away. Oh, how he wanted to take it all away.

"Why, oh, why God? Please no." He was sobbing now. Uncontrollably sobbing. If he could only take it all away. But the only thing being taken away this night was his precious Autumn.

CHAPTER

TEN

It was well after midnight when Phin finally made the city limits of Shawnee and began to navigate the snowy streets. He was coming in on Highway 18 from the turnpike because it was a nice straight shot into town. At this hour there was no one on the snow-packed roads, so he took his time moving up Harrison Street, which was a main artery in the city, and then turned right onto MacArthur. He guessed there was maybe three to four inches of powder on the ground, the snow still coming down.

Up ahead was his street, Broadway Avenue. He said a short prayer thanking God he'd made it home safely. Thoughts of Autumn were still fresh in his mind. Phin wondered if he would always be this sad. They say time heals wounds, but he didn't really believe that anymore, at least for some wounds. Passing Rose Garden Park, he was nearly there. He began to relax, suddenly aware of the tension in his shoulders and neck. He'd had a death grip on the steering wheel the whole way, he realized. A wave of exhaustion started to roll over him. He couldn't wait to hit the sack and close his eyes. Sleep. Yes, that's what he needed. *And please God no dreams. Not tonight.*

Phin still prayed, but in his honest moments he truly wondered if God had abandoned him. In his truly, truly honest moments he wondered if God was even there. *Imagine that,* he thought, *an ordained minister and professor of the Bible at a Christian university that doesn't believe in God.* How sad. How utterly pathetic. He was beating himself up now. It was too late to be thinking this way. Of course he still believed in God. And he had found a measure of happiness and professional satisfaction in his job at the university. He did love working with his students. They were, in some ways, his only family now. But it was a life lived in the shadows compared to what his life *had* been - with his precious Autumn. *His E.* Why had God allowed this to happen? He could have stopped it, right? How many times had he punished himself for ever agreeing to move back to the States when they wanted to start a family? And then, Oklahoma? Ah well. This is where he was, and this is where he would stay. Until...unless...the Garden of Eden. God's Garden of Eden. Yes, his quest was personal on a level no one understood. That no one *could* understand. If there was even a possibility. *Oh, the possibility!* This was the thought that dominated Phin, that drove him with a passion unequaled. He was getting himself worked up now, and he didn't need that either. No, not tonight.

His small house came into view. 1906 N. Broadway Avenue. He gave the Corolla a little extra gas to encourage it into the driveway. He didn't park in the garage as it contained box after box from his former life. Items he would just rather forget, never having the strength to work through. He shut off the engine, gathering his leather satchel and coat. His feet crunched in the snow as he made his way to the door. He was extra careful not to slip on the powder-covered sidewalk, his leather-soled Clarks wingtips providing no traction at all. They were a favorite of his that he'd now have to carefully dry out.

Holding his coat and bag under one arm, he fumbled with his keys, working the lock on the front door. He found it curious that there were footprints in the snow, right through the yard, ending at the small porch. *Hmmm....maybe the mailman or UPS guy. But no package? Probably just some kids.* He let the thought pass. It was freezing, the wind chill biting. The door eased open with a bit of a squeak. *Yep, still need to fix that.* He turned on a few lights in the living room as he tossed his armload onto the couch. Flipping on the gas fireplace, Phin kicked off his shoes and placed them on the hearth next to the flames.

Phin's house was a bachelor pad for sure. Lots and lots of items and artifacts from his time as a missionary and from his and Autumn's travels around the globe. Wood carvings on a shelf here, pottery on a table there. A fine Persian rug as the centerpiece of the living room. He probably shouldn't walk on it, but Phin didn't really care anymore. There was a certain haphazard coziness to the house. He wasn't a slob. Things were clean and somewhat orderly in their own way. He paid a house cleaner to come in once a month to really work the place over.

When he had students over, which was often, they just loved roaming around and looking at everything. "Is this real, Dr. Crook?" was a common question. "What about this?" and "Oh, my gosh! I've seen one of these on the internet!" Phin enjoyed the enthusiasm. What good were things if you had no one to share them with? Each item had a story, and the students gave Phin the opportunity to share it once again.

Fingering a small knife with a leather-wrapped handle that was on the fireplace mantel, Phin recalled how he had been four days into the Amazonia region on the Colombian-Peruvian border. A remote indigenous tribe had invited him and Autumn to stay with them in their village. The couple had delighted the people by taking Polaroid snapshots of the children and families, giving them the pictures as a keepsake. For all of them, it was the first time they had ever seen pictures of themselves. Ever. The children squealed with delight; the adults would just hold the pictures and stare in awe. Before leaving, Phin and Autumn had given them seed packets for growing more and better vegetables, and in return they had given Phin this knife. It wasn't a spectacular story. But to a college student it sounded like the adventure of a lifetime. The word on campus was that Phin's house was like a museum, and he was like a real-life Indiana Jones. Not exactly the case, Phin knew. But it brought him pleasure to share his past life with them.

Phin spent the next ten minutes or so washing his face and changing into some sweats. The kitchen was located just through the living room at the back of the house. Normally, he would unwind by lighting up his favorite Peterson pipe stuffed with a bowl of Molto Dulce pipe tobacco. Not tonight. It was simply too late. He, instead, made himself a peanut butter and jelly sandwich, and poured a cold glass of milk to wash it down - probably his favorite midnight snack. He was starving, but he didn't want a full meal at this hour - just something to take the edge off. He plopped himself down on the couch and dug out his MacBook for a quick check of his email, and then he'd be off to bed.

There were messages from the Hobbs College - basic faculty communication. He skipped over those along with some spam. There was an email from his bank, his payroll voucher, some personal emails from friends overseas - probably just checking on him - but nothing that looked too critical.

Phin was focused on looking at the list of messages when he heard a soft crunch. It came from directly overhead. Upstairs somewhere. The only things up there were his office, a spare bedroom, and a small bathroom. He stopped, listening carefully.

Pop!

There it came again. Then *pop, pop!*

Footsteps! He knew it. Someone was up there. Phin's mind raced. The image of the footprints in the snow came crashing back into his head. Footprints leading up *to* the house but no prints leading *away. How could I have been so stupid?* he thought.

What to do? What to do? Phin knew exactly what to do. He carefully laid his laptop on the couch. Then, ever so quietly, he eased himself up, reaching over to his leather satchel. He moved quickly, but it seemed like time had grown sluggish. Putting his hand into the bag, he kept his eyes trained on the stairway that rose up into a dark second floor.

A shuffle and more noise... *pop, creek, pop...*

Whoever was up there wasn't being as careful anymore. Phin knew he was running out of time. He found what he wanted in the bag, his hand grabbing a Ruger .357 magnum revolver. He had determined three years ago that he would never again be a victim. Lifting the weapon, gripped in both hands now, he turned and faced the stairs full on.

"I'm armed and I've called the police!"

Nothing but silence.

Phin waited for a full minute and still there was nothing. Sweat was beading on his forehead. He was struggling, his mind racing trying to decide what he should do. The intruder might know he hadn't called the police because it was obvious he had not been in a conversation on the phone. In fact, he'd not spoken a word at all since coming home.

"Look, I know you're up there. Come down now before this gets out of hand!" He tried to make himself sound more brave than he felt. He could feel his heart pounding in his chest.

This was ridiculous. Maybe he was hearing things. His imagination had gotten the better of him and now here he was, *alone* in his own house, pointing a gun at the stairs. Phin lowered the firearm and was beginning to relax, having convinced himself he was just overtired. That's when he heard the footfalls. There was no doubt.

Thud, thud, thud, thud....

He could hear them crossing the ceiling right over his head. Then out into the hallway toward the top of the stairs.

Thud, thud, thud, thud...

The steps of the intruder kept coming without a pause.

Phin immediately brought the revolver back up, his heart racing once again. "Come on down nice and slow!" He called out. "No sudden movements or I WILL SHOOT!"

And then...the sounds of creaking steps at the top of the stairs. Hard footfalls descending one step at a time. Phin saw black boots first, coming down from the darkness like some evil apparition. They stopped...as if deciding if they should come on down or go back up.

"Let's go! Nice and slow!" The boots, attached to the home invader, whoever he was, stood there just a moment longer. Phin's head was beginning to spin, wondering what he would do if the man in the black boots just continued to stand there. He didn't have to wonder long. The feet began to move again. Very slowly, one deliberate step at a time, down the final seven or eight steps. As they did, the midnight visitor came into view. He was dressed in black military-style pants with cargo pockets on the sides. His top was tight-fitting and looked like it was designed for flexibility and all-weather conditions. It was black also, as were the gloves he was wearing. And the stocking cap. And the full-face neoprene cover. And the sunglasses. Yes, sunglasses. All black from head to toe.

Phin's intruder stood there now, at the bottom of the stairs, not even bothering to raise his hands. He appeared to be unarmed, which gave Phin a bit of confidence. Although it was difficult to measure him up, he looked to be about Phin's height, in good physical condition if the muscle tone showing through his athletic top was any indication.

"Okay. *Don't move*," Phin commanded, gun pointed square at the man in black's chest. "I don't know why you are here and I don't care but -"

Before Phin could finish his sentence, the intruder launched himself with cat-like quickness. In only a split second, he covered the six feet that separated the two of them. He had raised both of his hands and arms above his head and, in the same motion, brought them down with crushing force on Phin's arms. Phin had been perhaps a bit quicker than his now attacker had anticipated. He pulled the trigger just as the attacker made contact and before the gun went flying. *Got him!* That was Phin's thought as the force of the blow sent him to the ground. But the man in black seemed unfazed. Phin was incredulous.

Laying on top of his Persian rug at the foot of his couch, Phin was attempting to gather his wits as the intruder made for the front door. He flung it open and then... he *stopped*...as if trying to decide his next move. Phin was nearly to his feet trying to locate the gun when the man in black turned and bolted back *into* the house. He snatched Phin's MacBook from the couch and made for the kitchen. Panicked by the surprise move, Phin jumped over the couch and ran toward the kitchen just in time to see the thief shoot through the back door, out into the night.

Phin tore after him. Not the wisest thing to do, but he was thinking of his computer. *I've got a lifetime of material – pictures of Autumn, videos, research, class notes – all on that computer.* This was all he could think about as he shot out the back door into the snow. He was still in his stocking feet, but ignored the feeling of ice cold quickly seeping through the thin layer of cotton.

By the footprints in the snow, he saw that the man in black had gone right and around toward the driveway and the front of the house. He took off in pursuit. As he came to the front of the house, Phin paused at his car, trying to assess any movement. He was crazy to think he was going to catch this guy, he knew. All of a sudden he heard shuffling, and out of the corner of his eye he caught movement on the porch. He looked over just as the man in black disappeared back *inside* the house.

"Hey! What the -" Phin kicked up powder as he tried to gain traction getting to the front door. He made the porch just as the door slammed, followed by the click of the deadbolt. Uselessly, Phin worked the knob and began wildly kicking the door. *Who is this guy? What kind of home invader goes back* into *a house?!* Phin was mystified as he feverishly threw his body into the front door of his own house.

He could hear rustling around in the living room. He moved over to make out what was going on inside. There was a front window to the living room, covered with a thin curtain making movement inside visible. He could hear sliding and scrapping and the...the distinct sound of keys on a piano being randomly hit. *What?!* This guy was sliding the piano in front of the entry door. Autumn's piano.

Phin could not believe what he was seeing. As the realization hit him - that the intruder was trying to barricade himself *in* the house - he suddenly knew that meant he wanted to keep Phin *out* of the house.

The back door! It was still open. Phin took off back around the house, his feet beginning to feel numb from the snowpack stuck to his socks. He shot down the side of the house and made the corner, moving fast toward the back patio. Light from the kitchen shone brightly through the still open door.

Slam! Click!

The back door was thrown shut before Phin could even get there. More scrapping as the man in black pushed the refrigerator into place, blocking any attempt to breach the back entrance. Phin was reeling inside. His gun and his phone were still in the house. He had nothing with him. Not even a coat or shoes. He was helpless. That's when it hit him. This was the man in black's plan the whole time. He'd opened the front door on purpose, intending the whole time to flee out the back, knowing Phin would make chase because of his computer. He needed Phin out of the house so that he could finish.

But finish what? Phin thought. None of this made any sense.

A few lights had come on from the neighboring houses because of the commotion. "Hey Phin, that you?" It was Sam, Phin's immediate neighbor to the right, sticking his head out his back door.

"Yeah, Sam, it's me. Hey, call the cops. I've got someone who's broken into my house."

"Why are you in your socks, Phin? Are you okay? What's going on? I thought I heard a gunshot."

"Just call the police, Sam. Please, okay? And make it quick!" Sam disappeared back into his house.

There was about a two-inch space where Phin was able to see into the house, through the window on the back door, past the fridge. He could see right through the kitchen and into the living room. A mental quiet fell over Phin as he looked with strange curiosity at the man in black. *What's he doing in there?* The intruder, attacker, thief - whoever he was - moved with patience and calm through the living room. He opened a few drawers, shuffled through some papers, not really finding anything that caught his eye. Satisfied with his survey of the room, he turned his attention back to Phin's MacBook. He set it up on top of the piano, again, in no hurry. At one point he made a glance back at the kitchen where Phin could do nothing but watch. His lack of hurry was extremely disquieting. *Surely he knows the authorities are on their way.*

Then, to Phin's horror, the man unzipped a pocket on the side of his pants and pulled out a USB jump drive. He plugged it into Phin's computer and began to type. He then took a small step back and folded his arms, waiting. *He's copying my files! He stealing my data!*

"Hey! Hey, hey, hey!" Phin began to yell. Frantic. He was pounding on the back door this time. Kicking and screaming. "Stop! You can't do that! Why are you doing this?! STOP RIGHT NOW!"

Sirens were beginning to pierce the night as the man in black uncrossed his arms, hit a few more keys and then unplugged the jump drive. He turned once again toward Phin...and then he waved. As if to say *thanks* and *goodbye.* He leaned into the piano that he'd used to block the front door, beginning to slide it out of the way. Eyes wide with realization, Phin took off one more time toward the front of the house. He came around the final corner just as the man in black shot out of the front door and leapt off the porch. He tore through the front yard, the snow doing nothing to slow him down.

Phin was not deterred. Without thinking, he ran through the snowy yard in pursuit. *What am I going to do if I catch him?* He had no idea, but that wasn't going to stop him from trying. He could just make out the blue light, reflecting off the snow that continued to fall. The police were maybe a couple of blocks back, coming as fast as they could, sirens louder now. Phin was out on the sidewalk. He felt like he was actually gaining on the man in black. *That shouldn't be happening,* Phin thought, but he kept on, lungs and legs burning. He couldn't feel his feet at all now. If he could just trip him up, slow him down somehow. Until the police could arrive. He only needed to hold him a minute or so. He was maybe three feet back and still closing the distance.

Phin made the decision to throw himself at the man in black's feet, like a from-behind-tackle in football. But before Phin could make his move, the man in black stopped. It was a quick, unexpected, impossible stop. Phin bowled into the back of the man and bounced off. Stunned. Phin was trying to clear his head when the man in black turned, grabbing him full on, one black-gloved hand on each shoulder.

In the next moment nothing happened.

With the sirens approaching and the snow falling, Phin and the man in black just stood on the sidewalk facing each other. Phin squinted, trying as hard as he could to stare through the sunglasses - to see the man's eyes. That's when the man in black slammed his head into Phin's and then *everything* went black.

CHAPTER ELEVEN

They say that in dreams new worlds are born.

Dr. Mark Sayer wondered what kind of new world Charles LaPhage was living in at the moment. Certainly it was better than the world of the awake that he was about to experience yet again.

It was the dead of night, but Dr. Sayer didn't sleep well anyway. He had dutifully made his way to the penthouse apartment on the top floor of the LaPhage Industries tower in Fort Worth, Texas.

It was time for the awakening.

The apartment was where Ruth lived with her father. It was fully-appointed with modern décor and the latest in smart technology. Ruth had her own bedroom, while her father had a separate suite that was more akin to an ICU unit in a hospital than anything that looked like home. It was all necessary.

Incapacitated was the word used for public purposes with the media and for the Board of Trustees of LaPhage Industries. Charles LaPhage, the founder of LaPhage Industries, was incapacitated. He had remained that way for the past three years, ever since Charles and Mary had taken that fateful plunge off the canyon road in Utah.

Mary had been killed but Charles had not been so lucky. Thrown from the Land Rover as it hit the bottom of the ravine, the vehicle rolled on top of Charles before bursting into flames. The small creek the vehicle settled in served to douse the flames that continually licked at Charles' body, only for them to surge again and again. Steam and smoke rose simultaneously as passersby made their way down the slope to attempt a rescue.

Not until first responders arrived was the fire brought under control, and then the hard work of extracting Charles' and Mary's bodies commenced. The paramedics had been shocked to find that, while Mary had been burned to death, Charles was still breathing. The creek had saved his life - whatever kind of life there was left to be saved.

Charles had suffered burns over the entirety of his body. He was unrecognizable. In fact, the paramedics had no idea at all who they were saving. In addition, the lower half of Charles' body had been crushed under the weight of the Land Rover. The rescue team knew it was a hopeless cause. No one could ultimately survive such trauma to the body. Nevertheless, they dutifully performed their job of extraction, and Charles was airlifted to Intermountain LDS Hospital in downtown Salt Lake City.

Dr. Mark Sayer was the first to be informed of the tragedy once the hospital made identification and reached out to him in Texas. As the LaPhage's personal physician and most trusted family friend, he was the emergency contact for Charles and Mary.

Dr. Sayer immediately took the company Learjet, and ninety minutes later, was on the ground in Utah - twenty minutes after that, he was by Charles' side. Dr. Sayer was not just a physician, he was also a devoted confidant of the LaPhage family. Upon seeing Charles' condition, he began to pull the public relations strings.

What the media was told and what the world would learn was that Charles and Mary LaPhage had been in a one-vehicle accident while traveling on vacation in Utah. Period. No other details.

The day after this statement had been released, LaPhage Industries would release a follow-up press release to the media explaining that Mary LaPhage had sadly passed away from injuries inflicted by the accident. The statement would go on to recount the magnificent life of Mary, reminding the public that she was the one that introduced the world to the wonders of the LaPhage Limb.

There, of course, were quotes of reflection and sympathy from those close to the LaPhages, and even a quote from her dear husband, Charles, lamenting the loss of his bride. The press release ended with a word about Charles being unavailable for further comment because he was still recovering from his own injuries.

The same day as the press release about Mary's death, Dr. Sayer marshaled the full and considerable assets of LaPhage Industries to have Charles released from Intermountain LDS Hospital and flown on a customized medical jet to Fort Worth to be cared for in LaPhage's own state-of-the-art medical treatment facility. Non-disclosures had been signed, monies had exchanged hands, and LaPhage attorneys had employed a variety of other techniques to ensure that the truth about Charles LaPhage's dire condition did not become public.

Incapacitated. That had been the official word used in the days and weeks that followed the accident.

It had been the official word for the last three years now.

The board of trustees was obviously worried. Worried about who was in charge. Worried about market confidence in LaPhage stock. Worried about LaPhage stockholders. And so the call went out to Ruth. *Could she come home? Would she come home?* The appeal was earnest and pleading.

Ruth refused to entertain the idea at first. She didn't want to leave Europe and the path she was forging for herself. She wanted to be free, needed to be free, from her father's ambitions. She had ambitions of her own, and the two often collided.

Enter Dr. Mark Sayer. His call to Ruth swung the pendulum in her mind. Not until talking to Sayer did she truly understand the real meaning of *incapacitated.*

Charles LaPhage was in a medically-induced coma. The second and third degree burns over his body were so extensive that if he were allowed to wake up he would go mad. He was fighting infection and was facing numerous skin grafting surgeries, if he could even survive to that point.

But the real problem was his crushed lower half. His legs were mangled, burned, and impossible to recover. So was his pelvic region all the way to his abdomen.

Thus Ruth LaPhage came home.

She came home to take control of her father's interests and to take care of her father's life, a life that hung in the balance for the better part of a year.

Charles LaPhage did survive under the watch care of Dr. Sayer, employing the full cadre of LaPhage Industries' resources. His body miraculously fought off the infections from the burns, although he remained severely scarred and hairless, his arms ending in stumps with the loss of all ten fingers. His eyes, no longer with lids, were continuously lubricated by tiny tubes that ran along his temples.

He was unrecognizable from the Charles LaPhage of old.

He would also lose to amputation: the lower half of his body, his entire pelvis, his small and large intestines, and his stomach. One kidney and a third of his liver were able to be saved.

In short, what kept Charles LaPhage alive was technology. He was fed nutrients by technology, his blood was cleaned by technology, his muscles were stimulated by technology to avoid atrophy, and his consciousness was regulated by technology.

Dr. Sayer and Ruth would never forget, could never forget, the awful first time Charles was roused from his medically-induced coma to face his new reality. He was still badly burned and barely kept alive. The moment he came to, his body tensed and he began to scream. A blood-curdling, mind-ripping scream.

"Aaahhhhhhhhhhhh!!!!!! Noooooooooooo!!!! AAAHHHHHHHHH!!!" His heart rate and blood pressure spiked. He was at risk of stroking out. With quick work, Dr. Sayer put him back under.

They waited three more months before trying again.

The second time, his vitals spiked again but stayed within acceptable limits. He moaned and cried. The only words anyone in the room could recognize was the phrase repeated over and over through his groaning agony, *"Hell...oh the hell....the burning...the fire...oh the hell....the burning...the fire....,"* over and over he repeated.

A small group of LaPhage psychologists surmised that he was reliving the last conscious moments of the accident. Laying in the creek burning. The fire being put out by the lapping water, only to be reignited as the vehicle burned. Charles pinned underneath, helpless and aware the whole time that he was burning, that Mary was burning. Alive.

Over the last three years, a routine had been developed. Charles LaPhage was now stable, but his physical life was truly a living hell. His body was broken and smashed beyond any hope of recovery. He had been settled into a personalized medical suite on the top floor where Sayer was with him at this moment. Ruth was always close at hand. His life was a rhythm of machines that kept him physically alive. Every seven hours, on the hour, he would be awakened. This awake time would last precisely one hour before he was put back to sleep. Each time he was awake, it would be his old friend, Dr. Mark Sayer, who would be there to greet him - many times with Ruth by his side.

These three precious hours of awake time, within each twenty-four hour day, were designed to keep Charles LaPage engaged in reality - to be able to say to the board of trustees that the founder of LaPhage Industries was alive and stable, just *incapacitated*. This had seemed to satisfy the board and the shareholders, although only a select few knew the true extent of the situation.

Charles LaPhage had changed as well. He was no longer the Charles that friends and family remembered. Oh, there were moments of lucidity where the personality of the old Charles showed through, but they were laced with moments of incoherence and meanness. When you took time to look into his eyes, those dark green eyes that no longer had lids or lashes, eyes that eternally stared even when he was asleep, there was a *look*. An almost sinister look of a man who had truly been to hell and back, who had stared evil and the demons of hell in the face and had been changed. And not for the good. Those eyes were now foreboding and carried with them a hint of darkness itself.

"Charles, can you hear me? Are you awake? Come on Charles, it's me, Mark." Dr. Sayer was gently coaxing Charles LaPhage out of his latest round of sleep. It was just right at midnight. He eased the plunger into the IV with the precise amount of chemical designed to bring awareness. Charles' eyes began to dart around, moving back and forth. He couldn't blink, but this is how Dr. Sayer knew he was awake.

"Yes, Mark, so good to see you," there was a lightness to Charles' voice as he began to speak. Amazingly the one part of his body that survived the trauma of the accident was his vocal chords. The strong, golden voice of Charles LaPhage came forth from the monstrous half body with tubes and wires running in and out of it. "How are you my good friend? I had the most amazing dream. Where is Ruth? I must tell her about it!"

"She will be along shortly, Charles, perhaps before it's time to go back to sleep."

"Dreams are wheams, and they float swiftly on the seams! Ha, yes they do! Don't you think so, Mark?"

"Of course they do, Charles. Of course they do." LaPhage looked to be in another one of his incoherent states.

"Tell me my good friend, how is Ruth doing with the company? Please tell me the board trusts her, that they are letting her run with matters." Now it was coherent Charles. Gentle concern in his voice.

"She is well, Charles. And yes, the board is very satisfied with the job she is doing. She represents your interests well. You would be proud."

"I don't trust the board, Mark. We must do away with them all! Today! Will you take care of this for me? It must be done! Today."

"Certainly, Charles. It will be done." This was a recurring theme with LaPhage - mistrust of his board.

"Ruth, only Ruth. She's the only one that can be trusted. She knows what to do. She knows me, Mark! She knows all about me. I am scared of her. Ohhhh.....she terrifies me. Can I trust her, Mark? I don't think I can trust her!" Extreme paranoia now.

"Charles, Ruth loves you. Yes, you can trust her. She will never betray you. Never. In fact, she's been away today working for you. We all work for you, Charles. You are the one in charge. No one else."

"Yes, of course. Thank you, Mark. You are a dear friend indeed.

Always. You have always been there for me and Mary. Thank you my good friend. Thank you."

"You are welcome, Charles."

"Can I see Mary today? I miss her so. I think she's in the kitchen now preparing lunch. Please, Mark, tell her to come here."

"She's not in the kitchen, Charles," said Sayer with soothing compassion. "But you will see her soon. Perhaps when you go back to sleep you will see her. I am sure she's waiting for you now."

"Of course, yes, how silly of me. She's dead. Thank you for reminding me, Mark. We have dinner plans in just two hours. I will see her then."

And so it was with Charles LaPhage. Here, and then not here, and then here again - only a shadow of his former self - all the while the feeling that something dark was hovering just underneath the surface.

"Hello, Daddy." The soft padding of Ruth's feet could be heard coming up behind Dr. Sayer. She had obviously made her way quietly into the penthouse and slipped her shoes off after a long day. "I was hoping I would make it back in time, while you were still awake."

"Ruth, oh Ruth, it's been so long my darling!" The excitement in Charles' voice seemed genuine. Dr. Sayer took a step back in deference to Ruth's presence, a smile on his face, grateful that she had arrived in time for this awakening. It had been three days since she had last made one of the one-hour sessions. Not because she didn't want to, he knew, but because of the demands of running an entity like LaPhage Industries.

"I'm here now, Daddy. How are you?" Ruth said as she eased in close to her father's side.

"Oh, I am just fantastic. I fired the board today, Ruth. Mark will take care of it for us. And your mother and I have dinner plans later today. Isn't that wonderful? You should join us! She would be delighted to see you."

"Not today, Daddy. You go on without me. I have to run LaPhage Industries, remember? Especially now that you've fired that silly board." Ruth was so good at humoring her father with a warmth and compassion that never ceased to impress Dr. Sayer.

"Ruth!" Charles excited all of a sudden. "Ruth, I had the most amazing dream! Come closer, I must tell you." There was real urgency in his voice as he raised his stumpy arms, coaxing Ruth to come. "Ruth, it was about the Garden. Ruth, listen to me. You must find it." There was a change in Charles' voice and presence as his eyes bore into Ruth's. Something had shifted inside of him. He was fully in the moment. Coherent and aware.

"Yes, I know Daddy. I am working on it."

"I hope you are. Listen, Ruth. I know what is going on. I know so much more than any of you think I do. I've *seen* things Ruth. I've seen the shadow of God. I've been to hell and back. You must believe me! It is so critical!"

Ruth was tense as her father began once again with this line of conversation that had dominated his lucid moments the last six months.

"I know, I know it's critical -"

"No, you don't, Ruth," Charles came back, cutting his daughter off. "You don't understand. You can't understand how immensely important this is. But I must make you understand. There is a Garden, Ruth. *The Garden of Eden.* Read the Bible, it's all there. You must find it, Ruth. You must find the Garden of Eden. In its center is a tree. The Tree of Life. It's in the Bible, I tell you. It's not a myth. I thought it was but it is not. I've seen things, Ruth. That tree must be found. It's important. More important than you could ever imagine."

LaPhage's voice was rising with intensity. "Say it Ruth. Say the words so I know you understand. *The Tree of Life.*"

"Yes, Daddy, the Tree of Life. I understand."

"No! No you don't! I can see it in your eyes, Ruth. You still don't understand. There is a war Ruth. I've seen it. A war between God and Evil. It's so real. Oh, it's so, so real. More real than anything around us in this world. But Ruth, there is a gateway. Climb Jacob's Ladder to the Tree. YOU MUST FIND IT."

Ruth stared, mesmerized by the sincerity of her father's words. This had been his fixation. The Garden of Eden. The Tree of Life. *What world do your dreams take you to, Daddy?* thought Ruth as she leaned in close, her lips just a foot from the hole in the side of her father's head that had once been an ear. She began to whisper so as to keep Dr. Sayer from hearing. Some things just had to remain between a father and daughter.

"I'm working on it, Daddy," she breathed excitedly so that only he could hear. "I think I've found the one person who can help us. I think we can find the Garden of Eden!" Charles LaPhage's heart began to beat more rapidly in his chest, his muscles tensing on their own.

"Tell me, my child. I must know!"

"I will know more soon. But I believe you, Daddy. You're right, I don't understand all of what you've seen and experienced, but I believe you. If it's out there somewhere, I will find it for you. I will find the Garden of Eden."

"And the Tree of Life, Ruth!" Charles was pushing out a loud whisper, trying to match her quiet tone, but clearly too worked up to speak so as not to be heard by Dr. Sayer. "You must find the Tree of Life. It's the key to the war. It's the gateway. You must be *careful!*"

"I will know more soon, Daddy. I promise. I will know more and then you can tell me what to do."

Charles LaPhage began to relax, his eyes losing their intensity. Ruth sensed a presence just behind her. Dr. Sayer had eased up close and was administering the sleep agent that would send LaPhage back to the world created by his dreams. For the next seven hours he would be at peace. At least that was the hope.

"Tell Mother I miss her, Daddy. Give her a kiss for me," whispered Ruth as she leaned down, placing a tender kiss on the scarred forehead of her father.

Then suddenly, as Ruth was pulling away, Charles' entire body tensed once again, back arching, his eyes rolling into the back of his head. He began to speak, this time his voice coming forth strong and clear:

Follow the River to the end of the sun,
Beware the eagle, the sword, the gun.
No man may enter, no man may leave,
You'll find healing and hell
from the fruit of the Tree.

And then Charles LaPhage fell into a deep sleep, his body collapsing into the softness of the bed. Ruth just stared, absorbing the meaning of her father's words. She gave Dr. Sayer a questioning glance, *What was that all about?*

"Most likely a residual effect of his forced wake-sleep pattern. He's having a hard time discerning what is real and what is a dream," replied Sayer, knowing what she had been thinking.

Ruth LaPhage wasn't so sure. She could not shake the nagging thought that her father had a firmer grip on reality than all the rest of them put together.

CHAPTER TWELVE

The sky was dark and ominous. Thunderclaps were rolling in the distance as flashes of lightening bolted across the awful canvas of clouds. It was hot and sticky. A soupy mess. Phineas slogged his way up the dirt path. Where am I? he thought. His head was so foggy. Yes, he'd been here before. Many times. But where was here? Everything surrounding him was covered in shadow. The grass, the trees, the flowers. All painted in an ashen gray. Like color itself had been wicked away from creation.

The path led up, toward a hilltop. He was walking into a hot breeze that seemed to blow harder with each step. He was alone. All alone. But faintly, in the distance, he caught echoes of voices. So many voices. Calling to him? He wasn't sure.

A sudden crash of lightening jolted him to his core. Thrown to the ground, his body and face planted into the dirt. Then the pain hit. So intense. Racking his whole body. What is happening to me?! *This too was a repeat. He'd lived this all before.*

His head was clearing now, but his body was frozen. Stuck to the ground. A few raindrops were beginning to fall now. Just a few. Like the giant puddle drops before a massive storm hits.

He had to get out of the rain. He had to find shelter. Phin could feel himself beginning to grow desperate. Desperate to move his body. To pick himself up. He had to move...now! Straining every muscle he had, he lifted himself onto all fours. Nausea swept over him and he gagged on his own bile. He could not get his feet under him. Why can't I stand? What's wrong with my body? *All he knew was that he had to get to the top of the hill, to get away from the storm.*

Slowly, oh, so slowly, he began to scrape and crawl up the path. Digging his fingers and hands into the dirt. Clawing his way up. One knee and one hand step at a time. Like a baby. Fear and dread consumed him as a massive weight that he could not explain worked to pull him down and away.

The crowd seemed to be growing louder, if ever so slightly.

More thunder and lightening.

Then the sky opened up. Pouring torrents of rain and wet splashed down upon the ground and upon Phin. His clothes became soaked, weighing him down even more. He was clawing his way up the now muddy path on his belly, overcome with shear terror and panic.

Then everything just...stopped.

Silence.

The only sound Phin could hear was that of his own labored breathing. The thunder, the wind, the crowd...they were all gone. In an instant.

Then Phin became aware of another sound. Something new. A voice. It was coming from...just in front of him? Yes, maybe just three feet away.

From the ground! No, not the ground - from a puddle of water just in front of him on the path. He had to get there. He had to hear. Something...someone was calling to him.

Pushing with his feet, sliding through the mud like a beached fish, Phin came up slowly to the puddle. He wanted to look, but he was scared. Oh, so scared. But he'd come this far. He couldn't not look. He slowly moved his head directly over the puddle of water that had now grown silent.

To his surprise he saw....himself.

Yes, it was his own reflection staring back at him.

A ray of light from the sun began to crack the clouds open, his reflection becoming more distinct.

Phin began to laugh. Mostly at himself. He must be going mad!

But Phin's reflection did not echo his laughter. In fact, it didn't reflect Phin at all. It simply stared back at Phin like a corpse staring from the grave.

Phin's fear returned in an instant, the reflection of Phin opening its mouth and uttering one haunting word... "REMEMBER"....

Phin screamed.

CHAPTER
THIRTEEN

P hin found himself staring up at the inside of an ambulance.
With sirens blaring, the emergency vehicle was sliding its way carefully through the snow-packed streets toward Shawnee Memorial Hospital.

He could feel the pressure of an IV in his left arm, the stiffness of a padded collar around his neck. He was laying on a backboard, aware of every jolt and jostle of the medical van as it drove on. Phin coughed, if for no other reason, just to send the message that he was awake. A smiling but serious face appeared.

"Okay...Mr. Crook, how do you feel? Can you hear me?"

"Yes," Phin tried nodding.

"Are you in any pain? We've given you a mild sedative to relax you."

"I don't think so," replied Phin. "What happened to me?"

"Well the police found you out cold on the sidewalk in front of your house. You were nearly frozen by the time we got there." Phin could feel the heat packs around him now, soothing his muscles, thawing him out.

"We're guessing you slipped while chasing whoever it was that broke into your house. You didn't even have shoes on, sir. Not a smart move," the medic retorted with that same smile on his face. Phin couldn't tell if he was being scolded or just being given the facts.

"You sure bruised up your face though. You might have a broken nose. And there's a pretty good lump on the back of your head too."

That's when it all came back. The man in black, the deception, locked out of his own home, the copying of his files onto a thumb drive. And then the chase through the yard out onto the sidewalk. As Phin thought about it now, it almost seemed that the man in black allowed himself to be caught. Finally, the head butt.

Yes, Phin remembered it all now. The big questions were who and why? Who was this man? Was he acting alone? Where was he now? Why Phin? What was so special about him and his files? Which files was he after? Should Phin be afraid? And what does all of this mean? All of these questions flooded Phin's mind in an instant.

What also flooded Phin's mind was the awareness of pain in his face and on the back of his head. He could feel the knot, his nose and eyes were definitely sore, and he recognized the coppery taste of blood in his mouth. There was the sensation of dried blood cracking on his skin as he began to work the muscles of his face - just an attempt to discern if everything was working properly. He was relieved to feel all of his teeth intact as he rubbed his tongue across them.

"Is this brace necessary?" asked Phin. As his head was clearing he was beginning to crave mobility.

"Just until we get to the hospital. Go ahead and move your feet for me."

Phin complied.

"Great! Any pain at all in your back, legs, or arms?"

"No, all feels normal. I'd just love to sit up if I could."

"Almost there, Mr. Crook. We will get you checked out. Do a few X-rays, and if all looks good we will get you on your way."

Less than five minutes later, the ambulance was unloading Phin onto a stretcher, the cold night air blasting him hard as they made their way into the emergency room and immediately to a curtained bay. By that time he was fully alert a thousand things were running through his mind. He needed to get back to his house and check his computer. He needed to do a walk-through of both the upstairs and downstairs to see if anything was missing, to try to figure out what exactly the data thief was after.

It didn't take long for Phin to be surrounded by a couple of graveyard shift nurses and a doctor. He was fairly sure he was okay besides being bruised up, and he was anxious to get going.

An hour later, he had answered all the questions the police had. They were handling the whole thing as a common breaking-and-entering event. That frustrated Phin. There was nothing common about what he had experienced tonight. But he also knew they had nothing they could really go on. The man in black, whoever he was, was meticulous. He was gloved-up so there were no prints to collect. The house wasn't ransacked in any way. Even the entry doors were unbroken. It was like the guy had just let himself in and when he was done he had let himself out. That was about the whole of it. So frustrating.

The police said that if he found anything missing or stolen to just let them know and they'd add it to the report. *Yeah, add it to the report. Like that'll do a lot of good*, he thought.

The X-rays came back negative. No broken bones. Even his nose seemed to be only banged up. The collar was removed, the IV was disconnected, and Phin was set to be discharged. Except for one small problem: he had no car. They would only release him into the care of another individual. *You've got to be kidding me,* thought Phin.

"You've got to be kidding me!" Max Allred was beside himself on the other end of the line. Phin didn't know who else to call. "It's nearly three o'clock in the morning and you're at the hospital because you chased a guy who broke into your house? Are you crazy?"

"Thanks for the empathy, Max," Phin replied weakly. "Look, I'm sorry, I know it's late, or early, or whatever. But they won't let me go unless someone comes and picks me up. You won the lottery. Can you *please* just come get me? I've had a really long day."

"Yeah, sure, give me a few minutes and I'll be headed that way," the line went dead.

A half hour later, Phin was inside Max's car all nice and toasty headed toward home. As soon as Max had seen Phin's face he had softened a bit.

"So I don't get it, you just come home from your lecture at ORU, you're actually in your house, chilling out, and then you hear this guy walking around upstairs?"

"Yes, that's exactly what happened," answered Phin.

He went on to unpack all the details as he could recall them. Including the many questions about who and why and what it all could mean. Max's concern began to match Phin's.

"I don't like it buddy. I don't like it one bit, not at all. This is super weird. Why would anybody be interested in a no-name professor at a small Baptist college in Oklahoma? No offense."

Phin just stared, "None taken...I think."

The two friends arrived at Phin's home, removed the yellow police tape from across the front porch and door, and took the next ten minutes to walk through the house. The only thing that seemed to be disturbed were the papers and files in Phin's upstairs study. The two assumed that when the intruder didn't find what he was looking for, he just waited until Phin got home so he could download the contents of Phin's MacBook, which, they discovered, was still laying on top of the piano.

Perhaps that had been his intention the whole time, to wait for Phin to come home so he could do just that. The man in black was hoping to wait upstairs until Phin had gone to bed. He would sneak down, copy the files in stealth, and leave without a trace. But Phin had stayed up just long enough - or the man in black had moved just the wrong way - and Phin knew someone was in the house. However it went down, all Phin was left with were questions and a banged-up head.

"Hey look, Phin," Max was speaking as he walked into the living room from checking the back door. "Why don't you come spend the night with us? Or what's left of it. Shelly won't mind at all. The university has already cancelled classes for tomorrow, and the public schools are closed, so we are all just going to be sleeping in anyway. You can take the guest bedroom and sleep as long as you want. Personally, I think you need it. You look awful. And I don't like the idea of you staying here tonight anyway."

Phin was about to hedge.

"Don't say no, Phin, just go pack a bag. The kids will love to see 'Uncle Phin' in the morning. Let Shelly make you a home-cooked meal. We can build a snowman. Just take a day off and away from it all. Look, you need this. Trust me."

Phin felt the fight drain from him. Max was right. He desperately needed to sleep, and being taken care of was something that sounded really good right about now.

What didn't sound good was what likely waited for him once he closed his eyes.

CHAPTER FOURTEEN

Phin had escaped the world of his dreams, if for just one night. He'd collapsed into bed and was sound asleep as soon as his head hit the pillow. By eleven o'clock the next morning, he was awake and feeling remarkably refreshed. He had laid in bed for another half hour, just listening to the movement in the house. The padding of children's feet running up and down the hall. The laughter and excitement over a blanket of snow covering the ground. It felt good to be in a house that had *life* in it. That was a feeling that Phin painfully missed. The feeling of *not* being alone.

As he lay in the warm softness of the sheets and blankets, Phin also reflected on the previous day. He'd never had a Monday quite like it. The low of the meeting in Dean Reynolds' office - questioning him, chastising him. Then the high of the ORU lecture. The stranger with his challenging questions and million-dollar offer. Followed by the emotional drive home in the snow. Ending with the violent confrontation with someone who had violated his personal space and had stolen data from his computer. The last part is what continued to confuse him. *What in the world do I have, that someone would want to break into my house and steal it from my computer?* Phin really was a no-name professor from a small Baptist college in Oklahoma. Max had been correct in that brutally honest assessment. He simply couldn't imagine anyone being interested in him in such a clandestine way.

Phin got up and showered and changed clothes. He felt like a new man when he walked out of the guest room.

"Uncle Phin!" a screaming blonde-headed, blue-eyed boy came bounding down the hall, throwing himself around Phin's legs.

"Hey! You glad to be out of school, Junior?" Phin hugged him in return.

Junior was Max and Shelly's youngest of two children, a real livewire, full of energy and vigor *all the time*. He was Max's namesake, so they just called him Junior. Phoebe was Max and Shelly's blonde-headed daughter who was exactly two years older than Junior. They were in first and third grade, respectively. Whereas Max was brown-headed and completely average in every way, Max's children were blonde and beautiful in the opposite direction. There was no doubt they got their genes from their very blonde and very pretty mother.

Phin was warmly greeted by Shelly and Max as he arrived in the main room where a hot fire was roaring in the fireplace.

"Hey, there he is! Did you sleep well?" asked Max.

"Like a baby. Thanks Max. And you too, Shelly. I'm so sorry for calling last night. I hope I didn't wake everyone up."

Shelly was quick to reply, "Nonsense. Who else would you have called? We're family, Phin. You know that. Our house is yours. You are always welcome here." Phin believed her.

The snowstorm had passed and it was a bright and sunny day, the snow almost blinding under its rays. Shelly had just finished working in the kitchen, and was ready for everyone to come to the table for a perfect lunch of grilled bacon and cheese sandwiches with tomato soup.

Phin could not remember a meal tasting so good, and it wasn't because of the food. It was because of everything. This is what Phin craved. He wasn't jealous of Max, but being around him and Shelly and the kids drove home to Phin how truly sad he was most all the time. But what could he do? His life was the life that had been handed to him. The life God had handed to him. Yes, there was unfinished business to be taken care of on that front as well...with God.

But first, he had to build a snowman!

← →

Max and Phin were sitting in the living room of Max's home later that afternoon. The kids were still outside playing in the snow, a couple of Energizer bunnies. Phin had quit trying to keep up a good two hours earlier, but he had succeeded in building a six-foot tall snowman, complete with charcoal eyes and a carrot nose to boot.

"How are you doing, Phin?" Max got around to asking while taking a sip of hot tea.

"Not bad actually, my face isn't as sore as I thought it might be today," replied Phin.

"No, I'm not talking about that. I want to know how you *really* are doing."

Phin looked down into his own cup of tea, a silent pause. "I'm fine, Max. About as good as can be expected I guess."

"I know you say that but, man, I gotta tell you, I worry about you. Both Shelly and I do. You're not the same since -"

"Since Autumn," interrupted Phin. "Yeah I know. Wouldn't you be if the same thing happened to Shelly?" Phin came across harsher than he intended. This wasn't Max's fault. He was just trying to help. "I'm sorry, Max. Please forgive me. I know you only mean it for the best. No, I guess I am not all right. I haven't been all right for three years now. I know they say time heals, but honestly, time has done nothing but torture me. I know it's not healthy to play *what-if,* but that's exactly what I do every single day. What if I had taken Autumn's hand and just run that night in the city? What if I had fought back harder? What if I had listened to my gut and just not even moved back to the United States? What if...what if...what if.... No, I'm not all right but I will be, one day, I suppose. Isn't that what you're going to tell me?"

Max didn't know what to say. He took another sip of tea, casting his gaze into the fire. Phin had not allowed himself to open up like this in a long time. Maybe never since what happened to Autumn that dreadful night.

Part of the reason was because, even in the face of death, life goes on. *It's funny how that works,* Phin often thought. Somebody famous dies. Somebody that is known around the world for their music, or movies, or charity, or innovation. Someone that the world proclaims can never be replaced and will be missed by all. Then two, maybe three weeks later, they are just a distant memory. Oh sure, those closest to them still mourn, but the rest of the world just goes on. Without skipping a beat. That's how it had been since that night with Autumn. There was shock and sadness and tears, and then more shock when it came to how Phin chose to handle matters. Her family was especially angry at Phin. He didn't care, though. He did what he had to do and that was that. But then the world just went on. Phin tried to go on with it, but the agony of his heart was never far.

He was now letting it all flow out verbally to his best friend. The reason for that was most likely because this was one of the few times when they both slowed down enough to talk. To really talk.

It was a snow day. Life takes on a different pace on a snow day. Nobody goes to work. Nobody gets out. Nobody checks email. They just play in the snow like when they were kids. They sit close to the comfort of a warm fire with a cup of Earl Grey in hand. *Oh, if life were only this simple all the time,* mused Phin.

"I want to ask you an honest question, Phin," Max spoke. He chose his words carefully before continuing. "Do you truly think that if you could find the Garden of Eden, it would fix everything that happened with Autumn?"

Phin chuckled, "That's the same question Reynolds asked me yesterday"

"No, it's not. He asked you if you believed the Garden still exists and *can* be found? I already know the answer to that question. At least I know what you believe is the answer to that question. I'm asking you a different question now. I'm asking if you really do believe that finding the Garden of Eden will fix everything that happened to you because of what happened to Autumn? Because that's what this is really all about, isn't it Phin? It's not just some academic obsession to prove the Bible and to prove God and to make your mark in the annals of biblical scholarship and archaeology. This is a personal obsession because it's personal on the deepest level possible. Isn't that right, Phin? Isn't that what you meant when you told Reynolds that this meant quote 'everything' to you?"

Now it was Phin's turn to take a sip of tea and stare into the fire. He didn't like the direction this was going. He'd been too transparent perhaps, opened up too much. But Max was safe, he knew. If there was anyone left in his life he could trust, it was Max. Still it was so hard to be vulnerable.

"Paradise on earth..." it was almost a whisper that escaped from Phin's lips.

"Sorry, didn't catch that," replied Max.

"Paradise on earth," Phin repeated in a normal voice, turning his head to look at his best friend. "That's what the Garden of Eden is supposed to be, Max. Paradise. A place of perfection. Perfect harmony between man and creation. Between man and God. Just look around us, Max. This world is falling apart. No, it's *tearing* itself apart. Murder, terrorism, rape, hunger. For crying out loud, over half a billion people on the planet still can't even get clean water to drink. Think about that for a moment. Children die every day from diseases that God never intended would inflict humanity. And don't get me started on abortion. The open season on the most innocent of all life. Instead of running to God, crying out to God, begging Him to fix it all, the world is more and more, all the time, running *from* Him. It's insanity."

Phin paused for a moment to breathe, to gather himself. Then he continued, "Look, I believe that the Bible is the Word of God. Inspired by God himself. I believe it is a *true* book. That means there was a real Garden of Eden, a place of pure and perfect paradise on earth. And since we still live on planet earth, that means it's still here, right? Somewhere...out there," Phin threw his arm toward the big bow window.

"Come on, Max, don't tell me that doesn't intrigue you. The idea that if there was a place on this planet somewhere, a place that had been *protected*. Protected from the pollution of sin and death and corruption and government and war and dictators. Protected from hunger and substance abuse and pedophilia and disease. A place where God and man could walk in unity and talk. Like you and I are talking right now. A place where you could ask God anything and he is there and will answer you. And it would be a real answer that makes sense, Max. Not some theological dribble that we say to make ourselves feel good, but a real answer to the question of why there is so much evil and suffering, and what he plans to do about it. But more than anything, it's a place where you could be safe. I mean truly safe, for the first time in your life. And if you're broken, God is there to literally hold you and take it all away. If such a place existed and held all those hopes and promises and more, wouldn't you do whatever it took to find it?" Phin sat back with that question hanging in the air, letting Max take it all in. They'd never had this level of discussion about the driving forces inside of Phin to find the Garden of Eden.

"Phin, I love you like a brother," Max began slowly. He leaned forward, eyes locked on his friend's. "So I'm going to say something I've never said and that you're not going to like. But I have to say it for your own good." He paused one more time. "You need to let...Autumn...go."

Phin's mouth parted just slightly, his eyes widening. "Let Autumn go? What are you talking about? This is not about Autumn!"

"Bull crud, Phin! It's all about Autumn, and the fact that you can't even see that is why you must let her go. It's way past time. You can't hold on like you are. It's not healthy."

"You're crazy! How dare you," it was Phin's turn to shoot back. But Max carried on. This had been a long time coming.

"So you're telling me that it's just a coincidence that this passion of yours, this noble question to find paradise on earth, just happened to begin at the same time you lost Autumn? You really expect me to believe that she's not the driving force behind it all?"

"I've not lost her, Max! I've not lost Autumn. She's still with me -"

"Yes, Phin, yes, you have! You have to realize this and let her go. What you are doing is not right and it's not healthy."

Phin was fuming. Controlling himself, he counted to three in his head, "Max, I don't want to talk about Autumn anymore. Not like this. Maybe it's not healthy, maybe it's not right. I don't know. But, please, I beg you, answer my question. Just about the Garden of Eden. Focus on the Garden. Don't question the *why* behind it. I'll be the first to agree, I'm screwed up, okay? I'm a mess and I'm still walking one day at a time. But the Garden, Max. Paradise on earth. If it's there...wouldn't you want to find it? Just for the possibility it holds?" Phin was pleading now, his sincerity unmistakable.

"Yes...I would, Phin. Yes, I would." Max relented quietly, once again looking into the fire. "But Phin, if the Garden of Eden still exits, wouldn't it have been found by now? Surely you don't believe that with over seven billion people on earth that we've just...missed it?"

Phin let out a short laugh, "Have you ever driven through Kansas, Max? Or the panhandle of Oklahoma, at that? Or how 'bout Arizona or Montana?" Phin had heard this line of questioning so many times before. "Brother, there is so much empty land still out there. Untouched and undeveloped by man. Shoot, there are parts of South America that have never even been touched by a single human soul as far as we know."

"Yeah, but we're not talking about Montana or the jungles of the Amazon Basin. We're talking about the Middle East, Phin. We're talking about one of the most ancient places on earth. Dominated by one human kingdom after another. Wherever the Garden was - and for the record I *do* believe that there was a real Garden - but wherever it was, it's surely not survived through the millennia."

All Phin could do was smile. He took another sip of his tea, now cool.

"Why are you smiling? I got you on that one, didn't I?" Max asked, smiling back.

"Genesis 3:24," replied Phin, still smiling.

"What do you mean, Genesis 3:24?"

"Look it up. No wait, I'll just quote it for you:

And at the east of the Garden of Eden, God placed the cherubim and a flaming sword that turned every way, to guard the way...."

A hush fell over the living room of Max Allred's house as Phin finished quoting the Holy Scripture passage from Genesis. The only sound was the continued crackling of the fire, the kids still laughing as they played outside in the snow.

"He's guarding it, Max. Protecting it," Phin's voice and words were calm and measured. "If God had simply intended to just take the Garden away, or to let it disappear, or whatever, then why didn't he just do that? Back in Genesis? But he didn't. He put up a barrier, a hedge around it. He placed holy angels to guard it. So unless you believe God changed his mind, or that the angels left their post, then it's still out there, Max. The Garden of Eden. Paradise on Earth. Just waiting to be found."

After a moment of introspection Max finally spoke, "Well, I'll be. You may have something there. I'll admit that. I want you to know, that for the record, I still believe what I said about Autumn. But that aside...yes...what you are saying has credibility. It's worth exploring. Yes," another thoughtful pause. "Yes...it is."

Phin was beaming, "Thanks buddy. This all sort of reminds me of our dorm room debates over theology when we were in college."

"Yeah, except you were always wrong!"

"No way! Never!" Phin threw a sock at his friend.

"So, Mr. Green Thumb, where exactly is this Garden that you're such an expert on?"

"You expect me to give that away?"

"Absolutely! Come on, I'm your best friend."

"Well about that -"

Phin was cut off by the chime of his phone. He pulled it out of his pocket and looked at the notification. It was an incoming message from an external priority email address that he had flagged. Phin opened the message, his face clearly disturbed as he read the contents.

"Oh great," he muttered to himself.

"What's wrong?" asked Max, sharing his concern.

"It's my brother."

"Remus?"

"Yeah. He needs to see me. Says it's important. He hashtagged it 911."

Phin did a quick calculation in his head. Over a year. That's how long it had been since he'd talked to Remus Crook. His only brother. Rolling his eyes, Phin drew in a deep breath. "Looks like I'm off to the state penitentiary this weekend."

CHAPTER
FIFTEEN

Sergeant Billy Warren stood on the roof of LaPhage Industries, arms crossed, staring into the distance of the eastern sky. He was wearing his traditional cargo-pocketed pants, dark brown in color, and military-issued desert boots. His torso filled a tight-fitting dry fit, long-sleeved black shirt. The wind was blowing ever so slightly as the sun was making its rise into the morning sky.

Warren was here to finish the mission. To see it through all the way to its end. He knew he was early, but a good Marine was never caught off-guard. Always ready early, and never late into action. A good Marine never questioned his orders. He simply executed. Sergeant Warren was good at executing. That didn't mean he didn't have questions though. He was human after all.

His employment for LaPhage Industries had seen his particular skill set used in a variety of ways. Most legal, some not. Last night's operation had fit into the latter, he was fairly certain. But a good Marine is also loyal. If the Marine Corps had drilled anything into his thick skull, it was loyalty. Loyalty to the country. Loyalty to the Corps. Loyalty to each other. Oh yes, Sergeant Billy Warren was loyal if nothing else. LaPhage Industries had given him a new lease on life and he was more than ready and willing to repay that debt with every ounce of loyalty in his being.

Warren could see it before he could hear it. The silhouette of the Bell UH-1Y Venom helicopter was making its way straight toward him, the sun directly behind it.

Just like freakin' Apocalypse Now, thought Warren. He even laughed out loud at the thought. Warren was a war movie junkie. Most of them were trash, he mused. But there were a few classics - real gems - that captured the essence of the warrior. *Apocalypse Now* was one of those gems by Warren's way of thinking.

The sound of the chopper began to grow, as did its outline. In another moment it had filled Warren's view as it came in hot and then pulled up to hover directly over top, settling in above the helipad. The sound of the Bell utility copter was now a deafening roar as it kicked a massive windfall down onto the building.

Sergeant Warren was the only person on the rooftop waiting for the arrival of the package. He made his move to meet the helicopter before it even touched down. Bits of grit and sand slapped at his face as he walked right up to the cargo door and ripped it open. The twin engines immediately began their wind down. Warren gave a quick and decisive thumbs up to the two other LaPhage carriers waiting inside. They returned the silent gesture the moment they recognized the sergeant.

"Any issues?!" called Warren over the top of the now declining roar of the engines.

"No sir!" came the reply. "The package was at the designated pickup point waiting on us, exactly as planned. We were in and out with no trouble at all. As easy as it gets, sir!"

Sir, registered Warren. That wasn't something an enlisted Marine like himself was ever called. He was *sergeant*, not *sir*. *Sir* was reserved for officers. But he wasn't in the Marines anymore. And this was a civilian operation, in spite of the military overtones. So *sir* is how everyone referred to him now. Not that he didn't like it! It was just another thing to laugh about to himself, that an old military grunt like him had risen to the level of a *sir*. Ha, yes, that was indeed something that made him laugh. His fellow Marines would surely be laughing about it with him if they could see it all now.

Warren jumped up onto the bed of the helicopter and moved to the rear where the storage equipment was kept. He quickly spotted what he was looking for. *Dang thing looks like a stinkin' coffin.*

There might have been a creepy aspect for most people as to what he was about to do, but Billy Warren wasn't most people. Without another thought he walked up to the 80-inch by 32-inch box. He located the keypad on the lower portion and punched in the security code, which immediately disengaged the lock with a soft click, felt more than heard. With great care, Warren lifted the lid. Not because he was afraid he was going to break it, but more so out of respect for the multi-million dollar cargo it contained.

He found himself staring down at a version of...himself.

Well, at least that's how he had begun to think of the Robatar. No one else had spent more time working with the Robatar. Being the Robatar. Warren wondered if this is what it would feel like to look at one's own corpse. He quickly put the thought out of his mind. *Finish the mission.* That was all he needed to be concerned with right now.

He made a quick visual once-over of the Robatar, still fully clad in all black, from head to toe. Including black facemask and sunglasses. His eyes next moved to the left-side cargo pocket. He reached down and worked the zipper, opening the pocket. Fishing around inside, his hand found what he was looking for.

"Right where I left you," Warren actually said aloud to no one in particular. He held up a USB thumb drive, turning it over between the fingers of his LaPhage Limb. Giving it a quick kiss with his lips, he did a one-eighty and moved to the exit, jumping quickly back onto the concrete rooftop and marching straight toward the entrance to the building.

Less than ten minutes later, Sergeant Warren was deep in the bowels of LaPhage Industries, standing outside the entrance to LP-6. After engaging the three-tiered security protocol, the door to the secret lab slid open. Stepping inside, it took just a moment for his eyes to adjust to the dimmed lighting. He spotted Oz Jenks and Tony Chen totally zoned out at their workstations, headphones on, completely absorbed in their work.

As he approached, it became more clear...not work, video games! Some first-person shooter by the look of it. Warren slammed the open palm of his hand down on the table next to Tony with a powerful *whack!*

Both Tony and Oz nearly jumped out of their skin. Oz about knocked over a Styrofoam cup likely filled with some kind of caffeine-loaded soda, and Tony's headphones went flying as they were jerked from his head while springing to his feet.

"What are you two geek-wads up to?" thundered Warren.

"Oh hey, Billy," Tony said nervously. "We are just...uh...running some simulations...."

"Yeah, okay, whatever. I don't really care what you girls do in your free time." Warren really didn't care. He knew the boys were good in their own world just like he was good in his. "I just came from the roof. The chopper flew in right on time and I was there to meet it."

"Awesome, yeah, we were waiting on you to bring us the data," replied Oz, looking nervously at Tony.

"That's right, we were just...killing time," it was Tony's turn to speak.

The truth is that Sergeant Billy Warren was the kind of man that made guys like Tony and Oz nervous. Whereas they spent the vast majority of their lives in a virtual world, Billy Warren spent his life in the real world. A world of wars, bombings, bullets, and missing limbs. Just being around a real Marine like Warren made them uncomfortable.

"Ask and ye shall receive," Warren held up the USB thumb drive for Oz and Tony to behold, as if it was some Holy Grail. "Look, I don't know what's on this thing and I really don't care. I've done my part. Mission accomplished as far as I'm concerned. It's now time for you boys to work your magic and produce for Miss LaPhage, whatever it is she needs from this thing."

"I'm not sure what all's on there either but I'm extremely curious." All heads turned toward the new voice. It was none other than Ruth LaPhage herself who had quietly entered the room.

"Ruthie! Well ain't this a pleasant surprise?" said Warren.

"Oh, uh, good morning, Miss LaPhage," Tony replied next.

"Yeah, great to see you? I think," it was Oz chiming in. The nervous factor exploded in the room for the two computer geniuses. They didn't get a lot of visitors anyway, but to have the sergeant, and now Ruth LaPhage, in the Lair at the same time was almost too much real-world sensory for Tony and Oz to handle at one time.

They both began to scramble, picking up wads of trash and cups and scooping it all into trash cans. Ruth just giggled.

"Relax, you two," she said in her token disarming manner. She walked toward the group. "Good morning to you all as well. Hi, Billy," she paused to look directly at Warren. "I heard you did another great job last night. Thanks so much. I always know we can count on you," laying a hand on Warren's real arm, she gave him a warm smile. There was a part of Warren, the gruff and tough Marine part, that melted away at the touch. Most people don't have that kind of effect on the sergeant, but Ruth LaPhage wasn't most people. Especially to Billy Warren.

"Sure thing, Ruthie, you know I'm always here to do whatever you need," Warren reached his own hand up to put it on top of Ruth's, but she was already pulling away.

His insides began to harden back up at the move. *What is it about her?* thought Warren. *Why do I let her get to me like that?* She just had a way about her that was spellbinding. Warren couldn't put his finger on it, but there was certainly something about her. He didn't like the fact that she did that to him - muddle up his insides. But he also *did* like it at the same time. She was having the same effect on Tony Chen and Oz Jenks. He suspected she had the same effect on all men.

Turning to her technology experts, Ruth began, "So obviously you've not had a chance to look at the data yet?"

"No, ma'am. We were just about to start right now." Oz reached over and Warren handed him the drive. He moved swiftly to a separate machine on a table behind the group, plugging the drive into the port. "It will take just a few minutes to download the contents and then we can begin a review."

"Perfect," replied Ruth as she walked up behind Oz and leaned over him, looking curiously at the screen. "So it's all there? Every file from his computer?"

"We'll know in a minute, but it should be. Let's see," Oz said as a progress meter was moving on the screen. "It's showing no corruption, so we for sure have clean data. But Miss LaPhage, it would really help if we knew what we were looking for."

"Whelp! That's my cue to leave!" proclaimed Warren. "You all have fun here in the Bat Cave looking for whatever."

"Thank you again, Billy," Ruth said, straightening back up to face Warren. "Just one more thing before you go." There was a look of concern on her face. "Our monitoring of the emergency frequencies last night showed that an ambulance was called along with the police. You didn't...uh...hurt anyone, did you?"

"The professor? Nah, he'll be fine. I gotta admit, though, he had a lot more spunk in him than I gave him credit for. Really created more of a ruckus than I would have wanted. Nearly woke the whole neighborhood up. I had to...sort of silence him."

The three others just stared at Warren.

"Silence him?" asked Tony.

"Oh...no! No...it's all good. I don't mean in *that* way! Crud, what kind of guy you think I am? No, he's fine, I promise. I'm sure he's makin' snow angels today." With a wink and a nod, Sergeant Billy Warren turned and made a quick exit from the Lab.

"That guys scares me," Tony whispered as the door slid shut.

"Don't worry about Billy, you two. He's good at what he does and we have an understanding. He's fine...I promise." Ruth was reassuring, as always. "So back to the data drive. What's it looking like, Oz?"

The curiosity over the drive had returned to the room. With Oz Jenks driving the keyboard and mouse, Ruth LaPhage and Tony Chen stood behind him, watching as various files were sorted.

"It looks like we've got your basic picture and video files. Lots of pictures of him with another woman. Probably his wife. She's pretty."

"I don't care about any of that. Look for files related to research. Anything on the Middle East, charts, graphs, etc. And the Bible."

Oz paused and looked up, "The Bible?"

Ruth huffed, "Don't ask why, Oz, just trust me. It's better you don't know everything right now." She placed a hand on his shoulder. It worked like magic. Like a compliant puppy, Oz went back to work. Tony watched the exchange. He was wishing she would put her hand on *his* shoulder.

"Well this could take some time, Miss LaPhage. I feel bad about making you wait."

"Okay, let's do this. Sort it all out like I asked. Then send me a copy of everything you find. Focus on the Middle East, the Bible, anything research-based, okay? If what I'm looking for is there, I'll know it when I see it."

"You got it."

It was Tony Chen's turn, "Uh, Miss LaPhage, one more thing before you go. If you have time?"

"Of course, Tony, what is it?" Her piercing green eyes and smile caused Chen to stammer.

"Yes, well, it's just. Well, Oz and I have a concern."

"A concern?" Ruth's smile faded as her brow furrowed.

Oz chimed in, "We were going through the post operation analysis of the campaign in Syria." Ruth turned, raising an eyebrow this time, as if to say *go on*.

"We found a...glitch," back to Tony.

"A glitch? What does that mean exactly? What kind of glitch?"

"Well, here's the thing," began Oz. "The initial stream of data that we look at every time we send the Robatar out for anything came back with some anomalous sectors. A glitch, right? It's the kind of thing we saw all the time back when we were beta testing the machine. So I ran a level two pushback analysis, just to dig into it and see if I could find the source."

"And?" asked Ruth, she was fully with them now. "What did you find?"

"The impossible," cut in Tony.

"What does that mean, the impossible?"

"He means that at the very end of the Syria campaign, the Robatar went...autonomous. It severed the link between itself and Billy. At that point, the good sergeant became an observer just like the rest of us. The Robatar was operating in full independent mode."

"But....that's impossible," the knowledge of what Tony and Oz were communicating was beginning to set in.

"That's what we're saying," said Oz. "It's theoretically impossible. At least for another generation. We are talking about full-on artificial intelligence. Total independence. With no human influence at all."

"Yes, completely untethered and unsteered by a human host," continued Tony.

"Okay," Ruth's mind was whirling, "to be clear, what you're saying is that the Robatar went rogue. That we lost control, right?"

"Exactly."

"But that's not supposed to happen, ever?" Ruth asked.

"It's not supposed to be *possible*, ever. At least in any way that we define what is possible for this generation of AI," concluded Oz.

"And this has never happened before, correct?" Ruth continued to question. She wanted to make sure she understood exactly what she was being told.

"No ma'am," continued Oz. "Tony and I immediately went back to every simulation and field test we've ever done with the Robatar. We dissected every glitch the machine has ever thrown at us, and nowhere in the data stream have we ever seen anything like this."

Ruth's brain was now swimming with the implications of what she was being presented. "Who all knows about this - besides us three in this room?"

"No one else," replied Oz. "We didn't know who to tell. We weren't even sure if we should say anything to you, but since you were here...well...it seemed the right thing to mention it."

"No, you did the right thing, guys. So you're sure it's *just* us in the loop on this? The Department of Defense folks don't know. No one knows, right?"

"That's right. Just us," answered Tony.

"So listen to me carefully," Ruth began. She had decided how she wanted to handle this. "You said this was a *glitch*. So that's how we are going to treat it, got it? A glitch. Nothing more, nothing less. But I want you to watch the Robatar closely. Run all your tests each time it comes back in. Do your pushback whatever. Go to level three, level four, whatever it takes. If you see anything like this again, come straight to me and no one else. And, under no circumstances are you to talk about this to anyone else. It's just between us three only. Understand?"

"Yes, ma'am."

"Yes, Miss LaPhage." Tony and Oz each replied in turn. "Just us three. The Three Amigos. Got it!" Tony was just a bit too eager. Oz rolled his eyes at his friend.

But Ruth LaPhage wasn't smiling. The gears were turning in her head. She didn't like the idea of not being in control. Especially of something as complex and expensive as the Robatar. And she absolutely didn't want her liaisons with the D.O.D, General Myers and Admiral Watkins, to get even a whiff of this. It could shut the whole project down. The military were fanatical about control. It had taken all of Ruth's cunning and persuasion to get the independence from the military she currently enjoyed in order to take Project BORG as far as they had.

There were other thoughts in Ruth's mind as well. She was an explorer at heart. She thrived on pushing the envelope. Tony Chen and Oz Jenks had called what happened to the Robatar a glitch. Not all glitches are bad, she mused. Sometimes a simple glitch can open the door to new possibilities. Yes, Ruth LaPhage would have to spend some time thinking about the possibilities of this particular *glitch*.

CHAPTER SIXTEEN

"This is a bad idea. You don't even have a driver's license!"

"Shut up! You don't need a driver's license to drive, you just need a car."

Remus Crook had always thought of his little brother as a chicken, but tonight that was going to change. In fact, that was the point of tonight. To drive the *chicken* out of Phineas.

"I'm telling you I don't like this, Remus. This is too big. We're going to get in so much trouble if we get caught."

"That's why we're not going to get caught, you wimp. Now be quiet and let me figure this out."

The two boys, Remus and Phineas Crook, were hunkered down in some bushes across the street from the Chevy dealership in their hometown of Moore, Oklahoma. It was late and it was a school night. Instead of studying for algebra, they were plotting the theft of a car. Remus, at the ripe old age of 15, was definitely the one steering the ship, pulling his reluctant brother, two years his junior, into what very possibly could turn into a disaster. But these weren't just any two young boys. No, these were the Crook Brothers. And that meant something. If not to the public at large, at least to them. But mostly to Remus.

The boys didn't have a bad reputation. In fact, quite the opposite. They were polite, kind, and respectful. They got decent grades and had good social graces. Remus was the more athletic of the two brothers. He liked to play summer baseball and during the school year, basketball was his sport of choice. He wasn't a great athlete, but he wasn't bad either, always finding a way to contribute to the team. Phineas, on the other hand, was always playing catch-up to his big brother. He tried all the same sports as Remus, but Phineas just didn't have the coordination or the physical build to be very good. What he really liked to do was read. Phineas was a bookworm - always finding a way to escape into some adventure through the words of someone else. Remus found it frustrating.

"You need to get your nose out of those books and into the real world!" he'd scold Phineas.

Phineas didn't care. He'd decided some time back that he would never be his brother, that he really didn't *want* to be his brother. Not that he had any idea of who or what he did want to be. He had just decided that it was okay for Remus to be Remus, and for him to be....well, whatever.

But they were both Crooks. *The Crook Brothers* was a term the other kids at school had adopted by way of teasing. The boys were well-liked for the most part by their peers; but kids will be kids, and Phineas and Remus just had one of those last names.

The funny thing was, through the years, wherever the Crook Brothers were, things had a tendency to go missing. In the very early years, it might've been something as innocent as the bag of candy from Mrs. Weather's desk drawer. The first grade teacher had Phineas as a student and always kept some sweets around to reward the kids for good grades on the weekly spelling test. Then one day the candy was just...gone. The same thing happened two weeks later. The thief remained a mystery.

That same year when Remus was in third grade, it was the stapler that disappeared from Mr. Holms' desk drawer. And not just once. But once *per month*, sometimes twice. It drove Mr. Holms crazy. By his count he lost twelve staplers that year, all just simply gone without a trace. He knew it had to be a student, and try as he might, he could never catch the thief. He even resorted to backpack searches, but to no avail.

And that's just how it was. A bag of candy, a stapler, a box of donuts from the teacher's lounge, the answer key to a test, the power cord to a computer, etc.

One winter every teacher in the school - every single one of them - over the course of one week, had a scarf go missing.

Another year, the entire faculty of the whole school had a rough time going home after work when they discovered at the end of the day that they each had someone else's car keys. It didn't matter if they carried their keys in their pockets like most men do, or in their purses like the ladies - every single teacher was in the possession of someone else's keys. Remus and Phineas would never forget that day. As they hung around waiting on the bus, they snickered and laughed as the teachers stood perplexed in the parking lot, staring back and forth between the cars and the keys in their hands. All they could do was shake their heads, trying to figure out what was going on. The bus arrived way before it was all sorted out. Remus and Phineas had heard that it took two solid hours before order was restored and everyone was headed toward home.

Through it all, the Crook Brothers were never implicated. Oh, there were times when an accusing eye might have been cast in their direction, but nothing ever stuck. They were like Teflon.

Now it was time for the big leagues.

Remus and Phineas were dressed in camo as they rustled around in the bushes, trying to stay quiet. It was late, past eleven o'clock. Remus used a set of binoculars he had borrowed from his father to peruse the parking lot and the showroom floor. There were security cameras, but the teens weren't really worried about those. The plan was to wear ski masks anyway. The big problem was the one security guard. Remus had been scoping out the dealership for a few weeks and knew that around eleven-fifteen every night the guard would walk outside and around to the north side of the building for a smoke break. He would typically spend about ten minutes away from his desk, which was inside the showroom. That was more than enough time by Remus' calculations.

"I don't understand why we are doing this," whispered Phineas.

Remus pulled his eyes away from the binoculars and gave his little brother a cold glare, "Because we can, Phineas. Because we can."

It was sort of the Crook Brothers' motto: Because we can.

Why do we have to take Mr. Holms' stapler for the ninth time? Because we can. Why do we need to steal the answer key to a test I'm gonna ace anyway? Because we can. Why do we have to swap every single set of car keys from every teacher? Because, Phineas, we can!

Phineas just rolled onto his back and let out a huff of air. He was so nervous. Candy and staplers were one thing. Stealing a car was another. Plus, Phineas didn't like any of it anyway. He'd rather be home right now, eating a peanut butter and jelly sandwich and reading *Lord of the Rings.*

"Okay, get up and get ready, Phin," ordered Remus. "It's almost time. The guard should be taking his smoke break any minute now. As soon as he rounds the corner we move." He paused to look down at Phineas. "Are you paying attention little brother? Don't screw this up," he hissed.

"Yeah, I'm paying attention. I'm ready," Phineas dug deep, putting on his best game face.

"Remember, follow close to me. We will go in low. Around the right side of the lot. Keep your head below the tops of the cars. They will give us the cover we need. Once we get to the door, you pick the lock while I watch. Then I'll take care of getting the car going while you watch. Once I get it started, you hit the button that opens the big glass doors. Then all you gotta do is jump in and I'll punch it. We'll be free and clear before Rent-a-Cop knows what's up!"

The plan was to take the car about five miles down the road and park it in the driveway of their principal's house. They would just walk away.

"I don't understand why we can't just boost a car in the lot, Remus," pleaded Phineas in one last-ditch effort to steer his brother to something less daring. "Like that Cavalier right there on the edge of the lot. We can do that no problem, even while the guard is inside. It'd be better that way."

"Don't be stupid, Phin. No way. We are going *inside*. Straight onto the showroom floor. That's where they keep the big money cars."

"And we're doing this -"

"Because we can," shot back Remus, cutting him off mid-sentence.

Because we can. Phineas just nodded. He was focusing now. If they were going to do this, then he needed to be focused. There was one thing he knew for certain: he didn't want to get caught.

Phineas moved into a squatting position, shoulder-to-shoulder with his big brother. His eyes were on the front door of the dealership as Remus raised the binoculars to his face for another close checkup.

With his naked eyes, Phin could himself make out the guard inside, behind the lobby front desk. He was moving around, like he was fiddling with something. Then he rose and casually walked around to the front of the desk. Pausing, he stretched big, with his hands over his head. Phineas didn't have the advantage of the binoculars, but he thought he could even make out a yawn.

Slowly, the guard sauntered toward the front door.

"He's moving! Get ready, Phin."

And then the guard stopped. He made a quick check of his pockets, patting them both front and back. He was missing something. He turned and walked back to the desk, bent over the front as if reaching for something. He pulled back up and Remus could see that it was his pack of cigarettes that he'd left behind. Remus smiled.

"Almost there. Get ready...get ready..." Remus was clearly excited. The adrenaline was flowing freely through both teens' bloodstreams.

The guard walked to the front glass entry door and reached down to unlock it. He let himself out, moving his hands to grasp his keys, which were fastened to his belt loop. He stretched them out via a retractable cable, and finding the right key, locked the door back.

Then he just stood there.

His head moved slowly from one side to the other. He was scanning the parking lot. Phin and Remus froze as his head suddenly stopped. The guard was staring straight in their direction. Remus was still watching through the binoculars, certain he was looking directly at him.

"Crap! Get down!" Remus dove, pulling his brother after him.

"He saw us, didn't he? He saw us."

"Just shut up!"

"Let's go! He made us, Remus. Let's get out of here."

"SHUT...UP!" he hissed through clenched teeth.

Ever so slowly, Remus lifted his head. The guard was already moving away toward his smoking corner.

"We're in the clear, Phin. It's all good. He's moving away."

Phineas' heart sank. He thought he was off the hook. He steeled himself, knowing Remus was determined, and that they were about to cross the line of no return. Raising the binoculars one final time, Remus could just make out the orange glow of the tip of a cigarette as it disappeared around the corner.

Ten minutes. The clock was ticking.

"Let's move, Phin!" Remus tore out of the bushes, pulling his ski mask over his face.

CHAPTER SEVENTEEN

Remus Crook sprinted across the road and ducked down behind the first car he came to at the edge of the lot. Phineas was right on his heels. Their hearts were pounding. They both raised up, making a quick look over the top of what they realized was a Chevy Malibu. Convinced all was still clear, they tore out around the car, working their way toward the right side of the lot, the opposite direction from where the guard was now enjoying his smoke. They didn't stop again until they were even with the front of the dealership building itself.

They were still at the edge of the lot, but behind a Chevy Silverado now. It was maybe thirty yards or so to the front door. Once they began to move again there would be no more cover. They would have to work quickly. In and out, just like they had planned it. *Well, like Remus had planned it*, thought Phin.

Remus gave Phineas a look as if to say: *This is it.* With a nod to his brother, he turned and the two teens moved, low and swift. They closed the final distance to the front door. Remus pulled up sharp with Phineas coming in low, sliding to a stop on his knees. His face was level with the lock mechanism on the door, and he was already unzipping his tool kit. Between the two of them, Phineas was the best with locks. He had a knack with the small tools that were the trade of the lock-pick. Anytime the two faced a door that needed to be breached, Remus always deferred to his little brother. He was a natural.

The clock was ticking as beads of sweat began to slide down Phineas' brow. He inserted the delicate tools into the lock, his nimble fingers reading the feel of the internal tumblers. *Click...click-click*...and then a light *Thwunk*....

Phin turned his hand over, the bolt to the locked door sliding back into its recess. It had taken less than twenty seconds. He rose and stepped back as Remus pulled the door open and glided inside. Phineas came next, stopping only to relock the door with the manual knob on the inside of the door.

Turning around, he couldn't see Remus. His heart raced. *Where did he go?* Just as panic was setting in, his eyes landed on his brother. He was standing at the far end of the showroom transfixed on their objective.

A jet black Corvette ZR-1.

The fastest, most powerful of the Corvette family. Price tag upwards of $90,000.

Why? Phineas thought again. But he knew the answer all too well. *Because we can.*

He moved up next to his brother and gave him a hard punch to the side as if to say, *let's go!* Remus broke from the trance he was in, moving up to the elegant driving machine. As expected, the door was unlocked. No need to lock a car that's locked inside a showroom. Remus smiled to himself. Everything was going smoothly, according to plan, as always.

Phineas took up his post next to the car as Remus slid inside. His job was simple now. Just keep his eyes open for the guard. He realized quickly, though, that they had not discussed what they would do if the guard came back early. All Phineas could think to do was run. Hopefully it wouldn't come to that. He trusted his brother. Remus always seemed to think of everything.

Remus had tucked his torso under the front steering column of the Corvette. Whereas Phineas was gifted at picking locks, Remus was good with wires - electronics, circuitry. He'd practiced on multiple cars the art of hot-wiring. Newer technologies had made matters more difficult, but Remus just viewed it as a challenge. The car they had chosen was no doubt outfitted with the latest in theft protection.

As the clock ticked, Phineas surmised that they were four minutes into the operation. That meant they had a max of six minutes left before the guard finished smoking and made his way back. Neither had said a word to each other thus far. When they were in the mode, the brothers tended to communicate wordlessly in an almost symbiotic relationship. But waiting was hard for Phineas. He could *feel* the clock ticking away. Time winding down.

"Remus!" he dared to whisper. "The clock -"

"Ssshhhh! I have to concentrate!" he shot back, still bent over, working feverishly. Phineas could see a splay of various colored wires dangling out from underneath the steering wheel. The thought that his brother had gotten himself in over his head shot through Phineas' mind. Along with it came a stab of fear.

"Remus! We're almost out of time. Please!"

"I said *can it*, Phin! Almost there. I've almost got it! Almost -"

The Corvette ZR-1 roared to life. And a roar it was with the glory of 375 horsepower behind its 5.7 L LT5 V8 engine. Phineas jumped at the sound. It felt deafening after the dead silence they'd been working in. His heart shot into his throat.

"The door, Phin! Get the door!" Remus yelled at his brother as he pulled himself out from under the dash, sliding behind the wheel.

Phineas sprinted the short distance to the sliding glass doors - the ones the dealership opened when they moved cars in and out of the building. He hit the big red button on the panel to the left of the set of doors. Turning around, he ran back to the car, his brother already having opened the passenger door. There was no sign of the guard, which registered ever so briefly in Phineas' mind as strange. But no sooner had that thought come to him then it was gone. His singular focus was getting out of there. He flew into the passenger's seat and slammed the door.

"Go, go, go!" he screamed.

"I've gotta wait for the doors to open!" Remus yelled back. It was true, the doors were still sliding open, much too slowly for either of them.

"Where's the guard?" Phineas asked his brother. "Why don't we see the guard? He has to know something's up!"

"I don't care about the guard. It doesn't matter. We're almost out of here!"

The doors were just opened wide enough for the Corvette to fit through. Remus threw the car into gear, giving it a touch of gas. He didn't want to gun it until he was clear of the doors though. Plus, it was true, he didn't have a driver's license, and his confidence in his driving skills wasn't as high as his hot-wiring skills; a Corvette ZR-1 wasn't something to take lightly.

The car eased forward, just clearing the doors. Remus made a turn to the left into the main lot, toward the direction of the Silverado they had last hidden behind. The exit to the lot lay directly in front of them.

They were clear!

Time to punch it!

But Remus never got the chance.

Two Moore City police cars came screaming into the car lot from the direction they were pointed. Remus was stunned. He hit the brakes, mind spinning. Time for Plan B. But he didn't have a Plan B. It never occurred to him that Plan A wouldn't work. Plan A had always worked. Candy, staplers, scarfs, answer keys, car keys. Each and every time, Plan A had been enough.

There was a tap on the driver's window. Remus and Phineas looked over. Staring down at them was the security guard, big smile on his face, grinning from ear to ear. That's when it hit Phineas. They'd never had a chance. The brothers had been made before they ever entered the building. That was the only explanation. Oh yes, the guard had moseyed around the corner of the building to take a smoke break...and to call the police.

All of this registered in Phineas' mind in a split second. In the next second, he flung his door open and tore out through the lot. He heard someone yelling after him. He didn't know if it was the police, the guard, or Remus. He didn't care. He just ran and ran and ran. He ran until he couldn't run anymore. And then he collapsed.

He found himself in a field, lungs sucking in air as fast as he could expel it. He still couldn't fathom what this would mean. After a period of time - Phineas had no idea how long it had been - he rose to his feet and walked home.

It was exactly midnight when he arrived. It seemed like all night, but it had only been one hour. The lights to the house were off as he expected they would be. He climbed the latticework to his and Remus' bedroom window. He eased it open, slipping inside. Quickly, Phineas stripped and washed his face. Putting on a fresh pair of shorts and a t-shirt, he sat on his bed, waiting on what, he didn't know. He didn't realize it at the time, but Phineas was experiencing a mild form of shock.

It was just a few minutes later that Phineas noticed the blue glare of police lights whirling as a cruiser pulled into his driveway.

Next came the doorbell.

There was a rustling and footfalls as one or both of his parents scrambled out of bed and down the stairs to answer the front door.

Phineas followed quietly, not wanting to see, but at the same time irresistibly drawn. He was certain they were coming for him. He'd be arrested, wouldn't he? His father would be so disappointed. What did they call a jail for teenagers? That's right, they called it *juvie*. For juvenile detention center. That's what he was now, a juvenile delinquent.

Phineas could hear his father talking to an unfamiliar voice, likely the officer who had come to get him. He eased his way down to the landing of the stairs where he could see everything happening at the front door. He stopped and starred in stunned silence, his mind racing to process what he was looking at.

There was his brother! Remus.

He was standing next to the police officer who was talking pleasantly to his father. The officer was even smiling. And Remus, he was...was that a smile on his face as well? Yes, it was. Then Remus' eye caught Phineas standing on the stairs. The smile faded as he recognized his brother.

Remus gave a nod, ever so slightly, to Phineas...and then a wink.

What the...? Phineas was completely confused.

Phineas' father was now talking easily with the officer. There were even a few laughs thrown in. Finally, Remus made his way to his father's side, who placed an arm around his son. He reached out and gave a warm handshake to the officer, who then reached over and tussled Remus' hair. With a final wave, the police officer turned and walked away, the door to their house closing behind him.

"Why don't you come on down, Phineas," his father commanded without even turning around. Phineas came all the way down the remaining steps, a look of confusion clearly on his face. "Well, boys, it looks like you were busy tonight."

"Yes sir," Phineas looked down.

"I'm sorry, Dad, it didn't go like I'd planned," a dejected Remus followed.

"That's the way life works, boys. Phineas, look at me. I want you both to look at me. It's okay. Do you understand me? You both have gifts. You are special. But sometimes no amount of gifting can get you out of the tightest of spaces. Tonight was a learning experience. That's how I want you to view it. Do you understand?"

That's when it dawned on Phineas that his father must have had some kind of pull with the local authorities. He didn't know how, but that was the only explanation. There were many mysteries surrounding his father, and this was yet another one.

"You mean you're not mad at us? Not at all?" asked Phineas.

"Mad at you? Phineas, how could I be mad at you for being what you were made to be? You are the Crook Brothers. That means something. You're still young, but one day you will understand fully what all that means. To be a Crook."

"I love you, Dad!" it was Remus giving their father a hug.

"I love you too, son. I love both of you. More than you know," he said, pulling Phineas into the embrace with his brother.

"We are the Crooks, boys," he declared. "And we do what we do..."

"Because we can," answered Remus proudly.

"That's right, son, *because we can!*"

CHAPTER EIGHTEEN

"All I can say is that we continue to be very pleased, Ms. LaPhage."

"Excellent, General, as are we on our end. The Robatar has been performing in every way as we had hoped, but honestly, even I have been surprised at how quickly it has all come together," Ruth LaPhage replied.

Ruth was in the private office of her top floor suite at LaPhage Industries. She was enjoying a secure video connection to the Pentagon where she had been having an animated discussion with General Myers and Admiral Watkins for the past half hour about the status of Project BORG. She continued, "All our post-operation data shows that Project BORG is stable and ready for continued real-world field exercises." Now she was lying. She had said nothing about the glitch in the post-operation data analysis. The glitch that had, but for a brief moment, indicated that the Robatar had independently severed its connection with Sergeant Warren and gone completely autonomous. Tony Chen and Oz Jenks continued to pour over the data, running numerous tests trying to find an explanation. They had even worked with the sergeant the last two days, running the Robatar through intense field exercises at the secluded LaPhage training facility in the desert outside of Roswell, New Mexico – trying to illicit a repeat of the glitch. But nothing. No repeat and no explanation.

In the end, Ruth had decided to shelve the particular version of the Robatar in which the glitch had occurred. Not destroy it, just mothball it...for now. And so that was why it was currently sitting in LP-6, *The Lair*, where it was freaking out Tony Chen and Oz Jenks every time they looked at it. Those two had watched way too many sci-fi movies and played too many virtual reality video games. The world of make believe and the world of reality were colliding a little too much for the two computer geeks. They didn't mind talking about it every time Ruth spoke with them about next steps. The next step, it had been decided, was to gear up the next Robatar in the series and prep it for a real-world test of its own.

There were now four Robatars in all. The first one, BORG-1, was decommissioned after a round of successful field tests on the AI software. The problem with BORG-1 was durability. It did not have the stamina required for the rugged nature of real-world scenarios. The Robatar had to be waterproof, able to withstand falls of at least thirty feet, shock resistant to bullets, and able to endure the heat of a fire. BORG-2 could do all of that, but it was clunky and not nearly nimble enough. What was needed was something more humanlike, which could move and imitate a real person. They had nailed it with BORG-3. This particular version of the Robatar was so eerily lifelike that at one point or another it had wigged everyone out who worked on the project. The team working on the project felt so good about BORG-3 that they ordered the manufacture of a second model of it. One of those had been destroyed in the Syria campaign when it detonated, killing the terrorists. The other model they had used with Billy, trying to repeat the glitch. It was that version of the Robatar, BORG-3, that was now decommissioned and hanging out with Tony and Oz as they worked to get BORG-4 up to speed and ready for its first training session. Very similar to BORG-3, BORG-4 was even more lifelike in the fluidity of its movement. It also had a longer internal battery life that could keep it in the field for up to two weeks. If all went well, the next step would be a real-world test.

Ruth was pushing for something very soon, which is why she was connected to General Myers and Admiral Watkins at this moment.

"We've got a couple of options to consider for a future exercise," General Myers was explaining. "We have a new target. This one in northern Iraq. Another leader of ISIS. We are still working the intel with our people on the ground, trying to determine location, patterns of movement, etc. We're not there yet, but we hope to be in a position to execute a kill-strike soon. So, we can do that the traditional way with a drone, or we can use it as an opportunity to send in the Robatar."

Ruth was liking what she was hearing. She had told the general and admiral that she wanted to move forward with the BORG-4 unit. She'd crossed her fingers, hoping they wouldn't question why, after such a successful outcome in Syria with version three. But Ruth was very good at exuding confidence. She had played it perfectly, as if this was part of their development strategy the whole time, to bring BORG-4 online and have a repeat success, equal to or greater to the one in Syria. "That way we will then have two Robatars and not just one that can be deployed," she had championed.

From a military standpoint, the general and admiral had taken the bait. It was always good to have a backup unit, they surmised. It made perfect sense. The idea of having two Robatars, two super-soldiers that could be deployed into a theater, was something they had not considered to date and it was very intriguing. The two Pentagon officials were ready to plow forward.

"The other option is less certain. Of equal importance, for sure, but in many ways riskier." Admiral Watkins was speaking now. Because he was a man of few words, when he spoke, the attention of those listening went up. For her part, Ruth was intrigued. "We are eager to launch an operation into North Korea for the sole purpose of gathering intel from within the Imperial Palace. Nothing like this has ever been attempted for obvious reasons. North Korea is completely cut off from the outside world, and we have no human assets of any kind on the ground. It's totally impossible...in the traditional sense. Like the other operation, we are not there yet, but we are talking about how the Robatar could be utilized in such a scenario."

"Well we can be ready on our end whenever you decide which operation best suits the government's best interests," Ruth answered.

"Very good," said General Myers. "We will be in touch soon, I hope. Take care, Ms. LaPhage, and again, thank you and your whole team for your fine work on Project BORG. You are doing a great service to your country. If I might dare to say...your father would be proud."

The conversation terminated with a smile and a nod from Ruth LaPhage as she sat back in her chair, contemplative. It was always a relief to end communications with the Pentagon on a good note. The relationship was solid, but Ruth was always uncertain, conscious that it could turn in a direction that was unfavorable to the interests of LaPhage Industries, to her interests.

Some in the inner circle had questioned the wisdom of bringing the military into the loop of Project BORG in the first place. LaPhage

Industries certainly was on the technological forefront of the program and didn't need the help of the government. But Project BORG was extremely expensive, and although LaPhage Industries' coffers were very full, it was certainly welcome to have the extra millions that such a complex project required. Plus, the Department of Defense offered something Ruth LaPhage could not generate on her own - access and opportunity. Access to case files that helped identify former military personnel who would be ideally suited to work on the project. People like Sergeant Billy Warren. And opportunity to put the Robatar in the most extreme scenarios, to truly see what it was capable of doing - real world tests that could make a difference. More than just rescue from natural and human disasters, but situations that could actually turn the tide of a nation. Operations like the Syria campaign and what General Myers and Admiral Watkins had just proposed to her as potential next steps. The whole thing thrilled Ruth as she reflected on it. Yes, her father absolutely would be proud.

She turned her attention back to her secondary computer monitor where she had been pouring over Dr. Phineas Crook's files. She was fascinated at the scope of his research on the Garden of Eden. It had not taken long to find what she was looking for once Oz sent the pre-selected data to her. Dr. Crook's work was voluminous, yet there were holes. The most obvious of which was the location of the Garden. She had the distinct sense that she still didn't have the whole picture, as if the good doctor was holding something back from her on purpose, which of course was impossible since he had no idea they were coming for the files to begin with, plus he had no idea who *they* were.

Her watch alarm went off, bringing her back to the moment. As she considered the whole idea of finding the Garden of Eden - the obsession of her father, Charles LaPhage - her watch reminded her that it was time. Not the designated time of the awakening. It was only eleven o'clock in the morning and the scheduled awakening was not for another four hours. This was a special time of her choosing. A time that no one, not even Dr. Sayer, knew about.

Ruth opened the bottom right drawer of her desk and withdrew a metal box. Undoing the latch, she lifted the lid and withdrew the two syringes that she had personally prepared beforehand. She rose and made her way through her office door and across the suite to her father's room, dropping one syringe in her lab coat pocket while palming the other in her left hand. Ruth knew that Dr. Sayer would never sanction what she was about to do. He was highly regimented when it came to the care of Charles LaPhage - with every aspect of his world, really. Ruth didn't care about any of that. Charles was her father. She was his daughter. There were moments when she just needed to spend time with him alone, without the watchful eye of Dr. Mark Sayer or any other LaPhage medical personnel watching over her shoulder. Besides, things were progressing with her search for finding the right person who could help them locate the Garden of Eden. She needed to talk to her father, to try to get through to the coherent version of the man, and to siphon out what special knowledge he had.

Ruth was certain that something more had happened to her father as a result of his accident years before. Something more than the mangling of his body. He had often said that he had been to hell and back. That he had seen things. Things that were too horrible to speak of. He also claimed to have gained some special knowledge. This had all led to her own obsession with finding the Garden of Eden and the Tree of Life that grew within its confines. Ruth believed him. Believed that he at least had crossed over into another dimension, and that because of his persistent state of sleep, still crossed from here to there at times. Wherever *there* might be. Ruth was not an overly religious person. She had never been raised in church or with a belief in God as the center of family life. That wasn't who the LaPhages were. But she did believe that there was something more to life and existence than what we can merely see and touch and examine in the natural world with pure science - a belief in the *super*natural, if that is what you want to call it. She believed that her father had somehow tapped into that supernatural world and the whole thing fascinated her. Her father had called it a gateway - the Garden and the Tree. He spoke of a war between Good and Evil or God and Evil or something of the sort. It was not completely clear, but she was driven to know more, to find the answer.

Ruth quietly opened and closed the door as she stepped into her father's room.

CHAPTER NINETEEN

W hy Ruth LaPhage was being so quiet she didn't know. Her father, Charles, was in a medically-induced sleep, and could not be awakened without the proper chemical mixture. Which is exactly what she held in her hand at that moment. Still moving with stealth, she eased up next to her father's bedside. He always looked the same. A crumpled and scarred mass of flesh connected to tubes and monitors. His dark green eyes ever-staring, unable to close because his eyelids had been scorched away in the accident. *He's not even human anymore*, Ruth contemplated as she stared at him. She knew that her real father, the essence of Charles LaPhage, lay inside the husk of the shell at which she was staring.

With great care she connected the syringe to his IV and pressed the plunger, sending the concoction that would bring him back to this world coursing through his veins. It worked quickly. In a matter of just seconds Charles spoke.

"Oh my dear Ruth! How wonderful it is to see you!"

"Hello, Daddy!" Ruth leaned over, placing a cool hand on his bare head, the warm glow of a smile on her face. "Did you sleep well?"

"I haven't been asleep darling. Your mother and I just finished the most marvelous run on a black diamond slope at Breckenridge." Her father and mother had loved to ski. He had likely been dreaming about one of their past trips. "You know we love Breckenridge so much. There is nothing like skiing the Rockies. You should join us, Ruth."

"That's an excellent idea, Daddy. Count me in," Ruth always humored her father's fantasies.

"You look like you are concerned about something, Ruth. Has Mark joined the side of the board? I told him to fire the board. He said he would. I knew I couldn't trust him! We can't trust Mark, Ruth. I've seen how he looks at me. He's evil!"

"Dr. Sayer is fine, Daddy. I keep an eye on everything he does. We can trust him, I promise." Ruth was working her magic to soothe her father. "But Daddy, I do need to talk to you about something very important."

"What is it, my sweet? Tell me, please."

"It's about the Garden of Eden -"

"The Garden!" Charles cut off his daughter. "You must find it Ruth! It is critical. Life and death. Heaven and hell. It all goes back to the Garden. You must believe that what I am telling you is the truth!"

"I do, Daddy. I do. I believe you. And I've been looking."

"You have? Yes! You have. Of course, you have. Tell me, my child. Tell me quickly what you have discovered. Do you know where it is?" Charles was bowed up in his bed, tense and focused. Ruth had no doubt that he was fully with her as she was with him. This is what she had hoped for, what she had needed from her father. Time to privately talk about her efforts to locate the mystical Garden of Eden and to mine her father for whatever secret knowledge he might have locked away in his mind.

"I've found someone, Daddy. Someone who I think can lead me, can lead us, to it."

"Yes! I knew it. I knew you would find someone, Ruth. Please tell me who this great explorer is. How did you find him?"

Ruth chuckled, "He's not a great explorer, Daddy. He's a theologian. His name is Dr. Phineas Crook. And he has spent years searching for the Garden of Eden. I've looked at his research and he thinks he knows, Daddy. He thinks he knows where it is."

"Where? Tell me Ruth, where is it? Let's go now. Call Marty and have him fuel the plane. We must board at once and go!"

"I don't know exactly, Daddy. His files aren't clear but I think he has it all figured out. I just need a bit more time and then we will know what he knows. I have a plan."

"Hahaha! Yes, a plan. That is what is needed. Good girl. Once you know where the Garden of Eden is, once you get the information from this Phineas Crook, listen to me, Ruth - once you know - you must kill him! He can't be trusted! I don't like his name. It's a bad name. No one can be trusted, I tell you. Kill him quickly and then go to the Garden."

"I understand Father. I will do what is necessary." Ruth had no intention of killing Phineas Crook, or anyone else, for that matter. On this point, she did not share her father's sentiment. She knew this part of him, the paranoid part, was not her real father. However, she was not above doing whatever was necessary, no matter how extreme, to get what she wanted. Ruth LaPhage was a woman used to having her way. "Daddy, I need you to listen to me. I need whatever information you can give me about the Garden of Eden. What have your dreams told you? What am I looking for if we find it?"

"Not if, Ruth - when! There is no 'if.'"

"Yes, Daddy, of course. We will find the Garden. I will make sure of it."

"You must. It contains the key!"

"That's what I need to know. What key?"

"The Tree of Life, Ruth. Within the Garden is the Tree of Life. It is the key. The gateway."

"The gateway to what, Daddy?" This was the crux of the whole thing. Ruth knew it. She leaned in, eyes drilling into her father's, trying to coax out what he knew, what he had seen.

"*Eternal life*," Charles whispered. "It is the gateway to eternal life. Whoever eats the fruit of the Tree of Life will live forever. Don't you see, Ruth? Don't you see how important this is? You must climb Jacob's Ladder and find the Tree and take its fruit and bring it to me."

Ruth did see. If what her father was saying was true, then finding the Garden of Eden and having access to the Tree of Life would be the greatest discovery in the history of the world. Ruth did a quick calculation in her mind of the implications. There were pharmaceutical considerations. What if the elements that made up the fruit from the Tree of Life could be synthesized? Then there was the humanitarian value of the fruit. Disease of all kinds could virtually be eliminated globally. What price would one pay to wield such power and might? Whoever controlled such a power as this would be...well they would be a god. The thought of it all was at once intoxicating. But Ruth also knew it would not be easy. Certainly she and her team couldn't just walk into the Garden and claim the prize. If it were as simple as that, then the Garden and the Tree of Life would have been found centuries ago. It must be hidden and extremely difficult to access. There was so much more she needed to know.

"Daddy, I need to know as much as you can tell me. You say you've seen the other side. Why is it so hard to find the Garden of Eden? Why has no one discovered it yet?"

"Aaaahhhhhhhhhhhh........" it was a guttural groan that rolled from her father's throat. Then, the same as before, it was as if he slipped into a trance:

> *The rivers converge on the cradle of life,*
> *Only those called can trespass without strife.*
> *Adam and Eve are reborn anew,*
> *You must find passage through the guardian*
> *To join the few.*

Ruth grabbed a pen and feverishly wrote down the text just as she had done the last time her father uttered a similar rhyme. There were clues here, she was sure of it, despite Dr. Sayer's insistence that it was all brought on by an unstable psyche.

"Daddy, are you still with me? I need you to keep talking. What did you mean when you said before that there is a battle? You mentioned good and evil." Ruth gently rubbed her father's arms with both hands, trying to bring him back to her. It seemed to be working.

"No! Between God and evil." Yes, he was definitely back. "The Garden of Eden belongs to God. It's his playground, but evil lurks close by. Beware, Ruth! Remember that the serpent speaks truth."

The serpent speaks truth? What did that mean? The serpent was the symbol of evil in the Bible. That much she knew. Ruth was working hard to process all that her father was throwing at her. Poems mixed with apocalyptic language. So much of it smacked of the mad ravings of a lunatic. But there was an undertone of truth and sanity that Ruth could feel. Plus, she trusted her father. She refused to believe that the essence of Charles LaPhage was lost forever. Maybe wandering and out of place, but not gone. And she felt - no she *knew* - that her father had seen and experienced the pathway that would bring him back to her permanently. She just needed to find the Garden of Eden.

"Daddy, I want you to rest easy now." Ruth was finished and she was beginning to sense that she had pushed her father as far as was healthy. He needed rest. Not his body, but his mind. It was still so fragile, she knew. "You've given me what I need. You've been so helpful like you always are. I love you." She leaned over, kissing him on his scarred forehead, as she always did before she let him drift away into his land of dreams.

"Ruth! I've made a decision!" Charles lifted his stubbed arms, trying to take hold of his daughter. He was not quite finished. "You must take me with you. Yes, of course. I never considered it before but I should have. You must take me with you to the Garden of Eden. No one can break through but me. That's why I've had the dreams. I've been *chosen*. That's why you came to me, isn't it? Because you know that I must go with you!"

This, of course, was impossible. Any attempt to relocate Charles LaPhage and his lump of flesh that was a pitiful excuse for a body would certainly be fatal. He was far too reliant on the delicate balance of life that the numerous machines he was connected to provided for him. It was absurd to even think about, Ruth knew.

"What a wonderful idea, Daddy! Yes, we shall journey to the Garden of Eden together."

"And we shall partake of the fruit of the Tree of Life, my sweet girl. We shall eat and live forever! Hahaha! Oh the joy. I can taste the fruit now. Oh, it's so sweet. Hahaha. Yes it is!"

She was beginning to lose him, she could tell. He was becoming delirious and unhinged. She quickly pulled from her lab coat pocket the second syringe. The one that would put him back to sleep.

"And your mother! She will go with us too, Ruth! We will be one big happy family. Forever! But not Mark. He can't go. He must not go. And you must kill the Crooked man as well. Oh yes, the plan is coming together...."

The last word came out as a sigh as Charles LaPhage faded away along with his ravings. Ruth sat back, glad that she had taken the time to pull her father awake for this brief but important time. She had gleaned much. But she was also glad it was over. There was nothing easy about any of this.

Little did she know that it was going to get harder. Much harder.

CHAPTER TWENTY

The Big Mac. That's what they called the Oklahoma State Penitentiary. It was a beautiful but cold Saturday morning and Phineas Crook was moving at 60 mph down Highway 270 toward McAlester, Oklahoma. Toward the state prison. Toward Remus. Yes, it had been over a year since he'd last seen his brother - Christmas, in fact - and it had not gone well. To be sure, Phin had not made the trek to the prison with the best of motives. It was an obligatory visit, mostly because of the holidays. A part of him felt sorry because, with their father now deceased and mother mentally ill, all they really had was each other.

The visit began in a good-naturedly way. Small talk about nothing, followed by Remus attempting to bring up stories from their childhood. Funny stuff like the jokes they played on people, or the things they had hidden or thought they had hidden from their parents. That's where the conversation began to go south; because the two boys, now men, had taken different roads in life. Whereas Remus looked on their upbringing with fondness, Phineas saw it as a path he had spent the last twenty years running from. And that's how it stood. Two brothers. The same heritage. Two completely different viewpoints.

Remus was doing hard time. Three years into a ten-year sentence. He likely would be out in only two more though. Phineas had no doubt his brother was a model inmate.

Remus' luck had finally run out for good when he was apprehended trying to steal the delivery of five million dollars worth of precious gemstones to a high-end jewelry broker in downtown Oklahoma City called McPhearsen's. As always, he was cocky and full of himself and was so sure he could not be caught. There was never anyone in a room full of people smarter than Remus, it seemed. At least that's the way it was in *his* mind. Unlike when they were teenagers, Remus now worked with a Plan B – just in case. That's because outfits like McPhearsen's have their own contingencies. You don't just move millions of dollars in diamonds and other precious stones without a backup plan to a backup plan to a backup plan. On this one, the jeweler had been one step ahead of Remus from the beginning. His brother had been caught red-handed, in his mock security uniform, with the stones in his possession. It was a slam-dunk case for the district attorney, and Remus was sent off to the slammer.

Phin made a quick pit stop at the Exxon in McAlester. A bathroom break and a diet Dr. Pepper and then he was back on the road. The Big Mac wasn't actually in McAlester proper as its address would indicate. It was closer to the tiny town of Stringtown, Oklahoma, another thirty plus miles south on Highway 69. The sun was just coming up as Phin pulled back onto the four-lane divided highway for the final push to the prison. He wanted to be there right at eight o'clock when visiting hours began, see what Remus so urgently needed to talk to him about, and then get back home to salvage what was left of his weekend.

He'd had another dream-slash-nightmare last night. They were coming nearly every night now. The details were still sparse upon waking. Dread, evil, thunderstorms, people yelling. It was all so fuzzy and disturbing. Phin was certain it meant something - something important - and it was gnawing at him to get to the bottom of it all. On top of the mental pain of the dreams, they left him physically exhausted when he finally awoke. It was a Catch-22. He craved rest and sleep while he was awake, but the only way to find relief was to lie down and close his eyes, which led to the dreams and more exhaustion. He felt like he was part of *The Walking Dead*.

The 911 message from Remus earlier in the week hadn't helped matters. It just brought back bad memories that he was constantly trying to run from. The heritage of a tainted family with a tainted legacy.

The Crook Family really was a family of crooks. That was the long and short of it. Phineas' surname told the whole story. Crook.

Most people take the designation of their last name for granted. The first and middle names of a child are chosen by the parents. Any name is up for grabs. He had always wondered why his parents chose the names Phineas for himself and Remus for his brother. Not the usual names for two boys living in Oklahoma, for sure. But that's what their parents picked so that's what he was stuck with. But the last name is set before birth. It's the name that is passed down generationally. No choice at all. Just a simple pre-determined designation. And the family surname can carry with it a legacy, depending on what is done with it. You can't hear the names Hatfields and McCoys without thinking about the two families of the late 1800s who infamously feuded along the Tug Fork of the Big Sandy River, right along the border of Kentucky and West Virginia. The two surnames are forever linked together for good or ill.

No one knows for sure where the whole concept of using a surname came from, but it seems to finds its origins somewhere way back during the time of the Roman Empire. How a particular last name was chosen appears to be clearer. Some surnames were tied to geographic features - names like: Hill, Green and Stone. Other names may have described physical features - Short, Brown, and White. But most surnames were drawn via vocation. Whatever a family *did* for work - and most vocations in the ancient and medieval world were passed on generationally - was simply what a person became known as. So a man with the first name of Robert who baked bread for a living would logically be called Robert Baker. Or a family who smelted metal and worked as blacksmiths for the local township would be known as the Smith family.

And then there was the Crook Family. Phineas knew all too well the history of his own family. Generationally they were literally a family of thieves. It is common for pride to run deep when it comes to the family business, and the Crooks were no different.

Adonis Crook was a proud man. He was proud of his family - particularly his two sons. And he was proud of his craft. He was also very good at it. The elder Crook was a giant in the eyes of his two young boys. Standing well over six feet tall, he had the good looks of a square jaw and broad shoulders. Phineas fondly remembered him with a swath of black hair that hung down nearly covering his left eye, except when he wore it slicked back with several dabs of pomade. His father could carry the look of a California surfer, or a sophisticated businessman – the likes of a James Bond-type character. No matter what persona he donned, he always carried an infectious charisma about him. These were just some of the reasons Adonis was so good at being a thief. He could be anyone he needed to be at any given moment, and he did it in a way that won over the crowd or the individual.

Before anyone was the wiser, his wallet was missing, her bank account drained, or their most treasured - and expensive - possession was gone from whatever lock or vault concealed it. Adonis Crook could work his way into any situation, become exactly who he needed to be, and extract whatever information he was looking for. And he had the technical skill to pull the heist.

His real expertise came with the theft of major works of art and jewelry. Growing up, the basement of the Crook home was a veritable rotation of paintings, sculptures, and exotic gems - all the result of Adonis' "work trips" around the globe. Nothing ever stayed long, though. The Crooks had national and international connections that moved the goods on the black market, yielding a very nice payday for the family. As a result, Phineas and Remus grew up in one of the nicest neighborhoods and homes in the unassuming city of Moore.

As a very young boy, Phineas had always wondered why he could never have friends over to their house. He could spend the day or night at other kids' houses, they just could not come to his. He would never forget the moment he came to understand why. He was eleven-years-old when his dad picked him up from school on a Friday afternoon.

"Phineas, we need to go for a drive," his father had explained.

Phineas was excited. Anytime he got one-on-one time with his dad was a gift. Not knowing what was to come, his heart thrilled as they drove away. His father took him to Earlywine Park where they found a lone bench.

"Phineas, I need to tell you a story," he began in the most serious of tones.

Over the next two hours, Adonis unpacked what he truly did for a living. Phineas had never put a whole lot of thought into it. When his friends asked what his dad did for a living, he just said he traveled for business. That, of course, was true. But somehow, he had been conditioned to not go any further with it in his own mind.

Sitting in the park, with the wind blowing ever so slightly, Phineas' world changed on that spring afternoon. His last name was not just a name.

"It's a calling," his father had explained. "Our family is one of the oldest lines in the world, Phineas. The Crooks can be traced back for more generations than I can begin to make clear to you right now. Today is just a beginning for you. You will come to know more, so much more, from this point forward."

Young Phineas' head spun as he took it all in. Somehow, though, he knew. He had always known, he thought, that there was something different, maybe even special, about his family.

"When I was just your age, my father - your grandfather - took me on a walk and told me the story of the Crooks, and what it meant to carry the name. To carry the calling. And from that moment forward, he began to teach me, to train me in the arts." By arts, Phineas knew that he was talking about the skill to steal and cheat others out of their belongings.

"That's what today is about, Phineas. It's time for you to know who you are, what you were born for. It's time for your education to take on a new dimension. I know this is a lot to take in, but your brother will be with you to help you as well."

"Remus knows?" Why had it not occurred to him before now?

"Of course! For two years now. He's been so excited for this day. He's been dying to share everything he's been learning with you. I gotta tell you, your brother has a real knack for wires and circuitry. So much today in the world of security is electronically-based, but I don't think any of it stands a chance to what your brother may be gifted to do."

Phineas was dumbstruck.

"You have a gift too, Phineas. You're a Crook. It's in your blood, I tell you. We just have to find your niche. But don't worry, I will teach you everything I know. Just like my father taught me, and his father before him, and so on - going back hundreds and hundreds of years. You'd be shocked to know how deep our family lineage goes, Phineas. I am so excited to finally be able to teach you and show you the way!" Adonis rubbed his son's fluff of hair, beaming with family pride. Phineas couldn't help but feel the thrill of excitement himself. But suddenly, he was struck with a sobering thought.

"But Dad...isn't it wrong?" his question was pure and sincere.

"Is what wrong, son?"

"All of it. Stealing. Isn't it just wrong to do that?" Phineas was nervous uttering the words. Somehow he instinctively knew he was treading on the most sensitive of ground.

"Phineas, look at me. Look into my eyes," his father's gaze bore into him with a warmth and intensity that he knew was nothing but love. "It is *never* wrong to be who you were created to be. Never. Do you understand me?"

"Yes sir," whispered Phineas.

"I need you to believe that, Phineas. Do you believe that? Do you believe your father?"

"Yes sir, I do," Phineas replied once again.

And he meant it.

CHAPTER TWENTY-ONE

The Big Mac was just coming into view on his right when Phineas slowed his car to make the turn off of the highway. *The yard* was the first thing he saw, ringed by fencing topped with razor wire. It was empty at this time of the morning. In fact, there were no signs of life at all, but Phin knew that behind the ominous walls of Oklahoma's penitentiary were approximately 750 souls doing time for every crime imaginable and some not so imaginable. The over one hundred year-old facility was classified medium-to-maximum security, so it held some truly bad guys. He liked to think Remus didn't fit into the particular class that needed maximum security.

The presence of several cars in the parking lot meant visiting lines were already beginning to form even though it was just past eight o'clock in the morning. Phineas quickly found his spot and took a deep breath as he exited his car to head toward security check-in. He really hated this place. Part of him couldn't help but be angry with his brother. But he wasn't sure if he was mad because Remus had gotten caught, or because his brother had chosen to follow the path of the family name. He was only a few yards from his car when he remembered his cell phone. Pulling it out of his jacket pocket, he hustled back to his car and threw it into the center console. He wouldn't be allowed to take it in anyway, and having it with him would just mean a more intrusive body search than normal.

Phineas navigated the security check-in without incident. He gave his brother's name and inmate ID number, and presented his driver's license. They crosschecked to make sure he was approved to visit one Remus Bartholomew Crook, and then allowed him to pass through the extremely sensitive metal detector. He was ushered into a holding area along with fifteen others who had checked in ahead of him. Then he waited. This was the worst part for Phineas. Just waiting to have your name called indicating that your "loved one" was ready. He never understood why it took so long. *What in the world could they actually be doing back behind those walls?* It was a prison after all. The room slowly filled over the next forty-five minutes. Phineas tried hard not to make eye contact with anyone, but that always proved to be impossible. For each person he looked at, the same thoughts entered his mind: I wonder who they are here to see. I wonder what terrible thing that person did to end up here, in the Big Mac. Phineas realized they were surely thinking the same thing about him.

What no one knew, of course, was that had Phineas chosen to embrace the story of his heritage, he very possibly could be the one on the other side of these walls, perhaps *with* his brother Remus.

Yes, he loved his father dearly, and there was a very real part of him that still idolized Adonis Crook, but Phineas had ultimately refused to "embrace who he was" as his father put it. The crossroads came when his father had been killed in Israel while attempting the theft of a cache of uncut diamonds as they were en route from the mine to a jeweler who would cut them and then sell them on the wholesale market. Uncut diamonds were a commodity in and of their own right because once stolen they would be impossible to trace. Cut diamonds are marked with laser engravings in such a way that they can be identified if stolen. Not so with uncut stones. They are not as valuable as cut stones but they are valuable enough. An unscrupulous jeweler who doesn't care what source the uncut stones come from will take the raw gemstones, cut them into any size and shape he wants, and then turn them back out onto the legitimate open market for a handsome profit. Stealing uncut diamonds was a way for Adonis Crook to turn a quick profit. He was in and out and on his way with his money in a matter of days, not having to worry about holding the inventory while it was cut, and while the authorities were hunting for them. But something had gone terribly wrong.

Phineas and Remus never got the whole story, they were sure. What they did know was that their father had stolen the collection of stones from the security car on an Israel Railways train. Disguised as a normal passenger, he had been apprehended while disembarking the train in Tel Aviv. The story goes that Adonis was reaching into his suit pocket, and somehow it was mistaken that he was going for a gun. A shot was fired and Adonis went down. The tragedy of it all was that Adonis never traveled with a weapon. In fact, he never used a gun or any kind of weapon in any of his thefts. He was adamantly opposed to physical violence. If ever caught, it was his personal oath that he would surrender and take his punishment. He taught his sons to do the same.

What had been thought to be a gun was nothing more than Adonis' black leather wallet. Attempts to save his life were futile, and just like that, the patriarch of the Crook family was dead. Phineas was eighteen years old. From that moment on, he had made his choice. He would go another way. Choose another path. A path as far in the opposite direction of the Crook Family legacy as possible, the path of full-time ministry as a pastor. How utterly ironic, Phin often thought. His father would surely be profoundly disappointed if he were still alive. His brother certainly was.

At just before nine o'clock, Phineas' name was finally called. He rose and made his way to the steel door where an officer waited to escort him to the visiting area. It was time to face Remus.

As Phineas entered the visiting room, his eyes scanned the various tables where inmates were meeting with relatives. It took only a second for his eyes to land on his brother, sitting alone at a table across the room with a guard right behind him. Remus made eye contact and rose to his feet, a big smile on his face. Phin walked across the room and found himself opening his arms for an embrace. The brothers hugged tightly, slapping each other on the back, then they each took their seats, the guard easing away toward an exit door.

"You look great, Phin. Thanks so much for coming."

"You too, Remus...you look good." And he did. His head was shaved and he was sporting a goatee, a few tattoos showing around his bulging biceps. It was obvious how his brother was using his free time. "So how are they treating you?" It was the standard small-talk question when you don't know what to say to your brother serving time in the state pen.

"Oh, it's fine. You know, four-star treatment courtesy of the state of Oklahoma," Remus wore a forced smile and looked down, fiddling his hands together. "So how have you been, Phin? You still doin' the Jesus thing? Teaching at that college over in Shawnee?"

"Yes...yes I am, at least as long as they will have me." Phin rolled his eyes. His brother never got tired of jabbing at him. Not just about walking away from the family, but walking toward "the Jesus thing" as he called it. Phin was pretty sure his brother didn't even believe in God, or if he did it was some diluted view of God as a higher power of sorts. Just like so many other people in the world.

"Uh oh, sounds like you might've stepped in it, little brother. You haven't reverted to your old sinful ways now, have you? Stolen something from the president's office?" Remus forced a quick laugh, playing with him. Not out of spite - he was just being Remus. This is always how it went when he visited.

"No, man. Nothing like that. It's just been a hard few years," replied Phin, as somber as he felt.

The smile faded from Remus' face at the reference to Autumn. "Look, Phin, I'm sorry. I was just messin' around. I know you've been through it and I'm sorry. I really am." Phin didn't know what to say to that so he said nothing. After an awkward moment of silence, Remus carried on, "I always thought I was the one cursed by God and that you were a *sinner saved by grace*." Remus held up his hands, making the sign of air quotes at that last part. "But looks like we are both cursed by God," Remus looked down again, finishing with an uncomfortable but quiet chuckle.

Phin really didn't know what to say to that. The tone of this visit was going in a different direction than his previous visits. While Remus said it in jest, Phin did feel like he was cursed by God. The Old Testament speaks about the judgment of God for a father's sins being visited on his offspring to the third and fourth generations. Is that what was happening here? Had God cursed his family? Was he doomed no matter what pathway he chose? If so, it was a good thing he and Autumn never had children. He would hate to pass the curse of the Crook Family legacy onto an innocent child.

Pulling himself together, Phin looked toward Remus and did his best to harden his shell. "Why am I here, Remus? Why did you send me a 911 message?" Looking at his brother, Phin could have sworn that he saw Remus' shoulders tense up, as if he were carrying a burden.

Lifting his head from his hands that continued to fidget with each other, Remus said, "I've been having dreams, Phin." His voice was a strained whisper and his eyes were wide. A bolt of electricity shot through Phineas at the mention of dreams. What was his brother talking about?

"Dreams?" was all he could utter in reply.

"Yes...dreams...nightmares, really," Remus' voice was slightly elevated above a whisper now, his body language becoming more agitated. "I've been having them for a while now. Probably more than a year - since our last visit. They started happening maybe once a week or so. But man, they've been getting worse. So much worse - like four or five times a week now."

"What kind of dreams, Remus? What happens in them?" He had Phineas' full attention now.

"Man, that's just it. I wake up and have no memory of anything. It's like it's right there in my hand and then it just disappears. But it's horrible, Phin. Whatever it is, it's bad... and it means something. Look at me little brother, I think it means something about *YOU!*" His voice rose with his last statement, causing several others to look in their direction. The guard gave them a look, followed by one step in their direction. Phineas raised his hand as if to say "all is well" and the guard moved back.

"What do you mean *me*?" It was Phineas who was whispering now.

"Look, I don't know exactly. Like I said, everything just fades away as soon as I wake up. But then it all changed this past Monday night."

Monday night. The night of lecture at ORU. The stranger challenging him during the Q & A. The snowstorm and the break-in at his house. The chase. The head butt and then the hospital emergency room. Monday night.

"Go on, Remus," Phin was desperate to know more. "What happened Monday night? What was different?"

"You, Phin! The dream was about *you*. At least I think it was. I woke up at like three in the morning, but this time I was able to hold on to a few pieces. Your face. I saw your face, Phin. And I was there with you, but it was about you, I know it."

Phin's mind was racing. *What else? What else did Remus know from his dreams?* So he said it. "What else, Remus? Tell me more." Phin's heart was pounding and he could feel his forehead just beginning to break out in tiny beads of perspiration.

"You've been having them too, haven't you?" Remus sat back, staring at his brother. "You have, haven't you? I knew it!" His hand came down hard on the table. More looks. Another move from the guard.

"It's okay," Phin said quickly. "We're all good here." The guard didn't look so convinced, and was now keeping a sharp eye on the two brothers. "I need to know what you saw, Remus. Tell me everything."

Leaning in, and once again his voice a whisper, Remus asked, "Phin, does the word: *Remember* – mean anything to you?"

It was like a floodgate opened in Phineas Crook's mind. With the uttering of that one word - REMEMBER - images, sounds, smells, all came rushing into his brain. He was overwhelmed. In an instant, Phin could hear the crowds in the distance. He could feel the pain as he was doubled over in the mud. A hill! He was climbing a hill. The dark clouds and the thunder. It all came to him in high-definition clarity. And then the reflection of himself. But it wasn't him, was it? It was him but not him - and the reflection had said that same word: REMEMBER. All of this became firmly planted in Phin's memory in an instant, never to be lost again. Phin staggered at the table, nearly falling out of his seat, grasping for the armrests. Remus' hand reached over to steady him.

"Whoa, little brother. You all right there?" The concern Remus had for his brother was sincere.

"Just give me a minute, will you?" Phin took a deep breath and righted himself. His vision was clearing.

"What's happening, Phin? What does it mean? You're the religious one. What is your God saying with all of this?"

"I don't know, Remus. I'm still trying to figure it all out."

"You're having them too - the dreams - tell me about them."

"I'm telling you, I'm trying to figure it out. Yes, I've had dreams. Bad ones. But for longer than you. Mine have been going on since Autumn."

"Autumn? Bro, that's like three years now, right?"

"Yeah, something like that. But I'm like you. I wake up and it's all gone."

"What happened just now? Something happened, didn't it? Something I said triggered something. Tell me!"

"It was that word: *Remember*. It's like when you said it, everything just flooded back in."

For the next ten minutes, Phin explained everything he was seeing in his dreams, that he could now *remember*. As he spoke of what he was seeing and experiencing, it triggered more recall for Remus.

"I'm climbing a hill too, Phin. A muddy path. People shouting in the distance. Just like what you are dreaming. But in my dream you are already at the top of the hill. And you're looking at something. I'm supposed to get to the top with you. I'm following you, little brother. How about that? You're the one leading the way for a change." Remus laughed again, trying to bring levity to the discussion, but they both knew this was no laughing matter. "This is important, isn't it, Phin? This all means something very important."

"Yes, I think it does. I just don't know what to do," replied Phin, staring into nothing, deep in thought. He was trying hard to connect the dots but he was certain he didn't have all the dots to connect yet.

"Let me ask you something, Phin," Remus broke his concentration. "Have you ever visited the family archives?"

Phin was surprised by the change in direction. "The family archives? What are you talking about, Remus? What does this have to do with the archives?"

The Crook Family Archives were located in the city of Jerusalem in Israel. They contained the full accounting of the Crook Family legacy, all the way back to its origin. Adonis Crook had told Phineas when he was eleven years old that the Crook lineage went back. Way back. Further than he could imagine. But he had only been made privy to the family lineage as far back as the founding of the United States and their immigration from Europe. His father kept a book with this part of the family history at their home in Moore. Phineas had looked at it many times. He had studied the names and locations and various exploits of the Crooks as they migrated across America. He had been instructed that once he turned eighteen, he was to make a pilgrimage of sorts to the Crook Family Archives in Jerusalem where he would learn more. Much more. But after his father's death, and Phineas' decision to walk away from the family business and heritage, the idea of visiting the archives no longer made sense.

"You've never been, have you?"

"Of course, not. Why would I? I'm a pastor and a teacher, Remus. Not a thief. What are you getting at?"

"REMEMBER....that's what *you* said to yourself in the dream. Maybe this is God's way of telling you to do just that. It's time for you to remember who you are, little brother. To embrace who you were meant to be."

"No way. There's no way I am believing that God wants me to

embrace a life totally contrary to him and everything he teaches. I can't accept that."

"Hey...I'm just sayin'. Don't be mad at me. It's the dreams, man. I'm just trying to figure it all out like you."

"Well, whatever it is, it's not about the Crook Family Archives."

The brothers spent another twenty minutes going over the details of each of their dreams one more time. There had also been some meaningless small talk, and then it was time to go. The brothers hugged once again and promised to communicate through the prison email system about anything new that might develop in their shared dreams going forward.

It had been a good visit. The best Phineas could ever recall. Probably because they were sharing something with these dreams, and they were both trying to figure it out together. For the first time in his life, Remus had treated him as an equal. Oh, he still called him *little brother*, and that was fine. He also continued to rib him about his belief in God. But something had changed with their relationship and he knew inside it would never be the same.

As Phineas drove away from the prison, he was dominated with thoughts of his dreams. Thoughts that were now firmly planted in his mind. He would not lose them again. Now that he and Remus had pulled back the veil on their dreams, they both wondered what would happen the next time they closed their eyes to sleep.

Phin was also haunted by that one word: Remember.

There was much more to that word than he had unearthed already. He was convinced of it. He was haunted by one other thought that he didn't want to admit to Remus. In order to find the answer to what his dreams meant, and what it was he was supposed to remember, he was going to have to make a trip to Jerusalem sooner rather than later.

CHAPTER TWENTY-TWO

Monday arrived without any fanfare. Phineas taught his three scheduled classes for the day, beginning with biblical hermeneutics, followed by a preaching lab, and finishing after lunch with his course on biblical backgrounds. In between he had worked to catch up on email and meet with a few students. The late February weather had turned warmer. Not warm as most would think of warm, but warm for this time of year. Temperatures in the mid-fifties and sunny days had wiped out any trace of last week's snow dump on the state. Phineas had also been sleeping well since his visit to the Big Mac to see his brother, Remus. No nightmares. No dreams of any kind. Just two long nights of wonderful, glorious sleep. Phineas felt reborn.

He was sitting in his office at his computer doing some prep work for the next day's classes when Max Allred stopped by to check on him.

"Hey, your face looks almost normal!" Max bellowed with hands over his head, holding onto the top of the doorframe.

Phin leaned back in his office chair with a smile on his face. "Normal's a good thing, right?"

"For most people, but I'm not so sure with you, my friend."

"Yeah, well, with friends like you who needs -"

"Easy there, buddy. I promise, I'm the best friend you've got around here, so be careful before you go and start talking about you-know-what," Max shot back as the two bantered.

"I'm just sayin'," retorted Phin.

"Seriously, though, Phin. You do look like you're feeling a lot better. I can see it all over you. You must be sleeping better, or your visit to see Remus must have gone better than expected."

"Both actually. I've slept like a baby the last couple of nights and I probably had the best conversation with my brother in years. Maybe ever."

"Really? You're serious?" asked Max. He was somewhat surprised because he knew the history between the two brothers and the tension that characterized their relationship.

Max knew Phin probably better than anyone else left alive. Phin had confided in Max years ago when they were college students, told him about his heritage and the taint of thievery that dominated his family line. Max didn't believe it at first. It seemed too fantastic to be true. But Phin had persisted and even taken Max home one weekend, violating the family code by allowing an outsider into the house. His mother was the only one that lived in the house since the death of Adonis, and she rarely ventured from the master suite. She had her own demons she battled in the quiet spaces of her mind, her relationship with her boys *unusual*, to say the least. Phin had shown

Max the family heritage book that his father kept for the boys, tracing the Crook Family line back to the founding of the United States. He'd taken him to the basement and showed off the lab where his father and Remus kept the various tools of the trade, so to speak.

There was even a small cache of stolen merchandise - a few paintings, a marble statue, some rare manuscripts, and various gold coinage and gemstones – that his father had left behind after his death. These were items that had never been turned back out onto the black market for profit. After the death of Adonis Crook, they just sat in the family basement as a testament to a life cut too short. The boys could not agree on what to do with the items. Phineas wanted to return them discreetly to their true owners, but didn't exactly know how to do that. He didn't even know how to find the rightful owners of some of the items. Remus wanted to sell them, of course. In the end they agreed to just leave them in the basement.

It was all enough to convince Max that his best friend was telling the truth about his most unique family. Phineas had made him swear to never tell anyone, and to his knowledge Max never had.

"Yes, I'm serious. And get this, Max. The reason Remus wanted to meet with me was because he's been having dreams too."

"No way! I don't believe it." Max replied with surprise. Besides his student assistant Jason Morris, Max was the only other person that Phin had ever confided in about his dreams. Now Remus knew, only because he too was having the same experiences. Max didn't know what to make of the dreams that his best friend had been experiencing. The fact that they were awful, but that he could never recall any of the details, led him to believe that it was all tied to some form of PTSD related to the loss of Autumn. He'd never seen two people more in love, and to have it so violently ripped away in a moment...well, it was no wonder that three years later Phineas was still experiencing personal trauma. At least that's the way that Max had sorted it out. But for his brother Remus to be having the same kind of dreams – well, that changed matters considerably.

"Yes, well, believe it. It's uncanny, Max. The details are virtually the same but with some interesting differences."

"Whoa, hold on. Details? I thought you couldn't remember anything about your dreams. Has something changed, Phin?"

"Oh yeah, sorry. I'm getting ahead of myself. I forgot. So much has happened in the last week. Listen, come in and close the door. Take a seat if you have a minute. I'll fill you in."

Max was not about to let this opportunity pass. Shutting the office door, he eased into the plush armchair that Phin kept in his office. He spread his hands before him as if to say, "I'm all ears."

Phin took the next half hour to fill Max in on his conversation with Remus and how, when he mentioned the word *remember*, it triggered an avalanche of memories related to the dreams. He remembered everything at this point, and still, two days later, nothing about what he recalled had faded. He left out the part of the conversation when Remus had suggested that Phin needed to visit the Crook Family Archives in Jerusalem. No need to muddy the waters with that little tidbit at this point, Phin believed.

"I gotta tell you, Phin. You've got one crazy weird family thing going." Max just sat there after absorbing all that Phin had shared with him, trying to make sense of it all. But that was just it, it didn't make sense. Not at all. Sure, it was comforting on one level to know that Phin wasn't insane or disturbed in some sort of mental fashion. The fact that his brother was independently having the same experience meant that something or someone outside of both of them was trying communicate with them. But for what reason? That was disturbing on a whole new level. It made Max believe that it would have been preferable if Phin's dreams *were* a result of his brokenness over Autumn. But this...this was something else altogether.

"Tell me about it. I thought I was going crazy...losing my mind. But now I know, Max, that this all means something. I just have to figure out what." Max continued to ponder the matter in silence. "Say," Phin was talking again, "you hungry? You wanna go grab some barbeque at Van's?"

"You bet!" The mention of food snapped Max out of his trance. "All you had to do was say Van's. Let me text Shelly to let her know what's going on and then we can split."

Phin began shutting down his office while Max sent the message to his wife. Phin, as always, had no one to send a message to. His time was only his own. The two men drove their own cars the short distance from campus over to the restaurant on Harrison Street. Van's Pig Stand has been a staple in the city of Shawnee since 1930, serving up all things barbeque. But they are best known for their hickory-smoked ribs. The smell of smoked meat permeates the dining room, and you can always count on taking it with you when you leave because your clothes will carry the smell for at least a day.

Phin and Max arrived at the same time and hustled into the restaurant to get out of the chilly air. It was still early for dinner - just after five o'clock - but the sun was already easing toward the horizon. Van's was not busy at this time of day, so the men had no problem finding a seat. Neither needed a menu as they knew exactly what they wanted. It would be a two-meat dinner of brisket and hot links for Phin, and Max eagerly ordered the ribs. Sweet tea was on tap for both, and the plan was to finish off dinner with a couple of slices of homemade chocolate pie. The mood was instantly good.

The two killed the time waiting on the food by swapping stories from college, reliving happier times. The food arrived and they dove in. The conversation took a turn for the serious, going back to what could possibly be the meaning of the dreams that Phin - and now they knew, Remus - had been having. Phin found it refreshing - therapeutic almost - to have someone with whom to unpack it all. Now that he could recall the details and had the added advantage of comparing the similarities and differences of the dreams, it felt really good to dissect it all with a friend, someone he trusted without reservation.

There was the ominous sky, the crowds screaming in the distance, the intense pain and dread and sense of evil that knocked Phin to his knees. Then there was the overwhelming sense that he had to do whatever it took to reach the top of the hill. Next came the rain and the climbing, crawling, and clawing up the muddy path. Only to end with the horrifying reflection of himself in a puddle of water, uttering that now haunting word: remember. What could it possibly mean that Remus had the same dream, the same feelings, and emotions and sense of dread as his little brother? The only exception - and it seemed so very important - was that in Remus' dream Phin had made it to the top of the hill. Remus' dream ends with Phin just standing there, on top of the hill, staring at *something*. It's Phin who, once again, utters the word: remember.

The big question now was: what did any of it mean? The pair exchanged a variety of ideas. The most obvious of which was that God himself was communicating with the brothers. The Bible is chock full of references and stories where God communicated to people through visions and dreams. The Old Testament in particular records the bizarre dreams of Joseph, which included the stars and sheaves of wheat bowing down to him. Later on, it's the servants of Pharaoh that have two dreams - one involving vines and grapes, and the other involving baskets of bread and other baked goods being devoured by birds. It was only Joseph who was able to interpret the meaning of the dreams. In the Book of Daniel, it is the man, Daniel, who interpreted the dreams of the Babylonian King, Nebuchadnezzar - dreams that the king could not even remember. Daniel was told by God of the dreams and then he revealed them to the king. Only at that point did the king *remember.* But these dreams themselves were also draped in mystery – visions of a massive statue with a head of gold, a torso of silver, thighs of bronze, legs of iron, and feet of iron and clay. Once again, only Daniel could provide the meaning after God gave it to him.

Phin and Max worked their way through the Bible, recalling these and more. Was it possible that what the brothers were experiencing fit into this category? If so, who could provide the interpretation? They would need a modern-day Joseph or Daniel it seemed.

Another idea they played with was that Phineas and Remus were having some strange sibling connection that revealed itself when they slept. This was not unheard of. While this phenomenon seemed to be more common between twins, there are records of it happening between other sibling pairs as well. Additionally, there is much anecdotal testimony of this link being realized when tragedy or death occurs with one sibling, while the other instantly feels that something horrible just happened. A brother dies in a car accident in Atlanta and at the exact same moment, his sister in San Francisco is overcome with a feeling of dread and tragedy and drops the cup of coffee she is sipping.

Finally, the two friends considered the possibility of demonic activity. Most people in the Western world scoff at the idea as one of ancient and medieval superstition. Only uneducated and uncivilized cultures would believe in such a thing as demons in our world today. Phin and Max both understood that such a position smacks of cultural snobbery, and they wanted to be careful to hold to a consistent worldview when it comes to the supernatural. The Bible speaks of God and angels, and it also speaks of Satan and demons. Phineas was always perplexed how a professing Christian could claim belief in the former without the latter, especially when both are thoroughly rooted in the biblical text. So was it possible that Phineas and Remus had been singled out for some sort of demonic targeting? If so, why? And still, what did it all mean? More questions and still no answers.

A final option the pair considered was that the whole thing was just one big coincidence. The two brothers just happened, for no reason at all, to be having strikingly similar dreams. While indeed possible, both agreed quickly that this was unlikely, and so they moved past this option, not to return to it.

Of all the ideas on the table, the one that made the most sense, and the one that Phineas hoped was indeed reality, was that God was behind it all. But this option also carried with it the most ominous of feelings. If God was the author and orchestrator of the shared dreams, there must be a purpose behind them. A purpose that demanded fulfillment. Phineas and Max found themselves thoroughly stumped as the chocolate pie arrived.

"Excuse me, Dr. Crook?" Phineas and Max looked up at the same time, both having just put forkfuls of chocolate smoothness into their mouths. "You are Dr. Phineas Crook, aren't you? I hope you don't mind me intruding."

CHAPTER TWENTY-THREE

Phin found himself staring into the eyes of a stunningly beautiful woman that looked to be in her mid-thirties. He quickly stood to his feet, his chair nearly tipping over backwards. Why was he being so eager? Max was standing as well.

"Yes...uh, hello. Yes, I'm Dr. Crook." Phineas swallowed his bite of pie quickly, wiping his mouth with his napkin while extending his hand in greeting.

"I just knew it!" She replied, taking his hand in turn. Phin was instantly aware of the warmth and softness of her hand. Yet her grip was firm and confident, but not too tight or overbearing. They shook hands, the grasp lingering for what most would consider just a bit too long. Phin found himself transfixed by her piercing green eyes as she returned his stare with equal intensity. She was undoubtedly gorgeous. Her red hair hung at shoulder length and gave her fair skin an almost angelic glow. Was there electricity passing between them? Of course not. Phin forced himself to end the handshake.

"My name is Ruth LaPhage. I was just finishing my dinner and noticed you eating here with your friend. I hope it's okay that I came over."

"Yes, of course, not a problem at all. This is my colleague, Dr. Max Allred." Phin gestured to Max, who shook hands and exchanged pleasantries with their visitor, but in a much more professional manner.

"Mrs. LaPhage, would you care to join us?" Phin asked, his hand indicating an empty chair at their table.

"Why, yes, I'd be delighted, and it's *Miss* LaPhage. I'm not married. But really, please just call me Ruth." Phin could have sworn that she threw him a signal with her eyes at the mention of her not being married. He shrugged it off as his mind playing tricks on him. The three took their seats.

"Can I get you a cup of coffee? Some water? Miss La..., I mean Ruth," Phin asked.

"Coffee would be nice, thank you." Phin motioned to their server and held up his coffee cup, indicating they would like a round.

"So Ruth, I'm sorry, but have we met before? I feel at a disadvantage as if I should know you from somewhere." Phin said this to get the ball rolling. He was certain he had never met Ruth LaPhage before. He would, no doubt, remember meeting someone so striking. She was indeed a very pretty woman, in obvious excellent health. Her posture was perfect and she held herself with an easy poise. The coffee arrived and she took a sip. She was wearing jeans with black Nike running shoes and a stylish pullover sweater that was a rich cream color.

"Oh no! My apologies, again. I need to explain myself. No, we have not met before, Dr. Crook."

"Phineas...or Phin. My friends call me Phin." He interjected. Phin caught an eye roll from Max, but he just shrugged it off.

"Well...*Phin*..." she said with a smile. "I am actually in town to try and meet with *you* tomorrow. I was going to call your office in the morning to set up an appointment. After checking in at the Holiday Inn Express down the road I asked the girl at the front desk for a great place to eat barbeque in town and she steered me right here. And wouldn't you know, as luck would have it, you and Dr. Allred came in right after I arrived. I sat and debated whether or not I should come over and introduce myself or just wait until tomorrow - and well - here I sit," Ruth reached over ever so subtly and gave Phin's left arm a brief touch and then she pulled back. Once again she was staring and smiling at him. Phin could swear that she was flirting with him. But that was crazy, right? What was wrong with him for even thinking this way?

"I'm sorry, Ruth," it was Max who chimed in. It was almost as if he had been forgotten in the initial exchange. Ruth turned and looked at Max as he went on, "I may have missed something. You're not from around here, right? So where is home and what brings you to Shawnee, Oklahoma, in search of the great Dr. Phineas Crook?" Max was speaking in a lighthearted manner, but there was also a serious curiosity to this Ruth LaPhage. Max was nearly certain that she had *not* been in the restaurant when they arrived. It was not a big dining room and there were not many people who were present ahead of them. As striking as she was with her red hair and good looks, he surely would have noticed had she been sitting alone when they walked in.

"Yes, thank you...what was it again...Max?" he nodded and smiled as if to say *yes*. It was clear, he was obviously the third wheel at this table. "I'm from Fort Worth, Texas, and I am the head of a collection of research entities called LaPhage Industries. Are you familiar with the LaPhage Limb?"

"Yes, absolutely," replied Phin. Who hadn't heard of the ground-breaking technology of the LaPhage Limb? It had made global news when it was released, and in the years since had changed the lives of countless individual amputees. "I knew I recognized the last name. So you are *that* LaPhage?"

"Well, my father is, and the LaPhage Limb was named specifically for my mother."

"Didn't I read something about your parents dying a few years ago in some horrible accident?" asked Max.

"Yes," Ruth looked down. "My mother was killed, but my father is still very much alive. Just incapacitated."

"I am so sorry. It must still be very painful," Phin replied with more understanding than Ruth could surely realize.

"Yes, I am sorry as well for your loss, Ruth. So, you now run the family business, so to speak?" Max continued to question.

"Yes, exactly. Which is what has brought me to Shawnee, Oklahoma, in search of the great Dr. Phineas Crook, as you put it, Max." Ruth had looked back up with that gleam in her eyes as she stared yet again at Phin. She had said Max's name, but it was Phin who had her attention.

"And the reason?" It was Max again.

"Excuse me?" replied Ruth, eyes still bearing into Phin's.

"That you're here, Ruth. Why exactly do you need to speak with Phin?"

"I've been following your work for some time, Phin. It's brilliant, if I must say so myself. I was at the lecture last Monday evening at ORU." At the mention of last Monday night and the presentation in Tulsa, Phin snapped out of the trance he had been in.

"You were in Tulsa last Monday night?" asked Phin.

"Yes, I was in town for another meeting and saw that you were giving a lecture. I just couldn't resist coming over to listen. It ended up costing me a day with the snowstorm that hit and all. I didn't get back to Fort Worth until Wednesday, but Phin, it was so worth it." She was sounding like some kind of groupie to Max at this point, which only raised his antenna even more. Something wasn't measuring up, and Phin was obviously too taken by her good looks and feminine wiles to see it.

"That still doesn't explain why you are here to see Phin," it was Max again. If Ruth was becoming annoyed with his questioning, she didn't show it.

"Because, Phin, I have a proposal for you." Although Max was asking the questions, she would not break eye contact with Phin, her answers always in his direction.

"A proposal?" Now Phin was curious as well. The spell looked to be broken and he seemed to be coming back to his senses, Max noticed. Ruth nevertheless continued to pour on the charm.

"Yes. I would like to hire you," Ruth leaned back with an even bigger smile on her face.

"Hire me? For what?"

"Well...to lead me to the Garden of Eden, of course!"

"You want me to take you to the Garden of Eden?"

"Unbelievable..." Max let out in a whispered huff, not meaning to be heard.

The smile on Ruth's face faded somewhat, "Look, I'm sorry, this isn't coming out right. I had planned to meet with you tomorrow, formally. I have my proposal all worked out. I'm just caught a little off-guard running into you tonight. Let me back up and explain myself."

"Yes, that would be nice," Max said. Phin eased back in his own chair as if he were ready to listen.

"As I mentioned earlier, LaPhage Industries is an umbrella entity that oversees several research endeavors. Our goal as a company is to improve the quality and length of life for every human being on planet earth. Ambitious, I know, but this is what drove my father, and it is what now drives me. The LaPhage Limb is the perfect, and most well known, example of what we are all about. To date, hundreds of thousands of amputees have rediscovered lives they thought were lost forever due to some awful accident or tragedy. But LaPhage Industries is involved in so many other efforts to improve the lives of real people. Like we have this tremendous project to desalinate water from the oceans to provide clean drinking water virtually anywhere in the world. It's amazing, really." Phineas and Max were listening intently as Ruth LaPhage continued on, trying to discern exactly where this was going, and how what LaPhage Industries was involved in related in any way to Phin's research on the Garden of Eden.

"That brings me, or I suppose I should say us, LaPhage Industries, to our interest in you, Phin. Your research into the continued existence of the Garden of Eden intrigues us. In particular the idea that the Garden contains the mythical Tree of Life. If you are right, that the Garden of Eden still exists, and can be found, *and* if it does, indeed, contain the Tree of Life, then the implications here are enormous. LaPhage Industries has a pharmaceutical research arm called Artemis Labs. You may have heard of it. Anyway, imagine if we found the Tree of Life and could bring its fruit back to the States. Let our scientists at Artemis break it down and see how it actually works. Then they can synthesize the active compounds, create a pill or a vaccine...are you following me, Phin? This is huge! Whatever is in that fruit, if it really exists, would change the world as we know it. No more cancer. No more diabetes or heart disease. We can wipe out AIDS for heaven's sake. Please tell me you understand what it is I'm saying here!"

Phin and Max were both silent.

"Well...say something." Ruth LaPhage was smiling enthusiastically.

"Money." Phin finally replied rather stoically.

"Excuse me?" The smile faded from Ruth's face, replaced by a furrowed brow.

"So this pill or vaccine or whatever it is that you propose that Artemis Labs creates, there will be a lot of money to make, won't there?"

Max followed up, "You want to use Phin to find the Garden and then you want to exploit whatever you find there to become richer than you already are. That's what Phin's trying to say."

Ruth was flabbergasted. She sat back with a look of utter shock on her face. She was not used to not getting her way. "No! You have me all wrong. I've got plenty of money. My family has made its fortune. Our goal now is to use our leverage and our financial base for the greater good. Gentlemen, we are talking about something that is bigger and greater than any of us - than all of us - could ever dream or imagine."

"But you would have to charge for it, right? There would be a price tag?" Max asked.

Again, Ruth was stumped by his reply. "Well, honestly, Max, I've not really thought that far. Yes, there are R& D costs. Sometimes a lot, millions even. Normally, those costs are recouped through the sale of whatever pharmaceutical drug is developed. Yes, that is all true. Artemis Labs operates like all other drug companies. But this...this is different."

Phin couldn't help but let a chuckle escape. Now Ruth LaPhage was the one becoming perturbed by the turn in the conversation.

"Is something funny, Phin?" she sat back, arms crossed.

"Artemis Labs. The goddess of fertility. That's who your drug company is named after. Did you even know that? I just found it humorous that a drug company named Artemis would attempt to bring a pill promising eternal life to the world's population, that's all."

"It was my father's idea. She represents *life* in Greek mythology," Ruth somberly countered.

"And that's the second time you've mentioned mythology. You referred to the 'mythical' Tree of Life earlier. Let me ask you something Miss LaPhage, do you believe in God?" Phin had decided to distance himself from her by using her last name.

"Honestly, no. I am an atheist. Or at least an agnostic. Are there things that I don't understand? Things that science cannot explain? Absolutely. So I am open to the supernatural, I suppose. But do I believe in God, as in the God of the Bible? Or a God that is up there or out there that rules over all of creation? No, I don't think so." Phin appreciated her honesty.

"Excuse me," it was Max. Once again he felt as if he had been shoved to the side in this discussion. "If you don't believe in God, then why on earth are you here, and how can you be talking to Phin about hiring him to go find the Garden of Eden, which is clearly talked about in the *Bible*? A book that was inspired by *God*?" Max put a special hard emphasis on the words Bible and God to make his point.

"Because, Max, while I don't believe in God, I do believe in myth," she turned her attention back to Phin and continued. "Just because something is myth doesn't mean that it's also not true. Or at least that it contains shades of truth. So, no, I don't believe in God and I don't believe the Bible as you gentlemen probably do. I respect your belief, don't get me wrong. I'm not one of those angry atheists that wants to kill Christmas for everybody," she took the opportunity to laugh at herself and try to recover some of the earlier levity, to take control of the direction of the conversation again. "But I also believe that books like the Bible find their origin in elements of truth. So I absolutely believe that the myth of the Garden of Eden and the Tree of Life is based on *something*. Do I believe that you can just pull an apple off of the Tree of Life and take a bite and live forever? No. But I do believe that if there is a Garden of Eden, then it likely contains some kind of special tree or vine or something we've perhaps never seen. Something that could provide great medicinal value."

Phin laughed again.

"Why do you keep laughing?!" Ruth reached over and slapped him on the shoulder, her attempt to be playful and keep him on the hook.

"I'm just laughing at the words you use when you talk about all of this."

"Perhaps you would like to enlighten me then," she teased back, clearly continuing to flirt.

"I'd be happy to!" The Garden of Eden was Phin's favorite topic of discussion, and he never missed an opportunity to set the record straight. "Most people assume that there was an apple tree in the Garden of Eden, and that it was forbidden or cursed. Many famous artists through the centuries have seized on this myth in their works. Like Lucas Cranach der Altere's famous painting, *Eve*, from around 1528. Google it and you will see that the artist clearly depicts the biblical Eve holding an apple while a serpent whispers in her ear. It's images like these that have perpetuated the myth of the apple tree. So there are already two big problems with the way you are talking about all of this, Ruth. First, we have no idea what kind of trees, fruit or otherwise, were growing in the Garden of Eden. There's nothing in the Bible to indicate any sort of typology. The idea of an apple tree is purely myth, and not one of the 'true' myths you are talking about. Second, the mythical apple tree, which really isn't an apple tree, is a completely different tree than the Tree of Life, which you're after. That tree is one we don't want to mess with if we ever did find the

Garden and could gain access to it. The real truth is, we have no idea what kind of fruit bears from the Tree of Life. Likely something no one has ever seen, since no one has found the Garden."

"Okay, I stand corrected," exclaimed Ruth with hands held up in surrender. "So I'll take my own apples with me when we head out to find the Garden of Eden."

"Hold on," Phin cut her off. "I'm not done yet."

"Why did I have the feeling that was the case?" Ruth replied.

"Oh, trust me, Ruth. He's just getting started." Max leaned back and took another bite of chocolate pie. He loved to watch his friend operate within his element.

"Well just one more thing I want to say about it all and then I'm done. Promise." He said this with a smile. He didn't want to beat their new friend up too badly. There was something about her he found likable, besides her good looks and charm. "So there's the idea that you mentioned, that eating from the Tree of Life brings eternal life. That's a myth as well, at least sort of. Once again, the text of Scripture indicates that while Adam and Eve lived in the Garden of Eden, they did eat from the Tree of Life. But the whole reason they were expelled was so that they could no longer have *access* to it. At the end of Genesis chapter three, God basically says that if they have the ability to eat from the Tree of Life anytime they want, then they would, indeed, live forever. But it's not a once-and-done thing. You have to *continue* to eat from the Tree of Life. The Book of Revelation gives us just a bit more information about the Tree of Life as well. In the final chapter of the book, we are told that at the end of time, when God recreates the earth, the Tree of Life will be freely available to all of God's children. And we are further told that the fruit from the Tree of Life is specifically for healing. So when you put it all together, you're closer to the truth than you realize, Ruth. The Tree of Life heals, and if a person continues to eat from it, then they actually will never die."

Ruth was all smiles as Phin concluded. "I knew I was right in coming to you, Phin." She reached over again, this time letting her hand rest on Phin's arm. She did not pull it back and he did not pull away. "Nobody knows more about this than you. I may not believe in God, but I believe *something* is out there. Something powerful and important. Something that will change us all if we can find it. I don't care about the money, Phin. Please believe me. Please help me. You are the only one that can."

"I'm sorry, Ruth. Really, I am. I appreciate the confidence, but my research and work on this is my own. I'm not sure the world is ready for what you are talking about. There's too much potential for abuse and market exclusivity. I've never thought about it on the level you have, but it all makes me very uncomfortable." Phin eased his arm away from her hand. He didn't want to. She was not an easy woman to disappoint, and part of him very much wanted to say yes. But his better judgment won out.

"Please reconsider. I am prepared to finance the whole operation. I have people, good people, that can be trusted, and we can go anywhere in the world that you lead us. Just point the way. Money is no object, Phin. And, of course, we would make it worth your effort. Just name your price."

Phin laughed yet again, "I'm not for sale, Ruth."

"I'm not trying to buy you. But it's worth it to me. It's worth it to the world."

"Look, thanks but no thanks. I am flattered and I appreciate the opportunity. I'm good where I'm at. I may go looking for the Garden of Eden one day, but it will be just me. By myself. Just to know that it's there. I'll document it all. The world will be able to see and know. But I am very certain that what is in the Garden of Eden is not for public consumption. There's a reason God ran humanity out."

"So that's it then?" Ruth replied.

"Yep, that's it. Nice to meet you, Ruth. I'm sorry this was a wasted trip for you."

"Oh, it was not a waste. I can promise you that. I'm pretty certain our paths will cross again, Phin. And soon. You will find that I can be very persuasive." She stood and shook Phin and Max's hands and bid them goodnight.

As she slipped out the door of Van's Pig Stand into the night, Phin looked over at his friend who gave him a raised eyebrow. Ruth LaPhage was a woman used to getting her way. Yes, their paths indeed were likely to cross again, he thought. He would be shocked if he knew how soon that was actually going to happen.

CHAPTER TWENTY-FOUR

*H*e had been here before. *Standing on a dirt path leading to the top of a hill. The crowd could be heard in the distance. A loud thunderclap slapped the sky above his head, causing him to hunker down. The presence of evil was palpable. He could feel it on his skin and smell it in the air. He could also feel the sweat rolling down his back, already soaking his shirt.*

It was so hot!

The air thick with humidity.

He had to get to the top of the hill, that much he knew. As he took a step forward the pain hit him in the gut. Like someone unseen took a sledgehammer and slammed it into him. He remembered this too. Yes, he remembered it all.

Phin attempted to stand upright, to not give in to the pain. He took another step forward, then another. The pain wracked his body again. This time he took a knee. What is going on? Why is this happening? The voices in the distance seemed to be calling to him, urging him forward. He had to keep going.

Just as before the sky opened up, large rain drops drenching him in seconds. He stood to his feet, pushing aside the pain coursing through his body. In a split second Phin made his decision. He ran! He had to get to the top! As quickly as possible. How did he know this? It didn't matter, he just did. Wham! Another unseen blow. This one to the head. He was knocked onto his back. Phin could taste blood in his mouth. He spat on the ground and clawed his way to his feet once again. BOOM! A flash of light and crack of thunder threw him to the muddy earth once again, this time on his face. Everything was working against him. Unseen blows, the powerful force of nature itself, all working to tear him apart. At least that's how it felt. Phin was on his feet yet again and running once more. More like a lopsy jog to be exact. His feet were sluggish like the demons of hell were reaching up from beneath the earth, grabbing hold of his legs. Down he went, this time a wave of nausea sweeping over him. He wretched onto the ground. He was so exhausted.

Everything stopped. The rain. The wind. The crowds.

Silence.

In front of him on the path was a puddle of water. The dreaded puddle of water he had seen so many times before when he had crawled this path. He couldn't not look. He had to see...again. He clawed his way forward and eased his head over the reflection in the water. His eyes stared back at him. His eyes. When he blinked, the reflection blinked. Phin laughed out loud and the reflection in the puddle mimicked his gestures. Time to move! Renewed from within, he was on his feet moving up the path.

This was new.

He had never made it this far before.

Phin could feel the beat of his heart as it threatened to pound out of his chest. One foot in front of the other, he finished the climb to the top of the path. As he crested the hill, he was stunned by what he saw on the other side. He was not sure what to expect, but this surely was not it. It was a crowd of people. A big crowd. Maybe fifty yards away, just down the slope from him. Thousands of people...like sand that carried on into the distance. There were people of all ages and races. Black, White, Asian, Indian, Hispanic and on and on. Every creed and tongue dressed in the clothing of their part of the world. Yes, it was as if the whole world was standing before him. Were these the voices he had heard? They were silent now, just staring at him.

"Phin! Hey Phin!"

Phin heard a familiar voice behind him and turned around. It was Remus! His brother was making his own way up the path, already near the top. Soaked to the bone just like he was.

"I knew that was you. What is this place? Where are we?" Remus was huffing as he finished his climb, joining his brother on top of the hill. They grasped each other in a bear hug.

"I have no idea. What are you doing here?" asked Phin, still taking everything in.

"What am I doing here? What are you doing here? And what is this place?"

"Man, I don't have a clue. But did you feel it on the way up?"

"What are you talking about? Feel what?"

"The evil. Man, it was thick, like this place is cursed. Well, the path anyway. Up here, though, it feels...I don't know...different."

"Bro, I have no idea what you are talking about. I just saw you on top of the hill here and knew I needed to walk that path and join you. Only crazy thing is it's raining down there but up here, it's clear."

"Wait, you didn't feel anything? Nothing? You just walked up the path?"

"Sure...didn't y -"

Remus was cut off as all of a sudden he doubled over in pain. *"Oooohhhh!!! Aaahhhh! Phin, give me a hand here,"* Remus struggled to say, reaching a hand out to his little brother.

Phin made a move toward Remus but was launched a good six feet away, landing on his back. He thudded to the ground with a hard umph that knocked the breath out of him. What the...??!!

"AAHH! Phin, help me!" Remus cried out in more pain. Phin lifted his head, trying hard to draw air into his lungs. There were two men standing over Remus, holding him down! They were dressed in black military-style uniforms, their faces covered with black cloaks similar to the ISIS death squads he had seen on TV. Where had they come from?! They had not been up here with them before, he was certain.

Phin struggled but couldn't get his arms and legs to move. Some kind of force was holding him down. Remus screamed again as the two men began to mercilessly beat him. A punch to the face, a kick to the groin. Remus was crying out for help, but there was nothing Phin could do. He looked over at the crowd and reached a hand toward the mob. They just stood there in complete silence and stared.

"What is wrong with you people?!" *Phin screamed. But they didn't even acknowledge Phin. What is going on?! What is this place? Why is this happening?*

At the height of his panic, Phin felt the overwhelming urge to do something counterintuitive. He relaxed. He let the ground hold him. Staring up at the sky, a feeling of warmth spread over him, and then a thought popped into his head. No...not a thought. A word. One word: REMEMBER.

"Remember..." Phin whispered to himself. Or to Remus. Or to whoever could hear him and would listen.

"Phin...please," Remus' strained voice brought Phin back to the moment. He lifted his head and stared at his brother. Confusion and shock

overwhelmed him as he watched, helplessly, as one of the two men opened a black duffle bag while the other man lay on top of Remus, pinning him to the ground. The one with the duffle stretched out Remus' left arm and held it firm within his grip. With his other hand, he pulled out of the duffle...what? A drill! A power drill. Remus' face went white. He began to buck and shake, sweat pouring off of his brow.

"PHIN!!!!"

But Phin only stared. Frozen.

The man with the drill gave the trigger a couple of devious squeezes. VWEEE! VWEEE! It made the quick whining sound drills make. The man's face was covered, but Phin swore that he could make out a smile underneath as he eased the drill bit onto the palm of Remus' hand. Showing no mercy at all, he pulled the trigger and bore down with the drill.

Remus cried out in agony.

Phin screamed.

CHAPTER
TWENTY-FIVE

"I like what you've done with the social media content from the lecture last week, Jason. The video clips, still pics with quotes, it's all top notch - really beyond what I expected. Thanks so much." Phin and Jason Morris were walking across campus toward the Geiger Center from Raley Chapel after Wednesday morning chapel. A herd of students surrounded them as the larger part of the group was all headed in the same direction, either toward Shawnee Hall for their next class or to the Geiger Center for something to drink, check their mailbox, or just to veg.

"I'm glad you like it all, Dr. Crook. And it's not a problem. I just want you to remember to give me a stellar recommendation one day when I'm ready for a real job," replied Jason with one of those looks in his eyes that says, *you owe me.* Phin didn't mind. The truth was he really did owe Jason. Phin may have been the brains behind all of his research that most labeled crazy, but Jason was the tech genius that actually made it all look sane and legit, and disseminated it to the world via Facebook, Twitter, Instagram, Snapchat and some other platforms that Phin had no clue about.

"Well, whatever recommendation you ever need will not be a problem, Jason. You know that. I want to help you in any way I can. Honestly, I don't know what I'll do without you come graduation. You're gonna be hard to replace!" Phin clapped Jason on the back and got a warm smile in return. "So tell me, you still planning on doing the dig in Israel this summer after you walk?" Phin was referring to the archaeological dig that was ongoing in the Caesarea Philippi region of northern Israel. Each summer, the dig was open to aspiring young archaeologists who wanted to spend twelve weeks digging in and sifting dirt, looking for shards of ancient mosaics, pottery, bones, etc. – anything that would shed light on the culture of the New Testament period being investigated. Jason had been saving money since his sophomore year at OBU with the hope of joining the effort.

"Yes, sir! I paid my final deposit a couple of weeks ago. I'm all set, I guess. Can't believe it's really going to happen. It's been more like a dream than reality this whole time," replied Jason.

The mention of dreams jolted Phin as they continued walking. The dreams were back, and more horrible than ever before. It was as if his visit with Remus at the Big Mac had opened the door to the next chapter, one that was more gruesome than he could have imagined - helplessness and torture at the hands of what must be barbarians. What could it all mean? What was the purpose? Where could God be in such a vision? His doubts and questions about God continued to mount. Yet he kept it all to himself, save his recent conversation with

Max. He needed to put it all out of his mind for now. There would be time to dwell on his own personal demons later.

"You deserve it, Jason. This is not just a dream anymore for you. And you will have a fantastic experience in Israel. Listen, I'm going to put together a list of places to visit and contacts of people I know in country who can help you. I mean, really take care of you, and get you access to some unusual and off-the-grid locations. You will have a lot of free time on the weekends so I want you to make the most of it." Phin had promised this to Jason in passing before, but he wanted to make sure his young apprentice knew he was going to be true to his word.

"Well, that would be awesome, Dr. Crook. Thanks so much!" Jason's youthful enthusiasm was a balm for Phineas in his life right now. It was so refreshing to have that vicarious connection with someone so full of life, someone who was about to embark upon an adventure, and to relive past moments all over again through his eyes. Jason meant more to Phin than he would ever know.

The two were just walking through the doors to the lower GC when Phin's phone began to ring. It was Max. "Hey, sorry, Jason. Let me get this and I will catch up with you later."

"No problem, I'm gonna grab a quick something to drink and run to class anyway. See ya, Dr. Crook!" Jason jogged ahead as Phin stepped back outside and answered his phone.

"Phin, where are you? Are you on campus?" Was that concern in Max's voice?

"Of course I'm on campus, Max. Just walked out of chapel and was about to grab a snack in the GC."

"Forget that. We need you over here in Montgomery right now." Something was up, Phin was sure of it.

"Okay, Max, I was headed that way in just a minute. Who's we?"

"Just head here now, Phin. Come to Dean Reynolds' office. We're all here waiting on you."

"We? Who's we, Max? What's going on?" But Max had already ended the call.

The dean's office. Phin had a sinking feeling in his stomach. What had he done wrong this time? He was already walking toward the Oval in the direction of Montgomery Hall, trying to imagine what in the world this could be about. Three minutes later, Phin passed through the atrium of Montgomery and bounded up the stairs, which dumped him right outside of Clayton Reynolds' office. The door was shut, and as Phin raised his closed hand to knock, it opened quickly. Max had obviously been on the lookout for him.

"Hey, what's this all about -" Max held up his hand with a quick jerk to shush Phin.

"Yes, it's him," called Max over his shoulder to the occupants of the office. He turned back to Phin and silently mouthed the words, *I'm sorry*. Stepping aside, he motioned for Phin to enter.

As he moved across the threshold of the Dean's office, he was met with a loud and hearty, "There he is!" Clayton Reynolds was on his feet quickly in front of Phin, grabbing his right hand and shaking it furiously. "The man of the hour has arrived! Come on in Dr. Crook. We've just been talking about you." Phin was caught completely off-guard. This was not the reception he had anticipated. Still trying to recover, his eyes fell next on Dr. Neal MacDonald. That would be *President* Dr. Neal MacDonald - the president of the university - here in the dean's office. He was wearing a smile across his face as he joined Dean Reynolds' side and offered his own hand to shake Phin's. Dr. Neal MacDonald was a tall man in his sixties and physically fit. He looked very much the role of president of a university with short black hair that he parted on the right and combed to the side. His black goatee matched his black hair and near black eyes.

"How are you, Dr. Crook? Thanks so much for joining us on short notice. We've had an eventful morning here on Bison Hill and we just couldn't wait to bring you into the loop," President MacDonald chimed in with enough enthusiasm to equal the dean's. This was most unusual indeed. Phin rarely spent time with President MacDonald, and certainly not in Montgomery Hall. In fact, he couldn't ever remember a time he had seen the president of the university on this end of the Oval. He nearly always conducted his business and meetings across the Oval in his own office in Thurmond Hall; or he would be seen walking through the Geiger Center hob-knobbing with students, one of his favorite pastimes. Neal MacDonald was an excellent president and one respected and liked by faculty and students alike. Phin had just never spent much, if any, time with him. And now, here he was, in the dean's office in Montgomery Hall, just a stone's throw down the corridor from Phin's own office, shaking hands and talking as if they were best friends. Yet in all of this, Phin couldn't help but feel like he was the one out of place. Reynolds and MacDonald were both in suits, and even Max had been given some sort of heads up because, he too, was sporting a tie and coat. Phin was in his usual winter attire of wrinkled khakis, a bland maroon shirt with no tie, and his Harris Tweed. All of a sudden he felt dumpy. Phin's head was spinning.

"The loop..." was all Phin could manage to speak.

"Excuse me?" It was President MacDonald asking in reply.

"The loop. You said you couldn't wait to bring me in the loop."

"Oh yes! Of course. Dr. Crook, please come on in and meet our guest." The two towering men in their crisp suits moved aside and motioned for Phin to step into the office toward a small conference table at one end. If Phin's head had been spinning thus far, it was now about to pop off of his shoulders. Standing with her back to the room looking out the window was one other person. Someone that instantly struck Phin as familiar. It was the red hair. Their *guest*. Phin was still processing all of this as Ruth LaPhage turned and made her own move from the window across the room to embrace Phin's hand. She was stunning. Phin was stupefied. Her hair was down this morning and she was wearing a smart looking navy blue pantsuit that complimented her athletic build. Very professional, yet very attractive.

"Dr. Crook, it is so very good to finally meet you *formally*," she said, wearing a sly smile on her face.

CHAPTER TWENTY-SIX

Phin took Ruth LaPhage's hand. It was instantly electric and at the same time disarming. *What is it about this woman? What game is she playing?* Phin thought to himself. The way she introduced herself bothered him - the use of the word *formally*. She knew precisely that this was their second meeting in less than forty-eight hours, but this little fact was only known to her, Phin, and Max.

"It's equally nice to make your acquaintance, Ms....?"

"LaPhage. Ruth LaPhage. But just call me Ruth."

"Certainly, Ruth," Phin replied, pulling his hand from hers, breaking the spell. He intentionally did not offer permission for her to use his first name in front of his colleagues. "So, what brings us all together?" Phin had regained control and was seeking to assert himself on some level. He felt like he knew very well what was bringing them all together. But he was willing to play along and see where this would lead.

"Let's all have a seat and let me explain what our morning discussions have involved. Sort of bring you up to speed, Dr. Crook. I think you will be delighted," President MacDonald answered. They all found themselves taking a seat at Dean Reynolds' table. It was a round-top oak table about six feet in diameter with comfortable chairs. Water bottles had already been placed at each seat, the configuration such that each person could easily see the other four at the same time.

President Neal MacDonald was clearly in charge of this meeting and began, "Dr. Crook, we had the opportunity to meet with Ms. LaPhage -"

"Ruth," she cut him off with a smile and a twinkle of her green eyes.

"Yes, of course. We met with *Ruth*, this morning for quite some time. She is a remarkable young entrepreneur with great vision. She heads a consortium of companies, all under the umbrella of LaPhage Industries. You may have heard of the LaPhage Limb, Dr. Crook." Phin just nodded at MacDonald's statement. Yes, he knew all of this. They just didn't know he knew. He and Max and Ruth. Ruth and Phin were both doing an admirable job of playing along as if this were a first meeting between them. Max not so much. He had his head down much of the time, looking tense. He had already drained half his bottle of water. Phin couldn't help but wonder what kind of strings Ruth LaPhage had pulled to get an early morning audience with the president of the university and the dean of the Hobbs College. Both men were busy, and you don't just walk in off the street and ask to meet. Yet, somehow she had done it. Well now that she was here, he was hooked by curiosity. Phin wanted to see how this thing would end up and how it involved him.

"Ruth has a wide range of interests both personal and professional as it relates to the various research projects managed by LaPhage Industries."

"A wide range of interests. Oh, I see," Phin chimed in with just a slight touch of sarcasm to his words.

Dean Reynolds gave Phin a funny look of annoyance as if to say, *What's going on with you?* President MacDonald seemed to not notice as he continued on. "That's right. And it seems, Dr. Crook, that one of her special areas of personal interest is the Bible - specifically the search for certain biblical artifacts. So Ruth has come to us because she wants to enlist your assistance in helping her on a specific search."

"Well, I'd be happy to help." Phin had decided to have some fun with the situation. "But I hate that there's been so much to-do over coming to see me. My best assistance would be to steer her to Southwestern Seminary in Fort Worth. Isn't that where LaPhage Industries is located, Ruth?" Phin was poking at her. She gave nothing away except that same smile of hers. Phin continued, "Southwestern has the most extensive collection of biblical artifacts of any evangelical seminary that I know. They even have their own collection of Dead Sea Scroll fragments. They are the envy of many other academic institutions. I've done some of my own work with their collection. Plus, they are involved in two major dig operations in the Middle East. They are the most connected group I know to steer you to. I'm just sorry you came all the way to Oklahoma to find that what you are looking for is just down the road from your headquarters."

There was a silence in the room as the group absorbed Phin's near-rude response. Ruth was the one to break the moment, "Thank you, Phin. It's okay if I call you Phin, isn't it?" She didn't wait for an answer before continuing on. "I am well aware of the collection at Southwestern. I'm afraid President MacDonald hasn't been specific enough. You see, what I need is something that only you can provide." Phin had a sinking feeling in his stomach. He knew what was coming next.

"Yes, Dr. Crook," it was MacDonald, working his way back into the conversation. "Ruth has come to us, OBU, because she needs what only one of our faculty members can provide. Namely what only *you* can provide. Dr. Crook, look at me." MacDonald leaned in from his seat, his gaze boring into Phin. "Ruth has been following your research for quite some time. *Your* research, Dr. Crook. She has come to us because she wants to *hire* you. She has studied your work and likes what she sees. She believes, Dr. Crook. She wants you to lead her to the Garden of Eden."

He had known it was coming, but even so, Phin sat speechless.

"This is the opportunity we've been waiting for, Phin," it was Reynolds this time. Phin nearly laughed at his use of the word *we*. He'd been derided and ridiculed. He'd nearly been censured because of his belief and public work on finding the Garden of Eden. Now, all of a sudden, it was *we*. There was no *we*, only Phin...by himself. The same way it had always been since losing Autumn.

"Neal and Clayton have been incredibly gracious and accommodating, Phin. You see, I am very serious about my need for you and you alone to help me find the Garden of Eden. Clearly, you know more about where it might be than anyone else in the world. Your work on the Garden is compelling. I share your passion for finding the Garden of Eden, Phin. But I know that what you lack is resources. Well, what you lack, I have aplenty. Money is no object. We can travel anywhere and put together a team of your choosing. You would be completely in charge. I'll follow your lead. And I'm ready to go *now*. I see no reason to wait, and Neal and Clayton agree."

"Wait, slow down please," Phin had lost control again. He was being put on the spot in front of his peers. He'd been so insistent on pursuing the Garden of Eden, and had stubbornly resisted any attempt from his dean, president, and even the board of trustees, to rein him in. Now here he sat, with two of his biggest doubters all of a sudden on his side. He was being painted into a corner. If he said no to Ruth LaPhage's obvious attempt at manipulation, he'd never have a leg to stand on going forward in terms of continuing his work, his way. Phin had only one play as he saw it.

"I'm very flattered, Ruth. Really I am. But I am a professor first, and a researcher second. I'm in the middle of a semester of classes. I have students who are counting on me. Plus, I have summer commitments with the university. In fact, I've got at least four more years before I qualify for a sabbatical. That would be the first time I could consider your generous offer."

Not looking very happy at Phineas' attitude, Reynolds chose the moment to weigh in. "We've discussed this as well, Dr. Crook. The president, Dr. Allred, and I are all in agreement. This is an exceptional opportunity for you and we don't want you to miss it. Spring break is just three weeks away. We believe this would be the perfect time to take a sabbatical of sorts. We will make arrangements for your classes to be covered. You'd likely be back by summer time, but if not, it wouldn't be a problem to give you that time as well. We see no barriers to this."

Phin could not believe what he was hearing. It was unheard of to give a professor leave from their classes in the middle of a term. Only in cases of family tragedy would such a thing be considered. There was only one explanation. They were trying to rid themselves of the embarrassment of Dr. Phineas T. Crook and his kooky theories about the Garden of Eden. It was a no-lose scenario for the school. If he failed, and they certainly believed he would fail, he would be disgraced and embarrassed. It would be academic suicide given his outspoken and public touting and insistence that the Garden of Eden truly did still exist. It would be an easy step to simply not have him return to the classroom come the fall. No one would question the school's decision, not even the students. But if he did do it, if he did find the Garden of Eden, then it would be a coup for the school to have him on their faculty - the all-of-a-sudden very prestigious Dr. Phineas T. Crook. Phin nearly laughed out loud thinking about how the matter had all been orchestrated. But there was one move he had. Just one that allowed him to maintain some semblance of control. He took a deep breath.

"No."

"Excuse me?" asked MacDonald.

"I said no. Or I suppose I should say: No, thank you."

"I don't understand, Dr. Crook," the president of OBU looked perplexed. Reynolds looked like he was about to explode. Max just looked down and took another drink of water from his bottle. Only Ruth LaPhage appeared perfectly calm. Almost as if she had expected Phin's answer.

"I'm sorry, Dr. MacDonald. I'm not trying to be unclear. My answer is no. I am not interested in helping Ms. LaPhage find the Garden of Eden. I appreciate the opportunity and I appreciate the interest you have in my research, Ruth. But I must decline. I have other priorities, and leaving in three weeks to hunt for the Garden of Eden just does not fit my timetable."

President Neal MacDonald was quick to respond to Phineas' near insubordination. "Dr. Crook, perhaps you have misunderstood this morning. Perhaps we have been the ones that have been unclear. So let me be crystal clear. Ms. LaPhage has graciously traveled from Fort Worth, Texas, to our campus here in Shawnee, Oklahoma. She has done so in order to establish a significant relationship with Oklahoma Baptist University. Just this morning, she presented to myself a check, a very generous check, for our capital fund to the tune of one million dollars." MacDonald made a point of calling out the financial amount

228

with a special emphasis, so that it would sink in. It was a huge gift for a school like OBU, for any school really. "In addition, she has donated another $250,000 to the endowment of the Sam and Martha Goodman chair. The same chair that you, Dr. Crook, currently occupy. In addition to all of that, she has offered to subsidize the cost of your replacement for the balance of the spring semester. And this very wonderful friend of the university has just told you that she will fund, to any level, the very search that you have poured yourself and this university's reputation into – namely the quest for the Garden of Eden. So, Dr. Crook, we summoned you here this morning not to *ask* you, but to *tell* you. Consider this a reassignment of your duties. You will be taking a leave of absence beginning spring break, and you will avail yourself and your research to Ms. LaPhage and prayerfully fulfill both your and her dreams as it relates to this quest. Am I clear? And at the risk of applying undue pressure, a little gratitude would be in order, I think."

There was a pause. Once again, silence settled over the group as everyone in the room was waiting to see what Phin's response would be. It was checkmate. Phin knew it. Ruth LaPhage knew it. Her composure during his dressing down was unwavering. She was one formidable woman. But what rattled Phin to his core was the gift. Not the gift itself but the specific amount - one million dollars. The same amount shouted out by his challenger at the ORU lecture just over a week ago. Ruth had said she'd been at that same lecture. What was going on? Clearly more than Phin could wrap his mind around in that moment. Phin reached for his bottle of water and broke the seal, unscrewing the cap and setting it calmly on the table. He took a long drink. Everyone continued to stare at him. There was only one thing left for him to say.

"Well, then. Let's go find the Garden of Eden!"

CHAPTER
TWENTY-SEVEN

Three weeks passed quickly. Phin was in his car driving away from LaPhage Industries headquarters in Fort Worth, Texas. He was headed back to Shawnee, but had decided to make one stop on the way home, a personal one. He'd be going through Plano anyway, so it made sense. In fact, he couldn't not stop.

Phin had just finished his final organizational meeting with Ruth LaPhage and the team that would be going in search of the Garden of Eden. It had gone well enough. Next week they would be on a plane headed overseas.

Phin's nightmarish dreams, however, had continued. Not every night, but enough nights that he found his energy level less than he wanted. Especially with the coming trip. He would need to dig deep on this one. Not just because he was physically down, but because of the circumstances that forced the issue. This was not how he wanted to go in search of the Garden of Eden. Ruth LaPhage was at the same time infuriating and captivating. He despised the tactics she used to force his hand into cooperating on this quest. Yet, when he was in her presence, there was something about her that was nearly irresistible. He found himself wanting to do his best to accommodate her wishes. There was an attraction, no doubt, which caused him to feel extremely guilty. What would Autumn think? It was all a massive head game that was almost too much.

Remus was also putting pressure on him. How was it possible that his brother, who was locked away in the state pen, could create another press point? Well, that was Remus. Phin started getting emails from his brother two days after what Phin began to refer to as his "next chapter" dream. The one where both brothers are on top of the hill, and then the torture begins. Remus had also had his version of the same dream. Except, according to Remus, he was waking up with real pain across his body, especially on the palms of his hands. Phin didn't even know what to do with that. Was Remus just being overly dramatic? Possibly. He was definitely the more extroverted and flamboyant of the two brothers. Remus also liked the spotlight. But there was a desperation in the emails. Phin recalled the closing lines from one he received just last week:

Phin, I don't know what is going on, but I'm scared little bro. I'm scared it's going to get worse and I have no idea where this thing is going. You have to do something, Phin! It's all about you. I just know it. You have to figure it out and fix it. I'm stuck. I'm helpless behind these bars. What a God-forsaken place this is that I live in. If God really is real and if he's out there and if he cares about me like I know you believe, then why would he subject me to a place like the Big Mac? There are some truly evil people in here.

They deserve this place. But not me, little bro. I'm not saying I'm innocent, but man, this place.... I've been able to stay sane by working out, keeping to myself, and sleeping. I can't wait to go to sleep each night because it's the one way, the only way, I can escape this place. But not with these dreams. Not anymore. What's happening to me on top of that hill in the dream is worse than anything I've ever experienced here. And whatever is going on is crossing over into the real world! I'm beat up, man. Inside and outside. YOU HAVE TO DO SOMETHING, PHIN. Please, figure this out. I'm counting on you.

-- Remus

Phin had no idea what to do. He felt as helpless as Remus. And he now had no time to do anything about it. He had been sucked into, no, he had been coerced, that's what it came down to - he had been coerced - into joining Ruth LaPhage on her personal joyride to find the Garden of Eden. But what scared and, if he was honest, excited Phin about Ruth was her end game. She was going after the Tree of Life. That was something Phin had never proposed to himself in his own research. All Phin ever wanted to do was *find* the Garden of Eden. Journey around it, record it, and film its boundary. He believed the Bible when it said that God had placed angels to guard the entrance to keep man out. There was an inherit divine warning involved - a warning to not even *try* to enter the Garden. Not only could it be impossible, but it could also be deadly. But Ruth was unfazed. She didn't believe in the Bible the same way as Phin. She'd made that very clear. Oh, she believed that the "myth" of the Bible pointed to something real, but she was not fearful. Not in the least. She had a plan, she had explained.

Just hours earlier, Phin had walked into LaPhage Industries for the first time. They had spent the last few weeks making decisions regarding who would be on the search team for the Garden. Those conversations had all taken place via email and video conferencing. Ruth had said it was all Phin's choice and he could have whoever he wanted on the team. But predictably, Ruth had inserted herself early on to make "suggestions." President MacDonald and Dean Reynolds had made themselves abundantly clear. *Do whatever this woman wants. Don't rock the boat. She's now a friend of the university.* So Phin had decided to go along to get along. Truthfully, it wasn't like Phin had a network of individuals whom he could call on for something like this. His intention, had he done it his way, was to one day go it alone. Make it a lone expedition. That was how he'd been raised as a Crook - to live the life of a thief in a very independent fashion. Trust no one. The only exception being family. Rely only on your own skill set and your personal mastery of the art of thievery. While Phin had walked away from that life, he still had those principles ingrained in him. He was used to flying solo. Oh, he had many connections around the world along with a nice network. But it was all for the sake of information. He had no one he'd dare bring into such a personal quest. Except one person.

Phin had insisted on including Max Allred on the team. Ruth didn't care, but MacDonald and Reynolds balked at the idea. They didn't mind being rid of Phin for a season, but the plan was never to send the associate dean of the Hobbs College.

"Too bad," Phin had said. "If I go, Max goes. Ruth said I could have anyone on the team I want. And I want Max."

Max nearly spit a mouthful of water onto Dean Reynolds' oak tabletop when Phin had mentioned his name. But Phin didn't care about that either. He was determined to have at least one person on the team that was *his* man. Someone he could trust. That man was Max. There wasn't much MacDonald and Reynolds could say to shut Phin down on this point, so in the end, they reluctantly agreed. Phin also got some measure of pleasure out of making the administration's life just a tiny bit uncomfortable having to shuffle Max's duties and classes for the remainder of the term, as well as his own.

So not only had Phin walked into LaPhage Industries for the first time earlier this morning, Max had walked in by his side.

"I still can't believe you talked me into this," he grumbled as they met in the parking lot. They had each driven down separately. Ruth had put them both up in the very nice Omni Fort Worth Downtown. Ruth insisted that Max bring Shelly and make it a weekend. As always, Phin was alone on the trip.

"I didn't talk you into anything, Max. I *forced* you onto the team, completely against your will." Phin slapped Max on the back.

"Yes, you did indeed, my friend. Yes, you did."

"Look, quit complaining, will you? You're my best friend and I'm not sure I completely trust this bunch down here in Fort Worth. I need you on this one, buddy."

"Well, I don't trust them either. And, I'm sorry, but Ruth definitely has a thing for you, Phin. You need to be careful around her, do you understand? Something's not quite right there."

"Once again, that's why you're here. I know with you around, I'll stay out of trouble."

Trouble. That's what bothered Max about this whole operation. Ruth was trouble, he just knew. He only wished Phin could see it. *Who knows*, he thought, *maybe he does.* Anyway, deep down, Max was excited about the trip. He needed a little adventure in his life and Shelly agreed. She trusted him with Phin and she trusted the two of them together. Max just wanted to know *where* it was they were going. In all the planning, Phin had kept what he believed to be the location of the Garden of Eden a secret. Even from Max. He had saved this final and most important tidbit of information for today's meeting. Phin had insisted he would only reveal where the team was going in its search for the Garden of Eden once they were all assembled together, in person, at LaPhage Industries. Well, that time had arrived.

The two men had been met in the foyer of the building by a man in a LaPhage security uniform named Benjamin. He had checked their identification and had run a fingerprint scan followed by a retina scan. "Building your security profile," he had explained. In short order, LaPhage security badges had been produced, which the men clipped to their shirts. They were then escorted to an elevator, which took them down. This surprised Phin and Max. For some reason, they had assumed they'd go *up* to some conference room with a majestic overlook of the city. They exited the elevator and Benjamin led them along a series of hallways and corners, through various security checkpoints that only he was able to get them past. Phin and Max shot glances to each other. They both started to have the sensation of being trapped. When it came time to get out of there, they weren't just going to be able to walk out on their own. They finally came to a door marked LP-13. Expecting Benjamin to navigate some elaborate protocol to gain admittance to the room, they were surprised when he reached up with his hand and simply knocked. A moment later the door opened and it was Ruth LaPhage.

"Ah, good! You're right on time. Come in, come in! Everyone is here and waiting."

She guided Phin and Max into the room. Phin noticed that as they entered, Benjamin turned and left. LP-13 was a well-lit large room with an enormous conference room-styled table in the middle. Leather high-back seats surrounded a rectangular table that had hard, sharp edges and was made of what appeared to be one big piece of white synthetic resin material. All four walls were adorned with massive video screens. Phin surmised that the whole room was embedded with the latest in technology, all at their fingertips should they need it.

There were five people already sitting around the table and Phin knew them all. This was the first time he'd been with them in person, but he'd interacted with all of them the past two weeks. The one person with whom he'd had no interaction was the mean-looking muscular man with a crew cut, khaki military-styled cargos, and tight-fitting short-sleeved black shirt. His left arm was clearly a LaPhage Limb. Phin had never seen one up close. This was Sergeant Billy Warren. Phin had read his profile. Ruth insisted that his place on the team was necessary for safety and security. Based on where Phin was taking them, he didn't disagree. There was a round of unnecessary introductions as the group stood, Max and Phin taking turns shaking hands with the sergeant, Tony Chen, Oz Jenks, and Dr. Mark Sayer.

They had decided to call themselves the GO Team. It was short for the Garden of Eden Team. The initials G.O.E. were simply pronounced *go*, so for practical reasons they just dropped the E and went with GO Team. It had a good sound to it. Of the seven of them on the GO Team, only five of them would actually travel to the field: Ruth, Phin, Max, Billy, and Oz. Dr. Sayer would stay home and be available to coordinate logistics with Tony, but more importantly to respond to any health issues that might arise while they were away. Phin had been told that neither Tony Chen nor Oz Jenks really wanted to be a part of the group that traveled, but Ruth insisted that one of them go along while the other stayed back and provided technical support. She didn't care which, and left it up to them to decide who would do which task. Since they both preferred the dim lighting of their home-away-from-home, LP-6, Phin had heard that the matter was settled based on the high score of a game of the old arcade classic, Donkey Kong. Seeing them both in person, he got it. They were definitely computer nerds. He had his doubts about taking either one into the field, but Ruth was insistent. What Ruth wants, Ruth gets.

"It is nice to finally meet you all," Phin began, trying to sound more confident than he felt. "Thank you for taking the time to be with us today." He winced inside, realizing how silly he likely sounded. No one in here really had a choice. Except for Max, Phin's "handpicked" team had really been selected by Ruth.

"Where exactly are we headed, Dr. Crook? I'm tired of all this beatin' around the bush. Just tell us, for cryin' out loud!" The gruff voice of Sergeant Warren cut in and echoed the likely sentiment of the rest of the group.

"Thank you, Billy," it was Ruth now. "Yes, I believe we've gone as far as we can with preparations, Phin. I appreciate your desire and need to keep the location of where you believe the Garden of Eden to be a secret. But now it's time to know. Everyone in this room can be trusted completely. No one in here will speak to anyone about the matters discussed here. I've been extremely clear on this point. Everyone in this room, with the exception of Max - but this is where I trust you, Phin - everyone else has proven themselves to me on multiple occasions when it comes to the issue of confidentiality. You are among friends." *There she goes again. Turning on that irresistible charisma of hers.* Phin fought it hard but was nevertheless being pulled in. She was correct. It was time.

CHAPTER
TWENTY-EIGHT

Looking at Sergeant Warren and Ruth LaPhage, Phin took a deep breath and dove in. "Yes, you are both right. It's time. So let me begin. Oz...Tony...do you two have the screen ready?" Tony Chen held up his phone to indicate to Phin that all was ready as he touched the face of the device. The large screens around the room lit up with a passage from the Bible. "The Bible is our road map. You are looking at the text from Genesis 2:10-14. This is the premier passage in the Bible on the geographic location of the Garden of Eden." Phin began to read the text as the group followed on the screens:

A river flowed out of Eden to water the garden, and there it divided and became four rivers. The name of the first is the Pishon. It is the one that flowed around the whole land of Havilah, where there is gold. And the gold of that land is good; bdellium and onyx stone are there. The name of the second river is the Gihon. It is the one that flowed around the whole land of Cush. And the name of the third river is the Tigris, which flows east of Assyria. And the fourth river is the Euphrates.

"So, clearly what we have here are four rivers listed by name: the Pishon, the Gihon, the Tigris, and the Euphrates. We have no idea where the Pishon River is nor do we know where the ancient land of Havilah is. The second river, the Gihon, is also a mystery to us, although the land of Cush is believed to be modern-day Ethiopia. But even this is not certain. However, the third and fourth rivers...*these* rivers are our clue!" The excitement was beginning to build in Phin's voice, his mannerisms becoming more excited. The group's attention was fixed solidly on him. He had rehearsed this moment many times in his mind; now the time had arrived and they were eating out of his hand. His friend, Max, had never even heard any of this. Phin continued, "The Tigris and Euphrates Rivers are clearly seen on any map of the Middle East. They are major aquatic arteries. They both flow from Turkey in the north down through Syria and then into Iraq where they actually join together as one before dumping into the Persian Gulf."

"That's a lot of real estate, Doc," Warren commented with his usual sternness.

"Yes it is, Sergeant. But that's not the only clue that the Bible gives us. Notice that we are told very specifically that there is another river – an unnamed river that flows out of the Garden of Eden. Once it exits the Garden, that's when it divides into the four rivers mentioned. It's okay that we can't identify all four rivers on a map today. Names of rivers, cities, even nations change throughout history. I think we all get that. But the fact that the names Tigris and

Euphrates persist to today is enough. We simply need to follow these rivers north to their source. Eventually they will come together according to the Bible. Now, follow me closely here, because this is important: I'm going to put a detailed map on the screens of this Middle East region we've been discussing." As if on cue, the map appeared. "As we follow the Tigris and Euphrates Rivers north into Turkey, you will notice that both rivers pivot and make a turn to the east. But look here...." The image zoomed in and a red circle appeared on the map. "Inside this circle is the termination point, or in our case the place where these rivers begin. You will notice two things."

"The rivers don't join together!" exclaimed Ruth. It was clear on the map that this was the case.

"Exactly. One, they do not come together. At their source, they remain separated. Two, they both source out near the borders of Armenia and Iran. Also, this is the region where most scholars believe is the location of the biblical Mount Ararat. This is the mountain where Noah's ark landed and where he began the resettlement effort of the land after the Flood. So this general location seems to be consistent with what we know to be a source of other human activity in the Bible and in history."

"But if the rivers don't come together, Dr. Crook, then we have a problem. It looks like the Bible is wrong." It was a good point that Tony Chen was making. Phin had everyone right where he wanted them.

"You might think so, Tony. But remember, we are talking about geographic features that are thousands of years old. A lot has happened between the biblical account of Genesis 2 and today. The fact that the Tigris and Euphrates still exist at all is significant. And, yes, we don't see them joined....*today*. But that does not mean that they weren't *once* joined together. In fact, I believe the Bible is correct and that they were indeed joined together... in the distant past. The source points and the flow of the rivers today act as a compass for us. The rivers are *pointing* us in the direction of Eden. If we postulate that the water table was different thousands of years ago, then it's not only possible, but likely, that these two rivers drew their original source further to the east - and not only that, but that the rivers originally joined together and flowed from another single river. That unnamed river would be the river that flowed through the Garden of Eden."

"All sounds like good theory. But how do we prove that what you are saying is true, Dr. Crook? And further, how do we make a determination about the ancient and original flow of these rivers?" It was Dr. Sayer weighing in with questions now.

"Thank you, Dr. Sayer. So I have a friend. Don't ask me who or how, but this friend works in the scientific community of the government of another nation. I was able to persuade him to fly a plane equipped with a lidar scanner over this region in a grid formation."

"A what kind of scanner?" Warren barked again.

"A lidar scanner. It's designed to probe the surface of the earth with laser light. A lidar scanner is able to map the ground beneath forests and vegetation and to see things that the naked eye just cannot see. Things like the remnants of ancient civilizations that have disappeared into the landscape. Or the ancient remnants of -"

"Riverbeds," finished Ruth.

"Yes...that is exactly right, Ruth. A lidar scanner can tell us where a river *used* to flow. We may not be able to see it with our eyes, but the subtle remnants of a riverbed always remain, if they ever existed, and the lidar scanner can show us."

"So what did you find, Doc? Cut to the chase," said Warren.

"Thank you, Sergeant. I'm about to do just that." Phin nodded at Tony one last time and the screens changed again. This time they showed the Tigris and the Euphrates Rivers extending on from their current source point. The animation showed the lines of the river growing to the east. At a point in extreme eastern Turkey, the Euphrates made a turn to the south and joined together with the Tigris becoming, now, one river. You could hear a collective gasp in the room. Phin was loving it. The animation continued as the one river entered into extreme northern Iran where it joined two other rivers. One from the north and one from the south. Four ancient rivers now joined together as one. Just as the text of Genesis had indicated. The tension in the room was palpable. Finally, the one river dipped just to the south where it terminated at its own source. A lake. Not just any lake, but a lake that is still in existence today. The far northern Iranian Lake Urmia.

"Oh my...," gasped Ruth LaPhage.

"Holy cow, Doc. It all fits," said Sergeant Warren.

Max Allred leaned back in his chair, looking quite impressed with his old college buddy.

"Yes, it does. It all fits," replied Phin with satisfaction.

Ruth LaPhage stood to her feet and placed the palms of both hands flat on the table, "Billy, begin working on the flight plan now. Gather the necessary gear for an expedition into northern Iran. I want anything and everything we might need. Proper clothing for us all. The works. Leave nothing out. Consult with Phin for specifics related to the search. Tony, Oz, begin looking at what we need to do to get in and out of Iran without being detected. I want to know all security and military assets the Iranians have on the ground, and how to avoid all of it. We don't need an international incident on our hands." Phin was in awe at how quickly and decisively Ruth moved. "Phin, I'm impressed. I had no doubt, but still, I am impressed nonetheless. Thank you. Okay, everyone. Let's talk details!"

And so they did for the next two hours. The GO Team finished over a lunch of sandwiches that Benjamin had delivered to LP-13.

Max and Phin said their goodbyes, but not for long. In just seven days, they would regroup and board a plane headed for the Middle East.

As Max headed out to pick up his wife, Phin was closing in on his detour to Plano. He exited the North Central Expressway just a block from his destination. His thoughts were on the Tree of Life. Something he had never really considered until Ruth LaPhage came along some three weeks ago. She was right. If it were possible to actually enter the Garden of Eden, such a find as the fruit from the Tree of Life would change everything. Phin still had major reservations. Was the world ready for the power of the Tree of Life? But Phin had a personal agenda that overshadowed his global reservations.

He had arrived. For the second time today he parked his car and exited. Unlike his inaugural visit to LaPhage Industries early that morning, he'd been here before. Many times. Once every two months, in fact. He wasn't required to come. He was compelled to come. His inner self is what drew him. A thread of hope that what once was lost could maybe, just maybe, be found again. If only God would have mercy.

Phin entered the lobby of SecondLife, Inc. He checked in, presenting his identification, and received his clearance. They knew him well because of his frequency of visitation. He rode the elevator to the fourth floor where he was met by a station host.

"Good day, Dr. Crook. Everything is ready. You'll be in Suite 3 today."

"Thanks, Barry. Really appreciate it."

"Sure thing. Anything you need, just let us know."

Phin was always impressed with the hospitality of SecondLife, Inc. It made him feel somewhat better about what he had chosen to do. He took a deep breath and entered Suite 3. It was a comfortable room with a window to the outside. It was a nice day, the sun shining brightly. The carpeted room smelled fresh, adorned with a homey collection of wall hangings and cozy furniture. In the middle of the suite was the main feature. A bed. It was dressed with a nice comforter and pillows. Not the institutional type, but the kind you would buy for your own house. Sitting on the bed was the POD - a sealed tube that Phin knew was carefully controlled to preserve its contents.

Taking one more deep breath, Phin walked over to the bed and stared down at the POD. The top was a Plexiglas window designed for viewing only. No touching. Phin was instantly overcome. Tears filled his eyes and began to flow. Oh, the love that broke his heart once again. He stared down at the most lovely vision of beauty he had ever known. She had been perfect. And now she was... she looked to be asleep, but Phin knew that she wasn't asleep. She was something else.

"Oh, my dear sweet, Autumn," Phin was able to croak out. "We need to talk."

CHAPTER TWENTY-NINE

"I don't like it, Ruth. I don't like it at all." Dr. Mark Sayer had been waiting outside of Charles LaPhage's medical suite as Ruth emerged from one of her non-protocol awakening sessions with her father. Sayer had suspected for some time that Ruth was doing this. After the morning GO Team meeting, he couldn't hold back from confronting her any longer.

"Oh, hello, Mark. You surprised me," replied Ruth. She seemed taken aback as she placed a hand over her heart. She was carrying the journal that she took to every awakening session with Charles. The journal where she recorded every detail that he uttered of his experiences on the other side. "What exactly is it you don't like?" She feigned ignorance.

"Let's not play games, Ruth. I know that you've been waking your father independently of what our medical team has advised. Three times a day. Once every seven hours, for one hour at a time. No more."

"You mean what *you* have advised, don't you, Mark?" Ruth questioned as her countenance took on a darker tone. She didn't like to be challenged. Especially by Dr. Mark Sayer. "The protocol was set by you. I'm not opposed to it, and I understand the wisdom behind it, but there is nothing wrong with a daughter spending some extra time alone with her father."

"It is an unnecessary risk."

"He is most at ease when he's talking to me. There is no risk, Mark. We just had a most pleasant conversation. He is resting comfortably again as we speak, his vitals all within the healthy range."

"That's just it, Ruth. He's not healthy. He's a broken man. He would be dead were it not for the resources of LaPhage and our medical experts alone. But as broken as his body is, it is his mind that most concerns me. Let's face it, shall we? We've avoided the subject far too long. Talked around it but never confronted it head-on. Ruth, your father is gone. The man that is in that room over your shoulder is nothing of the Charles LaPhage that hired me years ago and that I have spent my entire career serving. He's nothing like the man that raised you and loved you and loved his wife, Mary. What has happened to him is an utter tragedy and it's no fault of his own. But what we are continuing to do to him is even more of a tragedy, and the finger of blame can be pointed squarely at us."

Ruth listened as Dr. Sayer unloaded what must have been frustration building over the course of the last three years. She continued to appear calm on the outside, but on the inside she was seething. How dare he speak to her like this about her father - about anything really. Her father had made Mark Sayer what he was today - a leading and world-respected physician of the global entity, LaPhage Industries. Were it not for her father, he'd likely be digging out ingrown toenails and prescribing antibiotics to snotty-nosed little kids with ear infections in some general practice in the Midwest. A total unknown.

"Mark, I could not disagree with you more," she began calmly, not betraying the boiling kettle inside herself. Pointing toward the door to her father's medical suite she went on, "That man is Charles LaPhage. The same Charles LaPhage that made me, that made you...that made all of this," her arms sweeping the room. "Were it not for him, none of this and none of us would be here today. Are things different? Yes. Has he changed? Yes. It's a tragedy. No one feels it more than I do. I had my own plans, my own dreams. But I've laid it all aside to come back home and take care of the family business. It's what my father wanted, so I intend to honor him. It's what the board begged of me, and so I intend to honor their wishes. And even you, Mark...you were the one that was the most vocal about me coming home."

"This is not about my belief in you, Ruth," Mark inserted. Although in recent days, he'd begun to question her own mindset. The link with her father and this obsession with finding the Garden of Eden was totally outside the lane of logic to a man like Mark Sayer. How could anyone trust the ravings of a man who had degenerated into near lunacy? That was how he saw it, but he certainly had kept those thoughts to himself. His words today were the closest he had come to betraying how he truly felt.

"Oh, but it *is* about your belief in me, Mark," Ruth countered with force and determination. She was not done yet. "And it's about your belief in my father. You think he's gone. I get that. But I am telling you that he is not. I'm his daughter, Mark," she said, pounding her chest with force. "I know him better than anyone. Anyone. And I am telling you that he is *not* gone and that he is *not* crazy. Confused at times, yes. But, my gosh, Mark, wouldn't your grip on reality be skewed if you were kept in a comatic dreamland and then ripped into reality three times a day?"

"That's exactly what I'm talking about Ruth. It puts a tremendous stress and strain on him every time we perform an awakening. That's why we only do it three times a day. But what you are doing...well, it's erratic and serves only to make him worse."

"Make him worse?" Ruth nearly yelled. "What do you mean, make him worse? Mark, I'm trying to make him *better*. We've been going along status quo for nearly three years. We've been playing it your way. Under the current protocol my father simply exists. He is neither getting better nor is he declining. I'm trying to move the needle, Mark."

"Oh, you may move the needle, Ruth. But I'm not sure you will like where it ends up," Sayer continued to challenge.

"Well of course it's a risk. My father was a man willing to take risks. That's why LaPhage is what it is, Mark. Not because he played it safe. I am my father's daughter and I'm willing to take the risk."

"Even if it costs you your father's life?"

"What are you saying, Mark? That I'm killing my father?"

"What I'm saying is this: every time we perform an awakening on your father and he gets excited, which is nearly always, it puts stress on his body. I'm not sure you appreciate the delicate balance we are maintaining with the shell we have left to work with. So, yes, there is the risk that you, or we, push him too far. Wake him up too often, or upset him too much, and then we send his body over a cliff from which he can't be saved. But I want you to consider another alternative, Ruth. Let's say that you do move the needle, as you put it. Let's say that we can more and more acclimate Charles to the land of the living. Let's just say that we reach a point where Charles is stable enough physically to be more awake than asleep. Well, if we do reach that point, which, for the record, I don't think we can, but if we do, then, my dear Ruth, he would no longer be incapacitated, would he? Your control of LaPhage Industries is predicated on Charles being unable to run the company himself. However, if he is fully awake and aware, then that means he's back in and you are out. At that point, my big question is, which Charles LaPhage do we have with us running the show? The Charles LaPhage that's in that room right there is paranoid and believes everyone is against him. The Charles LaPhage in that room wants to fire the board of his own company, for heaven's sake. Do you...do *we*, really want a mad man running LaPhage Industries?"

Ruth laughed out loud. She couldn't contain herself any longer. She could tell that Dr. Sayer did not take her response well. He was shaking ever so slightly. In most cases, Ruth would turn on her charm - the magic spell that she knew she held over men. But not with Mark Sayer. He'd been around since she was a little girl. Seen her grow up through the teen years and into womanhood. He knew her and her ways all too well, so any attempt to woo him would be useless. She had chosen instead to meet force with force. And when necessary, like now, be dismissive.

"Mark, you are the one being paranoid. Look, my father is not well. That is a given. But there is more of him here than we are all giving him credit for. I know his body is shattered beyond repair. But I'm not worried about killing him. His spirit is strong. He *wants* to live, Mark. And as far as him regaining control of LaPhage Industries, well, that would be up to you and me I think. You are his physician. It would be up to you to communicate to the board that he is of sound mind and body and fit to resume his duties as chairman and CEO of LaPhage. I think you and I both know we are a long way from that ever happening. So that means that LaPhage Industries is safe and secure in my hands." Ruth ended with a smile and open palms. Dr.

Sayer was not comforted by her last statement. More and more he was becoming uncomfortable with Ruth's interests and use of the resources of LaPhage Industries. But he also wasn't in any position to do anything about it. "I'm glad we've had this chat, Mark. Truly, I am. It's been good to lay this all on the table - how we each feel - to reach a new understanding. We do have a new understanding, don't we, Mark?"

"Yes, Ruth. I think we do." What else could the good doctor say at this point?

"Good, because I want to talk to you about something else. Something I can't do by myself but that I need your help with." There was more? Dr. Sayer took a deep breath as Ruth dove in, "I think it's time we change the protocol for my father. He's done very well with my extra interactions with him. In fact, I'd say he's doing better mentally than I've seen since the accident. His periods of lucidity are growing longer and more stable." Sayer wasn't sure he agreed with her assessment, but he let her go on. "So I want to begin preparations for something bold."

"Something bold?" Dr. Sayer asked. He didn't like the sound of the word *bold*.

"Yes. Now, as you know I will be accompanying the GO Team next week as we head to Northern Iran. Listen to me, Mark. If we find the Garden of Eden, if we really do find it, then there may come a point I need my father. To know what he knows. Look, let's go sit down at my table in the next room and let me lay out for you what I have in mind."

They spent the next hour together. Ruth brought Dr. Sayer up to speed on some of the things she'd been learning from her father's visions in her extra awakening sessions with him. She was careful not to share everything - just enough for him to get the idea of Charles' critical connection to the Garden of Eden. Dr. Sayer wasn't convinced that what he was experiencing was real. While the search for the Garden was certainly real enough, and the work of Dr. Crook was compelling, in all likelihood, Charles' rantings about the Garden of Eden were driven by his own mad thoughts and dreams. But it didn't matter what the doctor thought. All that mattered was that Ruth believed in her father's visions and that was enough. She would not be dissuaded.

For her part, Ruth didn't fully trust Mark Sayer. He had been an important confidant of her father's, that was true enough. And he was loyal. Loyal to Charles. She knew very well that said loyalty did not extend to her, at least not fully. He would do his best to serve Ruth and protect her interests because she was the daughter of Charles. That's where his allegiance to her ended, though, and she knew it. She had to be careful with Dr. Mark Sayer. But she also needed him. No one was more on the inside of much of the goings-on of LaPhage Industries than he was. Certainly no one besides Ruth was more privy to the reality of Charles LaPhage's true condition. Whether she liked it or not, she was stuck with him. The one trump card she had in her pocket was that Dr. Sayer would do everything within his power to preserve Charles LaPhage's life. As bold as her plan was, Dr. Sayer would be forced to go along with it no matter what his better judgment told him. Ruth's judgment was the only thing that mattered. And the doctor's undying loyalty to Charles may just end up being the key that would pull the whole thing off.

Mark Sayer slipped out of the penthouse apartment, leaving Ruth and Charles behind. He still could not believe what he'd just heard. It was crazy. *She* was crazy. But what choice did he have? He was bound by his own sense of honor and loyalty to do his best work for

LaPhage Industries and for Charles personally. She'd known that and used it to her advantage. He had no idea where any of this would go. The search for the Garden of Eden. Ruth's schemes to involve her father. But there was one thing he felt certain of - it would not end well.

CHAPTER
THIRTY

Phin would have given anything to be able to hold his dearly beloved wife again. Instead, the best he could do was stare at her body through the Plexiglas window of her coffin-type POD. He placed his hand on the glass, willing that it could penetrate the cold barrier and he could stroke the softness of her cheek. Ten inches. That was the distance that could not be crossed. This would be as close as he could get, and it would have to do.

"Oh, Autumn. My dear sweet, E. I love you so much. So much has happened since my last visit that I need to tell you about." The grief always shattered Phin anew when he came to visit Autumn in her POD at SecondLife, Inc.

Many times when he made this visit - every time actually - he questioned the wisdom of his decision. Perhaps Max was right. He should let her go. But he couldn't bring himself to do it. Not as long as there was hope, no matter how small the sliver.

To say there had been a backlash to Phin's decision to employ the services of SecondLife, Inc. would be an understatement. Her family was furious. They were equally broken in their grief, but they saw no sense in prolonging what they believed to be the inevitable. "It's not natural," her mother had said. "You call yourself a man of God and here you are thumbing your nose at the proper order of things," her brother had accused. Her father wouldn't speak to Phin at all. He didn't trust himself not to say something even worse that he'd regret. There had been legal action. But SecondLife, Inc. was a legitimate "health care provider" and "sustainer of life," and so the case had no standing and went nowhere. Phin was her husband and legally he had the right to do the very thing that her family said he didn't.

Phin's own family and friends had been no less forgiving. For Max in particular, the whole subject of Autumn and SecondLife, Inc. was a continual sore spot. "You just need to let her go, Phin. It's not healthy for you to hang on." Max's words were an echo in his head, especially during times like this, when he would come and visit Autumn.

There was no breath in her lungs. At least none that he could see. No rise and fall of her chest. No fogging on the underside of the Plexiglas as she exhaled. She looked exactly as she had the day she had been placed in the POD three years earlier, perfectly beautiful in her favorite red dress. Makeup applied just as she would do it before going out for the day. Not too much - just a touch here and a touch there to accentuate her natural beauty. Her brown hair had been prepared to hang down in soft waves that hugged the side of her face and ended at her delicate shoulders. Perfect. His wife was perfect. Except she wasn't. Oh, she wasn't dead. Just very close to it. Much closer to death than she was to life.

Phin recalled that horrible, awful night when she had been shot. The bullet from the .38 special revolver had torn mercilessly through her insides. Her liver, a kidney, stomach, and intestines had been shredded, as if a mini-atomic bomb had gone off inside her. Her spinal cord had been nicked as well, causing certain nerve damage. By the time paramedics were able to transport her to the hospital, she had lost a tremendous amount of blood. She had never regained consciousness and quickly moved into a state of coma. The doctors worked furiously to stop the bleeding, but so much damage had been done - too much to repair. Sitting in the hallway of the emergency room in downtown Oklahoma City, Phin was covered in blood and didn't know what to do. So he prayed. He prayed to God to save his wife. "Please Lord, if you are really there, please let her live. Heal her, Lord. Please, I beg you."

"Excuse me, are you Autumn Crook's husband?" Phin looked up from his prayer and focused on the man in the doctor's coat standing over him. His vision had trouble focusing. He had cried so much his eyes were swollen.

"Yes, that's me," Phin said rising to his feet. He wobbled, having to catch himself. He was bruised from his own beating, but he didn't care about that right now. He refused to let the paramedics treat him. All he cared about was Autumn. She was the one that needed everyone's undivided attention.

"I'm Dr. Jennings. I've been the physician attending to your wife. I'm sorry to have to tell you - "

"Ohhh, nooo...," it was a groan that escaped from Phin as he steadied himself on the shoulder of the doctor. "No, please don't tell me she's gone."

Dr. Jennings had great compassion in his eyes as he took Phin by the arm, "Let's sit down, Mr. Crook. No, she's not gone. But I must tell you, her condition is grave and she is in decline. I won't lie to you because you need to spend these final hours with your wife and not here in the hallway.

"Final hours?" Phin asked. He was confused.

"Yes, I'm afraid there is nothing more we can do. Your wife will not survive the night. But she is resting now. You can go and be with her, be by her side until she passes."

Phin couldn't believe what he was hearing. There was no way this was happening. How could he just go and sit by his wife's side while she died? But what choice did he have? He was led to the room where Autumn lay. It was a cold, sanitized hospital room like one might expect - no warmth at all. Phin gently touched the side of Autumn's face, the coolness of her skin indicating that she was closer to death than life, her breathing shallow. She was leaving this world for the next. Leaving Phin. He began to sob again. He sat quietly by his wife, holding her hand and gently stroking her hair, for how long he didn't know. Time had lost meaning. Max and Shelly arrived. Phin had called and left a voicemail on their phone, and they had come as soon as they had gotten the message. They all cried and hugged and cried some more.

Sometime in the wee hours of the morning, a palliative care nurse asked to speak with Phin at the nurse's station. He was reluctant to leave Autumn's side, but Max and Shelly assured him that they would fetch him if there were any changes in her condition. What the nurse wanted to discuss with Phin would change everything.

"Mr. Crook, I need to tell you that your wife is a candidate for a new form of medical care. One that may prolong her life." Phin didn't understand what he was hearing.

"I'm sorry, nurse..."

"Maggie. Just call me Maggie."

"I'm sorry, Maggie. I don't understand. Dr. Jennings said that all that could be done for Autumn had been done. She's dying and there's nothing left to do."

"Yes, well, that is true in one sense, but in another sense there are still options. Or, I suppose I should say, there is one option." Phin continued to look confused. "Dr. Jennings is right. We've done all that we can for your wife...today. But that doesn't mean that something couldn't be done someday."

"Someday? I don't think you understand. My wife is dying. She won't even live through the night. You people need to communicate better. Excuse me, but I need to be by her side. Not out here talking."

"Please, Mr. Crook. Hear me out. Have you heard of SecondLife, Inc.?" Phin could vaguely recall seeing something about it on the Internet. Seems like it had to do with freezing people, or some such nonsense. It sounded like science fiction. The nurse placed a pamphlet into Phin's hand with the SecondLife, Inc. logo on the front. "Please take a few minutes to read this. My job is not to advocate for one form of treatment over another, but instead to make sure you know what your options are. In this case you have two. Option one is to do nothing more than what we've been able to already do. Your wife is dying. You've been informed correctly. She will not survive the night. But there is one other option available to you. Option two: SecondLife, Inc. They are a life preservation medical service. The literature I gave you will provide an overview, and there is a hotline you can call to discuss your wife's case in more detail. Basically, they can place your wife into a sort of state of suspended animation. The technology is still new, but has been approved by the FDA after years of testing. Basically, SecondLife, Inc. has perfected a process whereby they can slow your wife's bodily functions using an initial chemical cocktail delivered directly into her bloodstream. This is followed by a cooling process in a stasis tube. They call it a POD. In this way she remains perfectly preserved as she currently is right now. This doesn't heal her, please understand. What it does is buy you time, as much time as you need really. Years if it is necessary. I don't think there's a limit. Science and medicine are constantly in a state of evolution. New treatments are being developed on a monthly basis. We can't do any more for your wife today, but next year, five years from now, we may be able to. Should medicine catch up to your wife's needs, then she can be brought back and treated, her organs repaired. There are no guarantees, you understand. Time, Mr. Crook. That's all we are talking about. If at any point you decide that you don't want to go any further with SecondLife, Inc. then you can simply let her go. Think of it as life support, which we do all the time with patients. Sometimes traditional life support buys the body time to heal and recover and sometimes it does not. That's when the family terminates treatment or 'pulls the plug' as they say."

"I didn't know -" Phin sputtered, trying to process what Nurse Maggie was presenting him. "I didn't know something like this existed...was even possible." He was staring at the pamphlet.

"Well, as I said, it's very new and it's not inexpensive. Frankly, not many people have taken advantage of the treatment. Maybe less than one hundred nationally. And not everyone is a candidate. But your wife is, and that is why I am required to inform you of this option. I'm not telling you what to do, mind you, just -"

"Yes, I heard you. Just letting me know my options."

"That's right. But we are also on a clock. Your wife will pass soon. Within hours. So if this is something you want to do, we need to know quickly. Preparations must be made as soon as possible. Luckily, our hospital is a certified SecondLife, Inc. provider and most patients who take advantage of the service do so on a moment's notice. That's because we are nearly always talking about life and death cases when time is of the essence."

It didn't take Phin thirty minutes to make up his mind. He'd prayed to God to preserve Autumn's life. He'd prayed for hope. Now SecondLife, Inc. was the only lifeline of hope he had. He seized it and pulled the trigger. Maggie picked up the phone and within minutes, a team arrived and began the transfer process to a SecondLife, Inc. unit. Max and Shelly didn't understand what was going on. They'd never heard of SecondLife, Inc., and when Phin told them what was happening, they tried to slow him down. But there was no time, he explained. He had a desperate, wild look in his eye, and they were unable to change his mind. They weren't even sure that night if they *should* change his mind. Not until after Autumn had been PODed - that's what they called the process of placing a person in a POD - did they begin to have serious reservations as to the ethical nature of such a thing as SecondLife, Inc.

What if it took ten or twenty years for medicine to arrive at the point where Autumn's life could be saved? She'd be brought back to the land of the living and cured, and then what? Phin and her family and friends would all be twenty years older. Her parents may even be dead. Was this what Autumn would want? To come back to a world that had grown old and moved on without her? There were so many implications to the SecondLife, Inc. decision that needed to be considered. But it was too late now.

Phin sat looking at his wife, thinking back through all of this. He had no idea the night he made the decision that Autumn would need to ultimately be housed at the SecondLife, Inc. master facility in Plano, Texas. But that had ended up being okay too. The drive wasn't that far. They had been a class operation from the get-go, treating he and Autumn with over-the-top respect and dignity. He'd been able to bring her red dress to Plano, along with recent pictures, and they'd been able to prepare her as she appeared to him now in her POD. She didn't stay in Suite 3 all the time. They had another place, a location somewhere in the facility, where all the PODs/patients were kept. When a family member wanted to visit their loved one, they simply called ahead and the correct POD was brought to a room like Suite 3. Phin was allowed to stay as long as he wanted. He could listen to music, eat a meal, even watch television. It all seemed very warm and hospitable, if artificial.

"I don't know if what I've done is right or wrong, Autumn. But here we are. Please forgive me my darling, if I've done you wrong. I love you so much. I can't let you go." Feelings of guilt had crept into Phin's mind the last three years – feelings that he'd violated God's law by artificially holding onto Autumn. He'd thought more than once that he should terminate his SecondLife, Inc. agreement and let Autumn go. That's certainly what everyone else thought he should do. *Let her go, Phin, and have a proper funeral like what everyone else does in these situations.* He would become irate if anyone suggested that she was already dead, which had happened more than once. She wasn't dead, even if she wasn't quite alive. He preferred simply to refer to the whole situation regarding Autumn in terms of loss. He would say that he'd lost his wife. That he'd lost Autumn. He insisted that others use the same lingo, because that is exactly how he felt. Even though her body was in front of him and contained life, it was as if she'd gone away to a place he could not go. Not heaven, and not hell - somewhere in between. Not a purgatory - he believed in no such thing. Where she was had no category. That is why he thought of her as lost. His job was to find her and bring her back. To find his lost E.

"Autumn, my dear. I am about to go on a journey and I won't be back for awhile. I am caught up in something not of my choosing. But I've made some decisions. Decisions that will have consequences for us both. Please, if there is some part of you that can sense my presence, that knows I am here talking to you right now, please pray for me Autumn. Pray that God would go with me and that he would forgive me if I am wrong. I've got to do some things that I don't want to do and after that I am going to do some things that I have to do. I have no idea how this will end. And I may lose you forever in the process."

Phin lay his head gently on the window of the POD. His face just ten inches from hers. Ten inches. So close, yet so far. And then he sobbed.

CHAPTER
THIRTY-ONE

Destination number one was Ataturk International Airport in Istanbul, Turkey. Ataturk is a highly modern airport that sees the nations of the world pass through it daily. There would be nothing unusual about a group of American "tourists" entering the country through the normal channels of immigration and customs. While this would still place the GO Team a good 800 miles from their likely destination, it was the best and most logical starting point. The Middle East is not known for the stability of the countries that compose its makeup. While Iran is one of the stable few, flying into Tehran was out of the question. Turkey is more or less on friendly terms with the United States, so it made sense. Plus having the space to organize the additional necessary logistics would be easy from the Turkish side.

Phin and Max had caught a quick flight from Oklahoma City on Sunday, joining the rest of the GO Team at DFW airport, where they flew out on a standard United Airlines flight at 3:55 p.m. Ruth LaPhage had the resources to fly them privately, but all agreed that flying a U.S. carrier would attract less attention. That was exactly the goal they were trying to achieve. They wanted to stay off the radar.

After a ten-hour flight to Germany and a three-hour layover, they were on final approach into Ataturk. Phin had been in Turkey three other times, before and after he and Autumn married. He'd been through the airport in Istanbul more times than he could count so he knew it well. The plane touched down easily and made its way to the jet bridge. The team had been scattered around the cabin in two groups of pairs and a single during their two flights from Dallas. Max with Oz. Ruth with Phin, of course. And Sergeant Warren by himself. Ruth had booked Max, Oz, and Warren in coach, placing herself and Phin in first class. Max wasn't surprised, warning his friend to behave himself on the long flight.

While laying over in Germany he had tried to rib Phin, "Boy, must be nice to fly over the ocean in first class."

Without missing a beat, Phin shot back, "You have no idea, Max. I had lobster for dinner. And the seats fold down into a real bed! I got a solid six hours and then woke up to Belgian waffles, ham steak - the works."

"Shut up," Max turned sour. "Totally not fair. You were always the teacher's pet, even in college." The two laughed and then let it go. Ruth tried hard to engage him, Phin told Max, but he really did spend the majority of the flight sleeping. He felt refreshed even if his friend didn't. On the flight from Germany to Istanbul, the seating in first class was more standard, and Phin decided to indulge Ruth's attempts at conversation. He'd found her very pleasant, and they talked about a variety of subjects on the shorter flight. Family, education, places they'd each traveled to, etc. He found they had more in common than he would have thought. If he were honest with himself, he would admit that he enjoyed her company immensely, and that it was nice to have someone to talk to who was genuinely interested in him. It had been a long time. But he also knew he needed to be careful.

Immigration was not an issue for the group. Oz had been held longer than the rest. It was routine, Phin knew, but he got a kick out of watching the young man nervously answer the agent's questions about why he was in the country, how long he planned to stay, and on it went for about ten minutes. After being passed through, Phin threw his arm around Oz's shoulders, poking him playfully, "I thought this whole operation was going to be over before we could get out of the airport!"

Oz rolled his eyes, "Man, that scared me to death. I don't think he believed me at all when I told him we were here to just sightsee. He had a funny look in his eyes." The armpits of Oz's Batman t-shirt were soaked through.

"Relax, you did great. It's all standard, Oz. Trust me," he finished with a clap on the back. "And you might think about changing shirts!"

The team gathered up and made their way through the terminal. It was midafternoon and the airport was crowded. They were all hungry, and there were several delicious-looking restaurants they passed that called to them. Phin had eaten at Caffé Nero more than once. He loved their fare of Turkish sandwiches and pastries. But they settled instead for a fast cup of coffee from, of all places, a Starbucks. They wanted to get out of the airport as quickly as possible. They could have gone ahead and arranged for their next flight from Ataturk, but they had decided it was better to blend into the population of the city. They could more easily and quickly disappear, then arrange for a local private party to take them on to their next destination.

They were met outside the airport by a driving service that Ruth had prearranged. The group and their luggage fit nicely into the minivan driven by a man named Ocar. He drove them across the city where they checked into the Niles Hotel on the European side. The plan was to spend the night and continue on first thing in the morning. The Niles Hotel was one of a thousand hotels in Istanbul, and would be easy for them to relax in without attracting any undue attention. Not too fancy, it was perfect with its thirty-nine guest rooms and quick walking distance to several good eating establishments. When it came to rooming, Max and Phin shared a room, as did Warren and Oz. Neither Oz nor the sergeant seemed all too happy about the pairing. Ruth, as expected, had a room all her own.

The team went together for dinner to a local restaurant about a five-minute walk away. It was a crisp fifty-eight degrees, but walking in the cool air felt good after the long hours of travel in cramped spaces. They hit the jackpot with dinner. As the sun was setting, they dined on tasty Iskender Kebab. A delicious skewer of meat placed on top of freshly cooked pide bread and all of it covered with tomato sauce, butter, and yogurt. Even Oz, who had asked if there was a McDonalds, liked the dish. They sat at a round table with the windows opened to the street, enjoying their food. It was warm inside and cool outside, all of it making for a cozy atmosphere.

The group laughed and began to poke fun at one another. They were all very different, but they had been brought together for a common purpose: to find the Garden of Eden. They had spoken little about their objective since departing. There would be time enough for that later. Phin always loved how travel brought a group of people together, even people who had little to nothing in common. There was something about the shared experience of new places, people, food, and drink, that acted like a bonding agent.

Shortly after sunset, as the team was finishing dinner with a round of hot tea, the Muslim clarion call to prayer could be heard emanating from the speaker system of a minaret that was close by. They watched curiously as the Muslim population on the streets and in the restaurant stopped what they were doing, unrolled prayer rugs, and knelt down facing in the direction of Mecca to pray.

"I just don't get it," said Sergeant Warren, just a little too loudly. He looked genuinely put out.

"Don't get what?" asked Ruth.

"All this prayer stuff the Muslims do."

"It's their act of devotion to Allah," Max chimed in. He taught a class at OBU on world religions as well as a class on worldview. He was very well-versed in the customs of Islam.

"Well, I'd be curious what you two theologues think about all of this," he looked at Phin and Max.

"Think about all of what?" asked Phin.

"This," he said with his hand sweeping toward the crowds of people bowed in prayer. "All these towelheads bowing down to God." He used air quotes for the word 'God.' Phin cringed at his use of the slur directed toward the Muslim population, many of whom were within earshot.

Warren went on, "You don't believe the way they do... about God I mean. I know *I* don't. I'm not saying I'm religious or anything. But you two are the experts here on this stuff. So just wondering what you make of it all."

"Well, first of all," it was Max who took the lead. "This is their country and they have every right to worship whomever and however they want."

"But you don't believe the way they do, do you?" Oz broke in, interested in the conversation.

"No, I don't," Max went on. "I mean, obviously Phin and I

believe in God. But we are Christians. That means we believe certain things *about* God."

"Such as?"

"Well, namely that the God of the Bible is the one true and living God. Muslims might say they and we, meaning Muslims and Christians, believe in the same God. But when you really start looking at what Muslims believe about God and what Christians believe about God, it's very different."

"Okay, but in what way?" Oz continued to press.

"Yes, this is fascinating, gentlemen," Ruth chimed in. "I'd like to hear more. Continue on, Max."

"Well for starters, the Muslim concept of God is one based on fear. Allah is a god to be revered for sure, but he is also a god of great fear. When you talk to Muslims about Allah, they are a scared people. They never know for sure if Allah is pleased or happy with them. If he is upset or unhappy with them for any reason, then he will send them to hell. But if they've lived a life that pleases him, then they go to heaven. They even have this belief that after death, we all must cross a chasm walking on the barest of thin ropes. Flames leap up from the chasm while paradise waits on the other side, if one can only cross. If Allah is displeased with you for any reason because of something you did or didn't do in life, or even because of something you do while crossing the chasm, then all he has to do is flick the rope with his mighty finger, sending you plunging into the depths of the flames and hell itself. So you can see that such a view of God is ripe with incredible fear. A Muslim, then, must live every moment of their life doing all they can to please Allah. The call to prayer we are witnessing is just one of these 'works' they must devote themselves to." The evening call to prayer was finishing and movement in the streets was returning to normal as people began to rise and roll up their prayer rugs.

Drawn in by Max's explanation, Oz had more to say. "I know a lot of what you talked about is different than Christianity. I mean Christians don't do anything like this prayer stuff we just saw. But I used to go to church with my grandmother and I remember the preacher talking about the 'fear of the Lord.' So how's that really any different? Part of my deal with God is that in the end all religions may be different, but they are basically the same. They ask for people to blindly follow a God that no one has ever seen, but when all is said and done, how do you know he's even there and if he is there, how do you know you've got it right? About who he is and all, I mean. Christians think they're right. Muslims think they're right. Maybe nobody's right and it's all a big waste of time." Oz finished his sincere diatribe. It was easy to see that he was an honest skeptic.

"Boy, there *is* more going on upstairs with you than those computer games of yours, isn't there?" Sergeant Warren looked impressed. "I'm with Mr. Geek 100% on this one. I don't go for the God thing cuz there's no way to know who's right and who's wrong. It's all messed up as far as I'm concerned. Just a big waste of time."

"Oz, you said a lot. Maybe more than you even realized. I think everything you mentioned is worth talking about. For my part, as a Christian, if I truly do believe in what I say I believe in, then I should be willing to talk about it and answer the tough questions. So let me give it a shot if everybody's cool with it." This was Max's wheelhouse and Phin was more than willing to let him drive the bus on this one. Ruth and Oz indicated they were ready to hear more. The night was young and they were in no hurry. Sergeant Warren tried his best to seem less interested, although Phin suspected that he too was eager to hear more.

"Let me start by talking about what you heard growing up at your grandmother's church. The Bible does indeed talk about the 'fear of the Lord.' It's a phrase commonly used in the Bible. But for Jews and

Christians, the fear of the Lord has more to do with reverence and respect than about being scared of God. You see, because God is the creator of all life and basically everything that exists, he deserves the respect of his creation. That's us. And if we fail to give him his proper respect and reverence, then there is also an aspect of God's character that we should be afraid of. Just like Muslims, Christians believe in an eternal hell, but a huge difference is that we believe that God doesn't want to send anyone there at all. In fact, he has gone to great lengths for people to find freedom from the tyranny of this hell. Further - and this is important - for Christians, the only people that end up in hell are those who willfully choose to reject God and live a life without God. The ultimate definition of hell is separation from God. So in the end, what God does for people who reject him is grant their greatest wish - an eternity without him. But as I said, the Christian God is desperate to change this. If the Muslim view of God can be defined by fear, then the Christian view of God is defined by the word love. God loves us so much that he sent his son, Jesus, to take on the punishment that we deserve for rejecting God."

"Jesus!" Sergeant Warren cut in. "I knew we'd get around to him. I'm all in with Jesus. He was a cool dude. I just don't need the God and church and Bible stuff."

Max laughed but not in a deriding way, "Well it all sort of goes together, Sergeant."

"Not for me it doesn't."

"Well there's a lot to get into for sure. But since I brought up Jesus, let me say that he becomes another huge difference between Muslims and Christians."

"Yeah, right, because Muslims don't believe in Jesus, do they?" asked Oz.

"Actually, they do," answered Max. "But it's *what* they believe about Jesus that is the key. To Muslims, Jesus is a great prophet. He is worthy to be listened to, but he is not the pathway to heaven or anything like that. The prophet Muhammad is greater than Jesus to a Muslim. But to Christians, Jesus is the son of God. He is literally God in human form."

"Told you." It was Warren cutting in again. "Jesus is the dude!"

Max tried to ignore him as he went on, "Jesus is the key to avoiding hell and finding eternal life. The Bible says that there is no other name under heaven by which a person is saved than the name of Jesus. And here's the great part - once a person says they believe in Jesus in this way and they give their life to following him, then there is no fear at all of what happens after death. God is waiting on the other side of life to embrace you as a son or daughter. No fear. Just love." Max sat back and concluded, "So all of this and more makes Christianity far different than Islam."

"Very well said, Dr. Allred," Ruth finally spoke up with a soft clapping of her hands. "But the question still remains: How are we to know who is right and who is wrong? It doesn't really matter if we like the story of one myth over the other. They can't both be true."

"Excellent point, Ruth." Phin took this as his cue to jump into the mix. "But neither does that mean that they are both wrong. Just because you don't know the truth doesn't mean that the truth doesn't exist."

"But how do you know?" Oz was asking. "That's what she's saying. There's really no way to know for sure which one is right, or maybe they both are wrong and something else is right. It's all about how we can know."

"That's right, Oz. I agree with you one hundred percent. You and Ruth both. Surely there is a way we can know. And I believe that there is. Any system of faith should be able to stand the test, to be able to answer these hard questions, as Max said earlier. The starting point, once again, goes back to God. The first question that has to be asked and answered is the question: Is there a God? I believe that an honest assessment of the science and facts will point to an absolute yes. There is a God."

"Okay, you guys are starting to bore me now. I'm gonna take a walk. You all have fun." Billy Warren rose and moved toward the exit.

"I'll see you in the morning, Billy. Remember we start at 7:00 a.m. sharp," Ruth called after him.

"Oh, don't worry. I promise I'll be the one waiting on all of you," he called back as he walked out into the night.

The rest of the group spent another hour drinking tea and eating a delicious dessert of Turkish Delight, of all things, while they worked their way through the various arguments for the existence of God. It was all a very academic exercise that Oz and Ruth enjoyed. Neither ended up being convinced in the end it seemed. Ruth still stuck in her quasi atheistic-agnosticism, and Oz still floating between nothing and what he was exposed to from his childhood visits to his grandmother's church. Both seemed to have a growing appreciation for the two Jesus followers of the group, though. Theirs was not a mindless fanaticism or some generational religion passed down from their parents. No, they'd both come to what they called a reasonable faith in God and for that they were respected.

Phin's own questions about God remained deeper and more personal. Why had the God of love stripped him of his soul mate, his greatest earthly love? He didn't believe in the Muslim god of fear, yet it sure felt like he was being punished for something by God. Phin and Max walked back to the hotel with the other two and they all said their goodnights. Phin lay in bed listening to Max as he FaceTimed with Shelly. That's what he missed. Someone to share his life with. To share the deepest part of himself with. He listened as Max and Shelly traded inside jokes, talked about the kids, and called each other by pet names before signing off. Phin eventually escaped away into the land of sleep.

He bolted up in bed - the sheets soaked with sweat even though it was freezing in the room. Phin was afraid he might've woken up Max, but he could hear his steady breathing. He had not escaped into the land of sleep at all. He'd slipped into a replay of his nightmares. Oh, how awful he felt, sick to his stomach. It all was so real. He could still hear Remus' screams for help in his head. He needed to take a walk.

He slipped from his bed and eased his way out of the room into the hallway. He was on the third floor and decided to take the stairs down to the main level. There was no elevator. His watch said it was just after two in the morning and the hotel was quiet. He assumed the front door would be locked, and his plan was to relax for a bit in the lobby lounge until he felt sleepy again. He stopped on the first floor landing, though, as he heard sounds coming from below. He was about to turn and head back up when he recognized the voices.

"He doesn't know everything, does he Ruthie?" It was the sergeant. Phin strained to hear the reply.

"No, and he doesn't have to. I just need you to do what I need you to do on this mission, Billy. Nothing more, okay? And I need Phin to do what I need Phin to do. I'll make sure that happens. If everyone does what they are supposed to do, then we will be in and out with no complications."

"I still don't understand why the Allred guy is here. He's useless."

"Maybe so, but if his presence keeps Phin on track, then that's all that matters."

"Well, you're gonna have to explain some things to them both eventually. You can't keep them in the dark forever if we're gonna pull this off."

"Just leave that up to me. I've got everything under control."

Phin had heard enough. He quietly worked his way back up the stairs and to his room. Phin didn't know what all was going on. But he'd been aware of that since the meeting in the dean's office a month ago. There were too many oddities and coincidences. He'd heard enough tonight to affirm that the direction he'd chosen to travel was the right one. *She's got everything under control? We'll see.* That was Phin's last thought as he drifted back to sleep.

CHAPTER
THIRTY-TWO

It was just hours later when Phin and Max were up, showered and downstairs to join the rest of the group for a light breakfast of fruit and pastries. Phin's suspicions had been put on high alert after what he overheard the night before. What was it they weren't telling him? Phin took the opportunity before checking out of their room to fill in Max. He wanted as many eyes and ears on the other three as possible, especially Ruth and the sergeant. This was why he had insisted on Max joining the trip.

At seven o'clock sharp, Ocar arrived with his minivan and they all loaded up. Day two's itinerary involved a four-and-a-half hour drive to the Turkish capital city of Ankara. They were traveling light thus far, each with one large duffel that contained their clothing and some basic travel gear, all designed to make them look like tourists to anyone that might have stopped them in the airports to check their luggage. In Ankara, the operation would ramp up. They should be able to cover the two hundred and eighty miles and arrive easily by noon. Ruth had engaged her cadre of resources, which involved various payouts of cash, in order to secure a private hangar at the capital city's airport. The rest of their gear for the expedition should be waiting on them there, having been flown direct from the United States, marked as a shipment of "humanitarian supplies."

They made their way out of the metropolis of Istanbul, and were soon in the countryside of Turkey. It was a beautiful land and a perfect time of the year for the kind of travel they were doing. Sunny skies and cool days were on tap. Sergeant Warren had taken the front seat next to Ocar. That left Ruth, Phin, and Max sitting on the main bench seat with Phin in the middle. Oz positioned himself in the back and looked to be working away on his laptop, ear-buds securely in place. The team chatted at first, but everyone eventually slipped into the private space of their own heads as the miles ticked away.

Phin found himself thinking about the people in his life. Autumn was never far from him. When he closed his eyes, her beautiful face was there to meet his. Her smile. Her skin. The softness of her hair. One thing that Phin had noticed over the three years since the accident was that he had begun to lose his memory of what her voice sounded like. He used to recall specific conversations just so he could relive her talking to him once again. But time had dulled the details of much of those conversations, including the tone and pitch of her voice. Oh, how he missed her words. Her touch. Her love. Eventually, he had to place Autumn into a small compartment of his heart and move on. It was too painful to dwell there for very long. He prayed she would forgive him for the choices he was making today.

Next he thought of Jason Morris, his student assistant. Why had

Jason come to mind on this of all days? He had no idea really. He knew that Jason would love to have been with him and Max on this trip. He felt terribly bad for having to lie to Jason about his sudden departure mid-semester, especially since it was Jason's last and he would be graduating in a matter of weeks. The group was prepared for this operation to last weeks if necessary. That's what they had geared up for. But Phin knew that it would not be that long. He fully intended to see Jason walk at commencement. And then...then he had a proposal for the young man he was certain he would not be able to turn down.

Remus was also never far from Phin's thoughts. How could he be? Not just because he was his big brother, but because of the dreams. Yes, the dreams that had come to be a continual torment to them both. He was still stumped as to why this was happening to both of them. He was convinced more than ever that God or some demon was behind it all. But for what purpose? The whole thing had the fingerprints of dark forces on it, Phin thought. But why would God allow this kind of evil to touch him? Phin had given his life to God and to the ministry and the education of God's people and the next generation. He didn't deserve this. He didn't deserve what had happened to Autumn. He wanted to trust God, but more and more he felt compelled to take matters into his own hands. That's really what he was doing now, wasn't it? Well, it was going to be an interesting ride to see how it all turned out, he concluded to himself.

At the halfway point to Ankara, they stopped for a stretch and a tank of fuel in the small village of Bolu. It was a picturesque town tucked into a series of rolling hills that reminded Phin of the Ozark mountains of Arkansas, where he used to camp with his family as a boy. Everything was so green and lush and the houses were quaint. They loaded up and drove past a gorgeous lake on the way out of town. He noticed several teenage boys fishing. Life looked slow and easy in this little hamlet. Phin thought that he should come back here and visit one day and do his own bit of fishing.

Just over two hours later they arrived at the Ankara airport and drove straight to the hangar Ruth had secured. The doors opened when they pulled up, as if on cue. Three men came directly toward them. Sergeant Warren jumped quickly out of the van and met them for an animated discussion. Things seemed to be in order. It looked like Warren was in charge, pointing with his hands back to the van and the open hangar. The rest of the group was unloading their luggage when Warren joined them.

"It's all good. Let them take our bags, okay? You all go on in. There's a restroom in the far back corner, and an office that has some food. Chicken and sodas, I think. Take it easy. Oz, you're with me. I wanna check out all the gear before we load it and take off. If there's anything we are missing, we can get it in Ankara this afternoon. Everyone just chill and we will let you know when we are good to go." Sergeant Warren was in his element. Full military mode. Leading, giving orders, making things happen. Phin and Max just looked at each other and shrugged their shoulders.

"Well...let's eat," Max finally said as he headed for the open hangar. Ruth and Phin laughed and fell in behind him. Oz looked dejected as they went for the food without him. Something told Phin that he was pretty hungry, but he'd have to wait for Warren to "dismiss" him. Ah well, the kid was young. He'd be okay.

They ate, and then out of curiosity joined Warren and Oz as they were doing an inventory of the equipment that LaPhage had sent over for them. There was a cache of small weapons that made Phin a little nervous, although he understood. They would be headed into one of the more unstable regions of the world. Some protection was not out of order. There was a lot of technical and computer gear. Phin struggled to understand what its purpose could be. He noticed Warren and Oz spending a lot of time looking it over and talking about it. As expected, there was a supply of food, cooking materials, sleeping bags, tarps, etc. Everything you'd need for a camping trip on steroids. There was one other item that puzzled Max and Phin both. A large rectangle crate still boarded up. They'd not taken time to open it, and it was sitting outside the cargo bay of their small plane, ready to be loaded. Phin finally decided to say something to Ruth.

"I'm a little concerned, Ruth."

"Oh hey, Phin," she seemed surprised as he approached her from behind. "Sorry, you caught me off guard." She quickly closed a tablet she'd been engrossed in. The move didn't go unnoticed by Phin.

"I was just saying that I'm a little worried about all this gear we are inventorying. There's only five of us. How are we going to move around with it all?"

"Good question. Yes, the original intention was for the GO Team to be us five on the ground with Mark and Tony back home providing support. But after we pulled the trigger on the supply list, Billy and I knew we would need help. So we've hired some porters who will take us and our supplies where we need to go."

"This is the first I've heard about bringing anyone else into the loop on our objective, Ruth. Makes me nervous." Phin didn't like unknown elements. He knew what lay ahead and he knew the dangers of where they would be trekking. He didn't like having people he didn't trust around him in this part of the world. And the trust he had for Ruth LaPhage and company was tenuous at best already.

"It will be fine, Phin. We need all that we've brought, and we are using cheap labor, that's all. We will maintain a base camp once we cross over into Iran. That's as far as the porters will go. They have no idea what we are doing and why we are doing it. The search for the Garden of Eden will be an unknown factor to them. They will be completely ignorant of the details. Just a small group of hirelings helping a group of adventure-seeking Americans. That will be the extent of their knowledge."

"So how many are we talking about Ruth?"

"Four men, that's it."

"Four more," Phin mused as he whispered the number. What choice did he have?

"Phin, look at me." Ruth had taken hold of his right hand and was facing him, standing very close. She put her other hand on his waist. It was a near intimate connection. "It's going to be okay. You can trust me. Please trust me. I've got it all under control." Then she hugged him. To his surprise, Phin embraced her back, if ever so slightly. He liked the physical connection. There was a magnetism to Ruth that was hard to resist. But the warning sirens were going off in his head. *I've got this all under control.* It was the same phrase she'd used last night when he overheard her talking with Sergeant Warren. They broke from their embrace and Ruth gave his arm a final squeeze as she turned to head toward the office. She threw him one final flirtatious look with her eyes as she walked away. *What is wrong with you, Phin?* He chastised himself.

"What is wrong with you, Phin?!" Max had sidled up next to him. "Okay, my friend, you told me I was along on this trip to keep you out of trouble. And I'm telling you, that woman is trouble. Good grief, Phin, think man! Last night...think about what you heard just last night. Things are going on and we are not in the loop!"

"I know, Max." Phin was frustrated, and not with his friend. "I know. I get it."

"She's a vixen, I tell you. A vixen."

"Yeah...you may be right," Phin's voice trailed off as he continued to stare toward the office where Ruth had retreated.

CHAPTER
THIRTY-THREE

It was midafternoon when Oz and Warren gave the thumbs up. It was time to load up and lift off. Part of the preplanning had been the arrangements made for a small plane and a pilot that would carry them to their final stopping point for the day, the city of Van, in extreme eastern Turkey. It was a short flight and placed them a mere seventy-five miles from the border with Iran. Another hangar had been arranged, as in Ankara, and the group would spend the night with the plane and supplies.

Phin knew the city of Van to be one of the oldest in Turkey, dating back at least a thousand years before Christ. He was able to catch a glimpse of the majestic Van Lake as the plane made its descent and landed. The runway itself was right on the lake's edge, which boasted an impressive view of a snow-capped mountain on the far side. Max and Phin knew it was impossible, but they both desperately wanted to break away and do a little exploring. The historic Van Fortress boasted an inscription with the name of Xerxes the Great on the cliffs below the structure. It would be a real moment to see the carving that bore the name of the great Persian king mentioned in the Book of Esther. But alas, it was not to be.

A cold blast of air hit them as they exited the plane that by now had pulled into the open hangar, waiting on them as planned. This one looked more like a beat-up old barn, located on the extreme southern edge of the airport, far away from the simple terminal and all other aviation. Just fine as far as they were concerned. It was quite a bit colder at the higher altitude. Sergeant Warren guessed just above freezing. Everyone except Warren broke out matching down-filled packables that would suit them just fine to twenty-two degrees below zero, more than enough for where they were headed. The sergeant seemed impervious to the temperatures.

The group went to work unloading the supplies and gear. Then to the surprise of everyone, the pilot announced he was flying back to Ankara. The agreement had been for him to stay the night and leave in the morning when their ground transportation arrived. But now that they had been delivered, and he'd been paid, he apparently had a change of heart. Warren had strong words with the man and clearly berated him for his lack of integrity. But the pilot would have none of it. He simply hastened his exit. Ten minutes later he taxied away, and for the first time since arriving in Turkey, the group felt alone. Ruth was unfazed, however. Ever the optimist, she reminded the group that it was just the five of them anyway, no matter how much support they may hire and utilize along the way.

It was late in the afternoon and the sun would be down soon. They were counting on the pilot to communicate with the local airport personnel and help arrange for food to be brought to them for dinner. It looked like they would be breaking into their freeze-dried packets sooner than expected.

Suddenly, Sergeant Warren announced, "Y'all wait here. Back in a minute." He then took off jogging toward the main terminal. Easily a good half-mile away. Ruth shrugged and Oz collapsed onto a pile of duffels, sticking his ear-buds in his ears while closing his eyes. Phin and Max decided to take a walk around the perimeter of the hangar and get the lay of the land.

About thirty minutes later, the two men could hear Ruth calling from the front of the hangar. "Guys, I think you need to get over here quick!" Was that worry in her voice? The two had settled down in the back of the hangar after their walk around, but were on their feet in seconds, sprinting to Ruth's side. There was a car headed in their direction.

"Someone's coming," she said as they pulled up next to her.

"What's the plan?" Max asked Ruth.

"The plan is cash. I've got a wad of it in my cargo pocket."

"I like that plan."

"Phin, can you go get one of the guns that we packed in?" She was telling more than asking.

"No time, Ruth. They're nearly here."

He was right. The car had sped up. It was a late model Saab, navy blue, and approaching - fast. It made a turn to their right, followed by a wide swing as it came back in and screeched to a halt ten feet from the group. The door swung open and the lone passenger, a one Sergeant Billy Warren, stepped out.

"Ride's here!" he bellowed.

"How did you? – never mind. Sorry I asked," said Phin.

"Hey, I'm the most valuable player on this here team of ours. No offense, Doc."

"None taken," both Phin and Max replied in unison. Max knew he'd been referring only to Phin though.

Oz came sauntering out of the hangar, having missed the whole exchange. "Sweet! Wheels. Where're we going for dinner?"

"Wait," Ruth exclaimed. "We can't just leave all our things here unattended."

"You all take the car and go find a nice place to eat. I've heard Ruthie here has a nice stash of cash. Spare no expense. I'll stay behind and guard everything. Just bring me something back. No hurry." Warren was already walking toward the hangar, having dropped the keys in Ruth's hand.

Phin wasted no time seizing the moment. He snatched the keys from Ruth, "You heard the man. Let's go get something to eat. And I know just the place!"

Phin really had no idea where to take the group for food. He had another place in mind: The Van Fortress. *A detour on the way to dinner* - that's what he'd told the group. No one objected. They arrived just as the sun was going down. The ancient Uratu structure was impressive as it stood on cliffs overlooking Lake Van. Phin knew right where to go, and the group worked quickly as daylight was fading fast. They scrambled through the ruins of the fortress to a set of ancient steps leading to the base of the battlement just at the shoreline. And there it was. Some sixty feet from the ground, carved into a niche in the rock wall was the perfectly preserved inscription bearing the name of Xerxes the Great. Max and Phin stood on the steps in awe before the inscription. Ruth and Oz caught up to them.

"What does it say, Phin?" asked Ruth.

"I'm a little rusty in cuneiform. Max, this is your area, isn't it?"

Without saying a word, Max moved to the front of the group and began to read:

I am Xerxes, the great king, king of kings, king of all kinds of peoples with all kinds of origins, king of this earth great and wide, the son of King Darius, the Achaemenid. King Xerxes says: King Darius, my father, by the grace of Ahuramazda built much that was good, and he gave orders to dig this niche out, but because he did not make an inscription, I ordered this inscription to be made. May Ahuramazda and the other gods protect me, my kingdom, and what I have made.

"Whoooa - that is so cool." Oz was the first to speak.

"Yeah, Oz, it is," replied Phin. "Very cool, indeed."

Phin went on to explain to Ruth and Oz the story of the book of Esther in the Bible. How a Jewish woman had married the great King Xerxes, the very same man that ordered this carving. And how God had used her influence as the wife of the king of the known world to save the entire Jewish population of Persia from the genocidal schemes of an evil court official named Haman. The inscription also went a generation deeper with the mention of King Darius, who, Phin explained, is mentioned in the biblical books of Haggai, Zechariah, Ezra, and Nehemiah.

"So you're telling me that these same historical figures mentioned by name, carved into this rock - some five hundred years before Christ - are the same men mentioned in the Bible? Amazing. I had no idea." Ruth just stared.

"No idea about what, Ruth?" Phin asked, believing he knew. He just wanted to hear her say it.

"That the Bible was this accurate with its history. I mean I've said I believe in the Bible to a degree. You know...that it contains shades of truth and such. But this...standing here, and seeing something like this and being able to touch it. Something not a part of the Bible at all, but connected so directly to it. It just makes you wonder -"

"What else in the Bible is literally true? Like everything written about the Garden of Eden?" Phin pressed.

"Yes, I suppose that would be the best way to say it."

It was dark now and the group was hungry. Sergeant Warren was waiting for them to return with food. They drove into the town of Van proper and found a small local restaurant close to the airport called, ErKOÇ Cag Kebap. They had no idea what the name meant but it served Turkish food through and through. They ate and then ordered a plate hefty on the meat side for Warren. Returning to the hangar, they found the sergeant had set up a camp of sorts - lights, sleeping roles, etc., all laid out inside. They closed themselves up tight for the night as Billy Warren dug into his dinner, all smiles.

Tomorrow the real adventure would begin.

CHAPTER
THIRTY-FOUR

The next morning, right after sunrise, two Toyota Land Cruisers pulled up in front of the dilapidated hangar. After a night kept awake by the sounds of rats scratching and all kinds of other creepy-crawlies, the GO Team was ready to go. Just as expected, four men exited vehicles. Sergeant Warren met them, and after some discussion that included a lot of broken English and an exchange of some paperwork, he was satisfied these were their men and all was on the up and up. A round of introductions followed. Their names were Raman, Nebez, Eland, and Ako. It was obvious they were Kurdish, which was not a surprise given they were in far eastern Turkey. There is no official nation of Kurdistan, but the area the Kurds consider their homeland extends from eastern Turkey into northwestern Iran. The same area they were headed. As Sergeant Warren had handled the logistics of finding and hiring these men through some of their contacts via the Pentagon, he had been assured these men would be extremely familiar with the terrain they were aiming for.

Although they were a short seventy-five mile straight shot out of Van to the border of Iran, they had no intention of taking this direct route. It would put them in the country too far south of where Phin believed the Garden of Eden was located. The night before in the little barren hangar void of electricity, Phin had gathered the group around by flashlight as they huddled over a map of the region. He reviewed the plan yet again.

"Now that we're finally here, let's go over things one more time. You will see that this map shows terrain, cities, roads, etc. But I've customized this version with an overlay of what the lidar scanner revealed. You can see these bold yellow lines are the extensions of the Tigris and Euphrates Rivers." Phin was drawing along the yellow lines with his finger. "You can see that the ancient and original flow of these rivers brings them together right...here." His finger landed on a junction where the two yellow lines joined together. "This joining together is right on the border of Turkey, Iran, and Armenia. So what we are going to do in the morning is drive north to this little town called Dogubayazil, maybe twenty miles from the shared border with Iran. The road continues on into Iran and crosses the border here. But we are not entering Iran by this route."

"That's right," Sergeant Warren broke in. "It's a major military checkpoint. We are clearly Americans. That, along with the gear we are toting, will get us immediately detained or worse." It was a sobering moment. The mood was instantly heavy as they all realized they were down to serious business. Iran has a history of putting American citizens in prison for little to no reason. A group of seemingly wealthy and well-equipped English speakers would be too tempting for the government not to use as political pawns. They could easily find themselves in an Iranian prison for years.

Phin continued on, "So before we get to the border, we are going to follow this dirt road that hugs the border and takes us into this range of mountains. This is hard and desolate land. You can see that the road is windy and narrow. The good news is that there is absolutely nothing out there. We will make our crossing into Iran here," he was pointing again, "and follow the road, which will dump us out in a valley well south of the checkpoint. We will likely see people, farms, etc. but hopefully no military. In general, this part of the world is no man's land. There's just not much here and hasn't been for many millennia. What we need to do is make our way to where the lidar scanner shows the now ancient remains of this one river." Phin was back to tracing along the yellow line. "At this point it's very simple. We follow this path as it winds its way south toward Lake Urmia - do our best to stay unseen by any locals. Total distance is no more than one hundred fifty miles. It could take a few weeks."

"One big family campout," Sergeant Warren added.

"I hate camping," Oz said. This was clearly not his cup of tea.

"But we won't make it all the way to Lake Urmia, right, Phin? The Bible indicates that the Garden of Eden is along a river, a river that flows *out* of the Garden. There's no mention of a lake."

"That's right, Ruth. If we make it to Lake Urmia -" Phin began.

"Then my good buddy here is wrong!" Max couldn't help himself.

Phin just stared at the map. They were all here because of him. The weight of the whole expedition was ultimately on his shoulders. The eyes of the administration back home at OBU were watching. His career was on the line. But this group believed, sort of. At least Ruth did. She was fully with him. Warren and Oz were there because of her - a financial arrangement, nothing more, nothing less. Max because they were friends, and he felt sorry for Phin. Now, Phin was feeling sorry for himself. Ah well, tomorrow was the day.

"We will find it," Ruth declared. The look in her eyes was hard. She was convinced. Phin was grateful.

By morning the four Kurds had joined the party. The whole group went to work loading the gear into and on top of the Land Cruisers. The vehicles were old, maybe twenty years or more, the sand-colored paint flecking off after years of hard use. But they looked solid enough to Phin, and Sergeant Warren didn't seem concerned. In short order they were on their way.

The GO Team took one vehicle, driven by the sergeant, followed by the second vehicle with the four porters. It took about four hours to cover the distance to Dogubayazil. They arrived around noon, cruising on through town. They didn't need the attention this close to the border with Iran that stopping would bring. They pulled over about five miles outside of town. The other vehicle had stopped in the hamlet and joined them about twenty minutes later with sacks of hot food. This would likely be the last prepared meal the group would eat for weeks. They spent a good hour enjoying their meal and gazing at a massive snow-covered mountain that loomed large to the north. It was so large they felt they were nearly at its base.

Oz had commented as the mountain came into view some miles back, "That is one huge mountain!"

"Mount Ararat," Phin had replied. "The same mountain that Noah's Ark settled on. At least most people believe that's the mountain."

"You mean, *the* Noah? Like from the Bible?" Oz asked, truly in awe.

Max laughed, "Yes, *the* Noah, Oz. Phin's right. That's the mountain. Imagine this whole area, the whole world really, covered in water, and only one man and his family escaping because God told them it was coming. They survive in a massive ship made with their own hands, and then a hundred and fifty or so days later land right over there." Max instructed, pointing at Mount Ararat. "They disembarked as the only humans left alive on the planet to start over, right here, in this same beautiful land we are driving through right now."

"Amazing," added Ruth.

"Yes, it is amazing, isn't it?" Phin chimed in.

"Wouldn't it be so exciting, Phin, to be the only two people left on earth with the responsibility, the privilege, of starting over and repopulating the planet? Sounds like it could be a lot of fun too!" She reached over and took Phin's hand into hers with a naughty look in her eyes. Phin was too shocked to pull away. "They were like a new Adam and Eve. And here we are, headed to find the Garden of Eden, where it all began with the real Adam and Eve. This is all just tremendously exciting."

The awkward moment ended as quickly as it had begun when Phin took his hand back. After they had finished eating lunch and enjoying the majestic view, Sergeant Warren gave them a five-minute warning. Time to depart.

It wasn't fifteen minutes later that they turned off of the paved road. The dirt road was easy enough to find, and they began their trek into the mountains that would lead them across the border. Actually, dirt *path* would have been a more accurate description. Sergeant Warren had been wise in his choice of vehicle. No doubt this was four-wheel country. The going was slow as the group rocked back and forth, the vehicles trudging their way up switchbacks and sharp turns. About an hour in, the altitude had increased significantly, and a drop-off to one side of the road would surely end the expedition and their lives. They stopped every hour to hour-and-a-half to stretch and work out the kinks. All the jostling and hammering of the axles against rocks and potholes was murder on their backs. The Kurds didn't seem any worse for wear. They were likely used to this kind of travel, although it boggled the team's minds that anyone could ever get used to such abuse. Even the sergeant looked a little put out.

Somewhere toward late afternoon they officially crossed into Iran. There was no checkpoint, no sign, no nothing. Just an alert on their GPS. They drove on until an hour before dark, finally stopping to set up camp. This would be the norm for the next couple of days until they joined the location on the map where the lidar scanner had indicated the one ancient riverbed flowing south. It was truly a wasteland where they were. No growth of any kind, thus no firewood, thus no fire. They cranked up some cooking stoves from their gear pack for a hot meal in anticipation of a cold night.

And cold it was, indeed. Phin could not remember a night as cold in his life when he finally extricated himself from his sleeping bag the following morning. Sleep had been impossible, the only upside being that meant no dreams. The rest of the team unfolded themselves as the sun rose, everyone desperate to get warm. Raman, Nebez, Eland, and Ako seemed to be in jovial moods. They fired up the stoves and in short order had a round of coffee for everyone, perfect to heat their inner cores. Breakfast was quick and simple - some bland biscuits and fruit - and they were back on the awful road once again, grateful to crank the heater and cram together for the benefit of shared body heat.

Before lunchtime of their first full day in Iran, they had exited the mountain path and were back at a lower altitude and warmer temperatures. They were south of the border's military checkpoint and were ready to make their way across country to the big yellow line on Phin's map. The dirt road improved considerably and they were able to pick up speed to as much as thirty miles per hour. The main paved highway they had exited in Turkey was a welcome reprieve when it came into view. They would have to cross it and head northeast in order to get to the next leg of the journey, the crossing point being a small unnamed village. Keeping their fingers crossed and heads hunkered down in the seats, they drove straight into the village, turning onto the highway. Their attempts to drive through the village unnoticed were futile.

"Crap, everyone is just stopping and looking," cried Sergeant Warren.

Phin lowered the jacket he was holding next to his head by the window to take a look. It was true. Just like in some movie, every man, woman, and child that was out and about or just sitting on a bench in the shade turned their heads and followed them with their eyes. Some of the kids even chased the two-vehicle convoy, waving their hands and shouting for money. *So much for not attracting attention,* Phin thought. He supposed they'd been crazy to think otherwise. How was it possible for two Toyota Land Cruisers packed with people on the inside and gear on the top racks to roll through any village in this part of the world and go unnoticed? As remote as they were and as primitive as the village looked, one thing Phin observed the people had were cell phones. It was impossible to go anywhere in the world anymore, he thought, and not see people with cell phones. No matter what else a group of people might lack in terms of clean water, food, indoor plumbing, or any other amenities, there would always be cell phones. Several people were actively talking on their phones as the group drove by.

"I hope they're not calling the bad guys," commented Oz.

"Yeah, me too," answered back Sergeant Warren. That was not comforting at all. The sergeant exuded a type of confidence that said he was pretty much ready for anything at any moment. When he got worried, it made the rest of them worried. No one else spoke as they shot through the little town. The other Land Cruiser was right on their bumper as they picked up speed on the pavement and rolled quickly through. In less than a mile they made a left turn back onto another dirt road and barreled out of the village, kicking up dust and dirt as they went. The group began to relax, if just a bit.

They moved along at a quick clip, the road in good condition. They saw no one else and passed no other vehicles. Soon they began to feel very remote. They crossed another paved highway and continued on their dirt path. Eventually the terrain became hillier, and they could tell they were once again rising in altitude. Everywhere they looked it was brown. Gone were the lush green meadows and hills of Turkey. This looked more like high desert. Occasionally Phin caught a glimpse of green in the distance indicating some source of water, but overall it was a barren land.

By evening, the Go Team was firmly in the mountains. As darkness fell, they arrived at a point in the road that intersected with Phin's yellow line on his map, the supposed riverbed where an unnamed river flowed eventually into the Garden of Eden.

"We're here, Sergeant," called out Phin from his middle seat. "Go ahead and let's pull off anywhere around here so we can set up camp for the night."

"*This* is it?" questioned Oz. "This is where the Garden of Eden is? Out here in this wasteland?"

"Well, not here exactly. That area, just up ahead, about fifty yards according to my GPS, is where we will pick up the trail. The Garden itself lies somewhere between here and Lake Urmia, some hundred miles or so to the south. Now the real work begins."

"Sheesh," exhaled Oz. "I should have spent more time on Donkey Kong." Everyone laughed, including Sergeant Warren. He gave the group a thumbs up and jumped out of the vehicle, beginning to give instructions to Raman, who he'd discerned was the leader of their four Kurdish friends. He also spoke the best English. Everyone went to work and soon they had a roadside camp set up and food cooking.

Lasagna was the main course. Raman, Nebez, Eland, and Ako had never eaten the Italian cuisine, and didn't seem to care too much for it. Of course, it had nothing to do with it being freeze dried. Max asked Raman about his family and the families of the other men. He had a wife and two young sons. Nebez's family, a wife and daughter, were killed by ISIS in Iraq where he had lived in Kurdish territory. He alone fled the massacre that had descended upon his village by the black wave of terror. Now he was living in Turkey, trying to carry on, to start over. He looked sad and now the group knew why. Sergeant Billy Warren shared his hatred for the radical Muslim group. Eland was the youngest of the group. Nineteen years old, although he looked to be in his mid-20s. He'd already lived a hard life. He needed the money and was friends with the older Ako, who was married with only a wife and no children. The four were pleasant enough and seemed to enjoy talking about their lives. Max pulled out his phone and showed the men pictures of Shelly and his own two children, Phoebe and Junior. They got a real kick out of the two kids' pictures, especially the ones from Halloween with Phoebe as a princess from one of the Disney movies - Max couldn't remember which - and Junior as a dinosaur.

It was a good night overall and the team talked and laughed well past dark. The sergeant took a walk around the perimeter, maybe thirty or so yards out, all the way around. "I want to get a feel for the area," he had said. When he returned, he suggested that they set up a watch throughout the night.

"We are still on the road, not a main road but it's still a road. You can see other tire tracks so we are not the only ones who've come through here recently. I don't want to be caught off guard while we are snoozing."

This, of course, made perfect sense. Warren himself offered to take the first and last shifts. He didn't need much sleep, he explained. Phin agreed to stand watch from midnight until three o'clock in the morning. With that decision made, Phin asked the sergeant to walk with him around the perimeter. If Phin was going to keep a watch on things, he wanted to familiarize himself just as Warren had. He also wanted to talk privately with the sergeant.

"Something tells me you don't trust our four hired hands," Phin commented as they walked along a path Warren had marked off earlier. They were carrying flashlights, careful to keep an eye out for snakes.

"What makes you say that?"

"Well, I noticed when it came to guard duty for the night, you didn't even remotely look in their direction. You didn't want them taking one of the shifts, did you?"

"Nah, they seem alright. I've been measuring them up since we left. We've got a connection in the Department of Defense back in the States who has a man on the ground in Turkey. He's the one that connected us to these four. He swears by them. That's normally good enough for me. But at the same time, it's not his butt that's in a sling if things aren't all kosher...if you know what I mean. I wanna watch them a few more days, especially now that we are officially off the grid."

"Well, I don't blame you. As far as I'm concerned, it's just the five of us, plus our two eyes in the sky back home when it comes time to need them. I'm grateful for the muscle of our four Kurdish friends, but my trust only goes so far."

"Dang, Doc! You are one paranoid dude, aren't you?"

"No more than you, Sergeant. No more than you."

"Well, I've got your back, Doc. Don't worry about a thing. And if you do start to worry about something, just let me know. Ol' Sarge will take care of things."

"Thanks, Sergeant. I really appreciate it." Phin was grateful. His appreciation and like of Sergeant Billy Warren was growing by the day. He could see why Ruth wanted him close.

"Say! You're okay, you know it, Doc? I wasn't sure at first, but, yeah...you're one of the good ones. Makes me feel kind of bad about that deal at your house. No hard feelings, huh?" Warren stuck out his hand for Phin to take.

Phin stopped dead cold as he met the sergeant's grasp. Confused, he said, "What's that? My house?"

"Crap! Hey, never mind. Look, you need to get some sleep. Midnight will be here before you know it." With that, Warren let go of his hand and walked off into the dark.

Phin made his way back to the group; they were already climbing into their sleeping bags. He grabbed his own and nestled down inside. Next to the fire things were cozy. He couldn't quit thinking about the sergeant's last comment about his house. Still trying to put the pieces together, he drifted off to sleep.

CHAPTER
THIRTY-FIVE

Phin was back and he was exhausted. He'd crested the hill yet again. He was beaten and bruised by unseen forces and by nature itself, which seemed determined to punish him. The dream was always the same. A sea of people waited on the other side of the slope, extending into the distance. They were silent, just staring at him. Just like before, they represented every creed and tongue, every nation it seemed. Flowing away into the distance as far as his eyes could see. Who are these people? Why are they here?

"Phin! Hey Phin!"

Yes! It was Remus. Of course it was Remus. Just like all the other times before. He ran up the same muddy path Phin had climbed and joined his brother in an embrace.

"What are you doing here, little bro?"

"What am I doing here?" replied Phin. "What are you *doing here?"*

"Hey we've..." Remus' voice trailed off as if in thought.

"We've been here before," finished Phin. "That's what you were going to say, isn't it? This place, those people, you and me...this is not the first time."

As recognition dawned on both the brothers, Remus' eyes grew wide. He knew what was coming next.

"RUN!" Remus yelled.

As if reading his mind, Phin had already made a move back the way they'd come. But it was too late. The unseen force pulled him up and back onto the top of the hill and slammed him to the ground. Remus was already screaming. Just as in countless other renditions of the dream, Remus was in the hands of the black-clad punishers. And he knew what was coming next. Phin, for his part, was helpless as always, held to the ground, destined to watch in horror. The one man in black pinned Remus to the ground as he screamed for help.

"NOOO! Please! I beg you...don't do it. No, not again!" he cried and wailed as the other man unzipped the duffle containing the power drill. He extracted it with perverse pleasure and gave it a whirl with the press of his finger.

"Stop! Why are you doing this?!!" Phin cried in a hopeless effort to prevent what they both knew was coming next.

"Phin! Help me, please. Don't let them, Phin! Ohhh! God, please help me!!!" Remus was desperate.

There was a pause. No wind. No noise of any kind. It was as if someone had hit pause on a video playback. Phin felt a warm calm flow over him. And then the word. That word. The same word that came to him over and over, each time he dreamed the dream. Not always at the same time or in the same place. But the word always revealed itself. This time, Phin heard it from somewhere new. This time it came from...within.

REMEMBER.

Phin felt it before he heard it. And then it was in his head.

REMEMBER.

Then it was in his mouth. His lips parted, tongue beginning to work. Phin uttered the word aloud. Slowly, deliberately, "Remember."

And then it was over. Someone unseen hit the play button.

Remus cried out in agony as evil clothed in black bore down on the palm of his hand with the full force of the drill. Phin let loose a guttural cry as he watched his brother buck and kick. The drill bit kicked up bits of skin and blood as it tore through the tiny bones, tendons, and cartilage of a human hand. Remus' hand clinched into an almost fist as his fingers attempted to grab hold of the end of the drill even as it did its damage. The devastation ended only as the bit of the drill came poking through the backside of his hand. The man working the drill backed it out quickly and then stood to his feet, staring down at Remus as if he was inspecting his fine work. Remus only moaned and then moved into a fetal position as the other man climbed off of him. He was cradling his mangled hand.

Phin hoped against all hope that it was over. That this nightmare had reached its conclusion. It was not to be so.

WHACK! It was a vicious kick to the head that signaled the beginning of whatever was coming next. Remus scrambled to get away, but both men dove in, delivering blow after blow.

All Phin could do was cry, tears streaming down his face. He continued to be held to the ground, unable to move by the unseen force that seemed to be directing this whole awful scene.

"I'm sorry, Remus," he croaked out. "I'm so sorry." He wasn't even sure if his brother could hear him.

The blows stopped and the man who had drilled the hole in Remus' hand fell on top of his brother. The two men dressed in black were trading places! The other took up the drill and went to work on Remus' other hand.

"NNNNOOOOO!!!!!!" cried out Remus.

"Ohhh...noooo...." Phin whispered though his tears. *"Please, God, make it stop. Please have mercy."*

The horror continued in a methodical manner. *Having finished drilling holes in each of Remus' hands, they turned their attention to his feet. Stripping him of his shoes and socks, they worked against what little strength Remus had left to run the wicked power tool through the bones and flesh of each foot.* The blood flowed freely. Remus was a mess when it was finished. His brother said nothing. He was curled up in a ball, shaking and moaning.

And then...what? The men pulled a chain saw out of the duffle. They fired the saw up in all its awful glory, smoke and fumes spitting from its exhaust. *What are they going to do with that? Not my brother, Phin thought. Please, no. Not Remus.*

The saw was not meant for Remus. Mysteriously, the men went to work on the one tree that stood on top of the hill. It was a large oak of some kind and it took time for them to fell it. More tools came from the duffle as they used wedges and hammers and handsaws to cut and split the logs and fashion its wood.

Oh. No.

Phin knew what was coming before it became clear. He looked up into the sky, begging it to not be so.

A cross.

The men fashioned a cross and then turned their attention back to Remus who had been oblivious to what was going on around him. They grabbed him and peeled his body apart, forcing him to uncurl.

"No!" he spit out. *"No. No. No. No. No!!!"* He was kicking and writhing. Trying to work his way out of their hands. It didn't matter. Remus was beaten and drilled and helpless and hopeless.

Phin was bucking against the force holding him to the ground as well. His situation was just as hopeless. *There was nothing he could do.* Pathetically, he watched as they fastened his brother to a cross.

They left the cross lying on the ground with Remus fixed to it. They backed away, admiring their work.

Now what? Phin thought. What more could they do?

He didn't have to wait long to find out. One of the men in black walked over to the duffle and picked up the drill. He tested it with two squeezes of his finger. VWEEE! VWEEE!

Satisfied, both men began to walk in Phin's direction.

"NOOOOOOO!"

CHAPTER
THIRTY-SIX

Phin shot awake with a jerk. To his surprise he found himself staring into the eyes of Ruth LaPhage.

"Shhh..." she whispered. "It's okay. I'm here." He could smell the sweet aroma of her breath and he found it instantly intoxicating. Her face was just inches from his, a visage of pure beauty. His heart was beating fast and hard, overcome by the experience of this new version of his dreams - more horrible than he could ever have imagined. But looking into the eyes of Ruth, the tenderness and compassion, and what was that? Yes...understanding. Phin found himself unable to tear himself away from her gaze as they lay on the ground next to each other and the still smoldering campfire. They were each in their own sleeping bag, although she had maneuvered her body to lean against his. Oz and Max were fast asleep as were the porters. Sergeant Warren was patrolling the perimeter. He could feel the warmth from her, and it was soothing. His heart began to calm, and still he stared.

Then....she kissed him. A soft, tender kiss that lasted for but a moment.

As she pulled her lips from his, she moved even closer and nuzzled her head into the fold of his neck and chest. Phin's heart raced again. *What is happening? This is wrong. I'm a married man. Autumn is waiting on me.* All of these thoughts raced through Phin's mind. He knew what he must do.

"I'm sorry, Ruth. I can't." She pulled her head up to look into his eyes once more. He was certain she would try to kiss him again if he stayed.

"Please, forgive me," he said. "My life is so complicated. There is so much going on, so much I must sort out. And I have to do it alone. I can't do this. It's not right."

There was hurt in her eyes and Phin felt guilty. But for what? What had he done? Before he thought about it a moment longer, before he was tempted to change his mind, he rolled away and sat up. Without looking back at her, he unzipped from his bag and stood up. The cold air beckoned him to return to the heat of her embrace, but he dared not make that move. Phin glanced at his watch. 11:45 p.m. It was nearly time for his shift, and he decided to relieve Sergeant Warren a few minutes early.

The next morning the GO Team began a repack of their gear in preparation for the coming days ahead. It was time to walk. Nothing was said between Ruth and Phin about the previous night. She acted perfectly normal when she woke up, greeting him along with the rest of the crew. She was her good-natured self. It made Phin wonder if it had happened at all, or if the whole exchange - the kiss - had been part of his dreams too. Ah well, it didn't matter now. Whatever happened - if anything *did* happen - meant nothing at all. He was here for a purpose. He was supposed to lead their group of five to the Garden of Eden.

Billy had put together five packs of hiking gear. The plan was not complicated. They would follow the big yellow line on Phin's map. This was the line that represented a supposed ancient river that would flow to the Garden of Eden. They would be walking upstream, although the river itself no longer existed. Just the remnants visible only in the lidar scanner report that Phin had produced. They were one hundred miles north of Lake Urmia where this ancient river would have had its source. The Garden of Eden must be located between where they stood now and the Lake. The goal would be to hike ten miles a day. Some days would be easier than others with the terrain and all. For the most part the geography was barren and brown, so anything green they ran across would be something to check out carefully. Beyond that, they really didn't know what they were looking for. It wouldn't be easy, Phin knew. If it was easy, the Garden would have been found ages ago. So while the plan itself was simple, they really had no idea what lay before them.

Oz Jenks pulled up his computer and made a satellite connection back to LaPhage Industries in Texas. He checked in with his tech-twin Tony Chen and also Dr. Mark Sayer, as he did each day. Now that they had arrived at this stage of the expedition, both of these men would be on call 24/7 in case they actually found the Garden of Eden. Phin and Max still didn't understand how they could be of any benefit to the group this far away, but Ruth had assured them both that their connection would be vital when the time came. Sergeant Warren followed that assessment with a firm, "Just trust her, okay?!" And that was enough to not bring it up anymore.

Warren had given a copy of the map to their Kurdish porters, one without the yellow line. They didn't want anyone to know the path they were taking. Phin had been insistent on that part, and he got no resistance. Working with Raman, Warren had identified a rendezvous point about fifty miles to the south. The four hired hands would stay back at this base camp that they had established. They would watch over the two Land Cruisers and the heavier gear, including the big rectangular crate that Phin and Max still puzzled over. In four days time, they would drive the back trails and wait for the GO Team at the agreed-upon spot. It would take the Go Team five to six days to get there by foot. That is where the group would resupply with food and prepare to carry on the hike if they did not find the Garden of Eden before then. If they did find the Garden, then they would take their time exploring and documenting, and then meet the porters at the same spot to aim for their exit out of Iran. Much of it would have to be played by ear, they knew. But at least it was a plan.

Shaking hands with the Kurds, everyone was all smiles as the GO Team threw on their packs and began the long walk away from their first base camp. The day was pleasant as the air temperature warmed under the spring sun. The hiking was easy and everyone in the group was generally in a good mood. The only one that complained was Oz. He was clearly not built for anything like what they were doing, and he looked rather silly in his oversized cargo pants, uncomfortable hikers, and green Incredible Hulk t-shirt. He wore a floppy, wide-rimmed tan hat with a string that dangled under his chin, while continually struggling with his backpack, which actually looked smaller and lighter than the rest of the crew's. Everyone else looked like they knew what they were doing - from the way they were dressed to the way they handled their packs - like they actually fit the roles they were playing in this little adventure.

The next four days were completely uneventful. Lots of walking. Lots of dry, desolate land. A few signs of life, every so often, as small farms were spotted in the distance. Farm would be a generous term. Usually tiny patches of green, probably growing just enough food for a family or two. A few livestock, maybe a scrawny cow or goat, a clump of chickens. Not much else. The group talked about all manners of subjects. They even sang songs. And then there were long stretches of silence. They covered a lot of ground easily, hitting their ten-mile-a-day goal.

On the evening of the fourth day, as the group was sitting around the campfire after a "delicious" dinner of rice and steak chunks in sauce, Ruth asked a surprising question.

"So, Max and Phin, as theologians, would you mind me asking you both a question I've been thinking a lot about lately?"

The two friends looked curiously at Ruth. They weren't used to the idea of them as "theologians" being the qualifier for their evening campfire discussions.

"Well sure, Ruth," Max replied.

"Go for it. I'm sure with our combined brain power we can answer what it is that's been on your mind," Phin said lightly.

"Great. Now don't laugh because it's an odd question, but I'll elaborate shortly. So what I'd like to know is this: What exactly is evil?"

This was not what anyone expected. Eyebrows around the circle rose, and the question even got the attention of Sergeant Warren and Oz.

Warren put down the knife he'd been using to whittle a piece of wood and leaned back. "Oh, this oughta be good," he said.

Max deferred to Phin. "Evil. Well, let's see," Phin began rubbing his chin. He had been stuffing a plug of tobacco into his favorite travel pipe, taking time to light it and draw on the stem, releasing a cloud of aromatic smoke before continuing. "Most people ask the *why* question. Why is there evil? Especially in the context of the existence of God and the belief that God is loving and good. Why, then, is there evil? Or why is there so *much* evil? But your question, Ruth, is more basic...more foundational really." Phin was getting warmed up, trying to buy himself a few minutes to gather his thoughts as to how he wanted to approach the answer. "I suppose the simplest, most direct answer is that evil exists because of free will."

"Bravo!" Max applauded. "Exactly what I would have said." Phin rolled his eyes at the fun his friend was having watching him handle the question.

"Free will," Ruth replied in thought. She was twirling a strand of red hair around her left index finger, thinking on Phin's answer. "So unpack the whole free will thing for me. How exactly does that work? And how does that answer the question of: *What* exactly is evil?"

"Well, oddly enough, this whole discussion is going to take us back to the Garden of Eden." The mention of the Garden only served to draw everyone in closer, hooked on Phin's every word. He continued, "You see, according to Genesis, at the beginning of time you had Adam and Eve living in the Garden of Eden, which was a literal paradise on earth. No sickness, no death, no suffering, nothing. Nothing that we would consider or label as evil. Mankind lived in perfect harmony and relationship with God. But then things went bad. Real bad."

"But how?" Oz broke in with the question. "If everything was good and perfect - a paradise, as you say - then where did the idea of 'bad' come from? I'm not sure that makes sense."

"Free will. That's what I'm getting at, Oz," Phin answered back. "The story of the fall of mankind begins with Adam and Eve living in a state of perfect harmony until one day when Eve has a conversation with a serpent."

"Okay, talking snakes! Listen to yourself, Doc. This is where all that Bible stuff you believe in starts sounding like something written by crazy people. And you gotta be crazy to buy it!" No one would ever accuse Billy Warren of being reverent when it came to talking about God or the Bible.

"Not just any serpent, Sergeant," Max shot back. "Let Phin continue."

"That's right," Phin went on. "This snake had been inhabited - taken over - by the spirit of a fallen angel, now turned master demon. You may have heard the name Satan before. That's who we're talking about."

"But how did this happen?" Ruth asked. "If the world, creation, whatever...if it's all perfect, how do you end up with, what did you call it? A fallen angel?"

"Free will. That's what I'm trying to say. It's all - evil that is - it's all traced back to free will. You see, when God created the angels, he created them with this thing called free will. Free will is the free option that all created beings have to either say *yes* or say *no* to God. Since God is good, and in him is no darkness, then saying *yes* to God is a good thing, and good things flow from God's creatures when they freely say *yes* by their own choice. And the exact opposite is true. When God's created beings say *no* to God, that's a bad thing. And bad things - all kinds of really bad things - happen when *no* is the answer to God. No is an act of rebellion against a good God. There is nothing good in saying *no* to God. In short, saying *no* to God is the seed from which evil is born. And that seed of evil was planted in the Garden of Eden by the serpent. The next thing we know, Eve, another of God's creations, exercises her free will to rebel against God, and she convinces her husband, Adam, to join her. From that point forward, evil begins to work and spread. Adam and Eve's relationship with God is broken. Paradise is lost, to quote Milton. God comes looking for them but they are hiding from him. They are ashamed at what they'd done. And here's the thing - the whole concept of shame was unknown until Adam and Eve exercised their free will to disobey God."

"Wait, wait, wait," it was Warren again. "What exactly did they do that was so bad? What was this freewill choice they made that messed everything up?"

Max jumped in to answer. "God had given Adam and Eve one rule. He told them not to eat from a certain tree in the center of the Garden. The Tree of the Knowledge of Good and Evil - that was its name. They could eat the fruit from every other tree - just not that one. And that was exactly what they did."

"They ate a piece of fruit off of a tree?!" Warren was incredulous. "That was their big sin? They didn't smoke pot or look at porn or get drunk and go chariot driving or anything like that? They just ate a piece of fruit? Man, I gotta tell you, that's ridiculous. Talking snakes and fruit that will send you to hell. This kind of stuff is exactly why I don't believe any of it. It doesn't even make sense."

"The point is not the fruit, Sergeant," it was Phin countering back at him. "The point is that God had established a rule. Just one law that had to be obeyed or not obeyed...by free will. It was sort of a test. Would the first man and woman trust God or not? Would they believe that he truly had the best in his mind and heart for them? Or would they believe the lie, that God was holding out on them and that they were missing something better? You see, I think the whole idea of making one tree off limits was brilliant on God's part. It was brilliantly simple. God didn't make trusting in him hard. There were not a bunch of hoops to jump through or a bunch of laws to follow. Only one. And they couldn't even get that one rule right. Their free will gave them the option of disobeying God, and that's exactly what they did. The rest of the Bible is all about the fallout of that choice to rebel against God. Evil entered the world. So the answer to your question, Ruth...what exactly is evil? The answer is this: Evil is everything broken and bad that we experience in this world because of the freewill choices of mankind."

"Why doesn't God just stop it? Free will, I mean." Oz was back, questioning again. "If God is all-powerful, then why does he put up with free will and all the junk - or, I mean evil - that comes with it. Wouldn't the loving thing be to get rid of free will and get rid of the evil?"

"Well, that's a really good question, Oz. What I'd say is this: God allows free will because that is the only way that love can be genuine."

"Okay, you lost me. We're talking about evil and now you're talking about love."

"Look at this way: Free will works both ways. We can freely choose to run *from* God or we can choose to run *to* God, to love him. Obviously, what God wants is for us to run *to* him and to love him. But without free will, that choice to love him wouldn't be a choice at all. We'd all be like pre-programmed robots. There would be zero satisfaction for God in that. I mean, would you really want a woman to love you, Oz, just because you gave her some love potion and she lost all ability to *freely* choose to love you?" Oz was shaking his head.

"I would!" It was Warren. "Sign me up for Love Potion #9!" Phin went on, ignoring his outburst and laughter.

"Of course you wouldn't. The only guarantee that love is genuine is if it's freely chosen. Free will. That's the key. God takes a risk, and evil is the result when we rebel, but the payoff of love is worth it."

Ruth was staring into the flames of the fire as Phin concluded and took a long puff on his pipe. After a few moments of silence Phin finally asked, "So what are you thinking, Ruth?"

"I'm thinking it makes sense..." her voice faded away. Her gaze was still transfixed on the fire, her mind clearly somewhere else.

Carefully, Phin asked in a soft voice, "What makes sense?"

"My father," her gaze broke from the fire and she looked up at Phin. "My father has seen things. He's told me things and everything you've said tonight is finally starting to make sense."

"I thought your father was incapacitated. What kinds of things is he seeing and talking about?" Phin questioned carefully. He knew the whole subject of Charles LaPhage's condition was a sensitive topic with her.

Ruth had a decision to make, but she had already decided. "Hold on a minute. I need to show you something." She got up and went to her pack, digging through it as if looking for something. Having found what she was looking for, she returned to the warmth of the fire with a journal.

"I am going to share with you all something that is extremely personal. Very private." She settled in between Max and Phin and opened the journal. "My father, Charles LaPhage, his condition is...complicated. It's difficult to explain, but he sees things. Or I suppose I should say that he has dreams. Wild fantastic dreams." At the mention of dreams, Phin became nervous. Max looked over at his friend. They were both thinking the same thing.

"Go on, Ruth," Max urged. "We are safe. I promise."

"Yes, I believe you. Thank you, Max. Oz and Billy, you are not to talk about anything I'm about to share. Do we all agree?"

"Yes, Ma'am," Warren was quick to answer. Oz nodded.

"As I said, for some time, my father has been having dreams or visions. The images are bizarre but they all surround the subject of the Garden of Eden. I believe my father has seen it, or at least the edge of it. I've written down in my journal some of these images and the things he says. Sometimes he will slip into a trance and utter out rhymes of sorts. It's all recorded in here. He talks about a war between God and Evil. I think I understand that part now. Thank you," she looked at Phin with sincerity. "He says that the Tree of Life is the gateway. I don't know what that means: gateway. He says it's the key to the war. Do you have any idea?"

"I'm not sure. The Tree of Life is many times associated with eternal life," Phin replied.

"Yes! That's what he said. It's right here." She was pointing to a specific line in the journal as she read, "*It is the gateway to eternal life.* Those were my father's exact words. I don't believe in eternal life myself, but that's not important right now. Do either of you know what Jacob's Ladder is?"

"It's the link between earth and heaven," Max was talking now. "It appears in Genesis 28 when the Hebrew patriarch Jacob fell asleep one evening. He had a vision of a ladder extending up into heaven. He heard the voice of God telling him that the land he was sleeping on was going to be given to him and his descendants. That land would become what you and I know of today as Israel. Does your father mention Jacob's Ladder?"

"Yes! He says that *you must climb Jacob's Ladder to find the Tree of Life,*" Ruth read from the journal again. "But he's not talking about the nation of Israel is he? What does this mean?"

"I have no idea," Phin replied. "What else do you have, Ruth?"

"I have these - I guess you would call them poems. Here, let me just read them to you and tell me if you can make any sense of them:

Follow the River to the end of the sun,
Beware the eagle, the sword, the gun.
No man may enter, no man may leave,
You'll find healing and hell
from the fruit of the Tree.

And then this one:

> *The rivers converge on the cradle of life,*
> *Only those called can trespass without strife.*
> *Adam and Eve are reborn anew,*
> *You must find passage through the guardian*
> *To join the few.*

"What kind of sense can you make of this? Does it mean anything to you at all?" She was clearly stressed, looking for some kind of understanding into the mind of her father.

"Let me look, if it's okay," Phin asked, reaching for the journal. He read it all again. *Follow the river. Rivers converge.* That made sense. That's what they were doing now. *Eagle, sword, gun.* Sorry, no clue. *Healing and hell.* Obviously this was a dangerous undertaking, but with great reward at stake. *You must find passage through the guardian.* He knew it would be difficult, if even possible at all, to enter the Garden. Breaching the entrance of the Garden of Eden had never been Phin's goal. Ruth, on the other hand was fixated on it. She wanted the fruit from the Tree of Life. After hearing of her father's obsession and dreams he now understood where that came from. *Adam and Eve are reborn anew.* That made no sense at all. Overall, more questions than answers.

Phin took time to unpack all of these thoughts to Ruth as the rest of the team listened. "I'm not sure what to do with all of this, Ruth," he said as he concluded his evaluation of the journal material. He wasn't even sure if what he was reading were the thoughts of a sane man, yet there were enough clues that indicated something might be going on with Charles LaPhage that went beyond their ability to understand. "We may not fully understand what your father is

313

telegraphing to us until we arrive at the Garden of Eden itself. As they say: hindsight is 20/20."

"Well that brings up a more pressing issue, boys and girls." Sergeant Warren couldn't resist jumping in. "Tomorrow we will rendezvous with our Kurdish friends. That means we are halfway to Lake Urmia. In other words, we are halfway to this whole operation being a bust, Doc."

"Or over halfway to the entrance of the Garden of Eden," Ruth countered, ever the optimist.

"All I'm sayin' is if we make it to Lake Urmia and we've not found a patch of green out here, then none of this means anything. No offense, Doc, but a theory's only as good as what it produces in the real world."

Sergeant Billy Warren was right. The pressure was building and Phin could feel it. The next six to seven days would put his credibility to the ultimate test. Phin was ready and he knew what was coming. He relit his pipe for one final smoke before stowing it and heading to bed.

CHAPTER THIRTY-SEVEN

"My feet are absolutely killing me!" Max had drifted to the back of their little five-man team to join Phin who was bringing up the rear. "How did I ever let you talk me into this?"

"Because you love me so much! And remember, you're here to keep me out of trouble," Phin jabbed back while casting an eye about fifteen yards ahead where Ruth LaPhage was in the lead.

"Well if we don't find this Garden of yours, you're gonna be in a heap of trouble that even I can't bail you out of," Max's tone had turned serious. "You know we are on the edge here, don't you Phin? I mean, I can't imagine there being any kind of life out here, much less a paradise on earth. I don't know man - I was hopeful when we started this little venture, but now that we are here and about halfway to the end of the line, it just doesn't feel very good...."

The pair walked along in silence. It was a warmer day than the last few, and the group was huffing as the terrain rose somewhat. For the most part they'd followed the natural flow of a series of valleys. It was easy to see that a river could have flowed in this region at one time. Their lack of progress had caused most of them to complain about their feet from walking, and shoulders from carrying the heavy packs. The only one who showed no sign of weakness was Sergeant Billy Warren. Predictable.

As if the long days of walking and the warmer temperatures weren't enough to sour moods, things got much worse when they reached their stopping point for the day - still no sign of a green lush Garden anywhere.

"Hey, where are they?" barked Oz. All he had talked about all day was how he was going to dive into the stash of candy bars and Mountain Dew he'd brought along but left with the vehicles. The Go Team had been able to spot the rendezvous point while they were a good half-mile away because the terrain had become flat with nothing to block sightlines. Max was the first to comment that he had a bad feeling when there was no sign of the two Land Cruisers in the distance. Finally, Oz had popped and let fly the question they were all asking in the sinking pits of their stomachs.

"Oh, this is not good, guys. This is not good," Oz continued.

"So much for being trustworthy," Phin spat. He'd thought something like this could happen but had not wanted to believe it actually would. As they arrived at the exact spot on the map where the four hired Kurds were to meet them, it was clear they were nowhere to be found, nor had they been there at all. There was zero sign of tire tracks, or any other kind of activity for that matter. They were all alone.

"Maybe they are just late. Is that possible, Billy?" Ruth asked the sergeant who had already pulled out his binoculars and was scanning the horizon in all directions.

"No, ma'am. We've clearly been hosed. They were supposed to be here a full day ahead of us, and they had been instructed to wait indefinitely for us in case we found the doc's hidden Garden and needed time to survey it. Nope. Something has definitely gone wrong."

"Well, what are we going to do about it? We can't die out here!" Oz was reaching near hysterics. "Somebody has to do something!" Sergeant Warren turned and slapped the tech whiz upside the head. Hard. His hat flew off, leaving Oz stunned.

"Pull your crap together, soldier! What we have here is a situation and we will WORK. THE. SITUATION. Am I understood?" Sergeant Warren towered over Oz who, for his part, didn't say a word but responded with a half-hearted salute. "That'll do. Now pick up your hat so you don't get sunburned. Don't need you turning wussy on me because you get a little red on the head. No offense, Ruthie." It was a serious situation, but all anyone wanted to do was laugh at the manner in which Warren had taken control. There was actually some measure of comfort in him exuding confidence in the midst of a very bad turn of events.

"So what do you propose, Sergeant?" asked Phin. "I think we're all open to your guidance in a situation like this."

"Well, I think this puts an end to our search for the Garden of Eden for starters," Max said. "Clearly we can't go on without our resupply of food and water."

"No way," thundered the sergeant in response to Max. "The mission goes on."

"I don't see how," Max shot back. "Look, Sergeant, we're not military like you. We are just regular people. We're not trained for something like what we have now."

"Look," Warren directed to Max, but he was speaking to the whole Go Team. "Our options are limited, but those limited options shouldn't change anything about our objective. We will be fine on food and water for a couple of days, easy. We packed extra meals for at least the next two days and longer if we ration. There are plenty of water sources along the way, just like we've seen the last week. Maybe they're mud holes, but your iodine tablets will take care of any creepy-crawlies you don't want in your digestive system."

"Along what way?" Phin asked. "Which way are you talking about?"

"The way forward, Doc. Nothing changes, do you hear me? You all will follow the same path we've been following. The yellow brick road on your special scanner map. That's the quickest route to Lake Urmia and civilization – a.k.a., our way out of here."

"But we don't have enough supplies to make it fifty more miles. We'll die out here in the middle of nothing," Max continued, unconvinced.

"No you won't. Because your gonna find the doc's magic Garden full of all kinds of fruits and vegetables. Isn't that right, Doc? And even if you don't - and I for one highly doubt you will, but what I think doesn't matter - but even if you don't, you will start hitting scattered farms and pockets of life ten to fifteen miles from the lake. You all can absolutely walk thirty-five miles if you have to."

"Wait, you keep saying *you*, Billy, not *we*. What are you thinking about yourself?" asked Ruth.

"Glad you asked, Ruthie. I'm gonna go that direction," Warren said, pointing off to the west. "Maybe those punks broke down, or maybe they can't read a map and are lost. But just in case they're out there, that's the direction they would have to be. If I find them, all is well. We will catch up to you. Ozzie, you'll take one sat phone and I'll take the other, and we will call each other every two hours to check in. If I don't find them in two days, then I will hoof it at an angle and catch up with you before you make the lake. Everybody got it?"

And everybody did get it. Sergeant Billy Warren was one hundred percent correct in his assessment and in his plan. Nothing else made sense but to keep going. It was their best chance to still find the Garden of Eden. But more importantly, it was their best chance of getting out alive.

The next morning the team sat somberly as they ate a scant breakfast of stale biscuits and dehydrated fruit chips, rationing already on their minds. Warren left right at sunrise as the rest of the Go Team began their trek, following the yellow line on Phin's map to the south once more.

They walked for two days.

Two days with no sign of anything. After the first day their fresh water was gone and they began to drink out of the mud holes, as the sergeant had called them. They ate as little as possible and hiked as quickly as their legs would carry them. It seemed clear to everyone in their now foursome - although no one dared to actually verbalize it - that the primary goal was now Lake Urmia and not the Garden of Eden. Even Ruth's ever-present optimism had seemed to dim. Her flirtatious overtures to Phin had stopped completely.

Then came day three. Two things happened - one bad and one good. When Oz wasn't able to reach the sergeant on the sat phone he knew it was bad. They'd been making sat phone connections every two hours except when they slept. Warren had seen no sign of the four Kurds or their two vehicles.

"I'm gonna spend the first half of tomorrow going a little further, and if I don't see nothin' then I'm gonna hump it double-time to catch up with you all." Warren had told Oz his plans the night before. But when Oz woke and made the morning call, Warren didn't answer. His panic rose as he tried multiple times with still no answer.

"Come on, Billy! Answer your phone!" Oz shouted. Ruth moved quickly to try to reassure him. Maybe he was still asleep. Or maybe his battery in his phone was dead. Or...and that was just it. No excuse they could think of seemed plausible. Not for a man like Sergeant Warren. The whole group was worried beyond words. Even though he'd not been physically with them since they'd split up, just the presence of Billy Warren was enough to give them all a dose of confidence that everything was going to turn out all right. Not being able to reach him was definitely a bad thing.

But a good thing followed close on its heels. As the group ate lunch on a small rise overlooking another shallow valley, Ruth had taken up their shared pair of binoculars and was fixated on something in the distance. The others talked and tried to find some lighthearted moments, but their thoughts were not far from what could possibly have happened to the sergeant.

"Ruth, you seem to have found something interesting. Mind sharing with the rest of us?" asked Phin. There was no response. After another moment, all three of them noticed her fixation. Phin asked again, "Ruth?"

"I think you should look at this, Phin. Maybe my eyes are playing tricks on me, but I don't think so." She handed the binoculars to Phin.

"What exactly am I looking for?" He was staring in the direction she'd been looking but wasn't sure he had a bead on her target.

Pointing, she indicated, "Right out there. Zoom completely in. Full power. I think you'll -"

"Holy cow! It's green! And a lot of it," he exclaimed.

"Yes, it is, isn't it?!" Ruth stood up. Without the help of the binoculars, there was no way she could make it out from this distance, but she continued to stare in the direction Phin was looking nonetheless.

"What's green, what are you seeing?" Max was on his feet as well.

"Something we definitely need to check out!" Phin was excited as he lowered the binoculars. "Everyone grab your packs. We don't have any time to waste!"

They needed no prodding. They flew down the rise. It was difficult not to run, and they had to work to contain their enthusiasm. Whatever they had seen was less than a mile away, but still far enough that they'd not seen it without some help. The fact that whatever they had seen was not directly along the path of their yellow line was not a problem for them either. What they needed right now, more than anything, was hope.

Half an hour later they were close. And the closer they got, the slower they began to walk. Ruth's heart was racing. Could this be it? Unfolding in front of them was a deep-cut valley full of lush green foliage. It reminded her of the jungles of South America she had visited once as a little girl. Clearly, what they had seen from the binoculars back on the rise was but a hint of what lay in front of them now. It would have been easy to miss unless it was stumbled upon. Max found that he had quit breathing, and he had to remind himself to inhale. A cool breeze wafted up from the trees in front of them, a nice relief to what was turning into a hot day.

"I can hear water running," Ruth said excitedly. "A river, Phin, just like you said!"

They continued their approach cautiously. Wasn't there suppose to be a guardian of some sort? Isn't that what the Bible said? But there was nothing indicating they couldn't just walk on in. They found a game trail that led down and into the forest, then disappeared quickly.

Phin was stunned. He'd believed and convinced others to believe, yet now that the moment had arrived, he couldn't help but think this was too good to be true. Had they really found the Garden of Eden? It had not been easy, yet it had not been that hard either. Something didn't feel right.

"Let's just be careful, everyone," Phin cautioned. He was the first to take a step onto the path, followed by the others. In minutes they were swallowed by the thick growth all around them. Their world had been transformed. Gone was the desert and its desolation. The sound of running water grew. Birds flew overhead, some with marvelous colors. The vibrancy of the foliage around them was like walking into a world of high definition 3D after living in a world of black and white. It felt...peaceful, even tranquil. The stress of the last week began to fall away from all four of them. All the hiking, sore feet and blisters, the crummy rations they'd been eating, the nasty water. None of it seemed to matter at this moment in time.

"My goodness, it's beautiful!" Max exclaimed. "Phin, my good friend, I'm sorry for everything I ever said to make fun of you. I think you may have been right all along, I think we may have found it." He put his arm around Phin and gave him a brotherly squeeze.

In short order they came upon the source of the running water they'd heard at the forest's edge. A small stream was pouring over a cascade of rocks, creating a small roar. The water was crystal clear. Oz was the first to throw his pack to the ground as he fell to his knees and plunged his whole head into the stream, taking in a long, cool drink.

"Oh man, that is good!" He whipped out of the water with a wild shake of his head and a whoop. "You guys have to get over here." And they did. Phin couldn't remember a more satisfying drink of water in his life.

"So what do we do now?" asked Max.

"We explore," Ruth was quick to reply. "This is it, gentlemen. This is what we came for. This *must* be the Garden of Eden. After the days and miles in what is clearly an inhospitable land, there is no explanation for why this...Garden is here, other than it's special. Look how hidden it is. I would have missed it had I not seen the tiniest line of green back on the rise. I *should* have missed it really. There's nothing out here. No road, trails, nothing. We are completely isolated from the world. We just need to take our time and see what we can find in this little piece of heaven."

"Paradise," muttered Phin.

"Yes," Ruth eased over next to Phin and took his hand with a squeeze. "Paradise it is."

The team filled their water containers and even took time to sponge bathe themselves. It had been too long since any of them had taken a shower, and they were surely smelling ripe. Refreshed, they waded across the stream and began to work their way deeper into the forest. There was no sign of human trespass that they could tell, yet the ground was not so overgrown that they couldn't easily maneuver and make good time exploring.

"Hey check out these palm trees!" Oz cried as he ran deeper into the Garden.

"Stay close, Oz!" Phin called to him.

"Not just any palm tree," he cried back, "these have some kind of fruit on them!"

Ruth rushed forward, "They're dates! And look, a bunch of them are lying around on the ground." She picked one up and took a bite.

"Wait, Ruth!" Phin was crying as he ran to her side.

"Oh, Phin, it's delicious! Here you must try one," she said, handing Phin another one.

"We have to be careful, Ruth. We can't just grab whatever we see and start eating," he cautioned.

"Oh, relax, will you? They're just dates. And we can use the energy. I promise, it's the best thing you've eaten since we left home." He relaxed and took the fruit and, sinking his teeth into one, had to agree. Sweetness and juice exploded in his mouth, like the soothing taste of honey.

"Oh my, that is really good." He admitted.

"Told you!" she said and then gave him a hug. Finding this oasis of paradise had certainly reignited her flirtatious ways toward Phin.

The group had their fill of dates, and then they noticed not far away, a grove of fig trees. It was the same as before. Wonderful fruit that was delicious to the taste buds. Those weren't the only fruit trees they found either. As they ventured deeper into the depths of the forest they found patches of wild grape vines and trees bearing olives, pomegranates, and almonds.

"Look, there's a patch over here of muskmelons. This place is unbelievable," Max called out. It *was* unbelievable. The team darted from one location to another, sampling nature's best. The whole thing reminded Phin of the scene from *Willie Wonka and the Chocolate Factory* when the winning children with the golden tickets first entered the factory and went crazy over all of the candy everywhere. That's what this felt like, only better.

"We need to keep going everyone," Ruth encouraged. "This place is huge and we have no idea how long it will take to explore it all." Refreshed and refueled, they all agreed, ready to see what else lay ahead.

The afternoon slipped by quickly and what they found was more. More of everything. They crossed a few more small streams, found more of the same fruits along with some they didn't recognize and were cautious not to eat. Ruth insisted they collect samples of everything to take back home. The sky darkened earlier in the Garden because of the canopy they were under. They decided they didn't have any choice but to make camp and build a fire in preparation to spend the night. That was fine with them. The prospect of sleeping in their private paradise was much more welcome than the dry dusty ground they'd endured since their arrival in this region of the world. They'd seen a few small animals - a couple of varieties of squirrels and some rabbits - but no sign of anything that looked dangerous. The team felt perfectly safe.

That would soon change.

CHAPTER

THIRTY-EIGHT

Phin woke from his sleep soaked in sweat. Again. He had no idea what time it was. It was dark and their small fire was only still smoldering with a few embers left glowing. Another dream. Worse than all the ones before. *What are you doing, God?* Phin prayed. He rubbed his hands together. They were sore to the touch, as were the tops and bottoms of his feet. This was crazy. What kind of dream manifested physically in the real world? But Phin had decided a long time ago these weren't ordinary dreams. He didn't know how much more he could take. He had to get to the bottom of it all and soon.

"AHHHH!!! Get it off! Get it off of me...somebody help!" Phin sat up fast as Oz cried out, flailing around in his sleeping bag. Ruth and Max had also bolted awake. Oz was trying desperately to free himself from his bag.

Phin was quickly by his side. "It's okay, Oz. You're just having a bad dream!"

"Oooww! It's biting me! Get it off!" It wasn't a dream at all. Oz's hand emerged from his sleeping bag holding a large black snake, hissing and flailing as much as Oz himself. He flung it aside in the direction of Ruth and Max, who scrambled to get away from the slithering creature.

"Snake!" cried Ruth. "Somebody kill it!"

"I got it!" Max was quick to his feet, already holding a machete the group had used to clear foliage and chop firewood. He danced up to the snake that was already working its way toward the edge of the camp, trying to make its escape. WHACK! The blade came down, cleanly severing its head from its body. "It's okay everybody. We're all good. He's dead."

"No we aren't," replied Phin. "Oz has been bitten." Phin was leaning over Oz, who was sitting up now; they both were examining his lower leg. Somebody hand me a flashlight. Ruth handed hers to Phin and they probed the wound. "It's a snake bite alright," Phin grimly confirmed.

"Oh man...this is not good," Oz managed to croak. He slapped the ground with his fist.

"Max, check the head of the snake and see if it's poisonous," Phin called to his friend.

"On it." Max shined his own light on the snake's parts. The body was still writhing even though the serpent was dead. Carefully, using the tip of the machete, he confirmed what none of them wanted to believe. "Triangle-shaped head, Phin. I don't know what kind of snake this is. Never seen one like it before. But it's clearly poisonous."

"Man...I'm gonna die!" Oz began to cry.

"You're not going to die, Oz. Look at me...in the eyes," Phin commanded the computer specialist. Oz obeyed, pulling his eyes from the snakebite on his right calf, looking at Phin. "We are going to get you out of here. You are *going* to be okay. I promise." But Phin knew the situation was grim. Depending on how much venom Oz had been injected with by the serpent's fangs, and depending on what kind of snake it was, Oz could have days, or just minutes. There was no way to know.

Phin had a good working knowledge of first aid. He spent the next half-hour treating and dressing the wound as best as he could. Oz took a shot of antibiotics as well. They considered giving him something to calm him down, but they needed him to have his wits about him for their journey out of the Garden. Quick, emergency-type help was what Oz required. They didn't need him to be dead weight. At the same time, he needed to stay calm, keep his heart rate down to prevent the venom from surging through his blood system. Ruth and Max broke camp and gathered their gear, having made the quick decision to move out. Waiting until morning was not an option Oz could afford. Time was of the essence. Everyone was anxious, which made clear thinking a challenge. *Boy, what we wouldn't do now to have Sergeant Warren with us*, Phin thought. He wondered what had become of him as well. For all the wonder of this Garden they'd found, things had gone from bad with Warren's disappearance to worse with Oz's injury - a snakebite of all things. In the Garden.

The Go Team began their retreat. To say that it was dark would be an understatement. Because of the thick canopy, no light from the night sky could break through. It was pitch black. The mood was thick and heavy as they stumbled their way, trying to retrace their path with only flashlights to guide their steps. Max let Oz support himself on his shoulders to take any pressure off of the bitten leg. Phin led the way with Ruth by his side. They moved as quickly as possible.

Nothing looked remotely familiar from the day before, and soon they had no idea if they were going in the correct direction at all. Phin did his best, but the more they walked the more disoriented he became.

"We're lost, aren't we?" Ruth whispered to Phin, careful not to let Oz hear.

"I think we are going in the general direction that we entered the Garden from, but I can't be certain. I don't recognize anything to be honest." They continued on in silence.

Just moments later, Ruth squeezed Phin's arm hard, "What is that up ahead?" She was pointing into the black distance.

"I don't see anything. What are you pointing at?" He had stopped and was staring.

"I thought I saw something. A light of some kind maybe," her heart was beating fast. "Turn your flashlight off." Phin complied. Darkness enveloped them.

"Hey, what's going on?" Oz cried. "Man, I'm starting to not feel so good, guys."

"Shhh!" Ruth came back. "Just be quiet for a minute."

And there it was. With their flashlights off, Phin was able to pick up on what Ruth had seen. A faint glow of light just up ahead. Maybe one hundred yards away through the thick forest.

"I think it's a fire!" Ruth exclaimed. "I'll bet it's Billy! He came looking for us and set up his own camp!"

"You may be right," Phin agreed.

"Come on, let's go. He'll know what to do." Ruth eagerly plowed forward and Phin tried to keep up. Something inside of him warned him to approach with caution. He grabbed Ruth from behind and slowed her down. She understood and they moved on more carefully, the light growing brighter with each step.

They came to a clearing, shocked at what they found. It wasn't the sergeant. Instead they found a small cottage with a thatch roof and logs for walls, probably made from materials in the forest around them. It was old but obviously well kept. And it was occupied. Light poured out of the windows on all sides like a lighthouse. Phin noticed a small vegetable garden on the far side of the clearing, along with an animal pen with a few chickens in it. A goat was tied to a small tree growing next to the house. Phin was taking all of this in, trying to make meaning of it when all of a sudden....

"Shma kea hstad? Aanja cheh makena?" A voice commanded from behind them. Phin whipped around to see the barrel of a wicked looking gun pointed at them. Oz screamed and Max lowered him quickly to the ground. *"Hrket nken aa mn bh shma shlake kenm!"* The man barked again. Phin and Ruth instantly put their hands in the air. Motioning with his gun, he wanted the group to move into the clearing and they complied immediately. Oz got up, limping his way along. As the man continued to bark orders and wave his gun toward them, they moved toward his cabin. This was obviously where he wanted them to go. About ten feet from the front door, he began yelling again. *"Peaaan. Peaaan. Baa peaaan."* Get down! Get down!, was the clear meaning. The group obeyed, and once on the ground, Phin was able to measure matters up. The man with the gun was old. Clearly of Persian descent, he wore the clothes of a Bedouin, his long beard falling to mid-chest flecked with more gray than black. His head was covered with a brown cap.

"He wants to know who we are and why we are here," Max whispered to the rest. "He's speaking to us in Farsi. I know just enough to pick up bits and pieces."

"Tell him we need help, Max. Tell him we mean no harm. We are just passing through and don't meant to threaten him in any way."

Max held his hands over his head and slowly got to his feet. The man allowed him to rise but was cautious, keeping his weapon trained on them. It was clear they weren't the danger he thought they might be when he first heard them traipsing through the forest. Max began to speak. Phin could tell he was introducing himself, identifying them as a group that had simply gotten lost and needed help. He pointed to Oz's leg and the bandage that covered it. Oz was soaked with sweat now, looking pale. Max made a motion with his hand, trying to describe the snakebite. The man understood and the more Max talked, the more his defenses came down. He leaned over Oz's leg and made a swirling motion with his own hand, indicating he wanted Max to remove the bandage. Max obeyed, shining the light on the wound. The man's eyes grew wide. He stood quickly and rushed inside his house. Phin could hear banging inside and he gave Ruth a look. Reemerging in the doorway, the old man called out, *"Baa. Baa."*

"He wants us to come inside," Max translated.

They picked Oz up and made their way into the modest home where the man had prepared a bed for him. He motioned for them to lay him down. His were simple living quarters. The cottage was a small one-room home with a kitchen in the corner and living space in the center. There was a door out the back, which likely led to a toilet of some sort. The floor was dirt. There were a few clothes in one corner and a table with books on top of it. Two lanterns hung on opposite sides, which provided the light that had drawn them like moths. They discovered that their host's name was Cyrus. He had gone to work in the kitchen, opening several jars and mixing together some sort of concoction.

"What's he doing, Max?" asked Oz weakly. "What's he making over there? It smells awful."

"He says he can help you, Oz. Just relax. I described the snake to him and he believes he knows what kind it is. It's a common but deadly snake in this forest but he says not to worry."

"Oh man...deadly. I knew it." Oz groaned and laid his head back.

Cyrus came over with two cups. One held a pasty green

substance that was the source of the foul stench. He applied a thick coating of it to the wound and re-bandaged it. The other contained a sweet smelling broth, and Cyrus motioned to Oz to drink the whole thing. Oz gave a wary eye to the others.

"Bottoms up, Oz. Take your medicine like a good boy," Ruth patted him on the arm. That was all the coaxing he needed. Oz drained the cup in one big gulp. Cyrus explained to Max that the bite was fresh and that they had found him quickly so the medicines he had given Oz should serve to heal him without any problem. Everyone was breathing a sigh of relief. It could have been so much worse. But the whole event of the snakebite, plus the presence of Cyrus living here in the forest caused the group to wonder all sort of things about this "Garden" they had found.

"Max, can you see if it's okay for me to ask Cyrus some questions about how long he's lived here and what he knows about this place?" Ruth beckoned.

Max was about to do just that but was interrupted by a fast *thumping* sound that broke the silence of the night. *Thump, thump, thump, thump*...it was growing louder by the second. Phin was up and out the door, looking into the sky.

"I think we've got big trouble!" He shouted back to the group as Ruth, Max, and Cyrus ran to join his side.

"*Nzama!*" spat Cyrus.

"He says it's the military," Max translated. Max and Cyrus began an animated exchange. "He says we must go...now. Before it's too late."

"Go? Where are we supposed to -"

But too late had arrived before Phin could finish his sentence. A military-style helicopter came swopping in over the clearing with a spotlight aimed down on the group. A voice was calling to them over a loudspeaker. The light was blinding, and they could only assume that machine guns were aimed on the group, ready to mow them down if they tried to run. A dozen soldiers all with automatic weapons burst into the clearing, yelling at the group in Farsi. The Iranian military had found them. Phin spun around in stunned silence. Where had Cyrus gone? The old man had disappeared.

CHAPTER THIRTY-NINE

The Iranians had muscled the Go Team through the forest to its exit. It had been a long two-hour slog. They had shown no mercy to Oz, who was clearly still suffering greatly from the effects of the snakebite. The medicine was only slowly working its helpful magic in his system; what he needed was more time and rest. No hope for that now. The group had not been allowed to talk during the extraction. As they came out of the forest, the sun was just peeking over the horizon. It was the dawn of a terrible new day, and they were back into the land of barren rock and dusty, dry terrain. A small caravan of military vehicles was waiting to load them up. In short order, they were bumping and bouncing their way across open country, prisoners of the Iranian government. Ruth sat sullen while Max gave his attention to Oz. Phin, for his part, was deep in thought.

By noon they arrived at a military outpost on the edge of Lake Urmia. Their group of four was roughhoused out of their vehicle that had grown swelteringly hot on the long drive. Drenched in stink and sweat, they were exhausted. A mean-looking guard shoved them toward a small cinder-block building with a metal roof. Unlocking the door, he slung them inside one-by-one and slammed the door shut.

"Welcome home ladies...and Ruthie." A familiar but weak voice welcomed them into the darkness of their cell.

"Billy! Is that you?" Ruth exclaimed with a twinge of hope in her voice. If anyone would know what to do in this situation it would be Billy Warren.

"The one and only. Yes, ma'am."

Ruth rushed to his side, her eyes still adjusting. The only light seeping in came from cracks in the ceiling where the metal roof met the stone blocks. Their prison was an oven, much hotter than the ride they had already endured. She pulled away from Warren, her eyes wide with horror. "Billy! What have they done to you?"

Sergeant Billy Warren was sitting on the ground. Sitting because he could not stand. His left leg and left arm were missing. His LaPhage Limbs. The soldiers who had taken Warren had stripped him of that which had given him new life. He was reduced to his former mangled self. He was also bloody all over, his face swollen and bruised. Whatever had happened, Billy Warren had put up the fight of his life.

"It's okay, Ruthie. I'll be all right. Don't worry about me," he said, mustering as much of the Warren bravado as he could. He was not convincing.

Phin got on his knees in front of Warren, "Sergeant, what happened? How did you end up here?"

Warren began weakly, "Yesterday morning, real early, like before sunrise, I woke up and saw two vehicles driving across the desert. I thought it might be the Kurds. They were maybe half a mile away. When I looked through my binocs, sure enough..." Warren stopped and coughed a couple of times - a dry, hacking cough. Bloody spittle sprayed from his lips. Phin wondered if he had internal bleeding from the beating he had taken. He continued on, "Sure enough, it was the Land Cruisers. So I fired off a flare to get their attention. They saw it right away and turned and headed straight at me. I thought, 'Here we go. We're all connected back up again.' But when they pulled up next to me, these Iranian military putzes spilled out. They were our vehicles all right, just no Kurds. They had the jump on me before I could do anything about it. I put up a fight as best I could. They shot me in the left leg." He paused to laugh, which led to another coughing fit. "The bullet didn't even slow me down. Not in the left leg. Then they shot me in the right." Phin looked down and that's when he saw the bloody wrap that Warren had improvised on his right leg. "They drug me here and that's when they took my left arm and leg. They could tell something was different about 'um. While they was pulling my limbs off me I saw three of the Kurds we hired. Ako was in charge. He was with Nebez and Eland. I think that was their names. Raman wasn't around. Either he took off on his own, is dead, or they paid him beforehand."

"Paid him?" Phin asked, confused.

"That's right. We were sold out, Doc. Those Iranian goons paid out wads of cash to Ako and his two other buddies and then they split. Saw it with my own eyes. And that's that. Now here we sit."

A sick feeling fell over the whole group. It was unclear what would happen from this point forward, but all agreed it would not be good. The Iranians were not known for showing mercy to people who violated their sovereign borders, especially Americans. The most likely scenario would be that they would become political prisoners, pawns in some future chess match between the United States and Iran. And who knew if Billy would survive his injuries? Plus, Oz was still not out of the woods and looked as weak as ever. Somebody was going to have to do something if they were to have any hope at all.

That somebody would end up being Phineas Crook and that something would surprise everyone in the group.

It became clear after a couple of hours that the Iranians were not going to move the Go Team that day. It had apparently grown too late. The only compassion they had shown the group was a bucket of drinkable water and five plates of slop that was supposed to be dinner. Still, it was enough to provide some energy. Warren and Oz had rested throughout the day, bearing the heat of their cell as much as was possible. About an hour after sunset, Phin could hear the sounds of talk and laughter coming from one direction, a fair distance from their cell shack. It was dinnertime, he surmised. He walked over to the door of their cell and knelt down. He took his time looking through different tiny holes that had been punched through the steel door. They looked like bullet holes. Satisfied, he slipped out of his left boot and dug around inside as if trying to fish out a rock. What he produced instead was a pair of small metal picks. Max held his breath as Ruth looked on in confusion. Phin took a minute more to look over the locking mechanism on the door, and then he went to work with the instruments from his boot. It wasn't a minute later that the sound of a soft click could be heard. Phin looked back over his shoulder with a devious smile on his face.

"Time to play ball," he said. "Stay here and I'll be back." With that, Phin opened the door to the cell and slipped out into the night. Ruth looked on in stunned silence. All Max could do was smile.

"How'd he do that? What's he trying to do?" Ruth directed her questions to Max.

"I have no idea but let's just say there's a lot about Phineas Crook that you don't know."

Phin was gone for nearly twenty minutes when he finally snuck his way back into the cell. They had begun to grow worried, breathing a sigh of relief when he appeared.

"Okay, listen to me carefully," he began with the instructions. "They're all eating dinner. At least most of them. And there's alcohol involved, which is good for us. I've secured an armored vehicle, one of theirs. It's parked on the far side of the compound from where they are holding us. No one is even looking in the direction of this building they have us in. They assume that there's no fight in us. Oz is clearly sick, and the sergeant can't even walk. You're a woman, Ruth, sorry, but in their culture that doesn't mean much, and Max and I are clearly not soldiers. So as far as they're concerned, we are all tucked away in here till tomorrow or until they decide to do something different with us. That's our advantage. I figure they will be busy eating for another half hour or so. So we move now. Follow me and I will lead us to the armored car. Max, you help Oz. Ruth, you and I will help the sergeant. Let's go!"

There were so many questions swirling through Ruth's mind. Where had this version of Bible professor Phineas Crook come from? What were they going to do once they got to the vehicle that Phin had identified? She didn't have the chance to ask any of them because Phin and Max were in go-mode. Max already had Oz up and moving. He was asking questions about what was happening, looking like he had more strength than Phin would have thought, which was good. Max just told Oz to keep quiet and go with him. Phin had muscled Warren to his feet and was about to explain the situation.

"Yeah, Doc. I heard it all. You're our knight in shining armor. Whatever. I ain't in no shape to complain. And I sure as *you-know-what* ain't gonna hang around here if there's any kind of shot of flipping our situation. Ruthie, get over here, sweetie, and help me out. I'm ready to roll."

The Go Team was on the go once again. They moved out of the cell and around the back of the small unit. Phin had them pause while he snuck back around and relocked the door - just in case a guard walked by and pulled on it. Then they took off toward the edge of the compound. The going was surprisingly easy. It was dark. The moon had not yet risen. The further they slinked away, the quieter the noise from the mess hall grew. Soon it was silent except for the crunch of their feet on the rocks and dirt. No one spoke. They came to a small motor pool, which was really nothing more than a haphazardly parked grouping of five armored-style vehicles and their two Land Cruisers. A guard lay on the ground, either dead or unconscious. Ruth was afraid to ask, but now she understood what Phin had meant when he said he had "secured" their vehicle.

"Phin!" she dared to whisper, stopping short and motioning to the Land Cruisers. "We should take one of those. They have all our gear in them."

"We can't risk it. If they find that we are gone, that's the first thing they will be looking for. Plus, no one will stop us if we are in one of those things," he countered, pointing at the Iranian vehicle, official decals on its sides. Ruth understood and didn't push it further.

"Everybody load up. Max, you and I are going to have to try and push this thing down the road a bit before I try to start it. I don't want the noise drawing attention."

It was all the two men could do to make the armored car budge. At first they both doubted it was possible, but the asphalt it was parked on made the difference and once they had it rolling just a bit, it became easier to pick up some speed. Ruth steered as they silently rolled out onto a paved road. No one was around to observe their clandestine operation. After five minutes of hard, adrenaline-laced pushing, they finally felt at ease.

"Did you happen to lift a set of keys off that guard back there, Doc?" asked Warren. His spirit was returning.

"I looked but no luck. It doesn't matter, though." In another surprise to Ruth, Phin worked his way under the dash of the vehicle and began pulling out wires. Moments later, the machine roared to life.

Phin gave Ruth another beaming smile, "You wanna drive or me?"

CHAPTER FORTY

The Go Team shot up the highway north toward the border with Turkey. They passed other vehicles along the way, even other military cars, but just as Phin had suggested, no one bothered with them. They motored on unhindered because of the Iranian vehicle they were driving. It was only one hundred miles to the border, and they would be there quickly at their current pace.

"What's the plan for when we arrive at the border?" Ruth finally asked Phin. She was still somewhat in awe, impressed at how he had unexpectedly taken control and orchestrated their break from the Iranian detention outpost. She was even more surprised with his skill at hotwiring the armored vehicle they had stolen. Surely he was thinking ahead, already full of ideas on how they would handle the fortified border crossing.

"We don't have a lot of choice as I see it. We need to get out of the country as quickly as possible. The longer we stay the more likely we will get caught. They're going to open that cell door and check on us eventually, and when they do the jig is up. Plus, Oz and the sergeant need medical attention as soon as possible."

"So the plan?" she asked again.

"The plan is to roll up to the checkpoint at the border like we are intending to pull off and park. Then I'm just gonna gun it. Catch them off guard...hopefully. There will be gunfire from both sides of the border. The Turkish military isn't going to be too keen on an Iranian-branded armored vehicle just cruising into their territory. But as long as its small-arms fire we should be okay. This thing is built like a tank, but it's a risk, I won't lie."

"Solid plan, Doc," chimed in Warren from the back. "I like how you think."

They saw it before they heard it. As their conversation continued about how to make the crossing into Turkey, the night sky lit up with a stunning bright orange flash. Next came the long rumble like thunder. Phin pulled the vehicle off the road and turned it so they could look back. A huge explosion could be seen in the distance, from just about where they had come.

"Whoa!" exclaimed Max. "That's some ball of fire. What in the world caused something like that?"

Sergeant Warren looked at Ruth. They were both thinking the same thing. Warren spoke first. "The crate?"

"Yes, the crate. It has to be," replied Ruth.

"Stupid idiots."

"It was inevitable - either by accident or by us remotely. There's no way we could have left it behind for them to keep."

"The crate?" Phin broke in. "In the Land Cruiser? What was in it?"

"That was our secret weapon, Doc. No need to worry about it now. It's gone and this operation is over."

More questions added to a list of other unanswered questions for Phin. There was always more to Ruth LaPhage than what appeared on the surface. Ah well, as Warren had declared, this whole episode was over. Time to move on. They had more pressing concerns just up ahead.

"That explosion is going to play in our favor," Phin announced. "It'll be chaos back there for a while. The Iranians will be mobilizing any and all personnel in the area to the scene. It may just be the break we need."

Phin pulled back onto the highway and hit the accelerator. They drove along in silence.

"That wasn't the Garden of Eden, was it Phin?" Ruth finally asked the question they had all been thinking. For all its wonder and beauty, what they had found was clearly not the ancient Garden of Eden spoken of in the Bible. Paradise on earth would never be inhabited by poisonous snakes. A holy garden protected and guarded by God himself would not be the home of an old Persian man trying to escape society. Surely something as precious as the Garden could not be so easily breached and violated by the military forces of any nation. All they had found, it seemed, was an oasis in the desert.

"No...it wasn't," Phin answered in confirmation. He was somber in his tone.

"It's not here either, is it? In Iran?"

"No, Ruth. I don't believe it is."

"You don't know where it is, do you, Phin?" This last question was a gut shot. It represented Ruth's complete loss of confidence in him. The whole reason she had sought him out in the first place. All the money spent. The hopes and dreams gone. Two men beaten and bruised in back of the vehicle he was driving, his best friend watching and listening - a front row seat to his undoing. Phin had failed. Soon everyone would know.

Very quietly he answered what the group already knew, "No...I do not." He squeezed the steering wheel tight and drove on into the distance. No one spoke the rest of the way.

They eventually met and were passed by a convoy of Iranian military vehicles like their own, rushing south toward the explosion at the outpost near Lake Urmia. They carried on, however, pushing the speed of the vehicle as fast as it would go. The checkpoint came into view. There were bright lights shining on both sides of the border. They could see into Turkey. They were so close. But the Turkish military was on high alert. They had seen the explosion in the night sky as well, and had watched as the Iranians scrambled and headed south. They had no idea what was going on, but they were taking no chances. People could be very trigger-happy in this part of the world.

Phin had been correct. The mass confusion to their south left only a skeleton crew of Iranian soldiers at the border crossing. As he approached, he slowed the vehicle, careful not to make a threatening move. They were virtually ignored.

"Everyone get down," he ordered the group. They complied without having to be asked twice.

When Phin was only fifty yards from the crossing, he put his head down and mashed the pedal. The maneuver worked beautifully on the Iranian side. They had not expected one of their own armored vehicles to make a run for the border. With only a few dozen yards to cross, there was no time to react.

The same was not the case on the Turkish side of the border.

A hale of gunfire erupted across the front of the vehicle. The Turks had identified the vehicle as a threat. Perhaps a suicide bomber.

The explosion of gunfire was relentless. The sound was deafening inside as round after round bounced off the plated armor. None of them breached the interior though. Phin prayed and kept his head down as the windshield splintered. He couldn't see anything anyway. He just kept the vehicle pointed forward and begged God that it would hold. He felt a violent thud as one of the tires blew apart. Still the vehicle lumbered on. Surely he had crossed the border, right? His foot was still on the pedal and he could finally perceive that the gunfire was now pelting the back of the vehicle. They'd made it! They were in Turkey. Another BOOM and a rear tire was gone. The vehicle carried on ever so slowly. They only had one option, and Phin had known it would come to this anyway. He hit the brakes hard and killed the engine. He rushed to the back of the vehicle and ordered everyone away from the door. He flung it open, said a prayer, and stepped into the open doorway with hands held up in surrender. He was going to sacrifice himself in order to save his friends if necessary.

The firing stopped. Phin had closed his eyes, afraid to look. Now he opened them to find the bullet-ridden vehicle surrounded by Turkish soldiers, all with weapons trained on him. One threatening move and they would open fire.

Phin said the first words that came to his mouth, "Don't shoot! I am an American! We need help!"

The group of armed soldiers parted. A lone unarmed man moved through, walking toward Phin - the commanding officer, no doubt. He stopped just feet from Phin, measuring him up and down. "My name is Phineas Crook. I am a college professor in the United States of America. We have been held captive in Iran. We need your protection."

The Turkish commander took one more step forward. In a surprise move, he extended a hand, speaking in English, "Mr. Crook, I am Captain Omer Berat. Welcome to Turkey. You are safe here."

Phin lowered his hands, accepting the captain's gesture of welcome. He breathed a sigh of relief. They had escaped Iran.

CHAPTER FORTY-ONE

Phin took his time snaking through the crowded streets of the Jewish Quarter in the Old City of Jerusalem. There were at least three kinds of people surrounding him during this early afternoon hour. The Hasidic Jews in their distinct black clothing, long beards, and curls coming off the sides of their temples was one group. Another group was the Jews who were less strict in how they lived out and practiced the faith. Then, of course, there were the tourists. Always the tourists, at pretty much any location of interest throughout the nation of Israel. The Holy City was home to three of the world's religions: Judaism, Christianity, and Islam. But there would be no Muslims where Phin was today. Not in this quarter of the city.

The presence of military was also unmistakable. Both young men and young women in the classic olive of the Israeli Defense Forces were never far away - all armed with automatic weapons. Their presence could easily lead one to the conclusion that Israel is a dangerous place. To be sure, there is never a shortage of nations, groups, and individuals who want to see Israel utterly wiped off the face of the planet. But Phin actually found the military presence calming, as if, in a contrary sort of way, Israel was one of the safest places on Earth.

The smells of fresh baked bread, nuts, and honey dominated Phin's senses as he was carried along toward his destination. He'd already eaten a wonderful kosher brunch at the hotel in Tel Aviv where he was staying, but the warm scents made his stomach pang just the same. He was greeted with smiles and salutations from a menagerie of shop owners, some catering to locals and others to tourists. Phin was neither. He was here on a mission.

It had only been three days since their harrowing run across the border from Iran into Turkey. Captain Beret had been a man of his word. After confirming the identities of the Go Team members via their passports and VISAs, he had given them immediate aid and protection. Ruth made a series of phone calls and within hours, the United States State Department had involved embassy personnel in Istanbul. Arrangements were made to fly the team from Van directly to Istanbul where Sergeant Warren and Oz Jenks were currently convalescing. The sergeant had needed minor surgery to stop the internal bleeding Phin had suspected he was suffering from, a result of his intense beating. Tony Chen was on his way with two new LaPhage Limbs for the retired Marine. Oz had made a remarkable turnaround after being admitted. Not from anything the hospital did so much as the salve on his leg, created and applied by the mysterious old man known only as Cyrus. The doctors were amazed at his recovery, given the type of venom he'd been injected with. Both were resting comfortably and would be headed home within another day or so.

There was nothing more for Phin and Max to do. Ruth had vowed to stay and fly home with the others as a group. They were her people after all. But Phin and Max no longer had a place with LaPhage Industries. The quest for the Garden of Eden had failed. The only thing that seemed fitting to do was say goodbye. Surprisingly to Phin, Ruth LaPhage didn't seem all that upset. The financial loss alone would stagger most people. The tens of thousands of dollars on the expedition alone was a hefty price, but when you figured in the million plus dollars in "gifts" to OBU, Phin was certain he would see a different Ruth than he'd experienced thus far. If anything, she was melancholy, seemingly resigned to the failure as if it had been somewhat expected, even though she had been so hopeful of actually finding the Garden. Max thought she was just grateful to have escaped Iran with everyone alive. The outcome could have been, should have been, much worse. There was also the thought that she was suffering some mild form of PTSD from their ordeal. He cautioned his friend that her tune might change once she made it back to the States and life returned to normal. Phin didn't think so. He had said his goodbyes to Ruth and she even gave him a hug. One of those embraces that lasted just a bit too long. Then he was gone. Max and Phin went immediately to the airport. Max had assumed they'd be on the same flights home to Oklahoma, but Phin announced once they were at Ataturk International that he was not going home directly. He had a detour he needed to take first.

Now, as he rounded the corner from Hayei Olam Street onto Misgav Ladach Street, Phin identified the alley he was looking for. Stepping away from the crowds making their way toward the Western Wall, he came to a small unassuming shop. The sign on the door read House of Reuben in Hebrew. One tiny window displayed an assortment of watches, clocks, and other timepieces. Phin pulled on a rickety wood door and stepped through. Once inside, he was greeted by a portly Jewish woman, her jet-black hair in a bun. She quickly realized Phin spoke only English and changed to accommodate.

"It is time," Phin plainly said.

"It is time for what, friend?" she asked in return.

"It is *my* time." Phin rolled up the sleeve on his right arm. On the inner side of the biceps, just at the bottom before the muscle met the triceps was a small birthmark. Very distinct in shape and color, it looked exactly like a red spike with a red dot at the point. The dot and the spike didn't touch. It was striking for two reasons. One, the distinct shape. Most birthmarks are ambiguous. And two, his brother and father had the same mark in the same location. Phin had been told by his father that all Crooks historically had the same marking. A genetic phenomenon that was unexplainable. But it served one helpful purpose: it identified clearly those who were allowed to have access to the Crook Family Archives.

Upon hearing the correct reply to her question and seeing the birthmark, the woman introduced herself as Mary and beckoned Phin to follow her. She led him through a curtained doorway in the back of the shop. They threaded through a musty storage room of boxes containing clock parts and an assortment of other junk items for which Phin could see no purpose. A large shelf turned out to be hinged to reveal a door behind it. Mary entered a code on a surprisingly sophisticated keypad system.

Once the door was open, Mary instructed, "Go, child. It is indeed your time. Learn who you are. Embrace who you were born to be." With that, Phin stepped into a dark stone corridor, and the door shut behind him.

A run of conduit connected lights every thirty feet. They were low-watt bulbs, making for an ominous feel as Phin walked. He came to a set of stairs that went down. Phin descended. Coming to a landing, he met a rusty ladder descending yet again into the depths of the earth. There was only one way to go: down. So Phin complied. On yet another landing, a second corridor led into the distance as far as Phin could see. He walked a good distance, not knowing exactly how far he had gone, but his sense of direction told him he must be deep under the Temple Mount itself. *How was it possible that this existed, unknown to the archaeologists doing their own excavating of the Temple Mount somewhere else under here?* Phin was astounded at the thought. He was walking through ancient history, dating back to the time of Christ at least - and likely beyond even that.

His father had left clear instructions to his sons - both he and Remus - on how to find the little clock shop in Jerusalem, the exact words to say, and showing the birthmark. This would gain any member of the Crook family entrance to the archives. Beyond that, Phin didn't know what to expect. He'd never been here before. In fact, he had avoided coming here. Remus had made the pilgrimage years before, but had uttered not a word of his discoveries. For whatever Phin thought he would find, this was not it. He walked on in darkness, turning a corner every so often. It was impossible to get lost because the path led only one direction. Phin was thankful he was not claustrophobic.

Finally, the cramped corridor opened into a large chamber. Rock hewn, it was tall, maybe thirty feet high and at least that large from wall to wall. No exit could be seen leading out of the room. There was a hole in the ceiling that led to somewhere. Phin couldn't know because there was no way to access it. Spread around the room were various tables, all mounded with books. And there was shelving. Lots of shelving, all containing volumes upon volumes of books. Phin was in a library of sorts. He could spend days...weeks, in here. *Where do I start?* he mused. But it was clear. In the center of the room was a table larger than all the others. And there were fewer books on this table. It seemed obvious this was the starting point, the place to begin his journey of discovery. Phin approached and counted ten large leather-bound tomes. They were old. Very old. Each was embossed with large Roman numerals on the cover, numbering one through ten. *Well, that keeps it simple*, Phin thought. It seemed logical that if he was going to trace his roots back to the beginning he should start with the last page of the volume with the Roman numeral X for ten on it, then work his way backward to Volume I. Cracking open the ancient book to its end page, he dove in.

What Phin saw captured his attention immediately. The book was handwritten in large ancient script that was easy to follow. No one page contained too much material making it hard to get lost. There were genealogies as expected, but also historical notations that traced migration patterns, acts of bold thievery throughout history, as well as Crooks who had served in prominent government and business positions, many times under assumed names other than the family surname.

The record that Adonis Crook kept at the family home in Moore, Oklahoma, was a mere overview of the Crook Family in the United States only. What Phin was looking at here was much more detailed, yet easy to follow, even as the script changed from English, to Latin, to Greek, all languages Phin knew well. As he moved from one volume to the next, it was as if he was walking back in time. These were his roots. In these pages was the chronicle of his heritage. More than once, he was tempted to jump straight to the first volume to see where his family began, but he disciplined himself to walk the path, the whole path. The hours passed and Phin lost track of time. He didn't need to eat. He didn't need to relieve himself. It was as if time itself had stopped deep underground, under the little time shop above him. How many hours passed, Phin did not know.

Finally, Volume I.

Phin had navigated into the deep history of the Crooks. In the previous nine volumes he had discovered that the Crooks could be traced all the way back to the land of Israel itself, which explained why it was the city of Jerusalem that housed the archives. His heartbeat quickened as he continued to walk backward. Israel had been the home through the millennia for numerous nations of peoples, not only the Jews. Phin discovered that some of the first Crooks had been Samaritans, that mixed race of people referred to in the New Testament of the Bible who were half-Jew and half-something else, most likely another Arab population relocated to the land of Israel during the time of the Babylonian Empire. The Samaritans were hated by the Jewish people, isolated to the ancient central Israeli region of Samaria, where they thus got their name. This was news to Phin - that his first ancestors were Samaritans. He'd never heard this. This meant he had Jewish blood. He continued to be riveted by what he read.

One thing he found fascinating in all of his study was that the common vocation of thievery had been consistently practiced and passed down from one generation to the next in the Crook Family. Phin also found one curiosity that struck him as unmistakable. It was common for most Crook men to have two sons. There may or may not be daughters, but there were always two sons. Sometimes twins and sometimes separated by one or more years, but wherever there was one son, there was always a second. But never three. How was that possible? Especially through all of two thousand years of genealogy. What was even more curious was that in certain generations of Crooks, not all, but in certain branches of certain generations, there would be an occasional instance of a Crook son who chose not to pursue the vocation of thievery. When such an occurrence happened, it was duly noted, and that particular branch of the Crooks would no longer be recorded *unless*, in a successive generation, a son in the lineage took up the vocation. At that point the genealogy would begin to be recorded once again. Phin marveled, wondering who it was that had kept these records for all these years. Who was keeping them now? Surely not Mary alone.

Phin was also astounded at the breadth of the Crook Family. There were Crooks literally all over the world at various levels of government, business, entertainment, health care, technology, and on and on. He had no idea until this day. *Was that family pride he was feeling as he read?*

As he turned the pages, one after another, toward the front of volume one, the story became more and more streamlined. The branches of the family, this deep in the history, this close to the origin, were so few. He was almost to the first page. Almost to the answer of where his family, the Crook Family, had begun. Phin had a nagging in his spirit. Something didn't quite feel right. It was as if all the pieces were in front of him but had not all fallen into place...yet. The image in his mind was too fuzzy to make out. But the more pages he turned, the more a picture was beginning to form. Phin's pulse pounded. His palms were moist. He was nearly there. He had a thought. It struck him out of nowhere. No, that's not right. Not nowhere. This had been building. Another page. It was a wild thought. Too insane to entertain. It wasn't possible.

He turned to the final page.

The first page.

And the awful truth stared him in the face.

Phin collapsed.

CHAPTER

FORTY-TWO

P*hin slowly came to. The pain was intense, too much to bear. He could hear screaming. It was Remus. His brother was hanging on a cross. Covered in his own blood. Naked and bare before the sea of faces spreading off into the distance. Something was wrong. Phin's head was still clearing. He couldn't think straight. Why couldn't he move his arms? His feet. Something not right there, either. He jolted and then understood. He was nailed to a cross too! Naked and bloodied. Both he and his brother. Hands and feet run through with a drill. The sadistic pleasure of the two hooded men in black. What was happening?* God, where are you?! *Phin cried in prayer.*

"PHIN!" *It was Remus.* "Phin! Oh it hurts, Phin...it hurts so bad.*

Why Phin? Why? What are we going to do? Why us, Phin?!"

"*I...don't...know," Phin replied. His throat was raw. It hurt to even talk.*

Phin bowed his head. "Why, Lord? Why? Please, Lord. Answer me. I need to know why!" Phin's pleas for why went beyond the dream. It went beyond the pain and the cross and Remus. It went deep. Oh, so deep. Why had he lost his father at such a young age? Why was his family different from other families? And then Autumn. His dear, precious E. The one good thing that had come into his life. His own personal paradise on earth. Why had God bothered to give him such a thing of beauty, on the inside and outside, as Autumn Eden Rose...only to rip her away? Why? Why did she deserve such a thing? If God loved Phin so much, then why all of this?

Why?

The wind picked up. A rumble began to roll. Thunder. No, not thunder. It was the roar of people. The faces of the people contorted into rage. They began to shout, and the shouts grew like a wave from the back of the crowd forward.

Lightening flashed across the sky. It blinded Phin for an instant.

And then it was silent. Slowly, Phin could see again. What he saw took his breath away. He and Remus were no longer alone. There was a third cross. Between the two brothers. And on that cross hung another man.

Beaten. Bruised. Drilled. Naked.

Time stood still for a second time that day. First, in the chamber below the little time shop in Jerusalem, and now on this hill as the three of them hung on crosses, naked before the world. Phin's worlds had collided. He understood all. Well, almost.

For all the beating and abuse that Phin and Remus had endured, the man between them had endured far more. A hundred times more. No, a thousand times more. His body so broken he scarcely looked human at all.

What had he done to deserve such treatment? Phin's heart broke with compassion for him.

The man lifted his head.

Then he turned it.

Toward Phin.

Slowly his eyes came up and locked with Phin's.

"You want to know why?" he said. His was a gentle voice, the sound to Phin's ears actually serving to ease the pain in his hands, feet, and joints. How was that possible?

"Everyone wants to know...why?" he spoke again. Phin had no response. He saw nothing but pure love in the eyes of this man. In that moment, he felt unworthy to be next to one such as this. To suffer next to him. What could he speak in the face of such love?

"Before the foundation of the world, I knew you, my child. I have always known you, Phin. I know the heart of every man. Every woman. Every child. Nothing is hidden from me."

"Don't listen to him, Phin! Close your ears!" Remus was screaming. "It's all lies! He doesn't care about you or me or anyone. He only cares about himself."

"You know the truth, Phin," his reply was gentle in the face of Remus' raging. "You know the truth, and if you embrace the truth, it will set you free."

"NOOO! It's a lie!" Remus was bucking and shouting. Phin could not comprehend where his brother's renewed energy had come from. "I know the truth, Phin! And the truth is that if he cared - if he really cared about you and me, then he would get us out of here. He'd cut us loose. Listen to your big brother, Phin. Don't follow this liar!" His brother carried on cursing and spewing.

"Remus!" Phin found his own burst of energy. "SHUT! UP! For once in your life quit thinking about yourself! This man...this man has done nothing wrong. He's done nothing to deserve this. But me," Phin hung his

head in shame for a moment before lifting it back up. "And you, Remus. We deserve this. We deserve every horrible and evil and wrong thing this world could throw at us." How Phin knew this he wasn't sure. He just knew that compared to this man he was hanging next to, he was dirty and unworthy. This man...he was something else. He was someone else. He was pure. Never had Phin felt so unclean than at this moment in his life, so close to something so pure. "We deserve it all, Remus...but not this man."

"I have known you from before the beginning, Phin. And I have loved you from before the beginning. Search your heart and know this to be true. You want to know why? Why there is so much evil in the midst of my love? The answer is simple. So utterly and completely simple."

"Please...tell me. I must know," Phin begged.

"But you already know, Phin. Answer these questions, my child: Why was your father shot while robbing a train? Why was your dear wife taken from you that night in Oklahoma City? Why are you obsessed with finding my Garden of Eden? And why...why Phin, did you come to Jerusalem, my Holy City? Why have all of these things happened? Search yourself. You know the answer. It is the same for each question."

Phin did know. "Because of a choice."

"Yes, of course. A choice. We all make choices of our own free will. Your father chose, of his own desires, to be a thief. Those men in the city chose to rob you and your wife, and then one of them chose to fire a gun. You have chosen to seek that which is forbidden in my Garden. And, yes, you made the choice to come to the archives. Each and every day, across the world, billions of people each make thousands of choices...many of them leading to suffering. You ask why? Why don't I do something about it? But I have, my child! I have. The price has been paid. It is finished. And so now you have another choice to make."

"More choices," Phin heaved. His heart was heavy. "I don't know if I can."

"Yes, Phin. You can. The hard part has been done for you. You *want to know who you are. Are you a Crook or something else? I tell you, Phin, people think they were born a certain way. To be this or to be that. But I say that people are called, not born. Phin, you are called to be mine. To follow me. That for which you think you were born means nothing any longer. You want to know if your wife can live again? I tell you she is already alive because of me. She is alive in me! The answer is not found in my Garden. That is an old story. Behold, I have written a new story! If you want to find your wife, you must let her go. But it's a choice, Phin. It's all a choice. Choose wisely, my child."*

All the pieces fell into place in that instant. Phin knew what choices were in front of him. He knew what was at stake and what he must choose. The dreams or visions had not been a curse at all. They had been a gift. A gift from God delivered through this man. And in one final moment of revelation, Phin looked the man in the eyes. He had but one thing to say. A request. From the depths of his heart. Wrapped up in one word. That word. A word that had followed him, haunted him, in his dreams. A word that finally fell into its proper place.

"Remember..." Phin began and then stopped.

"Yes, my child. Continue."

"Remember...me...when you come into your kingdom." The tears began to flow from Phin's eyes. Not tears of fear. Not tears of pain. Not tears of sorrow. These were tears of love.

The man smiled. In the midst of his own agony, he smiled at Phin. "Truly I tell you, not today, my child...but one day...yes, you will be with me...in Paradise."

Phin opened his eyes. His head lay on its side, cheek scrunched to the wood of the table. Volume one still lay open to its first page. He sat up and blinked twice, giving his head a shake. What he had just experienced was nothing short of incredible. Phin could not explain it other than to believe that he had crossed over to some otherworldly plane, not like this world, but in its own way more real. He had come face-to-face with the Son of God. Jesus. There was no doubt. The truth of the archives had brought it all together. He could never have guessed any of this.

The Crook family legacy had its beginning with two men. Two thieves who had hung on two crosses over two thousand years ago...next to another man on a third cross. And not just any man. He was the God-Man. Jesus. And these were not just any two thieves. They were *brothers*. Two brothers who had been caught in the act of stealing. Two brothers who had made a choice to build their lives and families around the art of thievery. It was common practice in the Roman Empire, when crucifying a man, to nail a sign above his head posting his crime. Above the head of Jesus had been a sign that read "King of the Jews." That had been his capital offense, to dare to be a king when the Jews already had a king installed by Caesar. But above the heads of the two thieves hung a different sign, with a different title. The Greek word for *crook*.

And that would be how the families of these two thief brothers would come to be known. The Crook family. The name and the vocation stuck. The intersection with Divinity those two brothers had that fateful day on a hill called Golgotha would go on to mark the successive generations of Crooks with a birthmark, two sons, and a choice.

Phin had made his. He'd made the choice years ago to walk away from that to which he was born, into something else. But now he was ready to embrace his calling.

He was also ready to make another choice. He was ready to let her go. He couldn't hold on to Autumn any longer. It wasn't right. It wasn't fair. It wasn't what God intended. In order to find her, he had to let her go.

He was ready.

But first, it was time to go and find the *real* Garden of Eden.

CHAPTER
FORTY-THREE

"Hold on! You're telling me that you knew the whole time the Garden of Eden *wasn't* in Iran?" Max Allred was furious with Phin. The two friends, along with student assistant Jason Morris, were huddled around a small table in the cramped spaces of Phin's private study carrel in the basement of the university's library, the Mabee Learning Center.

"That's right. Look, I'm sorry but there wasn't any other way," Phin replied.

"And you dragged me all the way to one of the most dangerous places on earth, knowing full well the risks, and knowing that there would be zero payoff? I'm a married man, Phin! I've got kids. I can't believe you'd do that to me." Phin had never seen his friend so angry.

He deserved what he was getting, he supposed. He had known it would be risky, but that was part of the plan. He had needed to orchestrate a search for the Garden of Eden that looked and felt legitimate. It had to be to a plausible location. And it had to be exotic. But most of all, it had to fail. It was the only way that Phin could see how he could convince Ruth LaPhage and her company that they had made a mistake in hiring him. Forcing him was more like it. He needed to be done with LaPhage Industries so he could move on.

The beat-down continued. "And you didn't think you could bring me into your little secret plan? I'm your best friend, Phin. Or at least I thought I was. You asked me to go with you. Insisted. Said you needed someone you could trust. Well, trust works both ways, buddy."

"I had no idea things would become dangerous, Max," Phin pleaded. "You have to believe me. I just thought we'd roam around in the barren region of northern Iran for a couple of weeks, find nothing, and then call it quits. Honestly, that was the idea the whole time." Phin had spent the last half hour unpacking everything with Max, bringing Jason into the loop for the first time on where the two men had spent the latter part of the spring semester and why. "I'm sorry about not telling you all of this ahead of time. I should have, okay? I just felt so out of control with LaPhage steering the ship. I needed it to be believable when things didn't work out. I needed you to be as disappointed as the rest of the team. I had always intended to tell you when we got back."

Jason Morris had been quietly listening as the two professors carried on with each other. The twenty-two year old finally had to speak. "I just can't believe you guys actually went looking for the Garden of Eden. Like, and I didn't know? And I've been as close to the project as anyone, Dr. Crook. Amazing."

"Not really," Max said.

"Excuse me?" Jason asked.

"We didn't really go looking for the Garden of Eden. It was all a lie, remember?"

"Still, I can't believe it. And LaPhage Industries paid for it all and they gave OBU a million bucks? Sheesh. All sounds like a movie or something."

"A bad movie. Believe me," quipped Max.

"So, does the school know the whole thing was a bust? I mean, they know you're back, right?"

Phin jumped in, "Yeah, they know. I've been dodging Dean Reynolds for the last week. But that's why I wanted to talk to you both privately down here." Phin had put a lot of thought into how he wanted to move forward. The failed effort in Iran had only been the first part of his plan. A ruse designed to shake loose LaPhage Industries. Ruth LaPhage had painted him into a corner back in February in front of the dean and the president of the university. He had no choice but to go and find the Garden of Eden. But he had never wanted it to be like this. His had been an academic pursuit. Ruth was after something more. She wanted the Tree of Life. She wanted to exploit the Garden for gain. She couched it all in the guise of helping humanity, but Phin didn't buy it in the end. Oh, she was persuasive. She had even planted a seed in Phin's mind. A seed that grew and almost consumed him. Because of Ruth's ideas, he had been tempted to exploit the Garden for his own personal gain. What if he could bring one fruit from the Tree of Life back and give it to Autumn? What if he could find a way to heal her and have her back, all for himself? The temptation of the Garden was so great. But then he had his experience in the Crook Family Archives. His vision had changed everything. No, he would not use the Garden and its fruit in that kind of way. He was back on track and thinking clearly, now that Ruth LaPhage was out of his life. But he needed to redeem his reputation.

He also needed to be done with his obsession in finding the Garden of Eden.

Max was right. His friend was oh, so right. He had been unhealthy. For three years he had not allowed himself to process, in the right way, the loss of Autumn. All that had changed now. His encounter with the Christ had changed everything. Yes, he would go and find the Garden of Eden. It would be a real search this time. He would walk its perimeter and record the whole expedition. He would not enter the Garden of Eden, though. It was off limits and he knew this to be true. It was no longer a place for man. He would document it all. Return and publish his findings. He would keep the location a secret, but he would restore his reputation. The first thing he would do when he returned would be to make one final visit to SecondLife, Inc. and say goodbye to his precious wife. He was ready to let her go. But to accomplish all of this, he needed help. He needed the two men sitting with him now.

"No more secrets, Max. And Jason, you graduate in a couple of weeks and I have a proposal for you. On this table is my research on the Garden of Eden. All of my research. I kept a collection of files on my laptop, but I'm just too old fashioned to trust a hard drive or the Cloud to keep it safe. I certainly didn't trust it to hold the greatest secret of all: the true location of the Garden of Eden. Down here is where I've kept all of that. And I am so glad now because when my home was broken into back in February, I had this feeling something was up. I'm convinced that LaPhage Industries was behind it, but I can't prove it."

"Wait," Max broke in, "you think it was LaPhage who stole the files from your computer?"

"Yes, I do. Sergeant Warren let something slip when we were in Iran one evening. He didn't come out and just say it, but he commented he was sorry about the deal at my house. Anyway, the day after the break-in, I came over to my carrel in the library and checked on these files right here and confirmed they had not been disturbed. I knew the secret to the real location of the Garden of Eden was still safe."

"So you've kept all the good stuff down here the whole time because you don't trust computers?" asked Jason.

"Something like that."

"But, Dr. Crook," Jason paused, trying to decide if he wanted to ask the question he was thinking. "What if there had been a *fire*?"

Phin just smiled and shook his head, "That's a good point, Jason...I never thought of that."

"Look, that doesn't matter now." Max reached forward and opened the thick file folder in front of him. It contained a map with lots of scribbled notes on it. "So after everything that's happened the last two months, you want me to still believe that you've got it all figured out, that you really do know where the Garden of Eden is, after you took me to where you knew it wasn't?"

"Yeah...something like that."

"Unbelievable." Max pushed back from the desk with a huff.

"Well, I'd like to know!" Jason grabbed the file. "Why don't you give it to us straight, Dr. Crook?"

"I'm glad you asked, Jason," Phin said with a smile and wink at Max. Max just rolled his eyes. He leaned forward and took the file from Jason. He started spreading out various maps and other documents. "Okay, so hang with me as I explain all of this. I've spent a lot of years getting to what we have here." Jason and Max were both listening - Max more interested than he was letting on. "So the Turkey/Iran theory was legit for a while. I really thought that's where the Garden of Eden had to be. Most scholars agree, even though it's never been found. That just led them to believe the Garden is no longer in existence."

"What about all that lidar scanner stuff you sold to LaPhage? About the Tigris and the Euphrates joining together?" asked Max.

"Oh, yeah. Well...I made all that up. The lidar scanner is a real thing, don't get me wrong. It's been used in South America to great success. Found all kinds of hidden ruins and whatnot. But the maps and lines and extensions of the river, I made all that up. Got Jason and his media friends to help me." He gave Jason a pat on the back.

"So that's what that was for. I didn't think you'd actually use it as a real map!"

"Okay, let me keep going. So, I dumped the Turkey/Iran theory a long time ago and went back to square one - and I mean the beginning - as in Genesis. The key to the location of the Garden of Eden is in Genesis chapters seven and eight."

"Hold it!" Max butted in. "That's the Flood account. What does Noah and the Flood have to do with the Garden of Eden?"

"Everything, Max." Phin was excited. He was gripping the sides of the desk with both hands, leaning forward. "Look, we've always assumed that Noah's ark landed somewhere in the same region of the world where it was built and began to float. But we should never do that when it comes to the Bible. We should never just assume anything. The ark floated for one hundred and fifty days, remember? A hundred and fifty days! That's a long time. It seems much more probable, likely even, that it drifted a long way from its point of origin. If that's true then Noah could have lived within four to five thousands miles from where the ark actually landed. And not just Noah, but his ancestors as well. All the way back to - "

"Adam and Eve," Max finished.

"Yes! Adam and Eve. Our big mistake has always been to assume that the Garden of Eden was somewhere in the Middle East or Asia Minor, and that all of humanity from Adam and Eve forward populated there first, and then spread out around the globe. But what if it didn't happen that way? What if the origin of mankind - of Adam and Eve and the Garden - was not in that part of the world at all? What if it was somewhere else altogether?"

"Like where, Dr. Crook?" Jason asked.

With a glean in his eyes, Phin answered, "Like Africa."

CHAPTER FORTY-FOUR

"Africa?!" Max shouted. "Phin you are crazy. No way is the Garden of Eden in Africa."

"No, I am not, Max. I am not crazy."

"The Tigris and Euphrates Rivers are in Turkey, Phin. We were just there!"

"No...two rivers *named* the Tigris and Euphrates are in Turkey."

"Right, so what are you getting at?"

"What I'm getting at is this: if Noah began in Africa, and then floated north over the course of approximately one hundred and fifty days, then when he landed on Mount Ararat, it would have been a foreign land to him. He and his wife and sons and their wives would have been struggling to make it a home. I think what they probably

369

did was name various geographic features in this new land after what they had known before. So they see a big river and they name it the Tigris. But it's not the original Tigris River." Phin could see that Max and Jason were struggling to follow his logic. "Look, think about it this way. How many cities in America are named after other, original cities in England or Spain or wherever those first settlers came from? It's what people do. The largest city in the United States is New York. Named after the city York in England. Same goes for Birmingham, Alabama - Boston, Massachusetts - London, Ohio - Manchester, New Hampshire - Portland, Maine - Rochester, New York – each city named after an English counterpart. So why is it crazy to think that when the flood waters receded and Noah and his family found themselves in unfamiliar surroundings, they began to name things like rivers after what they knew from their old homeland?

"And consider this: the flood was a worldwide catastrophic event. There is no way something like that could happen without it completely changing the geography and landscape of the planet's land masses. It would be expected that the way certain rivers flowed would change. So when the Bible talks in Genesis 2 about one river flowing out of the Garden of Eden, and that then it splits into four rivers - well, I think we could expect that the flow of those rivers would be changed after the Flood. So we have at least two things to think about. First, the Garden of Eden is in a totally different part of the world than we would ever suspect. And second, when we find it, there will be hints of the four rivers that used to flow in that region, but they would also likely be different."

"Like what you led us to believe in Turkey and Iran, with the lidar scanner and the Tigris and Euphrates flowing together?"

"Exactly! The theory is sound, Max. I just used it to lead Ruth LaPhage astray."

"So why Africa, Dr. Crook? And Africa is a big continent.

Exactly where in Africa would the Garden of Eden be?" Jason was fascinated with what Phin was laying before them. It was only a theory at this point, but he was hungry for more.

"Well, I began to run with this new idea - that the Garden of Eden could be anywhere in the world. I dove in hard. Followed numerous leads wherever they went until they fizzled out. But one day I was reviewing the writings of the ancient historian Josephus. Remember, he was commissioned by the Roman Empire to write an authorized Jewish history. At one point in his own research, he makes note that the ancient Gihon River is, in fact, the Nile River of today." Phin paused to let that little tidbit sink in.

"The Nile is in northern Africa," Max sat up. He was rubbing his temples, trying to work it out. "The Nile is also one of the largest rivers in the world, Phin. It makes sense that after a global flood it would survive even though its flow may have changed."

"That's right, Max!" Phin was leading and they were following. "The ancient Gihon River is one of the four rivers spoken of in relation to the Garden of Eden in Genesis 2. So if the Gihon of the Bible is really the Nile of today - "

"Then the Garden of Eden has to be in that region of Africa!" Jason finished.

"Well, it's a big river, Jason. But it narrows things down considerably for sure. The other three rivers mentioned in Genesis 2 may or may not still exist, but their names would surely be different today. They would no longer be called the Pishon, the Tigris, or the Euphrates. So I needed more to go on. Let me ask you both this: how familiar are you with the adventures of Stanley and Livingstone?" Phin inquired.

"Well, I mean I know that Dr. David Livingstone spent his career searching the heart of Africa for the source of the Nile River. And that Henry Stanley was a journalist who was hired to go find Livingstone when he didn't return from the expedition," Jason jumped in with the answer.

"Yes, you are right, Jason. The tale of Stanley and Livingstone is filled with real-life intrigue and mystery. You see, there was an obsession during the mid-to late-1800s among British explorers to be the first to identify the source of the Nile River. The African continent was a mystery to the world of that day. Henry Stanley, in his later years, coined the term 'Dark Continent' because so much was unknown about it.

"Dr. Livingstone was a legend in his own day, having become one of the first people to ever navigate across the whole continent - from the Atlantic to the Indian Ocean. The Royal Geographic Society commissioned him to find, once and for all, the source of the Nile. In his efforts he dropped out of all communication with the outside world for a period of six years. Many people believed he had died or been killed. Thus Henry Stanley, who was indeed a journalist, volunteered to go and find him. The world waited on pins and needles for word of his success or failure. Remember, this was a world with no email or cell phones. Travel took months, even years at times. It was a different day. After so many years with no word from Livingstone that he was even alive, Stanley had his detractors. Many thought it impossible that he could ever find one lone man who was lost on an entire continent the size of Africa."

"Like finding a needle in a haystack," Jason responded.

"You got it, Jason. Like finding a needle in a haystack. It took all of eight months, but Stanley finally found Livingstone in a small village called Ujiji, very close to Lake Tanganyika. Recognizing the old white doctor in a sea of black faces, Stanley approached him with that now famous line, 'Dr. Livingstone, I presume?' Stanley would go on to spend many more months with Dr. Livingstone, helping him map and explore the region. He eventually returned home to England. Alone.

Livingstone had no intention of returning to civilization. Henry Stanley came home to a hero's welcome. Vindicated in his efforts to do the impossible. He brought back with him a collection of journals and letters from Dr. Livingstone to present for safekeeping to the Royal Geographic Society."

"Okay, Phin. It's a fascinating lesson in history. But how does this all fit together? What about the Garden of Eden?" Max needed more to be convinced. He was about to get it.

"I've read the journals - Livingstone's personal record of his explorations. And not the journals that the public has access to. I've read the archived material that only a select few are privy to."

"And how did you pull that off? Wait, don't answer that," quipped Max.

"Let's just say I have connections. *Family* connections. What no one knows is that in his efforts to find the source of the Nile, Livingstone became sidetracked by another obsession. He began to hear talk among one isolated tribe of indigenous people that he stumbled across. They were not too keen on his presence, but he was sick at the time and he needed a place to heal and recover his strength. Anyway, this tribe fancied themselves as the guardians of a what they called in their language a 'holy forest.'" Phin paused to let this information sink in. "Livingstone records that this holy forest supposedly contained a fruit that was the key to eternal life and healing. But it was forbidden fruit. Being a former missionary, Livingstone began to wonder if this 'holy forest' could possibly be the lost Garden of Eden. His focus changed and he spent the latter years of his life trying to find it. The one journal I examined contained a small map, and with it some text. I just happened to snap a picture of it." Thumbing through the file on the table he went on, "Let's see. Ah, yes. Here it is." Phin spread out the printed copies of Livingstone's map and notes.

Max and Jason examined the documents with fascination. Nothing they were hearing about Livingstone, and a search for the Garden of Eden, had ever been a part of the historical account. This information, long buried in the archives of the Royal Geographic Society in London, was a bombshell. How Phin had managed to discover it was astounding.

The notes, in Livingstone's own hand, spelled out his encounter with the lone tribe that considered themselves guardians of the holy forest. They were not forthcoming with any information on how to find and enter it. But Livingstone had made multiple explorations of the region. His hand-drawn map showed the Nile River to the north, entering Lake Victoria. In parentheses, he had written the word "Gihon?" next to the label for the Nile. To the south of Lake Victoria, Livingstone had notations on his map indicating the presence of three rivers. Three. To Max and Jason's shock, Livingstone had labeled the three rivers Pishon, Tigris, and Euphrates, each with a question mark after the name. Incredibly, it seemed he was suggesting, or at least asking, whether or not these, along with the Nile, were the four rivers mentioned in Genesis 2. The same four rivers used to geographically locate the Garden of Eden. The three rivers did not connect into one on Livingstone's map, but his notes postulated that in the ancient past they could have. He'd walked the region and knew the contours and dimensions of the land like no other human being in his time. He had seen something that led him to this belief.

The location of the tribe of guardians was also marked on the map, still further south of the three rivers. And then there was a big X on the map. A simple notation screamed off the page to Max and Jason: *"G of E"?* The Garden of Eden. Livingstone knew where it was. Or at least he thought he knew. His notes chronicled two attempts to journey toward the X on the map. Both times ended in failure. Livingstone had become ill on his first attempt. His second attempt ended in a more mysterious fashion. He noted only that the pathway was "fraught with danger too steep for any man to endure." *What did that mean?* they wondered. His notes came to an end with no other explanation. History records that not long after, he would make his final journey to the small village of Ilala in Zambia where he would die of malaria and complications of dysentery.

"It all fits," Phin concluded. "My Flood theory says Noah lived and built his ark in a whole other part of the world than the Middle East. Some place one hundred and fifty days distance away as the ark would float. That means Adam and Eve and life on earth began in that same region. The true location of the Garden of Eden. Josephus names one of the four ancient rivers flowing from the Garden of Eden as the Nile River of today. That gets us to northern Africa. Then we have Livingstone. Arguably the greatest human explorer to ever live, and a man of God. A former missionary. He put all the pieces together, only he was never able to complete the journey. But he left us a map! We have his own map and his notes. All we have to do is go."

Jason and Max stared at the papers that were by this time spread all across the table. They both understood why Phin was convinced. The evidence was compelling.

"I want you both to go with me. I can't think of two other people in the whole world I want to share this experience with. Max, I am sorry about Iran. But this is real and this is everything. No more secrets. You know what I know. It won't be dangerous this time. We are headed to a stable part of the world." Turning to face Jason, "To you, my young apprentice, I am going to make a big ask. You graduate in two weeks. I told you I'd be there to see you walk. And I will. But the day after graduation I want you to join me and Max in finding the Garden of Eden. It will be the chance of a lifetime. I've already made some calls and you can start your dig in Israel late. It won't be a problem. I've even arranged for you to stay in-country for an extended time of study. And it won't cost you a dime."

Phin leaned back in his chair and folded his arms. "So what do you say?"

"I'm in!" exclaimed Jason. "No ifs, ands, or buts. I'm ready when you are, Dr. Crook."

"What about you, Max?"

Max leaned back, joining Phin's posture by crossing his own arms. He smiled ever so slightly and shook his head. "You know I can't let you go running off into the jungle or wherever this is without me. Who else is gonna keep you out of trouble? But I have a question. This map of Livingstone's is hand-drawn. Have you taken it and matched it to an actual map to test its accuracy?"

"You bet I have. And it's a perfect match. Livingstone was meticulous when it came to details. Even I am impressed. What we have here will lead us right to where we want to go."

"If it's okay, let me just ask," Jason chimed in. "I'm not real good with the geography of Africa. Where exactly will we be headed?"

"Great question, Jason. Pack your bags, gentlemen, because we are headed to Tanzania!"

CHAPTER
FORTY-FIVE

Graduation day came and went. With a diploma in one hand and a travel duffle in the other, Jason Morris boarded a flight from Oklahoma City to Dallas to Amsterdam to Kilimanjaro Airport in northern Tanzania. His seatmates none other than Dr. Phineas Crook and Dr. Max Allred, whom he was instructed to now call by their first names, Phin and Max. It would take some getting used to, he informed them.

Phin had successfully dodged any meaningful conversations with Dean Reynolds. Max's only word to his boss had been that Phin was working on his final report and would have it for the administration of the school to review later in the summer. No one knew they were headed to Africa.

Kilimanjaro International Airport may have had "international" in its name, but it was hardly that. Phin had been through here before and was always amused at the three-point turn the giant KLM Boeing 777 had to make once it came to the end of the runway, turning around for its taxi to the terminal. Passengers disembarked on the tarmac and walked in the open air to the small, hot processing area where VISAs were purchased for one hundred dollars cash, and shot records were verified by airport personnel.

Phin inhaled, taking a long deep breath into his lungs as he stepped outside the airport. He loved that smell. There was something...different about the African air. He never could quite put his finger on it. It was a good sensation.

Because it was after nine o'clock at night and the team had been traveling for over twenty-four hours, they hired a ride and went straight to the Airport Lodge, which was only minutes away. It was the perfect place to stretch out on a comfortable bed in one of the lodge's signature thatched roof huts, and to eat a good meal for breakfast come morning.

The next day, refreshed and ready to go, a Toyota Land Cruiser arrived for their usage while in-country. Max made a smart comment about Land Cruisers because of their previous exploit, but it was the perfect vehicle for where they were headed – spacious, rugged, and it held a lot of fuel. They drove from the lodge to Arusha. The bustling city of over four hundred thousand people was where they would spend the day gathering supplies and any gear they needed. They didn't need much though. The nature of their expedition necessitated only plenty of food, water, and camping gear. Phin had brought along a nice camera as well as some compact surveying equipment, and a leather-bound journal to take notes in. They planned for two weeks max if all went well. Livingstone's map and notes should get them quickly to the starting point for seeking out the Garden of Eden itself.

Phin was financing the whole operation out of his own personal funds. The plane tickets, the gear, lodging, meals, etc. It wasn't super expensive but it wasn't cheap either. Max had inquired as to how Phin was paying for it all, but he deflected. The truth was that Phin had access to a family trust left to him after his father's death. It contained several million dollars. But Phin had sworn it off, knowing how that money had been obtained. Remus lived off the trust freely, but not Phin. He had always viewed it as tainted. Only twice in his life had he dipped into the funds. Once, to pay for Autumn's expenses with SecondLife, Inc., and now, for this trip to find the Garden of Eden. Phin intended to never touch it again.

With everything easily collected, they spent the night at the Outback Lodge in Arusha. A modest traveler's hotel with good food. They sat around that night, telling stories and enjoying one another's company. Phin lit up his favorite travel pipe with a bowl of Captain Black Royal. He passed a small package to Jason, "A graduation gift for you, my friend." Jason tore the plain brown wrapping off. It was a pipe. A Peterson Dongal Rocky 03. Made in Ireland, it was a "thinking man's pipe."

Jason was overwhelmed. He turned the apple-shaped briar over in his hands, "Man, I don't know what to say, Dr.- I mean, Phin. Thank you so much."

"Welcome to the club, Jason." He slid a pouch of pipe tobacco over. "Light it up and see how it smokes." He did just that.

"You guys enjoy," Max squawked. "I tried once, Jason, but could never get into the hobby. I love the smell, but it's just not my thing. Plus, Shelly would never let me smoke in the house." The men laughed and continued to share stories late into the evening.

The next day the trio drove out of Arusha and swung up north through the small town of Karatu, then turned west toward the Ngorongoro Crater and finally out across the Serengeti. It was slow-going but they were not in a rush. The weather was perfect with sunny skies and temperatures in the low eighties.

The men marveled at the beauty of the land. They had arrived on the back end of the rainy season so the normally brown grasses of the plains popped with a vibrant green color. For a whole day they followed the tourist route dominated by safari vehicles from more than a dozen companies. Clusters of zebra, wildebeest, and cape buffalo were easy to spot. Jason couldn't quit taking pictures with his phone. He'd never seen anything like it. Eventually they turned off of the heavier trafficked routes and began to trek out into the lesser-known regions of north central Tanzania. The Serengeti was left behind and the land became noticeably more barren. A smattering of mud brick and tin-roofed houses could be seen in the distance. The people living out here got by on farming and meager livestock.

They stopped to spend the night in a village they identified on their map as Mbuga Lugunya. It was a tiny, yet typical, African village - children wearing little clothing, more mud brick homes and buildings, but overall not heavily populated. Phin guestimated maybe a dozen structures that made up the main thoroughfare through the village. There were obviously no accommodations, so they would sleep with their vehicle. They were, however, able to purchase a cooked meal from a local kitchen. Very few, if any, white people ever came through, so they attracted a lot of attention from pretty much everyone - especially the children who swarmed the three explorers. Max and Jason were surprised at the friendliness of the people - Phin, however, was not. He knew of the hospitality of most Africans from his time serving as a missionary.

The next three days were extremely slow-going. The roads they were forced to travel were narrow, rutted, and in some cases didn't look like roads at all - more like hiking or game trails. They were aiming toward the mark on Livingstone's map where he had encountered the isolated tribe that called themselves the guardians of the holy forest. That was nearly one hundred fifty years ago, though, and the chances this tribe was still in existence could be slim. But it was the best they had to go on as a place to start.

Eventually, there were no more roads or trails - at least not headed in the direction they needed to go. Lake Victoria was far to the north, and that was the direction they were now pointed per Livingstone's map. Phin, Max, and Jason stood outside their Land Cruiser surveying the terrain.

"Somewhere - out there - is the answer," Phin said. The day had become hot, hotter than any day before it. The three were wearing canvas hats with brims all the way around. They found themselves sweating even in the low humidity.

"We have to be a good fifty or so miles from where Livingstone said he encountered the guardians," Max had leaned over the hood of the all-terrain vehicle with his copy of their map. "That's a long way to walk, Phin. I say we go off road and see how far we can really take this thing before we have to leave her behind and hump it on foot." Both Phin and Jason agreed. The Land Cruiser was a hearty vehicle, ideal for the punishment of off-road travel. They would just need to go slow.

For three more days they lumbered across the open terrain. It was rocky, bumpy, and did a number on their backsides. But it was better than walking, they decided. Plus, they were able to sit in the shade and avoid the torture of the sun. On day four the skies opened up with rain and the going went even slower as the ground slicked up into a muddy mess. They prayed they would not get stuck or break down. There was no cell service and no one back home had a clue where they were. They were completely off the grid and totally alone. Nevertheless, the vehicle did its job and they carried on.

They were able to cover forty solid miles before they finally decided it was time to leave the Toyota behind and hike the rest of the way. They estimated they were five to ten miles from the isolated tribe they were seeking. And isolated they were. Phin doubted anybody ever came out here. They had seen no signs of human life for days. None of the traditional mud brick homes that typically dotted the landscape, no farms, no anything. They didn't want to just roll up in a 4X4 metal beast to a group of people who had never encountered anyone from the civilized world. Their mere presence was likely to be a surprise as it was.

Waking early in the morning just as the sun was rising, they gathered all their supplies - food, water, survey instruments, camera, and so forth, into their three packs, and off they went. Jason suggested they lock the vehicle and Max responded by slapping the back of his head and knocking his hat off.

It was close to noon when they found it. They walked upon what had to be Livingstone's village almost unawares. Village was really an overstatement. A boma of thicket and briars surrounded what looked like a collection of no more than ten small huts. The berm of protection made it hard to make out what was on the other side, but that was the best way to describe it, Phin thought: huts. They weren't fashioned from the typical mud bricks used throughout the rest of the country; these huts were merely mud-packed together with sticks and stubble, along with thatched roofs as opposed to sheet metal. They looked ancient. They could easily have walked past the boma and not seen the village inside had it not been for a black body, clothed only in a loin cloth, that darted through an opening and disappeared.

"Hold up!" Phin called. "Did you see that? Someone just ran inside that thicket."

"This has to be it! This has to be Livingstone's isolated tribe," Max was excited. "We are right on top of where he said it would be –

but man, look how hidden that is. If we weren't looking we would never think to stop."

Three men, also in loin clothes, emerged. They were each carrying a spear but had stoic expressions on their faces. Only twenty feet or so from Phin, Max, and Jason, they just stared, matching the three man-for-man.

"What do we do, guys?" Jason whispered.

"Let me see what I can do," Phin replied, letting his pack slip to the ground. He took a step forward with his hands in the air, indicating he meant no harm.

"Jumbo!" Phin exclaimed, the word for hello in Swahili. *"Sisi ni marafiki."* We are friends. Phin moved slowly forward to within just a few feet of the warriors. Their heads were bald and they wore large gauges in their lobes. Other than that, there were no other distinguishing marks on their bodies. The one in the middle made a quick step forward and lowered his spear. It was a quick jab that ended with the tip just at Phin's heart.

"Whoa, whoa, whoa!" shouted Max. He threw down his own pack and took a step forward with his hands up too. *"Jumbo! Jumbo!"* He didn't know Swahili, he was just repeating what Phin had said. "It's okay. We are not here to hurt anybody. We aren't a threat."

The other two Africans began to shout and point with their spears. It was impossible to understand their language but not their intent. Their communication was crystal clear. They wanted the three white men to leave - immediately. And they were being pointed in the direction from which they had come. Jason froze as did Max.

"What do we do, Phin? Tell us what to do," Max pleaded. Phin was looking into the eyes of the young, near-naked warrior still holding the spear, touching the fabric of his shirt with its razor-sharp pointed end.

"It's okay," Phin spoke in English, his voice calm and cool.

Without taking his eyes off the black face staring back at him, Phin took a chance. He reached down ever so slowly with his right hand, wrapping his palm and fingers around the wooden shaft of the spear, just below the metal tip. Then, with slow firm pressure, he eased it to the side. He could feel streams of perspiration running down his back. He had stopped breathing. The guardian of the boma did not resist. Was that a softening in his facial features that Phin saw? Speaking very softly, he repeated, "It's okay. It's okay. My name is Phin. Phin." He said his name with force, having lowered his left hand now, patting his chest. "Phin," he said a third time and then, turning his palm face-up and motioning to the man in front of him, he asked, "You? What's your name?"

The warrior withdrew his spear and held it once again at his side. He seemed to understand what Phin was asking. "Chuqua!" he said with force, pounding his own chest.

Phin smiled, "Chuqua!" He looked at Max and Jason and then pointed at Chuqua and said his name again. "Chuqua!"

"Chuqua!" shouted Jason with enthusiasm.

Max followed suit, "Chuqua."

"Jason!" the new college graduate said, pumping his own chest with vigor. "Jason!"

Trying to match his gusto, Max went next, "Max!"

Chuqua opened his mouth to speak. "Fffeen," he struggled to articulate, stepping forward and putting a hand on Phin's shoulder.

"That's right," he replied. "Phin."

"Pheen," the African said with more confidence. He walked over to Jason and stared at him a moment, thinking. "Jaaysin," he managed to say. Jason smiled and nodded his head. Chuqua slapped him on the shoulder as well, with a firm squeeze to finish. He next approached Max and took a bit more time thinking.

"Max," said Max to help him.

"Mmmask," Chuqua was able to form. Max smiled back and received the now customary shoulder squeeze. "Pheen. Jaaysin. Mmask," he proclaimed with pride.

The other two had watched the whole exchange and began to repeat the names of their three visitors over and over. The tension in the air had eased considerably. Phin knew that if he could humanize himself and his friends - put names to their faces - it could turn the tide. It was much harder to hate someone or be fearful of them if you knew them as a real person. Phin's instincts had been correct.

Chuqua picked up Phin's pack and began motioning for the group to come inside the boma. *"Kapua!"* he said pointing to the entrance. *"Kapua!"* One of the other warriors took the pack from Jason's back while the third one picked up Max's. The group moved along. This was more than Phin could have hoped for given their initial reception.

"I guess they're rolling the red carpet out for us," Max conceded and joined Phin at the entrance. Jason followed.

It had been an anxiety-filled exchange, and in the commotion of it all no one noticed the growing sound - or *rumble* would be more accurate. Phin picked up on it now. He looked back over his shoulder. Ahead of him inside the ringed thicket of branches lay the small collection of huts. Other men were gathering to see who Chuqua was bringing to them. As Phin looked back, he could see a cloud of dust growing.

"What *is* that?" he asked.

"What's what?" Max asked in return.

"That sound. Do you hear it? And look at that cloud. It sounds like something's coming this way."

"Out here? No way." But the sound had grown too loud to miss now. The three warriors immediately changed posture. They dropped the packs of their new friends. The other men inside the enclosure scrambled as well. It was like a hornet's nest had been kicked.

Without any warning, a massive Humvee type vehicle tore over a small hill about thirty yards away. It was much closer than they had imagined, quickly approaching. There was yelling and shoving and spears waving and threatening voices. So much was happening in a chaotic mash of just seconds. Jason was on his face on the ground somehow. Max made a run for it while Phin just stood watching.

The large armored monster aimed right toward the group at high speed. It came to a quick stop just feet away from the wild bunch of Africans panicked and spewing. A suffocating cloud of dirt surrounded the scene from the sudden stop. The front door flew open and a set of combat boots thudded to the ground.

"Did you girls call the cavalry?!"

What the??? Phin's mind spun. It was Sergeant Billy Warren! In Africa. Right in front of him. Before anyone could react, Warren took in the scene. He saw the spears and the yelling warriors and sensed disaster. His military instincts kicked in and he acted before he thought.

"Holy mother!" He drew his side arm and began firing wildly in the air. The warriors went crazy. One of them chunked his spear at Warren and nearly landed a blow. He fired into the ground in front of the man, sending him fleeing. The other two were already backing away, screaming and taunting with their own spears. Other warriors were spilling out of the entrance of the boma, armed with primitive weapons.

"You guys jump in! Fast!" Phin, Max, and Jason didn't need any coaxing. They grabbed their gear and sprinted for the Humvee. All hope of a peaceful encounter was lost. A side door flung open and the three men launched themselves into a black hole. Another spear flew toward the sergeant. He dodged its deadly trajectory and then returned fire. The last thing Phin saw was Chuqua as he took a shot in his upper shoulder and was spun around violently before landing hard on the ground.

"Nooo!" Phin cried out as the door to the Humvee slammed closed.

CHAPTER FORTY-SIX

Phin punched Sergeant Warren in the jaw as hard as he could. "What were you thinking?!"

The former Marine's reflexes were quick and the blow landed, but not full-on. He shoved Phin hard with both hands and came back at him, fists up. "Hey punk, I just saved your life!" Ruth LaPhage jumped between the two men as Max and Jason grabbed Phin and pulled him away.

"You guys take it easy, will you?" Max was shouting.

"Yeah, well there wouldn't be any saving to do if you hadn't come barreling in with that tank on four wheels!" Phin pointed to the Humvee and spat. He continued his efforts to get at Warren. The sergeant had piled into the front seat of the vehicle after getting Phin,

Max, and Jason inside and secured. Then he'd hit the accelerator and tore out away from the boma, as the natives pelted the Humvee with spears, rocks, and anything else they could find to throw at it. Warren drove as fast as he dared for a good five minutes before stopping. Phin had been yelling the whole time, insisting he wanted to get out.

"Back off, Billy!" Ruth yelled. She turned the sergeant around hard and shoved him in the back, away from the group. Facing Phin she said, "Phin, are you all okay? That's the most important thing right now." Ruth's voice immediately defused the brawl.

"Yes. As I said, we are all just fine. Everything is fine. Or I guess I should say it *was* fine. Until you all showed up." The group from LaPhage was small. It was only Billy Warren, Ruth LaPhage, and Tony Chen. Oz was still recovering from his snakebite in Texas, Phin surmised. "Why exactly *are* you here, Ruth? How did you even know how to find us?"

Ruth laughed. Not a condescending, in-your-face kind of laugh, but a warm we-are-all-friends laugh. "Come on, Phineas. We are here for the exact same reason you are. To find the Garden of Eden, for real this time, I might add. As to how we found you? We've been watching you ever since we all departed in Turkey. Your side trip to Jerusalem. Your private meetings with Max and...Jason Morris, I presume?" Ruth turned and asked of Jason.

Jason only nodded in return with a meek, "Yes, ma'am."

"Nice to meet you, Jason." She extended a hand of greeting and Jason took it and shook. "I'm sure Phin has told you about me. Welcome to our little adventure. You've probably already guessed that my big friend over there is retired Sergeant Billy Warren." Warren was dusting himself off after the scuffle, checking his jaw - a line of blood out of one corner of his mouth. "And this is Tony Chen. He's our technical specialist. Tony will keep us connected with two others back home that are a part of our little team."

"Our little team? Excuse me, Ruth," Phin broke in. "There is no 'our little team.' Max, Jason, and I are not working with anyone. And you've been following me? Unbelievable!" Phin was furious. He and Ruth had never had an exchange like this. Ruth was trying to remain calm, exuding her charms to get her way, but something had changed with Phin. Perhaps he'd been pushed too far this time. Ruth would have to push back.

"No, it's not unbelievable, Phineas. If you will recall, I have quite the investment in what we are doing. I intend to see this through to the end and get my money's worth. Not to be too formal about it all, but I've hired your services. Your institution has released you to work with me. So here we are. In Tanzania. I assume you know what you are doing this time. I think it's time you shared your plan with all of us." She ended with a smile.

"This is ridiculous," Phin spat and walked away.

"Let me go talk to him, Ruth," Max stepped in. "Jason, why don't you introduce yourself and get to know everyone. Give me and Phin a few minutes."

Phin knew when he was cornered and out of options. He and Max talked, his old friend calming him down. They had no choice but to keep going, with LaPhage Industries now in tow.

The group eventually loaded back into Warren's Humvee and waited for instructions from Phin. Using Livingstone's map as a guide, they skirted the edge of the tribe they had encountered. Phin wondered what had become of Chuqua. Was he even alive? Phin pointed them in the general direction to drive, explaining that they needed to find a small stream or a river.

Even in something as unstoppable as a Humvee, the going was slow given the terrain of rocks, brush, and uneven ground they were traversing, plus they were pulling a small utility trailer, Phin had discovered.

Just at sunset they found it. Definitely more of a stream than river. It would be easy to cross in the Humvee, if needed. The group quickly set up a camp. The utility trailer was loaded with all sorts of gear. It looked to Phin, Max, and Jason as if LaPhage had come prepared for anything.

Sergeant Warren played the role of Mr. Everything for the group of amateur explorers. He issued sleeping gear, gathered wood, began a small fire, put out camping chairs, set up a portable kitchen, and whipped up a delicious meal of real cooked beef slices, green beans, corn, and even peach cobbler.

"I gotta say, Sergeant, you certainly know that if you feed a man's belly you will win his heart," Max said.

"Well, we won't be eating like this every night, so don't get used to it. Just felt like we all needed something to get us on the same page and lift our spirits."

Tony and Jason had taken up talking to one another about all sorts of things tech-related. Tony showed Jason how they were linked to LaPhage Industries back in Texas, explaining the LaPhage proprietary satellites, one of which they'd positioned over their own location. The LaPhage computer geek was decked out in polyester red athletic shorts, an orange tank top, and knee-high white socks with blue stripes. He looked even more out of place in the field than his tech-twin Oz had weeks ago.

Phin ate in silence, just staring into the flames of the fire. As he was finishing his cobbler, Ruth joined him. She plopped down in one of the canvas chairs Warren had put out, scooting over toward Phin. She was carrying some sort of journal. There was a look in her eyes that said she had something to say and could hardly wait to share it.

"Max, why don't you and Jason bring your chairs over here? I need to show you all something." Jason broke away from Tony as Max pulled his own chair around. "Phin, I almost picked up the phone and called you the moment I discovered this," she said, patting the old worn journal.

Trying to look interested, Phin managed to reply, "Found what, Ruth?"

"I solved one of the riddles in my father's ravings about the Garden of Eden." She was bursting. "Jacob's Ladder. Do you remember when we talked about Jacob's Ladder?"

"Yes, I remember. Your father said something about climbing Jacob's Ladder to find the Garden, or get to the tree...something like that, right? Max, didn't you unpack Genesis 28 with her? The whole story of Jacob and his vision of a ladder coming down from heaven?"

"Yep, we went over all that, Ruth. Couldn't see how it connected," said Max.

"Well, I figured it out! Once we got home, I was having another conversation with my father about our trip to Iran. He said we had it wrong the whole time. That all I needed to do was climb Jacob's Ladder. Then it hit me. It's not about Genesis 28 at all. It's about this book," she held up the old journal with both hands. "*This* is Jacob's Ladder."

"That's Jacob's Ladder?" Phin asked, unconvinced.

"This is a journal that records the last days of the life of my older brother, Jacob LaPhage. We called him *Jake*."

"Wait, you have a brother?" asked Phin.

"Had a brother. Jake died in 1994. He was ten years older than me. I was only eleven at the time so I don't remember a whole lot. It was the summer time. He and a group of friends went around the world on the trip of a lifetime. My parents paid for the whole thing. Sort of a turning 21 gift. Their names were Chris Jackson, Ryan Fowler, and Alberto Garcia. Here, I have a picture of them." Ruth handed over a 5x7 color photo of four young men. They were standing at the entrance to a jet-way. Phin imagined this was the last picture taken of the boys as they boarded their flight that took them far from home. They looked so full of life. Ruth continued, "Anyway, their last leg of the trip was somewhere in Africa. We never knew where for sure. They just disappeared. My father pulled on every resource he could find, and pay for, to search for the boys, but he turned up nothing. He also hired a small army of locals throughout the region to keep an eye open for any clues as to what happened to Jake and his friends. He was willing to pay a hefty sum for anything they turned up. He suspected they may have fallen victim to thieves, kidnapping, or worse. If they had been robbed, he believed their gear might end up in one of the markets. Then one day, two years later, sure enough - this journal turned up in a thrift shop in Cairo."

"That's Jake's?" asked Jason.

"No, it belonged to Chris Jackson. It's not a record of the whole trip. Apparently, Chris decided to start writing down his thoughts toward the end, once they were in Africa - just a few days from heading home. Because of what Chris wrote in here, we know that Jake is dead. They all are. My father mourned for over a year. Jake was his only son." Ruth paused and looked down. Was that a tear in her eye? She continued more somber, "His love for my brother drove a wedge between us. I could never live up to Jake's memory. That's why I decided to leave home when I was ready to go to college. Not until my parents' accident did I come back. Dad always called this the Lost Boys Journal. That's why I didn't make the connection. But this is Jacob's Ladder. It all makes sense now. Phin, you have to read this. I never did until two weeks ago. It's astounding! They nearly found it and didn't even know it!"

"Found what, Ruth? You don't mean -"

"Yes! The Garden of Eden. Here, read it for yourself and let me know what you think." Ruth put the Lost Boys Journal into Phin's hand.

CHAPTER
FORTY-SEVEN

Afterward, Phin got up and took a walk some distance from the campsite. It was an astounding thing to read. Jacob's Ladder. He could never have guessed. Ruth had no idea how the journal made it from wherever the boys met their fate to Cairo, but it had been in a canvas bag wrapped in a waterproof cover. The bag itself showed signs of being in the water a long time. Charles LaPhage surmised it had fallen in some river and floated for who knows how long before it was found and sold for pennies into the markets of Cairo. That's when it had been found by one of Charles' men. That in and of itself had been a miracle.

Phin needed to walk and think. He'd left Max and Jason behind to read the journal for themselves. Amazingly, the lost boys had nearly stumbled onto the Garden of Eden. Ruth was correct. Chris Jackson had likely laid eyes on it himself. Everything the boys experienced fit with what they knew from Livingstone. The tribe the boys encountered had to have been the same one Livingstone spent time with, and the one the newly-formed Go Team had met earlier that day. Now they were camped by a river. Livingstone's map indicated he believed the Garden of Eden lay along this same river. Chris had followed the river to a Garden paradise. But what about the tragedy that struck the boys? Chris' writings about a strange creature stalking them and then attacking one of them haunted Phin. His heart had broken as he was riveted to the tale of Chris Jackson and his friends. He couldn't imagine what had led Chris to pen his last haunting words. The Bible indicated that cherubim angels guarded the Garden of Eden. Somehow it all tied together. Livingstone's failed and cryptic attempt to breach the Garden. The fate of the Lost Boys. The warnings in the Bible. Now Phin and his friends were walking that same razor's edge.

Phin continued to walk but was careful not to wander too far. One never knew what kind of wild animals likely roamed the African plains. He found himself looking up into the sky, wondering at the stars, which were all out of place on this side of the world. And he prayed. He prayed for wisdom and direction. Once again he felt swept along by forces out of his control.

There was a crunch of light footfalls approaching. He took in a deep breath, knowing what was coming. "They're beautiful aren't they? The stars." Ruth's presence enveloped him as she stepped up to his side.

"Yes, they are. They remind me of how big God is and how small I am," Phin replied.

"You really believe he's up there, don't you?"

"God?" Phin asked, turning to look at Ruth. She was, indeed, a beautiful woman. Her red hair was pulled back and her green eyes sparkled somehow, despite the darkness. Even in khaki shorts and boots with a safari top she was stunning. "Yes, I know he's up there. And he's in here," Phin placed his hand over his heart. "He's very real, Ruth. Very real and very personal. This whole thing we are doing here is real. It's not a game. What we are doing - finding the Garden of Eden - is serious business. And not just for us, but for God. If we are not respectful, if we don't understand the boundaries, the limits, it could end badly."

As if to change the subject, Ruth asked, "You feel taken advantage of, don't you? That I am here. That we are here. That you can't do this on your own and that you aren't the one in control."

Phin laughed. All of that was true but he replied in a different way. "I just can't believe you tracked me all the way from the time I left Turkey until you found us today. So, yes, I suppose violated is the better term. I feel violated."

She placed her arm in his and leaned in close. She smelled so good. Phin had to be careful. "Look, I didn't *track* you, silly. It's not like in the movies. There are no bugs or devices hidden in your clothes or home or anything. But I had this feeling the whole time we were in Turkey and then Iran. Actually, the thought first came to me when you laid out your plan to us back at our labs in Fort Worth. I thought you might pull something like this. Lead us on a wild goose chase just to fail and then dump us. Oh, I've believed in you the whole time, Phineas." She turned and looked deep into his eyes. "I still believe in you. More than you know. So I just kept an eye on you. To see if you made any moves." Phin arched an eyebrow. "Don't look so surprised. It didn't take any great effort of detective work. You're not as sly as you think you are. Once you booked plane tickets to Africa, I knew. I knew, Phin. And well...here we are."

Phin looked down at his feet, Ruth eased in even closer. "You are quite a woman, Ruth LaPhage. I don't think I've ever met anyone like you."

"I warned you - I'm used to getting what I want, Phin." She moved her face close to his, just inches apart. "We can do this. Together. Just you and me. We will find it as a team - all six of us. But it will just be you and me who go in. What do you say, Phin? Just the two of us in the Garden of Eden. Like Adam and Eve, reborn anew. What if I let my father go and what if you let your wife go? And it was just us?" At the mention of Autumn, Phin drew quickly away.

"What do you know about my wife, Ruth? What are you talking about?"

"Oh Phin," she tried to move back close. "There are no secrets from me. Didn't you know? SecondLife, Inc. is a subsidiary of LaPhage Industries. We are the brains behind the technology keeping your wife alive - and keeping my father alive, for that matter. But let's move on together, Phin. Just you and me." She reached for Phin, to put her arms around him.

"I can't, Ruth. I just can't." Phin's mind was spinning wildly. Ruth knew all about Autumn and SecondLife, Inc.? Oh my, she *was* SecondLife, Inc. How could he have been so stupid?

"Yes, you can! *We* can. Phin, listen to me. No secrets, remember? Not any longer. I told you I want to find the Tree of Life. All true. But Phin, I want to do one more thing. I want to find the other tree. The Tree of the Knowledge of Good and Evil!"

Phin nearly fell over. He took a step back, stumbling. "What are you talking about, Ruth? The Tree of the Knowledge of Good and Evil is forbidden by God! You can't. It's not possible!"

"Yes we can! We can. Together. Don't you see? The only reason God doesn't want us to eat from that tree is because he knows of the power. He knows we can be like him. We can become gods!" She had lost her mind. Phin was sure of it.

"No! Absolutely not. I will have no part of this, Ruth. We will end it right now. I'm done."

There was silence as Ruth stared back at Phin. Her face grew dark as she set her jaw. "I will find it, Phin. The Garden, the Tree. *Both* Trees. I'd rather do it with you. But mark my words, Dr. Crook, I will do it without you if I must. Why don't you think about it? Let's get back to the others. Come along, now. You don't want to be caught out here by yourself."

She turned and walked away. Phin followed, of course. What choice did he have? For good or ill he was stuck with Ruth LaPhage and company. She may be mad, indeed. If that was the case he truly didn't have any other choice. He needed to stay close. It might be his only way of saving them all.

CHAPTER
FORTY-EIGHT

"Hey! Hey! There you guys are!" Tony Chen was out of breath as he met Phin and Ruth walking back to camp. Phin realized they had ventured further away than they had intended. "You gotta come fast! Something is happening on the other side of the river. Sergeant Warren sent me to get you. Told me to run."

The three of them took off as fast as they could, being cautious not to trip or stumble in the darkness. They arrived to a blazing fire and an empty campsite.

"Where'd everyone go?" Phin exclaimed. He was on edge after reading the Lost Boys Journal.

"Follow me," Tony yelled back as he ran on through the campsite and past the Humvee. Ruth and Phin followed. Once they were past the fire their eyes adjusted and they saw Sergeant Warren close to the river with Jason and Max. Warren was holding a semi-automatic assault rifle. Phin pulled up next to the sergeant and was about to ask why the need for the firepower.

"Take it easy and stay close to me, Doc," Warren instructed with his hand held out.

"What's going on? Why are we down here by the riv-" Phin didn't finished his own sentence because he saw. Across the river a mere thirty yards from where their group was standing was a line of shadowy figures.

"It's them...the men from the tribe we had the run in with. Don't know how long they've been here. Just saw them when I was walking the perimeter." The warriors formed a line fifteen in number. They were all holding spears and facing the Go Team.

"I don't like this," Tony said. "Oz told me weird stuff like this went down in Iran."

"Not like this, Tony. This is different." Phin said. "Have you all noticed the foul smell in the air? Ever since we unloaded and made camp? Just like what Ruth's brother and his friends encountered. We are definitely in the right place."

"Or the wrong place," Jason said. He was clearly uneasy. "So what do we do?"

"We don't *do* anything," ordered Warren. "You all stick close to me. They charge and I'll take 'em all out." He patted his rifle as if it were his best friend.

"No sir, you won't!" Phin shot back. "In the air, Sergeant. Not at *or* into them. Am I understood? Tell him, Ruth. We are the ones trespassing."

"All I'm sayin', Doc, is if it comes down to us or them..." Warren said. He was not taking his eyes off the warriors.

Something began to happen. It was imperceptible at first, but

Max was the first to pick up on it. "Listen!" he whispered. "They're chanting something." It was unrecognizable, but the men were definitely making some sort of guttural sound, in rhythm. It grew louder, if ever so slightly. Growing and growing as the seconds ticked by.

Whomp! There was a stomp, in unison. First, with their right, then their left feet. *Whomp! Whomp! WHOMP! WHOMP!* Over and over. The movements became more exaggerated as did the chanting.

"It looks like some sort of ritual," Phin suggested.

"How will it end, Phin?" Ruth asked. "Are they casting some sort of curse on us?"

"I think it's a warning. They don't want us here, that's clear. I think they're invoking some sort of spirit or barrier."

The warriors formed a large circle and began to move counter-clockwise, violently wagging their heads. UP. Then DOWN. Up. Down. *WHOMP! WHOMP!* All to beat of their chanting. The air began to feel different. It was a warm night, but a chill swept across both sides of the river. Ruth wrapped her arms around herself. One of the warriors tore away from the circle, walking to the middle. It was difficult for the group to make out what was happening until a burst of flames erupted.

"Whoa! What is that about?" Max exclaimed. The group stared on in awe. What they were observing was very ancient, no doubt, and very strange.

"I don't feel right, guys," Tony said. "My head is light. I think I'm gonna puke."

"Just sit down, Tony. Take it easy," Jason coaxed. He had moved over to assist Tony.

"I gotta go back to the camp. I can't do this!" Tony took off.

"Hey, Tony! Don't man. We need to stay together," Jason called.

"Let him go," Warren said. "He'll be fine as long as he stays behind us. Ain't nothin' gettin' past me."

The fire grew, the flames now twice the height of the dancing and chanting warriors.

"What's fueling that fire? I don't see any wood." Max asked.

A scream shattered the night. A horrific, terrible scream. Inhuman in every way. The group took a step back, including Warren.

"What the - what is that?!" Ruth cried out. "It's so awful!"

The scream echoed down the riverbed a second time, this time louder and longer. The flames grew taller still. The warrior who had ignited the fire walked to the outside of the circle, down to the river's edge. He was now a short distance from the group. He stopped with his feet barely in the water, lifted his spear overhead with both hands, and let out a bloodcurdling yell, *"AAAAHHHHHEEEEEEEE!!!!!!!"*

It was Chuqua! Phin was certain of it. But how? How was it possible? He'd seen him go down, shot. He doubted if he was even alive. Had he somehow been miraculously healed? It was too much to comprehend.

Then the impossible.

Out of the raging fire, inside the circle of undulating men, the scream came once again. This time a beast rose from the flames - a black silhouette hovering over the top of the flames, at least thirty feet high now. A massive winged creature, larger than any eagle Phin had ever seen.

"God help us!" Max cried out, lifting his forearm in front of his face. The light from the fire intensified. It was impossible to make out any of the warriors now. The winged beast seemed to be growing in size. Or was it coming at them?!

"Everyone get back!" yelled Sergeant Warren over the cries of the bird. He let off a string of fire from his weapon. The group scrambled back. But, no, the creature wasn't coming toward them. It was growing. Larger and larger.

"What is that thing?!" Phin could barely hear Ruth over the screaming of the terrible beast.

Whatever it was - a terrible supernatural, otherworldly eagle beast - shot straight up into the night sky, pulling a trail of light or fire with it. Like a giant flaming sword, Phin thought. He had ideas in his head about all he was witnessing. Phin could hear Ruth and Max and even the sergeant gasp for air. The flight of the bird sucked the oxygen out of the atmosphere, like a vacuum. He was fighting to get his own breath. Falling to his knees, he tried to keep his eyes on the fire. The beast had gone. Simply up and away. The pillar of fire remained, at least a hundred feet into the air. But how? That's when Phin noticed that the warriors were gone. Vanished. Even Chuqua. Where was anyone's guess. The air came back into his lungs as he rose to his feet, slowly, so as not to get a head rush. The pillar of fire descended, like it was being sucked back into the earth. It took less than a minute and then it was gone. No trace left at all. The group stood looking, shaken to the core.

"What...was...that?" Warren was the first to speak.

"I think I have an idea." Phin answered timidly. Everyone turned to stare at him, eyes wide.

"You *know* what that was?" Ruth asked, incredulous.

"Yes," he hesitated, still in thought, "I think I do. Let's get back to our camp and I'll try to explain."

CHAPTER
FORTY-NINE

The group sat close around their campfire. It felt like the closer they could get to the flames, the safer they would be from whatever it was they had experienced. Even though it had all vanished - the terrible flying beast, the warriors, the fire in the sky - there was an unmistakable feeling shared by all that something had changed. It was clearly because of their presence. They were close. Oh, so close to the Garden of Eden. Phin knew it.

"The air really does stink here," Tony blurted out. He had recovered from his bout of sickness. He was sipping a hot cup of coffee that Sergeant Warren had whipped up. All of the others were drinking coffee as well, except for Phin. He was smoking his travel pipe, deep in thought.

"Keep the joe flowing, Sergeant," Max said. "I don't think anyone's sleeping tonight."

"You got that right. Not after whatever it was we saw down there." Jason said. "So, Dr. Crook, what's your theory? What was that thing we saw?"

"*Phin,* Jason. I've told you that it's Phin now," Phin replied.

"Sorry, I'm just used to Dr. Crook. Right now, I'm so jacked up, I gotta go with what's natural. If you know what I mean." Jason took another gulp of black coffee.

"Let's get to your theory, Phin." Ruth wanted to get back on track, to understand what had just happened.

Phin grabbed the canvas shoulder bag he carried with him when traveling and lifted the flap. He kept his pipe and tobacco, a journal, small camera, and a few other items on hand at all times. Fishing around inside he pulled out a worn black leather Bible, compact size, just large enough to cover the whole of one hand.

"We are told in the text of Scripture," Phin began, "that after God expelled Adam and Eve from the Garden of Eden, his intent was for man to never enter it again. So God established a guardian, a holy vessel, to watch over and protect the Garden. To keep us away." Phin looked at the faces staring back at him in turn. Max, Jason, the sergeant, Tony, and Ruth. They each leaned in, hanging on his every word. He could see the hunger in their eyes for some kind of explanation of what they had witnessed.

"An angel, right? Isn't that what the Bible says? That God placed an angel to guard the entrance to the Garden of Eden," asked Ruth.

"Generally, yes, Ruth. The Bible says that God placed an angel at the entrance to the Garden, but not just any angel. Let me read what it says in Genesis 3:

He (God) drove out man, and at the east of the garden of Eden he placed the cherubim and a flaming sword that turned every way to guard the way to the tree of life."

"Wait, what's a cherubim? Is that what it says? Cherubim? What exactly is that?" Sergeant Warren asked. He all of a sudden was highly interested in the Bible, thought Phin.

"That's my point. God didn't place just any angel to guard the Garden of Eden. He appointed cherubim. That's a specific type of angel," Phin answered.

"You mean there's more than one kind of angel? Man, I thought an angel was just an angel. You know, some fairy girl in a white robe with bird wings. Oh, and a golden ring floating over her head."

Phin chuckled and took a draw on his pipe. "That's because you've seen too many pictures or paintings of angels, Sergeant. Most people think the same way you do."

"Put me in that camp," Tony said. "I just thought all angels were the same."

"Well, that's not the case. When you take away Hollywood and mythology and look only at the Bible, you will get a completely different idea about God's army of angels. Think about it this way: just like in a human army, there are all kinds of soldiers. You have infantry, airborne, mechanized military tank soldiers, etc. It's not any different with God and his angels. The Bible lists at least four different kinds of angels, each with their own jobs or tasks. You have messenger angels. Their name says it all. They deliver messages from God to people."

"Like the angel Gabriel at Christmas time." Jason said, excited. He knew this from his own studies but wanted to help the conversation along.

"That's right, like the angel Gabriel. There is also the archangel. This is a high-command angel. Maybe the highest order of all the angels. The Bible gives us the name of Michael as one of these archangels. Then there are the seraphim. These are angels that serve in the presence of God himself. They offer praise and song and adoration to God. But the last category are the cherubim. These are big-time warrior angels. They are the business end of what God wants done on earth. They make things happen. So, this is the kind of angel that, we are told in Genesis, guards the Garden of Eden."

"Okay, thanks for the Sunday school lesson, Doc. But what's all this got to do with that action down by the river?" Warren was losing his patience.

"I think what we saw tonight was the summoning of a cherub. A holy angel sent by God to keep us out of the Garden of Eden."

"Whoa! Wait a minute. I didn't see no angel. I saw some crazy bird beast outta some horror movie."

"No, I don't think you did. Look, forget everything you think you know about what an angel looks like, okay? All those images you've seen your whole life where angels are feminine with golden haloes. It's all wrong. Trash." Phin was thumbing his way through his Bible again. "In the Book of Ezekiel - he was a prophet in the Old Testament - we see a description of a cherub. Listen to this:

As for the likeness of their faces, each had a human face. The four had the face of a lion on the right side, the four had the face of an ox on the left side, and the four had the face of an eagle. Such were their faces. And their wings were spread out above. Each creature had two wings."

"Man, this is blowing my mind. That doesn't sound anything like any angel I've heard of," Warren spouted.

"That's the point. The way I read the Bible, a cherub can take on any one of four forms: a man, an ox, a lion-"

"Or an eagle," finished Ruth. She was rubbing her temples with both hands.

"That's right. An eagle. But obviously not just any eagle. And going back to the book of Genesis, remember we are told that the cherubim hold a flaming sword. Was it just me or did anyone else-"

"Nope, not just you, Phin," Max jumped in. "I thought the same thing. It was like a giant flaming sword shooting into the sky."

"That's what I thought too," said Jason.

"Ditto. Me too," Tony joined the chorus. "Man, what have we gotten ourselves into?"

"And there's one more thing," said Phin. A collective groan made its way around the campfire. "The word *cherub* is singular, referring to one cherub angel. Genesis says the Garden of Eden is guarded by *cherubim*."

"Meaning?" asked Sergeant Warren.

"*Cherubim* is the plural form of the word." Phin let what he was saying sink in.

"You mean there's more than one of those bird monsters out there?" Max asked, incredulous.

"Oh, man...not good," Tony sighed.

"What I'm saying is there's more than one of something out there. Remember, a cherub can take on more than one form. An eagle is just one. There's also an ox, a lion...and a man."

Sergeant Warren picked up his rifle and began to reload it.

CHAPTER
FIFTY

The Go Team spent the next morning over breakfast laying out plans for how they wanted to approach the Garden of Eden. As the group suspected, none of the six of them got much sleep, preferring instead to sit in their canvas camping chairs in silence, taking turns adding wood to the fire. Phin dozed on and off, feeling the effects of a long previous day. He was fatigued, and by the looks of Max and Jason, they weren't doing much better. Ruth was her usual chipper self, overly excited to get to their destination. As soon as the sun cracked the horizon, she was up and stirring the rest of the group to get going. She was ready to move. Sergeant Warren looked unfazed, but he was military. He was used to long nights and no sleep. Tony had the appearance of a young man totally out of place, wishing he were anywhere else in the world but where he was. He also looked scared and was complaining about being lightheaded again. If anything, the odor around them had grown worse overnight.

"I think we must be close," Phin was saying. They were all gathered around a small field table, and Phin was leaned over a blown-up copy of the Livingstone map. "As best as I can figure, we are somewhere around here, right next to this river." He place a finger on the map to show the others. "I am guessing that Ruth's brother, Jake, and his friends also ended up somewhere close by, according to Chris Jackson's journal entries. They were by this same river. And somewhere on the other side is where he said he saw one of their group, Alberto, attacked and killed by something that he said looked like an eagle but different. I can only assume it's the same thing we saw last night."

"And your theory is that that eagle beast is a cherub angel placed here by God, right?" asked Max.

"Yes, I believe it could be. For sure." Phin answered his friend. Max took his hat off and wiped his brow, blowing out a puff of air. Phin continued, "So Chris Jackson says in his journal that he walked down river, the same side we are on now. He eventually came to a point where the terrain wouldn't let him go any further. I'm assuming the land rises up onto a bluff of some sort. He didn't want to climb it, so as he fled their camp after Alberto was killed, he swam across. He continued on downriver, and that's when he said he saw...let's see, I wrote it down in my own notes." Phin fished his journal out of his bag and flipped through it. "Here it is. Chris says, *'It's even greener and more lush here. I've entered a jungle almost.'* And then he writes, *'I looked back across the river and began to cry. There is a grove of trees, maybe just 75 yards on the other side. There's what looks like fruit hanging from them.'* According to the entry, he planned to cross back over the next day. But then...well, something awful happened. The journal comes to an end."

"Yeah, I can only guess," Sergeant Warren muttered. He was also deep in thought, absorbing all Phin was saying.

"Livingstone's map has the X marking the Garden of Eden downriver. Chris went downriver and found it. The Garden of Eden. I have no doubt now. That's the direction we must go and it can't be far. We can easily be there today."

"What about crossing the river?" Warren asked.

"We do it here," Phin replied. "The water is shallow and we can easily drive the Humvee across. There's no guarantee we can do it if we go further downstream. In fact, I doubt we can. Chris said he had to swim."

"So we cross over here?" asked Warren warily. "To the other side where that little shindig took place last night?"

"You got it, Sergeant." Phin confirmed.

Warren took a deep breath in. "Alrighty then...let's rock and roll!"

Breaking camp was quick. Warren worked to ready the Humvee and trailer. Ruth was on her laptop connecting with Dr. Sayer and Oz back in Texas, informing them about their plans, and making sure they were ready to provide support when called upon. Phin still didn't understand how they could help but he didn't pursue it. For all of Ruth's talk about no more secrets, he didn't believe it. There was always more to uncover when it came to Ruth LaPhage, he had decided. He was very concerned about her too. He had seen a glimpse into her heart last night. She was hungry for power. The Tree of the Knowledge of Good and Evil. It was crazy. Phin doubted they could breach the entrance to the Garden of Eden at all, but if Ruth had access to that particular tree and its fruit it would be disastrous. He had to prevent it at all cost. He was juggling so much in his head and he was tired. He prayed for God to give him the strength and wisdom he would need this day.

The Go Team completed preparations and piled into the

Humvee. Sergeant Warren fired it up and worked his way to the river's edge.

"Hold on to your underwear!" he called back over his shoulder, easing the metal behemoth into the water. It was not deep, maybe mid-thigh high if one were walking. But no one wanted to walk. The thought of the eagle beast out there made the inside of the Humvee the place to be.

The crossing went without incident. In fact, it was anticlimactic. On the other side, they stopped where last night's ritual had taken place and got out of the vehicle. There was nothing left but a massive scorch mark on the ground, about six feet across. The rocks were completely melted or charred. No one said a word. Phin couldn't help but keep an eye on the sky until they were safely back in the Humvee, continuing their trek.

They took their time heading downstream. Warren could have pushed it but there was no need.

Phin had Max and Jason taking pictures out of both sides of the vehicle as he was making his own notes in his journal. He wanted to record everything from this point on. As they moved on, Phin noticed the lushness of the vegetation was indeed increasing. The river also looked to be getting deeper, wider, the water flowing faster. Warren noticed the river as well and thumbs up'd Phin for the decision to make the crossing upstream. No way they could do it now.

Greener and lusher - Chris Jackson had been right in how he described it. By noon the area around them had become more jungle-like and less of an arid desert. They stopped for lunch and noticed immediately upon stepping out of the vehicle that the foul odor was gone. The air was rich and sweet, almost intoxicating.

Max and Jason were busy collecting plant samples and taking lots of photos. Sergeant Warren noted to Phin and Ruth it was going to be slow-going from this point forward. Lots of trees and vegetation.

"I'm gonna stick close to the water. Less growth there. Ruthie, you need to be thinking about what we're gonna do if we hit a point that we can't take the Humvee any further," Warren said.

"I already have. I don't think we will have much choice. We will have to unpack and use the inflatable."

"Yep, the raft. That's what I thought you'd say."

"You guys brought a raft?" Max asked, overhearing the conversation. He gave Jason and Phin a look.

"Oh, we brought more than that. Trust me, we're ready for anything." Warren wadded up the trash from his lunch. "Let's load up! Time is tickin' and the sun is sinkin'."

They were on their way once again. The sergeant maneuvered the Humvee right to the water's edge, the left wheels actually *in* the water at times. The growth of the jungle was becoming intense, encroaching more and more toward the river as they drove on. After an hour and maybe only two miles further, the jungle had forced them nearly all the way to the water.

"We can't go much further, guys!" boomed Warren. He was fighting the vehicle as it slipped in the mud and rocks.

Jason cried out, "Hey, what's that?!" He was in the back, pointing out the front window.

"What's what?" Warren shot back.

"I just saw someone...on the other side of the river. They were running."

"Stop the vehicle, Billy! Everyone out," ordered Ruth. She was frantic as she undid the latches to the door. The group spilled out of the right side, Ruth running to the front of the Humvee.

"We found it..." she murmured. "We found it!" calling back over her shoulder a second time. Phin joined her and stared across the river. Another fifty or so yards on up and across the river, set back a distance from its bank, was a grove of trees. "We found it, Phineas!" She grabbed Phin's arm and squeezed him close.

CHAPTER
FIFTY-ONE

"Somebody give me a pair of binoculars - quick," called Phin. Jason was by his side, shoving a pair into his hands. Phin raised them to his eyes, giving the area across the river a long appraisal.

"Well?" Ruth could hardly contain herself.

Smiling and continuing to look, Phin said, "There's fruit. All over the trees. Can't tell what kind but it's everywhere."

"It's the grove in Chris's journal! Has to be. The Tree of Life, Phin! The grove is full of the *Trees* of Life!" Ruth squealed like a teenage girl in love. Phin continued to look, adjusting the zoom on the binoculars. Without warning, a figure stepped into his vision. He jerked the binoculars down.

"What's wrong?" Max asked. He saw the look on his friend's face.

"Somebody's over there."

"I told you I saw someone running," said Jason. Phin raised the glasses to his eyes again and there he was. He couldn't believe what he was seeing - a young man, no more than twenty-one or twenty-two years of age. He was standing within the grove of trees looking in their direction. Blonde-headed, he was wearing a denim long-sleeved top and khaki shorts, brown leather boots cladding his feet. It's impossible, Phin thought. His mind raced back to the picture of the lost boys that Ruth had shown the group. He was looking at Chris Jackson. The resemblance was unmistakable. But it was impossible. The figure bolted into the trees. Phin fought to find him again.

"What is it, Phin?" Ruth asked. "Is it one of the warriors from the tribe?"

Phin lowered the binoculars, clearly disturbed. "I don't know. I'm not sure." He couldn't bring himself to say aloud what it was that his eyes had told him.

"Well, we aren't just going to stand around. Billy, get the inflatable ready." Ruth commanded.

"Whoa, whoa, whoa, hold on Ruth," Phin barked. "We need to think about this. We can't just go storming over there. It may not be safe. Think back to what we saw last night."

"Don't worry, Phin. We've got a plan. Remember, I always have a plan!" she gave him a wink. "Tony," she turned to look at the computer tech. "Time to break open the crates. I'll get the link established with Texas."

"You got it!" Tony jumped up, excited.

"Wait." Phin called. "Crates? What crates?" He and Max followed Tony, who was already opening the trailer. He leaned inside and gave a big heave. Out rolled a crate the size of a coffin. It thudded onto the ground. Phin and Max recognized it immediately. It was the same kind of crate they had hauled around Turkey and Iran. The same kind of crate Ruth and the sergeant had said exploded into a massive fireball the night they escaped.

"What is this?!" Phin demanded. "You brought one of these out here to Tanzania?"

"This," Ruth said, having joined them, laying a hand on the plywood top. "This is our secret weapon. This is how we are going to get into the Garden of Eden." Warren arrived and punched a code on the box. Then he and Tony unlatched the top and lifted it off. Phin nearly fell over. He was staring at a lifeless body. Not just any lifeless body, it was the same someone who had broken into his house back in February.

"I knew it!" Phin thundered. "I knew you were behind the break-in at my house, Ruth." He was furious, seeing red, unable to ever remember a time he had been this angry. "I don't even know what to say. This is unbelievable! Who *are* you people? What exactly *is* that thing?"

Max shook his head and looked at his friend, *"That's"* what broke into your house and sent you to the hospital? Sheesh...what kind of sick operation are you guys?" He directed the last question at Ruth.

Ruth held up both hands and began. "Phin, I told you there would be no more secrets. This is the biggest one of all. I just needed to wait until the right time to explain it to you. Give me a chance and I think you will understand." She pleaded and then proceeded to explain everything. Project BORG, the Robatar, how the AI worked with Billy Warren in control, the contract with the Department of Defense, the field testing, everything. She apologized profusely for the violation to his property. She just had to know, she went on, if Phin was even close to knowing where the Garden of Eden was or if he was just some crackpot. Sergeant Warren apologized as well. They had never intended to confront Phin directly or for him to be hurt. The plan had been to be in and out and for Phin to never know. Well, now he knew all.

"So your plan is to send this Robatar thing across the river and let it explore the Garden," Phin was trying his best to put his emotions aside and understand. It might actually work, he thought. A machine might have better luck than a human. And it would be safer, he admitted. He was still fuming about the personal violation, but decided this was no time to deal with that. It would have to wait.

"That's right. You and me are going to take the inflatable over with the Robatar. Stay close to shore but let it do all the work. It can retrieve samples and bring them back to us. We can see everything it sees on our handheld monitors. It will record everything on video," Ruth said.

"Max comes too," Phin was blunt. "I'm not going over with you and the Robatar unless Max comes." Ruth looked at Warren who nodded in return.

"Okay. No problem. Max, you're with us then."

The group began pulling gear and setting up. In only minutes, Tony had a whole mini-command center set up with two computers and the works. A second crate was unloaded with a second Robatar. Phin questioned and was told that the second one was for Sergeant Warren to control in case of an emergency. He would stay back and monitor the operations and if things went south, Tony would connect him and he would engage.

"Well who's going to control the first Robatar? The one going over with us?" Phin asked. He was confused. The way Ruth explained how the Robatar worked, there needed to be a human host controlling it.

Everyone looked at Ruth, waiting for her to answer. She took a deep breath, "My father...Charles LaPhage. He's the one that's going in with us. We've been preparing him for weeks to do this. I wouldn't be here without him. This has all been driven by his dreams and visions. It's only right that he should go in first."

Phin was stunned. He had understood Charles LaPhage to be incapacitated. But now it was out in the open. This was the grand scheme Ruth had planned all along. Dr. Sayer had been adamantly opposed - convinced the elder LaPhage could not handle it. But Ruth was determined. All had been readied for this moment back in Texas. The next time her father was awakened, he would have his body back. Well, not actually *his* body. But something better. He would *be* the Robatar.

The raft was down by the river ready to go, and Ruth didn't want to waste any more time talking. She made the connection with LaPhage Industries LP-6 and confirmed with Dr. Sayer and Oz Jenks that all was ready. Charles LaPhage was ready. Tony Chen ran the boot-up protocol on the Robatar. The black-clothed machine shuddered and then with smooth precision, stood up and stepped out of its transportation crate on its own.

"Okay, we are ready in five, four, three..." Tony counted down. Ruth, Phin, Max, Jason, and the sergeant all looked on as Tony's fingers flew over the keyboard. He was wearing a small wire headset, muttering back to Oz commands they didn't understand.

The Robatar jerked. Then it jerked again. It turned its head slowly, as if looking back and forth. Raising its left hand in front of its face, it flexed and released its fingers, turning the hand over and looking at it as if in wonder.

"Man, this is crazy," whispered Jason.

Ruth walked over and stood in front of the Robatar. "Daddy? Is that you?" she cautiously asked. The Robatar stepped forward and reached up with its arms outstretched. Ruth stepped into the embrace.

"It *is* you..." she sounded relieved. "I knew we could do it, I just knew it."

As strange as the scene was, it was a tender moment between father and daughter. She pulled back and looked into the Robatar's black-clad face. "We found it, Daddy!" Ruth said excitedly. "We found the Garden of Eden! It's just across the river." She pointed back over her right shoulder to the other side. The spell of the intimate moment was broken in an instant. The Robatar's head snapped in the direction Ruth had been pointing. It shoved her aside and began walking at a crisp pace toward the water, picking up speed until it was jogging.

"Wait! Daddy...Charles LaPhage!...Come back!" Ruth shouted, using her father's name.

The Robatar ignored her and continued on, diving head first into the river.

CHAPTER FIFTY-TWO

"Oz says they've got trouble!" Tony shouted. "Your father's vitals are off the charts, Ms. LaPhage! Dr. Sayer is saying we need to pull the plug. Now!"

"No!" Ruth's head whipped around. "Do no such thing under any circumstances. Come on, let's go!" She took off running toward the inflatable raft. Max and Phin joined in pursuit. Ruth was already in the boat, having started the small motor when they caught up to her. "Let's go, let's go! He's almost across!"

They tore out across the river after the Robatar. Making it halfway, they watched as the Robatar, or Charles LaPhage, stood up on the bank and jogged out of the water.

That's when the eagle descended.

Phin had not seen it coming. It landed hard on top of the Robatar, smashing it into the ground. Aided with machine-like strength, the Robatar was quick on its feet, wrapping its arms around the thick neck of the bird-beast. Its gold, red, and brown plumage became a feathery mess as the Robatar tore and grabbed and ripped at it. Phin could never have imagined anything like what he was witnessing. In the light of day the bird was both beautiful and terrifying at the same time. An eagle-type beast it was, but not exactly. Besides its enormous size, it sported four feet with paws and claws, very much like a lion or other cat-like animal.

The raft rammed the shore some fifty feet from the battle between Robatar and beast. "Come on! Now's our chance!" Ruth jumped out of the boat and tore off toward the grove of trees.

"Ruth! Come back!" Phin was frantic as he catapulted over the side of the raft onto dry land.

"Don't do it, Phin! Let her go!" Max shouted.

"Stay with the boat, Max. I've got to stop her!" he said as he ran in pursuit.

Max was out of the boat, trying to pull it onto the bank to keep it from floating away. It was too heavy for him and he was struggling, also careful to keep one eye on the fight happening over his shoulder as he tugged and heaved. The eagle creature was screeching its terrible squawk. Over and over, it was deafening to the ears. Things were happening too fast. Suddenly the raft slid easily out of the water. Max jerked around, surprised. Another Robatar was walking out of the water, having set the inflatable on dry ground. It was the second Robatar, the one controlled by Sergeant Billy Warren. Max's heart soared. It felt like the cavalry had just arrived in the nick of time.

Warren's Robatar gave a thumbs up to Max, then turned and sprinted toward the furious battle. It launched itself into the fray, the whole fight becoming a ball of carnage. The eagle was screaming and clawing and biting. The two Robatars were punching and kicking and squeezing the beast.

Max's attention was broken by more screaming back across the river. He turned and witnessed the final descent of another eagle. A second guardian creature sent to enforce the will of a holy God.

Tony Chen was frozen mid-scream at his computer setup. The beast landed full force on top of him. It was an awful sight as the young man squirmed to get out from under the creature. It ripped and tore with its vicious beak. An arm went flying into the air, landing yards away. Tony could do nothing more than flop. Then a sickening crunch and pop as the beak closed around his head. Max couldn't watch. Jason was running toward the river, yelling for help and crying. The last thing Max saw was his young friend, newly graduated from college, throw himself into the river.

Max took a massive blow to his back.

He never saw it coming. And then he was in the river too.

Phin left the fray behind in pursuit of Ruth. He expected her to stop in the grove of trees - all of them the Tree of Life. But she kept running - away from him and into the depths of the Garden. Phin paused at the entry to the grove. The Trees of Life were like nothing he had ever seen. Utterly beautiful. If one imagined the perfect tree in their mind, then this was just that, times one hundred. The fruit of the Trees was plentiful. A large orange-sized fruit, but purple in color, with a red knob on top where the stem connected to the tree itself. It was magnetic, drawing Phin. He was tempted to stop and pull one from a limb. He was so close. What would it feel like to have pure healing flowing through his body? To know that if he stayed and ate and never left that he would never die?

This is an old story. He heard the words of Jesus echoing in his head. *Behold, I have written a new story.* Phin could not stay and he could not eat. He had to find Ruth and they had to leave. He'd seen what he came for. The Garden of Eden did exist. It was still here and had been for all these millennia. But it was not the domain of man any longer.

"Ruth!" he called out. "Ruth, where are you?!"

"I'm here, Phin! Hurry! Come quickly!" Phin could hear Ruth calling to him from up ahead. He tore on through the Garden and burst forth into a clearing. The sun shown bright overhead. The air was calm and sweet. Standing in the middle of the Garden was one lone massive tree. However beautiful the Trees of Life were, they paled in comparison to this tree.

The Tree of the Knowledge of Good and Evil.

Phin had no doubt. It was the difference between black and white television, and high definition color. Phin pulled up short. Ruth was standing under the canopy of the magnificent giant. To Phin's shock and horror, a giant snake was intertwined through the branches of the tree, its head hanging down, hovering just off to the side of Ruth's head. Its tongue shot out and back in a sickening hiss, its mouth slightly parted as if it was whispering to Ruth. The body of the snake was blood red. It must be thirty or more feet long were it on the ground, Phin thought. Evil in the midst of good. That's what this was. No, Evil versus God was a more accurate way to describe what he was seeing.

"Phin, come quickly! Join me." Ruth had something in her hand. Phin's eyes grew wide with recognition. She lifted it toward him. He was twenty feet away, having slowly walked toward the woman. It was a fruit. A different fruit. He had never seen one like it before but he knew exactly what it was. "Let's do this together, Phin. Come let's eat!" Her eyes were crazy with lust.

"Don't do it, Ruth!" Phin cried. "Don't! It's not what you think it is. It's an empty promise. A lie."

"No!" she shouted. "You're the one that has been listening to lies. This is truth, Phin." She shoved the fruit toward him, its skin glistening a shining sick color of black, wrinkled all over. "This is the way it was meant to be. This is the way I want it to be. Just you and me, Phin. Like Adam and Eve! Don't you see? I leave my father behind. You leave Autumn behind. We can be one! We can rule paradise. We can rule the world! This fruit is the key. It is the gateway. When we eat our eyes will be open and we will be gods!"

Phin shook his head violently, trying to speak, but nothing would come out. She raised the fruit to her mouth and took a deep bite of skin and pulp. The snake opened its mouth wide and let out a deep and low sound of laughter.

"NOOOOO!!!!" Phin fell to his knees, tears streaming down his face.

"YES!!!!" Ruth whooped. "I see, Phin! I can see! Oh, I understand all now. Yes, my eyes are open! I can feel the power! It's not too late. Join me."

"No...no...no...no...," Phin muttered through his tears.

A choking sound. That's what Phin heard next. Ruth's eyes bulged and she dropped the fruit. Grabbing her throat, she made a gagging sound and began retching, her body heaving as she stood on her feet. The reaction had come so quickly. Phin rose and walked toward her, tears continuing to flow.

"Hhhelp...mmmee," she gazed at Phin, her hands stretched out toward him. A sad look had fallen over her face. She retched yet again, volumes pouring out onto the ground. Falling in her own filth, she began to convulse. Phin rushed to her side, not caring about the mess, and he took her in his arms. She bucked and threw up yet again. Phin marveled that one body could expel so much. But he already knew what it meant. Ruth LaPhage's fate was sealed. And then, suddenly, she was still. Her beautiful green eyes bore into his.

"Forgive me, Phin. I didn't know what I was doing," she managed to say. She was weak. It was as if in that moment she had come back to herself. The temptation of the Garden and its terrible fruit forgotten.

"I forgive you, Ruth," Phin muttered through his sobs. He brushed her red hair back from her face.

"Is it too late?" she wheezed. "Is it too late for God to forgive me?"

"No, it's not, Ruth. It's not too late for God to forgive you. Nothing can change...this..." he said looking around. "But, yes, God can forgive you. He will forgive you...if you ask. And then today, you will be with him in paradise." Phin said as he sobbed for the poor woman.

"No...you are wrong, Phineas Crook. I love you, but you are wrong." Her voice was a bare whisper. She was fading fast. "Do you know I love you? Of course you do. But you don't love me back. And neither does God. *I...am...lost....*" And then Ruth LaPhage was gone.

The clearing was silent. The snake had receded up into the heights of the Tree. Phin eased Ruth's head onto the ground and sat back. She had been so close, he knew. So close to the truth and to real salvation. But she had believed the lies and it had cost her her life and now her soul.

Phin pulled himself to his feet and stared down at the lifeless corpse that had been Ruth LaPhage. Once so beautiful and now so ugly. The poison of the fruit continued its rampage even after death as her body shriveled before his eyes. There was nothing left for him here. He turned and walked away.

As he approached the edge of the clearing, a blonde-headed

young man stepped out and in front of him, blocking his way. But Phin sensed no threat. He was spent...oh, so tired.

"It's you," Phin said weakly. "I saw you when I was on the other side of the river."

"And who do you think I am?" he smiled.

"Chris Jackson. But I don't know how it's possible."

The young man just smiled. He should be in his forties if Phin was right, but this man was clearly not even close to that.

"Let's just say all things are possible with God, and leave it at that." He continued to smile.

"I have so many questions," Phin continued, his shoulders hung. He had nothing left.

"There is no time. You have the answers you came for. All the other questions will have to wait for eternity. Now you must go." The young man had been holding Phin's canvas bag. He must have dropped it in the scramble to find Ruth. He handed it back to Phin, urging again, "Go, Phineas. Go. Leave now. Your friends are waiting."

"Are you coming with us? Can you come?" asked Phin.

"No. I am not coming. It is not for me to leave. God and I have an arrangement. I live in the old story for today, but one day I can enjoy the new story. Now - you really must go."

Phin didn't wait any longer. He continued past the young man and picked up speed. He dared one look back but was not surprised when he saw that the man was gone. He ran and ran. Through the Garden of Eden, past the grove of Trees of Life, not stopping until he found the river's edge.

The boat was gone!

Looking across the river in the direction of their Humvee, all he saw was a mangled mess of metal and debris. What had happened here? There was a rustle behind him, causing him to whip around. He found himself staring into the horrible face of the eagle beast. Its head was bowed low, only inches from his face.

The beast let out a horrible scream that overwhelmed Phin. His world went black. He felt himself fall backward and then he was covered by water.

CHAPTER FIFTY-THREE

Phin sat on the edge of the queen-size bed staring at his bare feet, toes trying to squeeze the Berber rug. He'd had his first shower in days. It felt good to be clean even though he was exhausted. He hoped for a good night's sleep but he had his doubts. Too much on his mind. Too much to process.

It had been three days. Three long days trudging downriver in the bottom of a rubber raft, baking in the sun.

He'd woken up three days ago to the soft purr of an engine. Lying on his side, his eyes squinting into a setting sun as he forced them to open. The splash of water sprinkled his face as the inflatable he was in bounced its way down the river. Jason Morris was at the motor, steering the craft.

"Good morning, sunshine," Phin struggled to pull himself up to the sound of Sergeant Warren leaning across the opposite side of the boat. "Or I guess I should say, good evening." He looked haggard. Like he'd been to war and back. His left arm was missing...again.

"Where are we?" Phin managed to ask. "Anybody got any water?" His throat was raw. Max crawled from the back of the raft to his friend's side and handed him a bottle of water.

"Here, drink some of this and take it easy," Max said. "You took in half the river I think. The sergeant here gave you a pretty good working over." That explained the soreness in his chest. He rubbed it tenderly as he took a swig from the bottle.

"What happened? Where's Tony?" Jason continued to pilot the boat and looked away. Warren gave Max a nod as if to say, *you tell him*.

"He's dead, Phin. Gone."

Phin shook his head in understanding. "So is Ruth."

"That's what we thought. You came to after we got the water out of your lungs. You told us she was dead. We were going to go back for the body but you said it wouldn't do any good. Then you were out again." Phin didn't remember waking up.

"What happened to her?" Warren somberly asked.

Phin shook his head sadly and recounted the race through the Garden of Eden to the Tree of the Knowledge of Good and Evil. How Phin had begged her not to take and eat its fruit. But she did. And suffered the pain of a horrible death. He left out the details.

"Wait, I don't understand." Jason asked, "You knew that Tree was poison? That it would kill her? How did you know, Dr. Crook?"

"Yeah," Warren added, "Adam and Eve ate the fruit from that tree and they didn't die. So why did Ruth and how did you know?" The sergeant looked defeated. Lower than Phin had ever seen him.

"Because God said so." Phin looked down into the bottom of the raft as he went on, "He told Adam and Eve that on the day they ate that fruit they would die. It's poison. I knew it was and I tried to warn her."

"But Adam and Eve didn't die," Warren pressed. "How do you explain that, Doc?"

"Mercy," said Phin. "God chose to have mercy on Adam and Eve. They would die later - of old age - but he chose to show them mercy and let them live out full lives."

"But not Ruth..." Max trailed off.

"No, not Ruth. And probably not anyone else. It's a dangerous thing to presume on the mercy of God. Ruth was consumed by a lust for power. She gambled...and lost." There was no satisfaction in Phin explaining this to the others. A part of him had hoped he was wrong about the fruit being deadly. Sadly, he wasn't.

Jason took the lead, filling in Phin on all the rest that had happened. After all, he was the only one who had witnessed everything.

Tony was dead, crushed and torn by the terrible beast eagle. Jason had jumped in the river to escape. He had known his only hope was to join Phin and Max and the Robatars on the other side. While swimming across, the fighting between the two Robatars and the first beast eagle had boiled over toward Max. The threesome slammed into him, throwing him in the river. Unconscious, he floated on his back downstream. Jason made it to the boat, maneuvered it into the river and took off after Max, reaching and pulling him to safety. As Jason made his way back upstream, he was surprised to see that the beast eagle and one of the Robatars had joined together and were fighting the second Robatar, the one Sergeant Warren was controlling.

Warren picked up the story from Jason. He and Charles LaPhage had been holding their own for most of the fight. But something happened to Charles' Robatar.

"It was like it turned off," the sergeant explained. "No power. It just collapsed on the ground. The creature picked it up in its claws and flung it aside. I thought the fight was down to just the two of us. But next thing I know, Charles is back on his feet and he's tackling *me*! Punching and pulling. Then the eagle thing was on me. I didn't stand a chance."

"They tore him to pieces," Jason interjected. "I mean literally tore him to pieces. Arms, legs, head - all went flying."

Warren continued, "Once the Robatar was shredded, it should have detonated. Taken that monster out. I have no idea why it didn't. Once the connection was lost and I woke up back by the Humvee. I surveyed the scene and saw what was left of Tony. Poor kid. He was a good one. I rolled out of my chair where I'd been plugged in, grabbed my LaPhage leg, and had just enough time to get it connected before two of those things came at me. I ran for my life and jumped in the river. Didn't even have time to grab my arm. Jason motored over and pulled me in. We took off downstream to get away from those birds. They were tearing into everything including the Humvee. Tore that sucker all kinds of up. That's when we heard another one of those demon eagles screaming and saw you go into the water, Doc. We came back, grabbed you, and then we were gone. End of story."

Phin took it all in without saying another word.

The four men spent that night and the next day going full-speed down the river. The inflatable was stocked with plenty of fuel and some meager rations. The mood was somber, no one doing much except spending time in his own thoughts. On the third day they dumped out next to a small village on the extreme south end of Lake Victoria. They begged a ride to the lakeside city of Mwanza. Phin was able to obtain cash from a local bank to pay for the ride and arrange for accommodations at the very nice Adden Palace Hotel. That's where he sat now, thinking back through the whole ordeal. This was not how he had ever imagined his search for the Garden of Eden would end. He was forlorn. All he wanted to do now was sleep. Tomorrow they would fly to Cairo and from there back home.

Phin had no idea what would be waiting for him. His career was up in the air, but he didn't care anymore. He had a visit he needed to make. To his wife. His dear sweet, darling Autumn Eden Rose. He needed to say goodbye - and then he would figure out what to do next.

As he leaned back on the bed, his head landed on his canvas bag. The one he traveled with. He'd thrown it on the bed when he came into the room, just before heading to the shower. It contained his journal, notes, Livingstone's map, and more. He'd not opened it since Chris Jackson or whoever had given it back to him. Chris Jackson. He shook his head. Impossible. Right? But then again, *all things are possible with God.* Phin pulled the bag to his chest and sat back up. Opening the top flap, he looked inside for his journal. He'd make a few notes before closing his eyes. To his surprise, the journal was gone. To his greater surprise, in its place...a fruit.

One fruit.

Large and purple with a red knob on top.

EPILOGUE

Summer had arrived and it was hot outside. Texas hot. But inside the lobby of SecondLife, Inc. the air conditioning was doing its job. Max and Shelly Allred sat with Phineas Crook in the comfortable chairs of the lobby, waiting patiently as preparations were being finalized.

Phin had come to say goodbye to his wife, Autumn. To release her into her eternal rest. He'd held on long enough. Too long, he knew. Now he was ready. Max and Shelly had driven down to be with him. They were his best friends in the world besides the love of his life who lay sleeping on the fourth floor. Max and Shelly had been with Phin the night of the accident over three years ago. *The night I lost my precious E,* he thought. They'd walked with him through the whole awful journey, and they were now with Phin to close this last chapter - to sit with him in his grief and to assist him in the final arrangements that would follow.

It had been three weeks since Phin, Jason, and Max had returned to Oklahoma. Phin spent the first week alone, just resting and recovering. So much had happened in the months since Ruth LaPhage came into his life, and he was utterly exhausted. Spent. Remus had gone silent, not responding to any of Phin's emails. He imagined his brother was processing their shared dream in his own way.

The university was eager to meet with him, to talk to him about all that had transpired in his search for the Garden of Eden. *Did you actually find it?* They wanted to know. *Did you bring back proof? Are you ready to finally publish your findings?* The notoriety that a discovery the scale of the Garden of Eden would bring to a school like Oklahoma Baptist University would be beyond measure. If Phin had failed, though, if he had been wrong...well, perhaps it was time to part ways.

But he'd found it, all right. The tale Phin told Dean Reynolds and President MacDonald was unbelievable to be sure, but Dr. Max Allred, associate dean of the Hobbs College, had corroborated ever detail. The problem was neither man had any proof beyond his good word. Yes, they'd taken dozens of photographs and made copious notes, but the camera equipment and all their personal gear had been lost in the melee by the river. There had simply been no time in the chaos of the moment to gather anything of value. They'd been lucky to escape with their lives. Of course, Phin's personal journal had disappeared from his bag as well.

The administration was appalled and nervous that people had died. It seemed prudent to terminate Dr. Phineas Crook and distance themselves from what had become a tragedy...until LaPhage Industries stepped back into the picture. As financiers of the expedition, and a "friend" of the university, having donated more than a million dollars to the school, they had inserted themselves quickly, or at least their attorneys had.

Ruth LaPhage was dead. The CEO and head of LaPhage Industries. So was Charles LaPhage. Phin had been shocked to hear this bit of news. He had an inside link to LaPhage Industries through Sergeant Warren, who relayed to Phin an amazing and disturbing piece of news. According to Oz Jenks, Charles LaPhage had arrested and died within fifteen minutes of being neurally connected to his Robatar. The stress and brain stimulation had overtaxed his system. Dr. Sayer had been correct in his warning to Ruth: her idea for her father and the Robatar would kill him. And so it had. That was tragic enough by itself. But when Charles had died, the Robatar should have shut down - become totally inactive. Obviously, that had not happened.

As Warren explained it to Phin and Max, instead of turning itself off, Charles' Robatar had changed course and attacked the sergeant's. Charles wasn't in control any longer - he wasn't the one attacking. The Robatar had gone rogue. Just like it had in Syria back in the winter campaign to take out a group of terrorists. But that was not supposed to be possible. *Where was it getting its commands? Who or what was controlling it?* Phin didn't say it, but he couldn't help but think it. According to the Bible, one of the faces of the cherubim...was the face of a *man*. Was it possible that God himself had stepped in? And where was the Robatar now? Phin decided it would do no good to dwell on it.

With both the founder and the CEO of LaPhage Industries dead, the company was scrambling to control the public relations news cycle. And with Ruth's death occurring overseas - with no body that could be recovered and buried - it only complicated matters further. The attorneys for LaPhage Industries insisted that Dr. Phineas Crook stay on at OBU in his current position with all privileges. Anything less would illicit more questions that no one wanted to answer. In addition, Phineas was forbidden, through a mound of documents written in legalese, from writing or publishing any kind of account related to an expedition in search of the Garden of Eden. In short, both Phineas and the university and all those related to the events in Tanzania were to act as if nothing had ever happened.

For his part, Phin was fine with that. He was glad to keep his job. At this point all he wanted was a quiet life of teaching and pouring into the lives of his students. The administration conceded, of course.

Jason Morris had bounced back quickly from his ordeal. He was young and full of life and, as of two days prior, on his way to Israel to begin his summer archaeological dig which would extend into the fall. He and Phin parted with a warm hug and promises of connecting when he returned.

Sergeant Billy Warren was back at LaPhage Industries in Fort Worth. As the lone LaPhage survivor of the expedition to Africa, he was spending more time than he wanted answering questions from the higher-ups. He had also taken on a fatherly role in consoling Oz Jenks after the death of his best friend, Tony Chen. The news of Tony's death had sent Oz into a dark place. Warren, who had seen his share of death and carnage on the battlefield, was doing his best to befriend the young computer scientist.

Upon being informed of the death of Ruth LaPhage, the Department of Defense, on orders from Admiral Watkins and General Myers, had swept into LP-6 and seized any and all technologies and data related to Project BORG and the Robatars. It was anyone's guess as to what would become of the powerful AI system built and steered by the late LaPhage.

The door to the elevator dinged, and Barry from SecondLife, Inc. stepped out to join Phin, Max, and Shelly in the lobby.

"Everything is ready, Dr. Crook. If you'll follow me, your wife is waiting," he said.

"Suite 3 today, Barry?" Phin asked as he stood. His adrenaline was flowing, his palms sweating. The moment had arrived.

"Yes, sir. Same as always. I know you like that one."

Max and Shelly stood as well. "What do you want from us, Phin?" Shelly asked.

"We can come with you, if you want. Or we can wait down here," said Max.

Phin appreciated these two more than they knew. "It just needs to be me. I hope you understand. I need to say goodbye, in my own way. I might be awhile," he said, lost in his own thoughts.

"Sure thing, buddy. Take your time. We will be here when you need us," Max said. They each gave him a long hug.

Phin entered the elevator and hit the button for the fourth floor as he'd done so many times before. But never like this. This was the last time. He would not return.

Exiting the elevator, he was met by Dr. Mark Sayer. "Hello Dr. Crook, you look well," he greeted Phin warmly. "She's ready for you."

"You disconnected her from the POD? She's back to...the way she was?" Phin didn't quite know how to ask it.

"That's right. She's back to the state she was in the night of the accident. Her body has been revived. We call it de-Poding, but you get the idea. She's still unconscious - her body is naturally shutting down. Just like the night of the accident. Left the way she is now, she will pass within the next few hours."

The two men began walking toward Suite 3, arriving at the door of the room a moment later. Reaching into the pocket of his lab coat, Dr. Sayer withdrew a syringe and held it in the palm of his hand.

"I did what you asked, Phin. There's no guarantee, obviously, but you won't be doing any harm if you go forward and use this. I can't say I'm much of a believer, but the story of what you all experienced in Africa...well, let's just say it's given me pause."

Phin took the syringe and examined its contents - a clear mixture tinged ever so slightly, a hint of purple.

"You extracted the juice of the fruit I gave you and mixed it with saline. Nothing else, right?" Phin asked.

"Just as you requested."

"And did you destroy what was left?"

"Didn't have to. Once we pierced the skin it began to shrivel. I've never seen anything quite like it. Within just a few minutes it was a dry husk. We were lucky to extract what's in your hand."

"Thank you," was all Phin could say. He turned and entered the room by himself.

Lying on the bed in the center of the suite, in her beautiful, favorite red dress, was his wife. His life. His Autumn. He walked to the edge of the bed. She looked perfect. Like the last time he'd seen her, except no more Plexiglass barrier. No more POD. He reached down and tenderly stroked her cheek. Her skin was cool to the touch, and pale. He noticed that her breathing was shallow. Her life was slipping away. He placed his hand gently on the side of her head - her brown hair silky soft to the touch - as he leaned down and kissed her lightly on the lips.

"I love you so much, my darling." His eyes were moist. "And I'm here to say goodbye. I'm sorry it took me so long to be ready for this day."

He looked at the syringe in his hand.

He knew what he was about to do would most likely mean nothing. But he had this nagging feeling that followed him, from the hotel on Lake Victoria, all the way to this moment. The fruit from the Tree of Life had been placed in his bag for a reason. For this reason. But how was he to know for sure? He couldn't. So it came down to *trust*. Was he willing to trust God no matter what may come? For good or ill. For life or death. Would he trust God?

Yes. He had decided. He was ready to trust.

Phin took the syringe and inserted it into the IV connected to

Autumn's arm. He pressed the plunger. Then he waited.

But not for long.

Autumn's lungs expanded, her chest rising high. Phin sat up, eyes wide. His own heartbeat accelerated. Was the color returning to her cheeks? He felt movement and looked to Autumn's side. Her hand had clenched itself into a fist. He reached up to take the side of her face in the palm of his hand. It felt...warmer? Yes, it was warmer than minutes before.

Autumn's eyes fluttered open. She stared at the ceiling for just a moment, as if she was trying to focus, and then she turned her head. She turned her head! Ever so slightly she turned and looked into the eyes of her husband, who by now was weeping.

"Oh, Phin...it's you" she said, her voice stronger than Phin would have suspected.

"Yes, my dear," he was stroking the side of her hair, "it's me. My dear sweet, E... it's me."

"I had the most amazing dream, Phin. I must tell you about it."

Phin could only laugh through his tears of joy, "So did I, my love... so did I."

Finding Eden

"And it shall come to pass afterward,
that I will pour out my Spirit on all flesh;
your sons and your daughters shall prophesy,
your old men shall dream dreams,
and your young men shall see visions."
- Joel 2:28

The End.

ACKNOWLEDGMENTS

I am thankful for my family for their support as I have taken the better part of a year to hammer out this work, my first novel. More than anything I have ever written, this book is the result of a lifetime of journeys and travels and people that have all had a profound impact on me. There are too many names and faces to try and list but they all hold a special place in my mind and heart and I am eternally grateful – I am a thankful man. None of the words written could have been possible without my wife, Julie. Her belief in the project and constant encouragement were the fuel that kept the fire burning and the fingertips clicking as I pounded out that first draft on my MacBook. She employed her excellent editing and proofing skills to wordsmith the text over the course of multiple readings. The novel is miles better because of her and where it falls short, I take the blame. I also want to thank my colleague in ministry, Andy Jennings, for serving as an early reader and applying his considerable erudition, helping me think through plot lines and serving to fine tune the final manuscript. For Tori Lasater's patient and excellent work on the cover artwork, I am also thankful. A special word of commendation for the excellent work of Martin Dugard whose wonderful book, *Into Africa: The Epic Adventures of Stanley and Livingstone*, captured me and provided a historical foundation and launching point for a detour down the rabbit hole in search of the Garden of Eden. The lidar scanner is real technology used for exactly the purposes described in this book. *National Geographic* has documented its use to great success in the discovery of long lost civilizations buried by time and jungle. This fictitious story about the Garden of Eden has ping-ponged around in my head for over a decade. So finally, thank *you*, dear reader, for diving into this adventure with me.

ABOUT THE AUTHOR

Jeffrey S. Crawford is teaching pastor and lead pastor of ministries at Cross Church in northwest Arkansas, one of the largest and fastest growing megachurches in North America. He holds a Doctorate of Education in Leadership from the Southern Baptist Theological Seminary, a Master of Divinity degree from Southwestern Baptist Theological Seminary, and a Bachelor of Arts in Philosophy from Oklahoma Baptist University. He has served for over thirty years in churches across Arkansas, Texas, Oklahoma, Louisiana, Utah, and Tennessee and enjoys traveling the globe on missionary journeys and interacting with the peoples of the world. He and his wife, Julie, have raised their four children in the foothills of the Ozarks where they make their home.